"Mercy, peace, and love
be yours in abundance" (Jude 2).
Many blessings,
Muriel McAvoy Morley

Nela Burnett

A Cottage in Akin

a novel

MURIEL MCAVOY MORLEY

Inspiring Voices®
A Service of **Guideposts**

Great Is Thy Faithfulness
Words by Thomas O. Chisholm
© 1923, ren. 1951 Hope Publishing Company, Carol Stream, IL 60188.
All rights reserved. Used by permission.

Inspiring Voices books may be ordered through booksellers or by contacting:

Inspiring Voices
1663 Liberty Drive
Bloomington, IN 47403
www.inspiringvoices.com
1 (866) 697-5313

Because of the dynamic nature of the Internet, any web addresses or links contained in this book may have changed since publication and may no longer be valid. The views expressed in this work are solely those of the author and do not necessarily reflect the views of the publisher, and the publisher hereby disclaims any responsibility for them.

ISBN: 978-1-4624-0766-8 (sc)
ISBN: 978-1-4624-0765-1 (e)

Library of Congress Control Number: 2013918333

Printed in the United States of America.

Inspiring Voices rev. date: 12/16/2013

Chapter 16: Passage from "A Mad Tea-Party," *Alice's Adventures in Wonderland* by Lewis Carroll (Pub. 1900).

Chapter 16 and *Chapter 27:* Poem "A word is dead when it is said" by Emily Dickinson (1830-1886).

Chapter 16: Poem "Hope is the thing with feathers" by Emily Dickinson (1830-1886).

Chapter 17: Poem "Jabberwocky" by Lewis Carroll (1832-1898).

Chapter 17: Poem "A bird came down the walk" by Emily Dickinson (1830-1886).

Chapter 17: Poem "The bee is not afraid of me" by Emily Dickinson (1830-1886).

Chapter 19: Poem "A drop fell on the apple tree" by Emily Dickinson (1830-1886).

Chapter 19: Poem "If you were coming in the fall" by Emily Dickinson (1830-1886).

Chapter 19: Poem "There came a wind like a bugle" by Emily Dickinson (1830-1886).

Chapter 19: Poem "An awful tempest mashed the air" by Emily Dickinson (1830-1886).

Chapter 19: Poem "The Slave's Dream" by Henry Wadsworth Longfellow (1807-1882).

Chapter 19: Poem "Hope" by Thomas Campbell (1777-1844).

Chapter 19: Poem "Gone, gone, sold and gone" by John Greenleaf Whittier (Reprinted in *Narrative of the Life of Frederick Douglass: An American Slave,* written by Himself. Boston. 1845.) (Actual title—"The Farewell of a Virginia Slave Mother to her Daughters Sold Into Southern Bondage," *The Works of Whittier, Vol. III.*)

Chapter 19: Poem "From the Chrysalis" by Emily Dickinson (1830-1886).

Chapter 19: Poem "On this long storm the rainbow rose" by Emily Dickinson (1830-1886).

Chapter 19: Poem "The Last Eve of Summer" (third verse) by John Greenleaf Whittier (1893, 1902) (*The Works of John Greenleaf Whittier, Complete*).

Chapter 20: Poem "I'll tell you how the sun rose" by Emily Dickinson (1830-1886).

Chapter 20: Poem "To fight aloud is very brave" by Emily Dickinson (1830-1886).

Chapter 20: Words to Negro Spiritual "Nobody Knows de Trouble I've Seen" (1926…)

Chapter 20: Poem "I'm nobody! Who are you?" by Emily Dickinson (1830-1886).

Chapter 20: Poem "The Plumpuppets" *The Rocking Horse* by Christopher Morley. 1919. (*Chimneysmoke*).

Chapter 20 and *Chapter 23:* Poem "I Never Saw a Moor" by Emily Dickinson (1830-1886).

Chapter 21: Poem "Water" by Hilda Conkling (© 1920).

Chapter 21 and *Chapter 60:* Words to song "That's Why They Call Me Shine" by Cecil Mack (1910).

Chapter 21: Poem "He Wishes for the Cloths of Heaven" by William Butler Yeats (1919).

Chapter 21: Passage from "Safe in Your Arms," *The Saints' Everlasting Rest,* by Richard Baxter (1615-1691).

Chapter 22: Words to hymn, "All the Way My Savior Leads Me" by Fanny J. Crosby (1820-1915).

Chapter 27: Poem "Heart not so heavy as mine" by Emily Dickinson (1830-1886).

Chapter 28: Words to song "The Star-Spangled Banner" (written 1814) by Francis Scott Key.

Chapter 32: Words to song "Caisson Song" (1904) by Edmund L. Grubert, R.M. Danford, & Wm. Bryden © 1921

Chapter 39 and *Chapter 70:* Poem "Hiawatha's Childhood," III of *The Song of Hiawatha* by Henry Wadsworth Longfellow (1807-1882).

Chapter 43: One line from song "I'm Late" by Bob Hilliard.

Chapter 48: Poem "I Hear America Singing" by Walt Whitman (*The Patriotic Poems of Walt Whitman*, Part III).

Chapter 57: Poem "I Heard a Bird Sing" by Oliver Herford.

Chapter 57 and *Epilogue:* (4 lines only)*:* Poem "The Coin" by Sara Teasdale (1920).

Chapter 60: Words to hymn, "Jesus Calls Us" by Mrs. Cecil F. Alexander.

Chapter 60: Poem "I shall know why when time is over" by Emily Dickinson (1830-1886).

Chapter 60: Words to hymn "Breathe on Me, Breath of God" by Edwin Hatch.

Chapter 67: Passage from Chapter 1 of *Little Women* by Louisa M. Alcott (1868, 1869, 1896…)

Chapter 78: Quote "Enough, if something from our hands have power…" by William Wordsworth (1770-1850).

Poems by fictional character in story, Agatha Jordan:

Chapter 19: "Stars"

Chapter 20: "Morning Time"

Chapter 21: "Your Dreams Are a Treasure"

Chapter 43: "God Made Us Friends"

Chapter 57: "Until We Meet Again, Dear Friends"

Poem by fictional character in story, Ponia Snow:

Chapters 74 and *84:* "Tender Mercies"

Folktale retelling by fictional author in story, June Lane Blair:

Chapters 69, 81, 83, 84: "When the People Soared Like Eagles"

Photo of author and husband on back cover by Earl McAvoy.

Photo of front-cover artist, Sandra Bergeron, is by Lifetouch / Olan Mills. All rights reserved. Used with permission of Lifetouch for commercial use by Inspiring Voices.

See Acknowledgements at end of book.

To the Almighty Author of All

Soli Deo Gloria

True hope is swift, and flies with swallow's wings.
—William Shakespeare

Prologue

June 2001

bigBIRDSareBACK
Ungainly pelicans grace waters all over Greeley
—*Greeley (Colo.) Tribune,* p.A1, Friday, June 1, 2001

Larvae's favorite food is
Weld County's worst noxious weed
—*Akin Scoop,* p.1, Friday, June 1, 2001

I tumble from my dreams into the quiet light of dawn.

The coffeemaker in the kitchen is brewing in low whispers, but in my half-sleep, it's a sprite rustling about the room flinging petals from an extraterrestrial bouquet. Five o'clock. I rouse and squint toward Charles' empty place beside me. I didn't even hear him leave the house for his early shift today. He works so hard. Bless him. I sit up in bed and my orange cat Agatha jumps up. She purrs, arches against my hand, and paces across my lap.

The wobbly chirp of a lone robin and the heady fragrance of my Autumn Bouquet rose hedge drift in through the open window.

The dream—what was it? It had been pleasant, yet doleful. Agatha snuggles her face beneath my chin, and I lean back against my pillow, pondering, stroking her.

I recall it now. I'm a child in the dream. The scents of apple blossoms waft in through the open windows of the school auditorium and coffee from the refreshment tables in the vestibule. People stir in their seats and fan themselves with their programs, a man coughs, a baby squeals, and a squeaky door opens at the back. A sweet, deep pulsation grips me as I slog my way up onto the stage toward a brown-as-dark-rye-bread elderly woman, sitting, waiting for me on the stage, her arms outstretched. My legs are like sticks with wooden feet that clunk across the stage. The air is thick like water. With great effort, I stroke with my arms in swimming motions and finally reach her. There is sadness as well as joy in her animated face, her tilted smile. I clasp my arms around her neck. She smells like spice and honeysuckle. Her cheek is yielding and cool, and her rhinestone earring presses like a thorn into my cheek—a cherished discomfort. Then I'm poised beside her, soaked in a hot chill. She recites a poem—casts it out over the audience like bread upon the waters.

And her voice is deep and rich and clear, an orchestra of tones and notes. She transforms the commonplace words into a sonata, a symphony, and then a lullaby just by the turn of her voice. A myriad of emotions plays across her splendid old features like clouds flinging shadows over the fields on a windy afternoon.

I smile at the dream—and the remembrance—of Auntie Odie, the dear woman who metamorphosed my life. Had my existence not become entwined with hers, I may not have survived—and I would not have traced the God-ordained design for my life.

I yawn, nudge Agatha off my lap. I get up and shuffle through the kitchen to the sun porch that overlooks the back yard.

House finches, house sparrows, and mourning doves gather to chat among themselves and worry the feeders and tins of seed. Black-capped chickadees dine at a feeder of sunflower seeds hanging in the saucer magnolia tree. Up in the maple and pine risers, robins and starlings, chests fluffed, practice their scales for the sunrise opera to come.

I head for the bathroom to slide into familiar clothes—jeans, cardinal-red tee and brown sandals.

In the mirror I fuss with my mass of pale curls and inspect the bridge of my nose, sunburned from yesterday's work in the garden. I am homely, it's true, but I look much younger than my fifty-nine years. The beauty experts say I should never wear red, but I do. Crimson, cochineal, fuchsia, magenta, and any other color I wish. Daffodil. Tangerine. Cobalt. Amaranth. The sheer pleasure of wearing a garden of colors outweighs the mischief they affect on my moon-white skin.

I run a brush through the tangles and look no better for my trouble. Dear Charles has never even noticed that I'm no beauty. Bless him.

★ ★ ★

Coffee, notebook, and pen in hand, I head for the sunporch and shoulder my way through the door to the back walk. Agatha strolls out ahead of me, confident in our daily routine. The morning is goldenizing itself in the waking sun. As I step along the garden walk, and through the arbor, I am baptized in a fragrance-blend of roses, dianthus, alyssum, and lily-of-the-valley.

I don't pause to examine the gardens for weeds like I usually do or to see if the foxtail-lily bulbs are coming up. Agatha leaps up onto the garden swing next to me. As I push us into motion, I drink in the air like a delicious gourmet beverage. A squirrel chatters and eats at the pie tin of seed on the fence rail. A robin eyes him, cocks her head, then chirples her ambivalent song.

The dawn slings ribbons, peachy gold, across the Colorado plains and ties up the roofs, chimneys and spires of our little town—and my gardens—like birthday packages. I journal my morning so far—simple, yet somehow profound.

Glory be! I notice Agatha, off the swing and stealing close to a cluster of finches and mourning doves pecking at seeds beneath a feeder.

"Agatha!" I scold, and she is scooped up and taken inside.

Embarrassed, Agatha slinks off to her kitty igloo, and I change into my Reeboks.

★ ★ ★

Swash! Swash! Two pelicans plunge their immense, vivid-yellow bills deep into the water. Soon the bills are raised, lower mandibles expanded. They swallow the fish whole—*gulp, gulp*—and the mandibles return to their original size as I snap away with my digital camera.

I'm one of many birdwatchers around the pond at Akin Park. So glad to be here to see the pelicans during one of their rare visits to Weld County. From my shady spot on a grassy swell, I notice for the first time that Pretty Pond is shaped like a pelican with wings folded. *Pelican Pond.* I'm warm from the brisk walk here, so the breeze feels good. The sky shimmers in the exact color of the star blooms on my blue phlox in the spring. I even imagine I smell blue phlox.

"Look! There's more!" a man shouts.

Looking to the east, I shield my eyes. Twenty or more pelicans in the morning sun, looking as if a glassblower had fashioned them in white and clear glass, soar in a *V* on expansive, black-edged wings. All at once, they flap in a hushed thunder of sound. Soon they still their wings into glass again as they soar over us, circle back, and then glide in for landings on Pretty Pond.

★ ★ ★

I pour out yesterday's lemonade—along with a couple dozen one-inch caterpillars. A few which haven't yet drowned, squirm themselves upright and ripple away. That's what I get for leaving my glass outside.

For a week I've noticed the painted lady caterpillars in shady areas of our property—on the sides of the house, on the walks, fences, trees, arbor, and on a few choice garden plants. Only one in the house so far. I remember at least three of these infestations of painted ladies in my lifetime. Many gardeners complain about them, hate them, and kill them off with Sevin. But I can hardly wait to see my garden lit up and alive with the gorgeous little winged wonders. They look like miniature monarchs—bright orange wings with black, brown, and white markings. To me, it's worth the damage to a few of my plants—strawberry, sunflower, and geranium mainly—to be blessed with the painted ladies' frail beauty.

While heading inside to cool off, I notice a caterpillar hanging on a potted geranium stem. It bobbles and twists. Fascinated, I stay and watch until it becomes a silvery chrysalid.

Maybe, in about a week, I'll be lucky enough to see it emerge.

★ ★ ★

At two p.m. I rock in my writing nook, reflecting on the day. Like the unfolding of this morning's dawn, a revelation is unfolding in me. It swells in my soul as incredibly as an embryo grows in the womb of its mother: I must write the story of Auntie Odie—how she entered and transformed my life.

But where do I begin? I ponder awhile.

Ah.

The Arrentz Place. When I was nine.

Chapter 1

1950

Expects Korean
War Will Last
Until Spring
—*Greeley Daily Tribune*, p. 3, Wed., Nov. 22, 1950

★ ★ ★

Akinites:
Traditional Thanksgiving
Celebrations Most Popular
—*Akin Scoop*, p. 1, Thurs., Nov. 23, 1950

Thursday, Thanksgiving, Nov. 23; dropped to 14° early Thursday; cold wind during night; high 27°; bright sunshine, light winds during day

Mama and I peered out the front window between the shelves full of bottles Gram had collected over her lifetime. Beyond Gram's houselike trellis, the farmyard, the cottonwood, and Grampy's field of winter rye shivering in the restless chill of the November day, and just beyond yonder fencerow and silo, the Gromans' red barn glinted like a flame in the midday sun.

"I'd give a lot to see that old gray tub pull into the farmyard," Mama said.

"Me too." I frowned. Gram and Grampy hated it when Mama called their Nash a tub.

She held her mouth in that pinched way, making her words sharp and flat like the wind that forced its way beneath the door. "Wonder what's keeping 'em."

With Gram and Grampy away, the silence had howled in our little farmhouse like the ocean in Gram's prize conch shell. Mama and I had stayed home to take care of the place while Gram and Grampy drove to Aunt Grace's funeral in North Platte, Nebraska. Aunt Grace was the last relative except for a few cousins and Gram's sister, Bella, in a rest home in Akin several miles away.

How joyous it would be when Gram and Grampy tromped through the doorway, greeting us with boisterous voices, laughing, and shedding their light and warmth—their very life—throughout the house.

Mama pushed her hair back from her eyes. "Might's well eat something. Go wash your hands and try to get a comb through that wild mop."

In the kitchen we spooned up helpings of turkey, dressing and yams, and then sat at the large table at one end of the front room. The whisper of our forks on Gram's Poppyware plates played a dirge with the whooshing wind against the house and the ticking of Gram's and Grampy's wall clock.

The phone rang our ring—two shorts and a long—as the wall clock struck three. Mama lifted the receiver, stifflike, and held it away from her ear.

Standing next to her I, too, heard the metallic words. "This is Sheriff Thomas. Ingrid, I'm afraid I have some bad news." Long pause. "I... uh, it's..."

Mama glanced down at me. "Spit it out."

"Ingrid, your parents died this morning."

Mama gasped and so did I.

"Your pa must've dozed off. Lost control on highway 138 a few miles southwest of Atwood." He cleared his throat. "Overturned three times."

Mama moved the receiver close to her ear, turned her back to me, and cupped her hand around the mouthpiece. "Where are they now?"

Shivering, I crouched on the hearthrug in front of the potbelly stove and covered my ears. I closed my eyes against Mama's talk with the sheriff and the fear that swelled inside me.

Mama hung up then slumped into Grampy's rocker. Mouth wide open, she cried emptylike— dry sobs from some place deep inside her. I worried that she might strangle, that she might not catch her breath. Then the tears exploded from her eyes, and she breathed again in great heaving gasps.

I studied her for a few minutes and wondered what to do. Her thin, rounded shoulders shook, arms rested in her lap, long and shapeless. Her gasps hung in the room like fog.

Gram and Grampy gone? Forever?

I longed to touch the quivering sleeve of my mother's blue-and-red-plaid housedress.

I inched across the floor on my knees. My hand raised up, and at last I allowed my hand—*gently now*—to touch her shoulder.

Mama's light-brown eyes dulled to hard gray as she glared at me through her tears, her mouth contorted. "Don't do that!"

My heart throbbed in my throat, and I struggled to breathe.

She leaped to her feet, stormed into Gram and Grampy's bedroom, and slammed the door. The rocker rocked as if Grampy were in it then stopped as if he had dozed off.

The lingering smells of our Thanksgiving dinner turned foul, and I swallowed down nausea. I climbed into Grampy's rocker and curled up in Gram's brown and orange afghan. I rocked, and with my finger traced its endless zig-zag design.

The pendulum on the wall clock thrummed in whispers, fire snapped in the potbelly, the rocker creaked, and Mama, off in Gram and Grampy's bedroom, wept and wailed.

★ ★ ★

Bong, bong, bong, bong, bong.

I stirred from the rocker. Five o'clock. The fire was down, the room cold. I found long underwear, sweater, and overalls in the bureau and changed out of my dress. Gram and Grampy's bedroom door was still closed. No sounds.

On with my cap, scarf and coat—I hated to be cold—and grabbed a clean bucket. Outside, I gulped the air, frigid but fresh. In the distant west only the highest peaks of the Rocky Mountains were visible above the cloak of gold-stained clouds.

The chickens cackled from the coop. I scattered feed, then forked hay into the stalls for the cows. I ran past the milk shed, past the hay barn to the elm tree towering beside the pasture gate where Polly and Pie huddled for warmth and chewed their cuds. They looked like chubby ladies chewing gum, waiting to place their orders at a soda fountain. When I opened the gate, they ambled toward the milk shed.

"Good girls."

Maybelle trotted from the far end of the pasture and nuzzled my shoulder. I combed my fingers through her jet-black mane. "You need a good brushing."

She raised her head up, then down.

"I'll feed you, soon as I milk Polly and Pie." I patted her dark muzzle and rubbed her ears. Her frosty breath encircled us like white smoke.

I set about milking Polly. When I gripped her teat with my cold hands, she flinched—and so did I. *Shpleet, shpleet, shpleet!* Polly's milk steamed as it hit the ice-cold bucket, and its warm, sweet scent filled the frigid air. It was good to be outside doing chores instead of being bathed in Mama's mournful sounds or suffocating in the silence. I tried to imagine what the rest of my life would be like without Gram and Grampy. I imagined Grampy there with me now in the barn, grinning and rubbing his chin. "That's right, sis," he'd say in his low, rough voice. "You got the touch."

Gram and Grampy were the ones who had loved me, cared for me for as long as I could remember, not Mama. Their love for me was pure like the milk flowing from Polly.

Mama and I had come to live with them when I was six months old. Soon after, Mama left and didn't come back for three years. She'd stayed several months only to leave again until she returned just last year. Gram was the mama of my heart, but she never let me call her Mama. "You done got a mama," she'd say.

The Arrentz Place—that's what everyone called it because the Arrentzes owned it—had been Gram and Grampy's home for twenty-five years. "Since before the Great Depression," Grampy always said.

That little farm on the plains of northeastern Colorado was home. Because of Gram and Grampy, life had been joyous for me—I was as contented as a cricket singing evensongs at the ripening of summer.

I recalled how Gram chuckled in her wheezy way. Sometimes she called me little bee. She'd say, "You just never stop flittin' here and there like a little ol' bee going from bloom to bloom." Gram wasn't the hugging type, but every once in a while she'd gather me in her plump arms and clasp me tight against her bosom. I'd close my eyes and smell the Vicks Vaporub she smeared on her soft thin lips. I'd wince as the brooch on her dress above her apron bib stenciled a lily into my cheek but tarried in that embrace, collecting the closeness in my heart.

Pie hollered in her moo-voice, eyeing me with one liquid-brown eye.

"Ya, Pie, now it's your turn." I moved to her side with my stool and bucket and set the bucket beneath her. She gave me a one-eyed gawk then went back to chewing her supper.

Comforting and familiar, ears twitching, Polly and Pie radiated warmth and blew steamy breath like hefty heaters.

I drew milk from Pie's teats and listened to the splooshing sound of the milk echoing in the tin pail, the cows' contented chewing, and the swishes of their tails.

Pie stomped her hoof. "M-m-m-a-a-a!"

Lowering my voice, I tried to sound like Grampy. "Almost finished, girl." I breathed in the earthy scents of the barn—hay, manure, cow flesh, and sweet milk.

"What will happen now that Grampy isn't here to farm the land?" I asked Pie. "Mr. Arrentz will probably rent to folks who can work it."

She munched her hay and gazed at me, a straw dangling from her lip.

"What will happen to you, Pie?"

She looked sad, intelligent, so I asked her, "And what will happen to Mama and me?"

Chapter 2

War Casualties
Of U.S. 29,996
—*Greeley Daily Tribune*, p. 1, Fri., Nov. 24, 1950

★ ★ ★

New Christmas Decorations
Adorn Downtown Akin
—*Akin Scoop*, p. 1, Sun., Nov. 26, 1950

Fair Sunday, 67°

Bob and Glenda Myers, small quiet people from up the road apiece, and their nine-year-old twins Maizy and Marvin, along with blustering Elmer and Grace Hill and their tribe of boys—Chester, Harley, Chad, and Charlie—came by Sunday afternoon to bring food and offer their condolences. Mama was a lone goldfish in her bowl, resting at the bottom, gulping for oxygen, while everyone else gathered around on the outside.

When the company rose to leave, Mama surprised us all when she said, "Don't go. Please. Tarry awhile longer."

Maizy, Marvin, and I—the nine-year-olds—took the Hill boys, ages four to eight, out to play and run for awhile. Little Charlie fell, so the rest of us escorted him, bawling, into the house, and I washed his knee and daubed it with Mercurochrome. Someone had started a fire in the potbelly, so we kids sat on the big braided rug as close to it as we were allowed.

Bob Myers hooked a thumb under the bib of his overalls and rubbed his free hand over his dark stubble of beard. "Need help with the milking, Ingrid?"

Mama looked at him as if she didn't even know we had cows.

Mrs. Myers gave him a gray look then glanced at Mama. "You know she does, Bob."

I stood up, my chin high. "I been feeding 'em and milking 'em."

"Well now." Mr. Myers looked at Mama, at his wife, then back at me. "Me and Marvin'll help you milk today. And we'll help you in the morning again after we milk our'n."

★ ★ ★

Mr. Myers milked Pie while Marvin milked Polly.

Elmer Hill leaned against the post and chewed a length of straw. "Did you hear the story 'bout the farmer who hit hisself in the head with a hammer?"

"Don't think so," Mr. Myers said.

"Well, this farmer is hammering hisself on the head, see, and he quits a minute and then he hammers hisself again. He keeps on a'goin' like that till a friend from down the road stops by and sees him. The friend asks him, 'Why do you keep hammering yourself on the head?' and the farmer says, 'Because it feels so good when I quit.'"

Mr. Myers and his twins chuckled, and I did too, in spite of myself.

Maizy helped Harley, Chad, and Charlie feed the chickens, and Chester and I gathered the eggs. "Raw-awk!" The hens didn't like Chester's help. We laughed until Hettie pecked him.

Mr. Myers and Mr. Hill chewed the fat in between Mr. Hill's jokes. It was fun having help from the neighbors. The men's small talk and Mr. Hill's jokes made it seem like nothing bad had happened—cheered me up somehow. We took the milk inside, and Mrs. Hill and Mrs. Myers strained it. Mama stood by and watched like a dazed goose.

Grace Hill, a stocky woman with a tanned, cherub face, smiled at Mama. "How 'bout if we jis all stay and have supper with ya? We brought plenty of food. Would ya like that?"

A sliver of a smile appeared on Mama's face, and she nodded.

Mrs. Myers took hold of Mama's hands and looked into her eyes. "Ingrid, why don't you come with us to the Christmas lighting program in Greeley? It's a beautiful evening, not too cold. Get you out."

"Do, Ingrid," Mrs. Hill said. "There's plenty of room in the back of the truck."

"Yeah, yeah, yeah!" Maizy and I jigged around the big table in the front room.

★ ★ ★

A dozen of us climbed into the bed of Mr. Hill's green Dodge truck. Mr. Myers rode in the cab with Mr. Hill. They probably swapped jokes and talked about weather extremes, sugar beet crops, tractor parts, and the war in Korea. In the truck bed out in the open air, bundled in quilts, Glenda Myers, Grace Hill, Mama, Maizy and Marvin Myers, the Hill boys, and I huddled like roly-polies.

The truck bumped and rattled along the dirt road, making us laugh and holler and complain happily. Even Mama smiled. On the paved highway, the ride smoothed out. Into the cooling air of twilight the "truck-bed chorus" brayed, "'You better watch out, you better not cry, you better not pout, I'm tellin' you why. Santa Claus is comin' to town!'" and "'Silent night, holy night, all is calm, all is bright...'" As the ball of sun rolled over the Rocky Mountain silhouettes on the western horizon, the day's warmth dwindled. Above us, vast furrows of cloud crops twinkled like tinsel.

Singing full-throated, covered with Gram's gray-and-red-woolen patchwork quilt, I felt swaddled in Gram and Grampy's presence. Many a time Grampy had hauled Gram and me, along with a few neighbors, in his truck to a picnic or a parade in Akin or Greeley or LaSalle or Kersey or some other nearby town. I closed my eyes and pretended Grampy was in the cab with Mr. Myers and Mr. Hill, and Gram was caroling with us in the back.

Nearing Lincoln Park in Greeley, the traffic slowed. Sedans and pickups, most of them crammed with people, moved slowly down the wide streets. Greeley police directed traffic, blowing whistles and waving their arms. We found a parking place two blocks away, and off we tromped toward the park carrying quilts, a jug of hot chocolate, and a package of paper cups.

We kids squirmed and giggled through Mayor Price Hopkins' welcoming speech, and the chamber of commerce president Mr. Scott's thanks to the Elks club and the Jaycees for helping to make the lighting program possible, and Mr. John Hallgren's announcement about the Jaycees' home-lighting contest.

The best part was when the king and queen of the ceremony, third graders at Lincoln School in Greeley, Ronny Gies and Rosalie Torrez, pulled the switch. Red, green, blue, white, and yellow lights flickered then blazed, illuminating the park and streets.

"Ooooooh," the crowd said en masse then broke into applause, yells, and whistles.

The Elkateers chorus sang "Winter Song," "Steal Away," "Oh Little Town of Bethlehem," and "Silent Night" while some in the audience hummed or sang along, me included. It was impossible to comprehend that Gram and Grampy weren't there with us enjoying the crowd, the lights, the sense of joyful anticipation at the coming of Christmas.

For the finale, "in honor of the U. S. troops fighting for freedom in Korea," the director, Merle Carpenter, and the Elkateers chorus led the crowd in singing "God Bless America" and "My Country, 'Tis of Thee."

On that sweet night, the darkness and sorrow distilled by the twinkling lights of Christmas and the presence of Mama and our kind neighbors, I sang every verse along with the crowd, loud and clear, with all my child-heart.

> "...Our fathers' God, to Thee,
> Author of liberty,
> To Thee we sing.
> Long may our land be bright
> With freedom's holy light;
> Protect us by Thy might,
> Great God, our King!"

Chapter 3

Thousands See
Yuletide Lights
Turned on Here
—*Greeley Daily Tribune*, p. 1, Mon., Nov. 27, 1950

★ ★ ★

Double Funeral of Long-Time
Area Farmers Set for Today
—*Akin Scoop*, p. 1, Tues., Nov. 28, 1950

Generally fair Tuesday; windy in afternoon

I awoke to morning light passing through Gram's bottles in the front window, effusing the room with colorful glow.

Gram and Grampy—their viewing was to be today at eleven and the funeral at one at Macy's in Greeley, then burial at Linn Grove.

Where was Mama?

I listened for sounds and heard only the gentle thump of the wall clock pendulum and somewhere a rooster crowing.

Mama's bed at the opposite end of the large front room was still made. Gram and Grampy's bedroom door stood open, bed empty, covers in disarray. In the kitchen the coffeepot sat cold and empty on the stove. Through the window I watched a flock of clangorous blackbirds swirl and swoop across the cornflower-blue sky and alight in the big cottonwood by the sheds at the south end of the farmyard.

I sat on my couch-bed in the front room, slid my bare feet into my oxfords, grabbed my coat off the hook by the back door and headed out. No sign of Polly or Pie in the pasture. Maybelle grazed down near the water tank and the chickens clucked contentedly in the coop.

In the milk shed Mama sat hunched on a milk stool. Her matted hair tucked under her coat collar and her back toward the partially open door, she yanked at Pie's teats.

Pie bellowed, stomped her hoof, and swung her head around toward Mama.

Schplatt! Schplatt! Schplatt! The milk blasted into the tin pail.

"I hate death! I hate life!" Mama's white fists worked the teats, as she spoke in savage whispers between sobs. "How did I get stuck with Ponia?" And she mumbled other things I couldn't make out. She was angry with me. But why? What did I do wrong?

I fled, shoestrings slapping my ankles until my shoes flew off. The cold ground bit at my feet. I stopped and struggled to step back into my shoes. I got them on and ran to the sheds around behind Grampy's tractor shed. The chirping of the blackbirds converted to startled cries, and with rapid wings they lifted like one great black hissing ghost into the hole of sky.

I leaned against the shed, pulled the lapel of my coat over my mouth and screamed.

And screamed.

Until it felt like my temples would burst open. Until my heart nearly exploded from my chest. "Ponia!"

Until Mama called me.

Hide!

★ ★ ★

I dragged a box, clanking like it had pans inside, across the dirt floor and shoved it against the shed door. A sound like a steam engine bearing down on me panted in my ears, then I realized it was myself, breathing.

"Ponia!" Mama's shrill voice sounded from the farmyard. Soon I heard her footsteps near the side window.

I ducked behind an antique wringer washer and peered between the rollers. She squinted and pressed her forehead against the dirty window to see in.

The air in the shed, frigid and still, entombed the putrefying odors of mouse droppings and must. Thick, filthy cobwebs clung to my hair, neck, and coat. I climbed over a box, in slow motion it seemed, and tried to squeeze between a dresser and the wall. The door pitched open in a clatter against the box of pans. I struggled to hold my breath, but it burst from my lungs, coarse and deafening.

The morning sun poured through the doorway, shooting rays around the black silhouette that was Mama. She eased the door closed behind her and the rays vanished. I saw her clearly now, leaning against the shed door. Like reflections we stared at each other, panting and shaking.

Mama stepped toward me over boxes and junk, breathing like a racehorse. Her brow furrowed into a sharp *v* and lightning flicked in her eyes. My knees gave way and I slumped to the floor. *Why? Why is this happening?* She towered above me in her brown coat, bare legs, and scuffed brown loafers. Her fists, at my eye level, clenched.

"Mama…" My cheeks burned like fire—she had struck me. But, no! She was poised like a statue, bronzed in the frail light sifting through the grimy window. She hadn't moved. I touched my cheek and it was wet. Blood? I looked at my damp fingers. Water. Who was crying?

And then a sound erupted from her—a sound like the cows made sometimes—half bawling, half breath. Mama extended her arms. Her words scratched the dead, chilly air. "Come 'ere."

She lurched toward me. I flinched and squeezed my eyes shut. I heard her breathing and a mouse rustling along the back wall.

She bent so close I could smell her stale breath and the musty scent of her coat.

Run!

But she had me by the arms. I opened my eyes and saw the twisted face of my mother. The skin crinkled over her bony face in a grimace, her thin lips pulled white and tight across her teeth—an evil smile. But, no, she was in agony. Then her eyes softened, tears spilled.

A pitying place deep inside me stirred then ballooned.

"There, there, Mama," I whispered. "There, there."

Chapter 4

1951

Russia Has
Atom Bomb,
Dean States
—*Greeley Daily Tribune*, p.1, Tues., Jan. 2, 1951

★ ★ ★

Chinese Tanks Barge Toward
Seoul Through Allied Lines
—*Akin Scoop*, p.1, Wed., Jan. 3, 1951

Wednesday's high 42°, low 18°; high winds

Today's *Akin Scoop* open to Classifieds, Mama searched the apartments-for-rent ads. I sat at the kitchen table next to her and rubbed my finger over the table's stenciled design—a black basket of red flowers.

Soon, I'd never again milk Polly and Pie. I wouldn't ride Maybelle like lightning across the pasture or kiss that coarse, flat place between her eyes or feel her soft, damp nuzzle on my hand as she took a sugar cube. And those silly chickens—I'd never scatter feed to Hettie and Molly and the others or hear them cluck-cluck, or watch them twitch their pink-combed heads forward and back and blink their pink lids over round, startled eyes. From town, I probably wouldn't be able to see the fields of corn and alfalfa and wheat and beets stretched out to kingdom come, clear to that distant place where land and sky rub shoulders.

The walls creaked and the windows whistled as a gust of wind blew against the house.

"Hope the weather cooperates for the auction," Mama said, "and for our ride to Akin next week."

I nodded.

Mama read every ad slowly. Reading was a puzzling chore for her and for me. I only pretended to look at the ads.

"There's probably more apartments and jobs in Greeley," Mama mumbled, talking mostly to herself. "But Greeley's getting so big. Akin's better, I think. And Aunt Bella's there. Might's well be near our only living relative."

Mama penciled circles around two ads. "These are pretty cheap." She tucked a lock of brown hair behind her ear, nudged the newspaper toward me, and studied me.

My face turned warm and I pretended to read in the circles.

"We'll get by if I can just get work," Mama said, "maybe as a waitress or a housekeeper."

The first apartment Mama called about was already rented. She rested her finger under the second ad.

FOR RENT- Furn.
one-rm. apt. with kitchenette,
share bath, 340 Tenth Avenue,
Ph. 276

Mama dialed. She gripped the black receiver, her knuckles white. She introduced herself and said she was calling about the apartment-for-rent ad. "Thirty-five dollars a month? Okay, we'll take it. Now don't rent it to nobody else. We'll be there Saturday."

Chapter 5

Six City Trucks
To Pick Up Old
Yuletide Trees
—*Greeley Daily Tribune*, p.1, Fri., Jan. 5, 1951

Dunkling Memorial Public
Library Reopens Monday After
Month-long Painting and Repairs
—*Akin Scoop*, p.1, Fri., Jan. 5, 1951

Snow Friday afternoon; icy roads at night

At ten-thirty Bud Binger the auctioneer—short, stout, wearing a plaid mackinaw and ten-gallon hat—pulled into the farmyard in his mud-caked Ford pickup. Several women from the Akin Ladies Aid arrived with steaming covered dishes, filling the cold air with aromas of onion, chicken, and fresh-baked bread. By eleven o'clock a crowd had gathered.

Mr. Binger climbed up on a flatbed. "Well folks. Let's get started, see if we can get this done 'fore the predicted snow blows in." He tipped Gram's wheelbarrow up on its front wheel, and the auction began with Mr. Binger rumbling the bidding along in something like a sputtery foreign language. One by one, Gram and Grampy's possessions were auctioned off—farm equipment, the animals, and almost everything inside the house—including the couch that had been my bed, and even Gram's bottle collection. Mama and I stationed ourselves apart from the crowd—stoic statues in the January cold, our frosted breath drifting away like dust—and watched neighbors, friends, and strangers cart off the pieces of Gram and Grampy's lives.

Mama barely spoke to the folks who expressed regrets. I could only stare and endure the parched pressure in my throat. Some of the women from the Ladies Aid had known Abigail, as they referred to Gram, and comforted us with smiles and gentle arm-squeezes—and few words, for which we were grateful.

Mama didn't sell Gram and Grampy's blue 1942 Ford truck. But she sold Gram's Singer sewing machine to Grace Hill who offered her twelve dollars for it before the auction. The few things we kept fit into Gram and Grampy's wooden trunk and Mama's old black suitcase. Grampy still owed on his tractor and owed the bank for two years of failed beet crops. "We won't have much of a blitherin' thing left to live on after the bills are paid," Mama said.

Mama kept the pendulum wall clock that bonged the hours. She settled it into the trunk, lovingly wrapped in Gram's handmade quilts along with other basic supplies.

Tomorrow Mama and I would set out for our new life in Akin.

Chapter 6

Navy To Double
Carrier Force
—*Greeley Daily Tribune*, p.1, Sat., Jan. 6, 1951

Icy Roads Cause
of Many Crashes
—*Greeley Daily Tribune*, p.1, Sat., Jan. 6, 1951

Saturday's high 26°, low 2°; snow and ice on ground from yesterday afternoon's storm

The Myers family loaded our trunk and suitcase onto the bed of the pickup, and Mr. Myers covered them with a tarp.

Smiling, Mrs. Myers handed Mama a basket draped with a tea towel. "Just a little lunch, Ingrid."

Mama's soft, "Oh, Glenda," was her thank you.

The way Mrs. Myers blinked her gray-blue eyes real slow and touched my cheek, I knew she was sad for us.

Our breaths wreathed our faces and we shivered in the cold sunshine.

Marvin saluted me. "See ya."

Maisy pulled her cap down over her forehead, nearly covering her teary eyes. "I hope you like Akin School."

I shuddered. "Thanks."

She handed me a small flat box. "If you write me, I'll write you."

Inside were pink sheets, matching envelopes, and postage stamps. We hugged. I thanked her and stared at my shoes.

"Just write plain," Maisy said, as if she had read my mind. "I don't spell good neither."

Marvin pointed at the pink stationery. "If you write to me, don't use those. Write to me on a Big Chief tablet or somethin' else."

We laughed, then Maisy hugged me tight and sniffed.

I reached toward Marvin. He bridged his arms between us. "I ain't huggin' no girl."

Maisy laughed and chased him. "Come on, give us a little hug."

Then they raced toward the warmth of their Studebaker, calling over their shoulders. "See ya, Poni."

Mama didn't cry at the auction or when we packed or when we said our good-byes. But after we drove down the road apiece, it looked like every pore on her face welled like springs. Wetness oozed onto her face, and she looked straight ahead saying nary a word as we bumped along the icy road. She gripped the steering wheel so tightly her hands trembled.

It was curious how the sun reflected in the driver's side-view mirror, cast a ray across Mama's reddened face, and transformed her tears to crystals. I stared at those gems, suspended, glistening. A grievous ache throbbed in my chest. I wanted to change places with the lunch basket and lean my head against her shoulder. But I knew better.

A drought blew hot inside me like the summer winds that whip dry heat and sand over the plains. It was peculiar, feeling that way, while Mama was so sodden. There we were, far apart, each in our own zones—she in her jungle, me in my desert.

Brindled fields spread out like quilts stitched with snowy threads and sewed in a nice straight seam along the horizon to the baby-blue-pique sky. The iced earth breathed fog up into the morning light as we passed the Hill place, the Rochester place, the Smith place…

Two horses—a chestnut-colored and a black—huddled against the cold in the Eastmans' pasture. I thought of Grampy's and my gentle Maybelle, how Mr. Rayner had struck her to get her into his horse trailer. Her eyes had gotten that wild look, as if a rattler had startled her. She had whinnied at me and tossed her mane. *Help! Rescue me, Poni!* she'd said with her eyes. But she was no longer ours, she was Mr. Rayner's. I had to let her go. We had to let everything go.

We had to set the past free.

★ ★ ★

We gassed up the truck at Syd's Sinclair Service Station in Sandy Creek, then trundled on down the highway.

"Only enough money left for a month's rent and a few groceries," Mama said.

When we came to a sign—*Akin*—with an arrow pointing west, and a sign below it—*Sixth Avenue*—Mama turned off the highway. Hamburger Hut squatted on the corner to the left, on the right a small Standard station. Mama dabbed her swollen face with a hanky and blew her nose.

Two blocks down the road Mama read a sign aloud, a filament of steel in her voice. "'Welcome to Akin, the home of Weld literaries.'"

A block down the street, nailed to a telephone pole, a homemade poster flapped in the breeze: *Literary Mon. 1/8 @ Larson Barn, 7 pm Publick invited.*

We had often driven to Akin for supplies and various events, but today it appeared new—strange.

Like centurions with outstretched arms, lofty barren trees guarded the large, old homes with wrap-around porches and extended eaves.

Next, a neighborhood of modest rectangular clapboard houses—friendly, cheerful. Two black cockers on leashes pulled an elderly woman wearing a sapphire-blue scarf. A thin, red-haired woman, hugging her white sweater to her, hurried out of a brown house with white shutters and called to the blue-scarfed woman. They greeted each other with grins, and then the thin woman petted the barking, bouncing cockers. I watched the neighbor women until they faded from my view and wished Mama and I could live on that block.

We passed two churches—Akin Assembly of God and First Baptist—on the north side of the road, nestled among small, plain houses. On our left, taking up half a block, was a dirty-white, flat-roofed building—John's Hardware and Lumber. Large open doors exposed rows of stacked-to-the-ceiling lumber. We drove by Crawley's Five and Dime, Francine's Fancies, Matthews' Drug Store, Landry's Laundry, Rex's Diner, and a few small shops.

Mama pointed to a two-story, red-brick structure on the right, surrounded by a large play yard and a high chain-link fence. "Your school."

A gust of wind set the swings swaying. Along one side of the play yard near the swings were a slide, two bars, a tetherball pole, a merry-go-round, and, on the corner, a backstop. *Akin School, est. 1905* was engraved above the school entrance in granite. A tiny store, Snodgrass Grocery, was directly across the street. So was Bud Green Furniture and Akin Scoop, the newspaper office.

"Will I ride a school bus?"

"You'll walk."

I smiled. "Where's our apartment?"

"A few blocks south of here."

We stopped at the light on Sixth and Harp Way, then continued west on Sixth. Just past Smith Dry Cleaning, we turned left into Zimmerman's Standard Service, pulled up in front of a pump and stopped.

A nice looking fellow, his hair and goatee the color of Maybelle, trotted out of the small station, a blue cloth swinging from his back pocket. He beamed at us, his brown eyes glinting in the sun. *Roger* was sewn near the left shoulder of his slate-blue coveralls. The ribbing of his long underwear showed at the neck, the same way Grampy's did in the winter.

Mama rolled down her window.

"Fill 'er up, Ma'am?" he asked.

"Well, yes, but…"

He smiled, waited.

Mama spoke haltingly. "I-I done filled up the tank in Sandy Creek. Won't take much to fill it again. I w-wonder, do you know of anyone who could help us move a trunk up to a second-floor apartment?"

Roger tugged at his goatee. "How big is it?"

Mama pointed toward the back of the truck.

Roger raised a corner of the tarp.

"Trouble is," Mama said, "I can't pay much."

"Where you from?"

A gust of cold wind blew through the open window. "About ten miles southeast of here—the Arrentz Place." Mama pulled her coat up around her neck.

Roger nodded. "I know the Arrentzes. Come in here all the time. You their daughter?"

Mama stared off through the front windshield. "Nope, Art and Abigail Parks'. They died in November. Ponia here, and me, we had a farm sale. We come to Akin to live, get work." Mama scrutinized Roger from under the rim of her brown felt hat. "Do you know of anybody?"

Roger grinned. "To haul up your trunk? Sure do." He trotted back toward the station and called over his shoulder, "Be right back."

He trotted out with a boy that had the same Maybelle-colored hair and brown eyes as Roger. Looked to be about fifteen.

"This here's my son, Billy."

Smiles and nods on both sides of the window.

"Billy and I'll haul it up for you. Where's your place?"

"Three-forty Tenth Avenue."

"Give us a minute to warm up our truck. We'll lead you there."

"But your station…"

Roger gestured toward an elderly man who gave a loose salute from the doorway. "Dad'll mind the station. Won't take long. We'll be back before business picks up at noon."

We followed Roger's red Dodge truck back down Sixth Avenue to Graham Way by the school. We turned right and drove south for four blocks. Turned right on Tenth and there we were, in front of a rambling, gray Victorian house with large peeling numbers near the front door, *340*. I liked the big wrap-around porch. Even had a porch swing.

Roger and Billy waited while Mama and I went inside and knocked on the door marked *Manager* beneath a fading *A*. A thin, elderly woman opened the door. She was a head taller than Mama with an inch of slip peeking from beneath her paisley skirt. Air, thick with must and garlic, assaulted the hallway. Heavy curtains were drawn over the windows.

"Ingrid Snow," Mama said pointing to her chest. "You're holding an apartment for us."

The woman looked us up and down and yelled over her shoulder into the dusk, "Harold! The new renters are here."

Harold was bald and stout, as short as his wife was tall. Black suspenders held up his gray, wrinkled pants. He pumped Mama's hand, smiling. "Harold Fens. How do you do," he said, and breathed the air thicker with the smell of garlic. He pointed up to his wife. "My wife Gertrude Fens. Welcome. Glad to have you."

Mama grunted, nodded, and took a step back.

The Fens eyed me but said nothing.

Harold Fens gave Mama two identical keys and led us up to our apartment. We creaked up the stairs to the second floor, right U-turn and creaked down the hallway to the end—apartment C, Mama's and my new home.

Roger and Billy carted the trunk up the stairs, muscles straining.

While Mama offered Roger a five-dollar bill with a shy thank you, Billy hurried back downstairs and carted up Mama's old black suitcase.

Roger gently pushed away her hand. "You can thank me by coming to our station when you need gas or your truck serviced."

"I can do that." Mama was still red and puffy around the eyes and nose, but her shy smile made her look pretty, even in her old brown coat and her hat pulled down around her face.

Roger and Billy Zimmerman shuffled out of the apartment. Roger halted and looked back at Mama. "Good luck finding work." He smiled and then pulled the door closed.

Mama and I listened to their heavy work shoes tromping down the creaky stairs and the sharp closing of the entrance door.

I glanced around the room that would be our home, then at Mama's tired eyes. She sighed. "Well, here we are."

I spread my lips over my teeth into what I hoped looked like a smile. "Here we are."

★ ★ ★

Mama and I unpacked the suitcase then ate some of the fried chicken, buttered bread, and peanut butter cookies that Glenda Myers had made for us. The thought of Mrs. Myers' kindness warmed me. I cupped my hand over the place where she had touched my cheek. And, oh, how I would miss Maizy and Marvin.

Late that afternoon, after we made our beds—Mama's on the couch and my mat on the floor, we crawled into them for naps. I slept until morning.

Chapter 7

President Truman Awards
Medal of Honor to
Soldier from Akin Area
—*Akin Scoop*, p.1, Sun., Jan. 7, 1951

Three Polio Victims
Meet with Volunteers
—*Akin Scoop*, p.1, Sun., Jan. 7, 1951

Sunday's high 34°, low 3°; snow and ice still on ground from Friday snow

January sunshine filtered through the frosted window. I lay in bed, eyes barely open, watching Mama. She was unpacking the trunk, wearing her long woolen socks, and over her faded lilac-colored chenille robe she wore her coat and hat. Her hair, dull as bark, had been gathered into a tangled ponytail and secured with a rubber band.

I could hear and smell someone next door frying bacon.

A pair of rhinos—or what sounded like a pair of rhinos—slammed the main door and tromped up the stairs. A man laughed, and a woman with a sing-song voice said, "Well, I do 'preciate the help, I surely do."

Another door in the hallway squeaked open. An older woman shouted, "Pipe down out here. Show some respect!" *Slam!*

Mama, with folded sheets and towels, walked past me but didn't notice her daughter was awake. She placed the linens in the bottom bureau drawer, shuffled back to the trunk, and lifted out the wall clock. It filled the small tabletop, even with both leaves up.

The floor creaked as Mama stepped back and forth between the kitchenette and the trunk, putting the few dishes away.

The room that was now Mama's and my home wasn't even as big as the front room at the Arrentz place. The ceiling was high and far away like gray sky. A light bulb hung from a long, brown cord threaded through a fat chain. The pull-string to turn the light on was long enough so even I could reach it if I stretched up my arm and stood on tiptoe. The radiator huffed and hissed. Even so, the room was chilly. No. Cold. I wished I had worn my stocking cap to bed. And I wished the bathroom didn't have to be clear down the hall even though, I had to admit, it was better than an outhouse any day.

I lay there, my body warm and comfortablelike under the quilts that Gram had made, and admired the frost fanning out on the sunlit window like silvery-white plumes. They looked like the plumes that had bobbed over the top of Gram's favorite black hat. She had worn that old hat summer, winter—every time we went to town. When Gram bent down to say something important to me or to offer me a stick of Clove gum, sometimes her silvery plumes tickled my face. I would squint and giggle, delighting in the tickly feeling, her closeness, and her clove breath. A brown sadness settled over my heart, remembering Gram like that.

Tap, tap, tap. Mama hammered a nail into the wall. "Get up, Ponia. Help me hang this clock."

I shut my eyes.

"Up! Now, Ponia Glass Snow."

★ ★ ★

We ate breakfast—oatmeal without milk. Then I washed the dishes that had been wrapped in newspaper while Mama washed the shelves in the kitchenette and swept the linoleum floor.

Then out of the blue Mama said, "Let's go visit your great Aunt Bella at the rest home. Go take a bath and get dressed."

That was my first bath in a regular tub. Whew! What fun! It was like swimming in a fancy-legged pool.

★ ★ ★

Mama answered the loud rap at our door.

It was Gertrude Fens, our new landlord. "Come and look at the mess your daughter made." She stomped off toward the bathroom. "Now! And bring a mop!"

★ ★ ★

Aunt Bella lived at the Akin Rest Home, an old converted manor house. Three gray-haired women slumped and slept in wheelchairs right by the front door. A bent, silver-haired man shuffled with a cane down the narrow corridor. A faint odor, similar to our chamber pot of a winter morning on the Arrentz place, accompanied us.

Mama walked into Aunt Bella's room ahead of me. It was a small room, just big enough for two narrow beds, a chiffonier, and a chifforobe. Aunt Bella lit up when she saw Mama, her eyes like donuts—round and surprised—in her pickle-shaped face.

"Ingrid!" she crowed, and rolled her wheelchair toward Mama. With a gnarled hand she gestured toward the bed. "Come! Come in. Sit down."

The bed sank down in a loud squeak with Mama's weight. She smiled her tight little smile.

Aunt Bella spotted me standing in the doorway. "And you brought little what'sername! Come. Come in. Sit down." She beckoned me with a bony arm, her eyes round and wide. The irises floated like little brown boats on gray ponds. I thought an eye doctor might've pushed her eyelids back during an examination and then forgot to pull them back down.

"Ponia," said Mama, "come say hello to your Aunt Bella."

Aunt Bella flung up her arms. "Ponia! That's it. Of course!"

I slid my steps across the bare wood floor and stopped just out of her reach. "Hello, Ma'am." I held out the bag of horehound candy Mama had purchased at the corner grocery.

She angled her gnarled finger toward her bosom. "*Ma'am!* This is your Aunt Bella!" Then she snatched the bag and peeked inside. "Horehounds! My favorite. Oh, thank you so much, dears." She popped one into her mouth, savored it a moment, then pushed it into her cheek like a chipmunk. "Now, Ponia, have you started school yet? Can you read yet?" I imagined her shrill voice scraping grooves into the airways.

I shook my head.

"Troubles with reading," Mama said, "like me."

"You should listen to your teachers, Ponia." She poked at my chest with a bony finger. "Don't you be a woolgatherer like your good-for-nothing father."

My father?

Mama glared at Aunt Bella, yanked me away, and plopped me down on the squeaky bed next to her. "Aunt Bella, please don't be bringing up old ghosts, especially around Ponia."

"I've always felt so terrible about him leaving you and your sweet little baby for that tramp…"

"Aunt Bella!" Mama scolded.

A pinkness blanketed Aunt Bella's odd, narrow face and she wrung her hands. "Forgive me, Ingrid." Her eyes stayed wide, stricken. Then she offered us her horehounds, which we politely refused.

Mama cleared her throat and changed the subject. "Well, the auction went good, considering everyone just about froze to death. And we done moved and settled in Akin for good now."

Aunt Bella spouted a quaky laugh. "Good! Now I'll have company every day." Mama and Aunt Bella talked awhile catching up on news. Mama gestured with her hands, even giggled. Sometimes—like now—Mama was a whole other person, like someone else had dropped into her skin for a visit.

We stayed longer than we'd planned and played a game of Parcheesi—half a game rather, as Aunt Bella was so distracting with her complaints and prattle that we finally quit. I sure had trouble believing Gram and Aunt Bella were sisters. Gram was soft and sweet and warm like a cinnamon bun fresh from the oven. Aunt Bella was firm and tart and cool like a dill pickle from the icebox.

Aunt Bella threw up her hands, and a squeal burst from her throat. I thought she might be having a heart attack. "You can't go yet," she gurgled. "You haven't met Wordsworth!"

At her instruction, Mama and I pushed her in her wheelchair back up the hall, past the main entrance to a door with a sign that read:

Denton and Wordsworth Daleshaw
Directors
Alice Cane, Secretary
Knock and come in.

Aunt Bella leaned forward in her chair and knocked. "Wordsworth! This is Belley and friends, here to see you!" Aunt Bella's whole countenance and presence had transformed—glowed. The door opened into a large, homey office. A pretty, deep-blue-eyed woman with long, thick, dark hair sat at a mahogany desk. "Good morning, Miss Chester," she said to Aunt Bella, smiling.

"Good morning, Alice dear," Aunt Bella said, "I want you to meet…"

"Well, howdy-do!" Across the room in front of a window, a man stood up—unfolding like a long foldout card—and walked around his desk. "How's one of my favorite girls?" He reached down and enclosed Aunt Bella's hand in his large ones then kissed her on the forehead.

I was shocked. It was clear that he genuinely liked Aunt Bella.

She laughed in her little squawky way. "Denton Daleshaw, I want you to meet my niece and grandniece, Ingrid and Ponia Snow."

Mr. Daleshaw's tallness and deep voice could've been intimidating, but for his cheerful countenance and the soothing quality of his voice. His neatly trimmed hair was nearly black and his mustache was gray, and he wore a blue-and-white striped shirt.

"How's my favorite girl?" asked someone who sounded a lot like Aunt Bella, but it wasn't Aunt Bella.

"Wordsworth!" Aunt Bella clasped her gnarled hands.

"Favorite girl! Favorite girl!"

Mama and I turned as an object swooped toward us, then over us—a bird!—and landed on Mr. Daleshaw's head.

We squinted and ducked. Mama covered the top of her head with her hands, and a goofy smile eclipsed her face.

Mr. Daleshaw chuckled. "Meet Wordsworth, Extraordinary Cockatiel and Assistant Director."

Wordsworth was light yellow, head to chest, his body grayish. A bright orangy peach spot rouged each of his cheeks. I felt an immediate kinship with the bird because his mostly yellow "hairdo"—his crest—was close in hue to my pale hair, and it sprang out of control just like my hair tended to do.

"Come to Belley, Wordsworth!" Aunt Bella called, holding up her finger.

A few flaps of his wings, and Wordsworth came home to roost, as it were, on her finger.

After Aunt Bella goo-gooed over Wordsworth, Mrs. Cane took him onto her finger. "Poni, would you like me to set Wordsworth on your head?"

"Will he poop in my hair?"

She laughed. "I don't think so."

I nodded and scrunched up my shoulders in anticipation.

Wordsworth scrambled onto my head. It felt funny. Down he flew to an *Akin Scoop* paper spread out on the floor. He did his business then flew back to my head as everyone hee-hawed.

The director patted my shoulder, still chuckling. "Wordsworth likes you, Poni. It usually takes him several visits before he'll sit on someone's head without being prompted."

"He also flew to the paper when he had to go," Mrs. Cane said, "instead of letting go on your head. That's the ultimate compliment."

"Whew!" I said. "I'm sure glad he likes me."

Mr. Daleshaw held up his finger for Wordsworth then carried the cockatiel to the top of the birdcage. "Thank you for making everyone feel so welcome, Woodsworth," he said. "You are *some* bird."

We all agreed. We thanked the director and assistant director, and their secretary for their time.

Mr. Daleshaw shook Mama's hand and beamed. "Ingrid, you're welcome here any time."

"And, Poni, that goes for you too," Mrs. Cane said. "Any friend of Wordsworth's is a friend of ours."

We left the office. Mama and I said good-bye to Aunt Bella, whose narrow old face was half taken up with grin, then headed for home.

Maybe Aunt Bella wasn't so much like a dill pickle after all. She wasn't soft and warm like a cinnamon bun—and Gram, but she had more cinnamon and sugar in her than I'd thought.

Chapter 8

Fair Monday, high 50°, low 6°

The tall, dark-haired secretary pointed a red fingernail toward the bottom line. "That's all, Mrs. Snow. She's registered. Just sign here and date it." She squinted down at me. "Nice little blue eyes. They're the color of the summer chicory along the road by my house."

Mama signed her name *Ingrid Helene Snow* and dated it.

"I'm Dorothea Pruzer," the secretary said. "Feel free to call if you have any questions, Mrs. Snow."

Mama scowled and nodded. She was probably thinking about the day ahead of her, looking for a job and all.

Mrs. Pruzer cleared her throat. "Welcome to Akin School, Ponia."

In her matching green skirt and sweater, Mrs. Pruzer looked like a stringbean ready to be picked as she leaned over the counter and pointed toward the office door. "Now, go left to the end of the hall, up the stairs and down the hall to room 204. It's on the left. Your teacher, Mrs. Kipp, and I came to this school the same year Herbert Hoover was elected President—she to teach, and I to run the office." She paused and smirked. I thought she might take a bow.

Face pinched and pale, hair clinging to her neck, Mama waved me towards the office door. "Go on now, and walk on home after school lets out."

In the empty hallway, Mama's footsteps shuffled away and out the door. Gray cold swept by me as if the Ice Queen had just passed. The door shut—*thunk*—behind her and echoed over my head.

Mrs. Pruzer shooed at me. "Go! Go on. You'll be fine." The wood floor might well have been pasture mud after a rainstorm. I could not raise my feet from the spot.

Tip, tap, tip tap. Mrs. Pruzer walked in her black high heels through a little gate and out to the hallway where she towered over me. "I'll take you up. Come with me." A nudge to my shoulder broke me free.

We climbed the wooden stairs. A high window at the landing framed the gray-and-blue mottled sky. Wind shuddered on the glass.

Mrs. Pruzer puffed like a locomotive and tugged at one of my curls. "My! That hair of yours looks like a puffball." She sniggered. "Cute though."

I hurried past her to the top of the stairs.

"Wait for me," Mrs. Pruzer said with a sharp-edged voice, "Just because you can prance up the stairs with your long, colt legs, doesn't mean I can.

"Here we are. Room 204!" Mrs. Pruzer's words echoed up the hall.

I cringed.

"A new student, Mrs. Kipp—Ponia Snow." Mrs. Pruzer's voice rained upon the quiet room with a clatter. "She just moved here from a farm near Sandy Creek. No father. Her mother brought her in." Mrs. Pruzer pursed her lips and raised a black, painted-on eyebrow.

Four rows of students gawked at me as though they were beholding a spook.

"Come in. Welcome." Mrs. Kipp's voice was pleasant and warm.

"Go on!" Mrs. Pruzer pushed me into the room and closed the door behind me.

Mrs. Kipp smiled from a comfortable face. The frames of her glasses and her hair matched—the color and texture of winter wheat. She wore a straight tweed skirt and bright blue blouse. "Here's a desk for you." She indicated a desk on the far side of the room by the windows.

I chewed my lip and hung onto my lunch sack and school box. Whispers and snickers flew around the room. A brown-haired boy with a turkey tail smirked and pointed at my twine-laced oxfords.

"Your name's Ponia?" Mrs. Kipp asked.

I nodded and murmured, "Poni."

"That's a pretty name, Poni. You may hang your coat on a hook over there by the door. Put your lunch bag on the shelf then take a seat."

I put away my things then walked as if through shattered glass toward the empty desk where Mrs. Kipp waited. More whispers, giggles.

"Class," said Mrs. Kipp, "you are to treat Poni like you'd want to be treated if you had just started in a new school. I expect all of you to be friendly and helpful."

As I slid into the seat, my bare legs chirruped on the varnished wood. A loud snort erupted at the back of the room and flurries of snickers passed through the rows.

Mrs. Kipp removed her wheat glasses. "*Class.*" She skimmed the room with brown eyes glowering.

A round girl in front scooted her desk. A skinny boy with porcupine hair coughed and cleared his throat. Then stillness settled like the lull between lightning and thunder.

Mrs. Kipp spoke to the girl seated across from me. "Martha, would you be Poni's friend today? Show her around?"

I looked over at her. Hair streamed down her back like black silk, and she wore a white pinafore over a full-skirted, plaid dress. She glanced at me, her enormous eyes the color of Gram's heavily spiced apple butter, then at Mrs. Kipp, and at the smirking pig-tailed girl to her right.

Martha squirmed in her seat, screwed up her face, and mumbled, "Yes, Ma'am."

After school, I ran the four blocks down Graham Way, holding tight to my library book and folded lunch sack. The frigid morning winds had subsided and the sky alternated between sunshine and a foglike haze.

The rambling old apartment house loomed before me like a great gray dragon rising out of the mist. How different from the cozy four-room farmhouse I had lived in until a few days ago.

A person on the first floor was frying chicken, someone else, cabbage. My lunch had been a slice of buttered and sugared bread, an apple, and a few sips of water from the hall fountain. Even the cabbage smelled heavenly.

A man's voice announced the news from the radio in apartment F at the top of the stairs. The toilet flushed in the only bathroom, which was between apartments E and D.

A podgy, elderly lady stepped out of apartment E and halted. "What are you doing in here, girl?" She peered over her thick glasses and flicked her hands toward me. "Shoo! Get on out of here!"

"But, I live here."

"What'd you say?" shouted the woman.

I clung to the wobbly rail. "I-I live here." Gram had worn a white bib apron like that, but nothing else about this woman was like Gram.

"Children do not belong here. You better not cause any trouble." The woman waddled into the bathroom and slammed the door.

Locked. Tapping on our apartment door, I spoke softly. "Mama, I'm home." I waited, listening. Maybe she was at a job interview.

The E lady came out of the bathroom and waddled into her apartment. I used the bathroom since it was available, then went back down the hall and stood at our apartment door and knocked hard. "Mama! It's me."

E door squeaked open. The woman's eyes rolled around like black marbles behind her thick glasses. "Pipe down!" *Slam!*

I stared at our door—the green paint soiled and peeling.

Bong, bong, bong, bong. From inside the apartment, Gram and Grampy's wall clock clamored from its new place on the gray wall.

That old clock had hung in the front room at the Arrentz place, perched like a large owl among the leaves and roses of the wallpaper. Beneath it, many an evening Gram and I had sat on the squishy, huckleberry-colored couch and listened to the radio. Grampy's chair cackled like a chicken as he listened and rocked, hands folded against his chin. Throughout the long Colorado winters the pot-bellied stove radiated warmth. I could smell the chicken frying in the kitchen and see Gram's weathered hands rolling out a piecrust and peeling potatoes.

"Mama." I knocked again and listened.

The cobwebs swayed in slow motion from the ceiling high above as a gust outside stirred the air. My eyes watered.

"Now don't you cry," Gram used to say to me when I fussed about something. Then Grampy would say, "Big girls don't cry, and cryin' don't help nobody anyway."

I swallowed down the pressure in my throat and blinked hard, pushing back thoughts of Mama leaving me at Gram and Grampy's all those times. She wouldn't leave me again, would she? She only left me before because she knew Gram and Grampy loved me and would take care of me.

I leaned back against the door and waited.

★ ★ ★

Thud! Back onto the floorboards I sprawled, my head spinning.

"Ponia!"

I opened my eyes. Someone stooped over me, hair forward, obscuring the face.

I stood up and rubbed my eyes. "Mama."

She shuffled past me. "I must have fallen asleep."

I picked up my book and followed. "I knocked loud."

Mama eyes were red and swollen. "I was sleeping." Her voice had turned cold. She wiped her eyes on the sleeve of her housedress.

I removed my coat as the clock bonged seven times.

She trudged to the kitchenette and pulled a can of Campbell's vegetable soup off the shelf. I smelled it from across the room as she opened the can, dumped it into Gram's dented saucepan, and set it on the hotplate.

"Want some soup?" she asked.

"Yes please." I studied the tattered lace edging on the collar and pockets of her housedress, feeling thankful she was here with me, not gone. "Did you find a job today, Mama?"

It looked like Mama asked the pan of soup, "Where'd you get that book?"

"Today was library day." I opened *Stuart Little* to the first page. "Mrs. Kipp is nice."

"Get spoons, Ponia."

I took two spoons from the shelf. "I want Gram's Poppyware bowl please."

Mama set the requested bowl full of steaming soup in front of me. "That teacher better not be too nice. She better make you behave. You been spoiled rotten."

I handed her a spoon. "Martha had to be my friend today."

Mama crushed a cracker between her palms then brushed it into her soup. "*Had* to be?"

"I could tell she doesn't like me much. But she tried to be nice."

Mama frowned. We blew and sipped the hot soup. I touched the chip on the edge of my bowl then traced the poppy design.

Mama's face smoothed out some. "What are you smiling about?"

I waved my spoon at her and said, "I was thinking about how Gram liked her Poppyware dishes—because they're the color of morning fog when the sun shines through. Gram's favorite kind of morning."

Mama waved her spoon back. "And because red poppies were her favorite flower."

"Gram liked the way I described the color of her Poppyware."

Mama's thin lips curled into a tight little smile. "You're very good with words, Poni."

My heart thumped in my chest. "But not when they're on a page."

Mama sighed. "Tell me about Martha."

"Well, Martha said it was pathetic that I can't hardly read. In the library today she read me the first chapter of *Stuart Little*. I liked it."

Mama was caught in her little smile. I wished I could say *freeze* and she would stay like that forever.

I tapped on the book and said, "These people—the Littles—had a son named Stuart. He was normal in every way except he was a mouse."

Mama stopped eating and listened.

"Mrs. Little made him teeny-weeny clothes, and he slept in a teeny-weeny box." I grinned. "The family really loved him, including his big brother, George, who was a regular kid. Stuart climbed down into the bathtub drain and rescued his mama's ring."

I drank the last drops of broth from the bowl.

"Ponia-a-a!" Mama scolded.

"Grampy always drank from his bowl."

A faraway look enfolded Mama's drawn face.

"Mama, you know what I've been wondering?"

"What?" Mama whispered.

"If I was a mouse, would you like me better?" A snicker escaped from Mama. Soup dripped onto her chin and down the front of her housedress.

I laughed and ran for the dishrag. Mama wiped her chin and dress. Then the smile faded and her eyes clouded.

Making Mama happy was like throwing a stone into a pond. The rings faded quickly.

"Mama." I paused, searching for just the right words. "Sometime—sometime can we talk about my dad?"

Mama frowned. "It's late. Get ready for bed."

"I would just like to know what he looked like, and maybe... maybe what happened to him?"

"He didn't look like much. And he left us—that's what happened." She got up and cleared the table.

I wiped off the table. "Where is he now?"

"That's anybody's guess. And we're through talking about him. Hear?"

Mama got that look, that kind of scary look. *Change the subject!* I wished I'd stuck with Stuart Little as the topic. "Martha says..." *What did Martha say?* "She says... Stuart Little had more adventures in one book than we'll have in our whole life."

"That's enough, Ponia. Get ready for bed."

I stood by the table holding the book like a placard. "Would you read chapter two?"

She turned off the light over the table, then spread sheets and quilts over the couch for her bed. "Get into your nightgown."

The wall clock struck eight just as I pulled my gown over my head. "Would you read to me, Mama?"

A sigh came from somewhere deep inside her. She patted the sofa. I sat close to her, cross-legged to warm my bare feet. I opened the book to chapter two then gazed up into Mama's face. The skin around her eyes was dark and bluish, her cheeks hollow. Reflections of the lamp formed golden butterflies in her cinnamon eyes.

Mama read haltingly in monotone. After only a few words she paused.

I waited.

She cleared her throat... and flung the book into my lap. "*You* should be reading this."

I opened the book again.

She pushed it closed. "Go to bed."

"But, I wanted..."

Mama waved her arm toward my mat. "Go."

I padded across the cold linoleum and crawled under Gram's quilts.

She turned off the floor lamp. The couch groaned as Mama adjusted, trying to get comfortable.

A gust of wind rattled the panes. Shivering, I hunkered down under the covers with my book and closed my eyes. The clock ticked, the radiator hissed, and down the hall the toilet flushed and a door closed—comforting sounds. Breathing in the quilts' musty scent, it was as if I was back in Gram's and Grampy's farmhouse in my sofa bed in the front room.

Soon Mama breathed deep and steady and I knew she was asleep.

I wondered at my mother's changes—like seasons. I had loved seasons on the farm. Spring set off a fireworks display of color and new life. Summer birdsong and cricket jazz rang out over the irrigated fields of corn and wheat and sugar beets and watermelon. Nippy fall mornings frosted browned cornstalks like icing on ladyfingers and decorated the porch with yellow and brown leaves. The sounds of crying geese, bawling cows, and snow-crunching boots caught between winter's snowy mittens and slid into my inner ear—quiet, cold, and close.

My throat bulged and ached from holding back the outcry of my own hurting heart. Mama and I were both in a kind of winter. Were winters of the heart, as in nature, always followed by spring? I hoped so.

I reckoned everybody had to go through the seasons many times in their lives.

Especially Mama.

Chapter 9

Korean Waifs
Get Started
In Orphanage
—*Greeley Daily Tribune*, p.7, Wed., Jan. 10, 1951

Help Needed from Akin
Residents in Polio Campaign
—*Akin Scoop*, p.1, Wed., Jan. 10, 1951

Wednesday's high 57°, low 23°; partly cloudy; windy in afternoon

Our substitute teacher, Mrs. Snuggs, announced that she would be taking us on the walking fieldtrip to the library as Mrs. Kipp had planned. She explained that the library was an old stone mansion that had been donated to the town by the family of Maurice Dunkling, "a pillar of the community," after he died. She pointed out that his great great grandson was a "beloved member" of our fourth grade class—Laurence Dunkling. The class looked at Laurence and snickered. His chin and nose turned scarlet, and he snickered too.

The Akin School fourth graders shivered in the cold shadows of the library. Stained-glass flowers in arching windows adorned the front length of the stone building. *Dunkling Memorial Public Library, 1899* was engraved in granite above the tall, arched entrance.

Mrs. Snuggs shushed us before we filed in. Bright warmth and the comfortable smell of books welcomed us. The stout, silver-haired docent ushered us into an open area where we sat on a velvety maroon rug, and she introduced us to the library.

After a tour of the library, Mrs. Perkins lined us up at the fountain for drinks then led us back to the maroon rug.

"And now, boys and girls, friends of the Dunkling Memorial Public Library are honored to present a literary for your enjoyment via our guest reader and storyteller for today, Mrs. Odessa Luckett."

We clapped as a tall, elderly Negro woman promenaded across the wood floor and onto the rug. She laughed, deep-throated and breathless, and floated gracefully to the front in her fluttering black dress. A flowery fragrance drifted in with her. Long earrings dangled and sparkled with colorful points of light in contrast to her skin, which was the color of dark-rye bread. And her hat! The brim, as broad as her shoulders, supported a wreath of ink-black plumes and immense blood-red flowers that waved like sea anemone with every turn of her head.

Mrs. Perkins carried in a large box covered with red paper and sat it on the floor beside the storyteller's chair. "Children, say hello to Mrs. Luckett."

We sing-songed, "Hello, Mrs. Luckett."

Her voice rippled like a mountain brook. "Good morning, young ladies and gentlemen. You may call me Auntie Odie, if you'd rather. Lots of people do."

"Good morning, Auntie Odie," Laurence said.

"Good morning, Auntie Odie," said the rest of us.

She laughed. "And good morning to you, librarians! *Welcome* to today's literary." Her black-coffee eyes roamed over her young audience and looked at each child. The way she said *welcome* was throaty and breathless like her laugh and I knew she meant it. Her eyes settled on me, and I felt like I had known her all my life.

I'd never seen a colored person up close before. I studied her—the rich darkness of her skin, the broad nose. Large teeth bordered the inside of her smile like a whitewashed garden fence. She bathed us in a tub of words with a voice so clean and fresh it was like a new language.

> "There is no frigate like a book
> To take us lands away,
> Nor any coursers like a page
> Of prancing poetry.
> This traverse may the poorest take
> Without oppress of toll;
> How frugal is the chariot
> That bears the human soul!

"Emily Dickinson." She paused then recited a short poem by Agatha Jordan and another by Robert Louis Stevenson. And then another Emily Dickinson poem, which I loved—

> "He ate and drank the precious words.
> His spirit grew robust;
> He knew no more that he was poor,
> Nor that his frame was dust.
> He danced along the dingy days.
> And this bequest of wings
> Was but a book. What liberty
> A loosened spirit brings!"

We clapped, she repositioned her hat then announced, "'The Highwayman' by Alfred Noyes—

> "The wind was a torrent of darkness among the gusty trees.
> The moon was a ghostly galleon tossed upon cloudy seas.
> The road was a ribbon of moonlight over the purple moor,
> And the highwayman came riding—
> > Riding— riding—
> The highwayman came riding, up to the old inn-door..."

The storyteller told on, verse after verse, her voice galloping with the highwayman up hills and through valleys. We sat, as straight and alert as prairie dogs, immersed in the classic quest—its rhythm and rhyme, the adventure, the love of it all—until the last lines cantered to a halt.

At Mrs. Snuggs' leading, we stood and clapped, along with Mrs. Perkins and others in the library. Odessa Luckett bowed, and her hat fell off.

Auntie Odie rested her weathered hand on the red box. Ezekiel Rademacher pointed to it. "What's in there?"

Mrs. Luckett—Auntie Odie—rolled her lips into an *o* and raised her scant eyebrows. "Why, young man, that's a secret." Then she laughed and removed her hat, resting it in her ample lap.

Underneath that big hat was a "wild mop" hairstyle a lot like mine—tight, uncooperative curls, not very long—only hers was mostly silver-gray with some dark sprinkled in. She smoothed back frayed strands that haloed her face. I imagined the other kids and I were like strands of hair that she gathered up into the spell of her performance. She opened the red box, and again we became Auntie Odie's captives.

She lifted out two hats—a man's wide-brimmed straw hat, and a lady's worn, black-felt pillbox, then she stood. "'The Fisherman and His Wife.'" She paused and looked down as though gathering energy and growing taller.

Putting on the straw hat, she talked to an imaginary person on her left in a potent southern accent, her voice deep like a man's. "'I'm goin' fishin', Isabel, same as always.'"

In one swift movement, Mrs. Luckett—Auntie Odie—switched to the pillbox hat, side-stepped to the place of the fisherman's wife and looked at an invisible husband. Her voice turned high and scratchy, but she kept the accent. "'Then go, just go, Samuel. Catch sumpin' big and good.'"

Auntie Odie removed the hat, looked straight at her young audience, and said in her normal, rich voice, "The fisherman left his miserable hovel and strolled down to the sea. He cast out his line and sat down." She put on the straw hat, sat in the chair, and cast out an invisible line with a barely perceptible smile. "Pretty soon he done caught hisself a bi-i-ig flounder." She strained to reel in the invisible fish.

"Flounder spoke." Auntie Odie removed the hat, her voice became gurgly and pathetic. "'Hark! Fisherman, please let me live! I am not a flounder, but an enchanted prince. I would taste dreadful. Please let me go.'"

On with the straw hat. "'Glory be! You is talking! Therefore, I has to believe you, Flounder. As hungry as we are, I'm a-goin' to let you go.' So he threw the fish back into the sea and went home, fishless, to Isabel."

Auntie Odie plopped the black pillbox on and looked to her right. "'Samuel! Did you catch any fish?'"

Switched to the straw hat and looked left. "'No, Isabel darlin'. Well, yes, I done caught a flounder, but he was really an enchanted prince, so I heaved him back into the sea.'"

Switched hats and looked right. "'Samuel, no! You didn't!'"

Switched and looked left. "'Yes, Isabel, I did!'"

Switched and looked right. "'You didn't!'"

She kept switching hats and voices and talked faster and faster. Her face looked like it was made of soft rubber the way she instantly changed expressions. We all roared, even Mrs. Snuggs. I laughed until my sides hurt.

When the story ended, I clapped so hard my hands stung.

"Now," Auntie Odie said, "I'll tell you a true story—a story about myself and my family, a story about slaves." She lifted a length of massive chain out of the red box and laid her big fancy hat inside it. She pulled a white soiled cloth from the box, folded it into a triangle, and tied it around her head knotting it on top at the front. "I am the daughter of slaves." Her voice was a cello, sweet and low.

"My parents, Thomas Simmons and Melvina Annie Douglass Simmons, were born into slavery in North Carolina, and so were their first seven children. They all bore the scars of abuse by their master. They told me the stories of scourgings, and sunup to sundown labor in the plantation fields. In 1865 they rejoiced, freed by the Union victory in the Civil War. In 1871 they bought a small farm.

"Ten years after the war was over, in 1875, my parents' eighth and last child, Odessa Simmons, was born, free." The storyteller sprouted a sweet-sad smile. "That lucky child was me. When I was three years old, my father died and my mother Melvina became sickly and could no longer do the work of farm life."

Some of the kids sniffed and their chins quivered. My throat got that familiar ache and I breathed in quick, shallow breaths.

"My oldest brothers, Horace, Samuel, and George, took over the farm in 1879. My mother and I—I was four years old then—traveled to Concord, North Carolina. Mother got a job as a house servant—housekeeper and cook—in a white family's home, the Moores'.

"Annette Moore loved and pampered me—'little Odessa' she called me—and her husband, Dr. Floyd Moore, did too when he was home, along with their own children, Betsy, Richard, and Elizabeth. The Moores read to their children and me, and I learned to read before my sixth birthday. Mother told me the old Negro tales of slavery, which had been passed down to her. By the time I was ten, about the age of you children, I had memorized hundreds of stories, poems, and Bible verses, and the book of Philippians from the Bible."

"I grew up and received a college education because of the Moores' generosity, became a teacher, and married William Luckett in 1900 at the age of twenty-five. We wanted to go to Africa as missionaries to our people, but the missionary board refused us. 'Coloreds are not allowed to be missionaries overseas,' we were told.

"My husband William and I had one child that died at birth. William died in 1915. I came to Akin and taught a few years, then retired to advance my interests in poetry, storytelling, gardening—and the appreciation of nature in general."

When Auntie Odie had finished, she asked if there were any questions. She called on Imogene Schott who was up on her knees waving her hand. Imogene had a tall solid build, reddish-black kinky hair, and smooth rosy-brown skin.

"Why? Why…" Imogene rocked on her knees and slung her head back to flip the yellow ribbon out of her eyes that had worked loose from its bow. "Why didn't they let y'all go to Africa if your folks came from there?"

Auntie Odie adjusted her scarf and narrowed her eyes toward the ceiling, thinking about Imogene's question. It was a hard one all right.

I expected Auntie Odie's voice to take on a bitter tone. Instead, it sounded mellow and smooth like a cello. "In America, white folks and black folks had lived three-hundred years as masters and slaves. People didn't even know what equality and fairness was anymore, so freedom took a lot of getting used to on both sides. Growing into freedom takes time, patience, and work."

Imogene didn't wait to be called on again. "Can I be a missionary to Africa when I grow up, if I wanna be? I'm half colored."

"I believe maybe you could. Things are slowly getting better for our people. It's not what it should be. But it is better."

Auntie Odie removed the scarf, replaced her big fancy hat on her head, and dropped the chain and white cloth back into the red box. She looked at Imogene. "Everyone—whether you're colored…" Her eyes skimmed the class then settled on me. The sunlight slanting through the stained glass window warmed me. She smiled. "Or whether you're white, the Declaration of Independence says we're all created equal, we have liberty, and can pursue happiness. I look forward to the day when all people are free to live good lives unhindered by the lightness or darkness of their skin." Auntie Odie adjusted her hat and straightened her shoulders. "Don't you?"

In unison, we proclaimed, "Yes!"

Chapter 10

Akin Storyteller Visits Schools
And Libraries Around Weld
—*Akin Scoop*, p.1, Fri., Jan. 12, 1951

★ ★ ★

Akin School Students, Teachers
Gearing Up For Annual
Silver Tongues Harvest
—*Akin Scoop*, p.2, Sat., Jan. 27, 1951

Mother Sees Four of Her Six Sons Go Off to War
—*Greeley Daily Tribune*, p.1, Sat., Jan. 27, 1951

Saturday's high 12°, low minus 6° (after yesterday's 66° high); ½" powdery snow in early a.m.

Spindly shadows from the bare maple danced on the window shades. Outside, a dog barked, people talked, hollered, laughed, honked cars, and slammed car doors.

I got out of bed—*ooh, freezing-cold floor*—and raised the shade. A light snow covered the ground and clung to roofs, trees, and bushes. Frigid cold seeped through the pane, and my breath turned to a circle of frost on the window. Men, women, and children, bundled in hats, earmuffs, scarves, coats, snowsuits, gloves, and boots, swarmed the white Victorian house across the street on Graham Way. A light fog, formed by warm bodies and breaths, hung over the yard like a scant ball of cotton. A sign, nailed to a birch tree, proclaimed *Estate Sale.*

Mama stretched and yawned on her couch bed. She slipped into her chenille robe then stood beside me. Icy air whistled in when Mama opened the window a crack, but we could hear better.

On the broad porch of the house, a ruddy-faced man in overalls, brown jacket, and a blizzard cap with the ear flaps down jibbered loudly. His rapidly repeated words and syllables sounded something like a yodel mixed with a gander clamoring orders to his family.

Mama and I chorused, "An auction."

From the time I was little, I had attended auctions. If Gram was driving down a road or a street and she spotted an auction, she braked and parked in the first spot she could find.

I grinned. "Can we get dressed and go over?"

"It's mighty cold."

"We could dress warm."

A hint of cheer burnished her voice. "Let's."

★ ★ ★

"Hmmm, smbdygimmeforty, forty." The auctioneer opened the lid of a tool box and displayed the contents. "Hm- smbdygimmeforty-forty. Do-I-hearfortydollars? Goinggoinggoinggonefrthirty-five. *Sold* for thirty-five dollars to the gentleman in the brown Stetson." The auctioneer whipped off his blizzard cap, wiped his balding head with a kerchief from his pocket, tied up the flaps, and slapped it back on. The gentleman wearing the Stetson smiled and ambled up to the porch to pay for and collect the tools.

I spotted Vanessa Perlmutter from my fourth grade class holding up a Bo-Peep lamp. "I want this," she said, whining to her parents. When she spotted me, she waved half-heartedly and flipped back her long blond braids.

A living room set was auctioned off for forty-seven dollars and two boxes of Dresden China for twenty-two fifty.

I walked up beside Mama who was inspecting boxes overflowing with fabric scraps, spools of thread, and other sewing supplies. We pulled our coats tighter around us. She rubbed her hand, red from the cold, over the shiny black curves of a Singer sewing machine. She had hated letting go of Gram's Singer at our own auction in December.

"Now that's a splendiferous machine," a woman's deep voice drawled.

We turned and looked up into a broad, white-toothed smile. "Dandy walnut cabinet too."

I grabbed the woman's black-gloved hand, my voice squeaked. "You're the storyteller at the library! You're Auntie Odie!"

She raised one eyebrow, tilted her head, and studied me with wide dark eyes.

An ornate gold-framed cameo was pinned to her coat—the profile of a delicate ivory face on ebony stone. Other than the cameo and large, gold hoop earrings, she was shades of brown and black—face, coat, legs and shoes—and she wore a fancy black felt hat. The three black plumes stuck straight up because of the way she had the hat pulled down around her face. I smiled remembering how Gram had worn her black hat pulled down like that when it was cold. *Dear Gram.*

Mama looked up, dazed, at Odessa Luckett, her hand still resting on the Singer.

"Have we met?" Auntie Odie asked me.

"At the library," I said. "You told us a story about a fisherman and a magic fish. And you told us your life story and you said 'The Highwayman' poem. I really liked that."

Her eyes glistened as she studied my face. "A couple weeks ago?"

"You told us poems by Emily Dickinson and Agatha Jordan and Robert Louis Stevenson."

Auntie Odie held my hands between her warm gloved ones. "Oh, child, I do so many visits around Weld County."

Her smile faded and she blinked her eyes. "What's your name?"

"Poni Snow." She looked so sorry about not remembering me, I smiled my brightest smile.

"Poni Snow," she said, wrapping my name in softness.

I looked down at my scuffed oxfords, and then at my legs covered with goosebumps from the cold. I glanced at Mama, but her eyes were on Odessa Luckett. Mama's light brown eyes shone like bronze in the bright sunlight, their color vivid against her brown felt hat. Her face was pink from the cold and her thin lips parted revealing small, uneven teeth.

"Oh…" Auntie Odie tilted her head, her eyes glinted. "Are you a curly towhead underneath that big ol' snowcap?"

I yanked off my cap. Static electrified my thatch of curls.

She laughed, deep-throated and breathless, just like she did that day at the library. She drawled, "Oh, I remember you, child, I do!"

My voice creaked, "You do?"

A quick look at Mama and I knew she, too, was intrigued—or at least curious.

Cupping my face in her gloved hands, Auntie Odie said, "I remember now, child. Why those little blue peepers of yours got so big and sparkled like sunlit ponds the whole time I spoke." She laughed again, higher, like a violin. "Why, the sun streamed in through the stained-glass window that day and set you aglow like a little angel fresh from heaven, your hair a sunlit halo."

Then she turned to Mama. "And all those sunlit colors alighting there on your little towhead, changing colors as the sun moved across the sky—well, it was a lovely sight."

Before Mama could step away, Auntie Odie clasped her hand and shook it. "I'm Odessa Luckett. A pleasure to meet you."

"Yes," Mama said softly and nodded. "Ingrid Snow."

Their eyes met and held for a moment, and then Mama looked away.

"This is a dandy machine, Mrs. Snow. Do you have a sewing machine?"

Mama smoothed some quilt squares. "We used to, my mother's. I should've hung onto it somehow."

"You sew then?" Auntie Odie asked.

Mama let a hint of smile curve into her thin face. "I kind of enjoy it." She cleared her throat. "Enjoyed."

"Do *you* sew?" I asked.

Auntie Odie laughed. "I used to sew. Some. Never came easy. Never cared for it. My mending pile is stacking up. Pretty soon I won't have anything to wear." Auntie Odie patted a mound of quilt squares. "Do you quilt?" she said to Mama.

"I used to. Some."

The women fell silent, eyeing the Singer.

Auntie Odie patted the machine. "I bet you could get this at a bargain price today."

Mama squinted in the sun, and then shaded her eyes with her hand. "Not today I won't. I've got to find work first." She took my arm and walked toward the street.

"Mrs. Snow… Ingrid." Auntie Odie followed us. "I wonder…"

We stopped and looked back at her.

Auntie Odie's face beamed. "If I can get that machine for hardscrabble, I'll give it to you. You'll catch me up on mending and finish the quilt my mother started years ago. That'll repay me for the machine. And you could sew for other people, too, and earn income. Do you cotton to that?"

Mama stood, ox-eyed. "You would do that?"

Auntie Odie laughed. "Lollapalooza! This'll be good for both of us."

"Here you are!" A man in a brown overcoat and business hat, about the same height as Auntie Odie, walked up to her.

"Fritz!" Auntie Odie said, "You been looking for me? I've been right here. Say, I'd like you to meet Ingrid Snow, and this is her daughter Poni."

He shook Mama's hand, then mine. "Fred Matthews—Fritz—here. Pleased to meet you."

Then Martha and her mother Olivia Matthews joined the group. Martha greeted me like we were old friends. She looked like a rose in her scarlet coat and hat and rosy-red cheeks. Mrs. Matthews, shivering even though bundled up in knit hat and long blue coat, was friendly too. Auntie Odie and the Matthews, it turned out, had been friends and neighbors for nearly thirty years and had come to the auction together.

Auntie Odie bid on a box of poetry books and got it for fifty cents. She showed Mr. and Mrs. Matthews and Mama—*Familiar Quotations* by John Bartlett, *Whittier's Poems,* and *The Poetical Works of Robert Burns.* Mama politely glanced through *Whittier's Poems* then put it back in the box.

By the time the auctioneer got to the sewing machine and cabinet, the morning had turned cloudy and bitter, but Auntie Odie did indeed make the purchase "for hardscrabble"—seventeen dollars. Auntie Odie also got a box of sewing supplies—thread, scissors and such—for fifty cents.

★ ★ ★

Mama tromped up our apartment stairs. Behind her, Martha and I toted the box of sewing supplies, feigning misery and giggling. Mr. Matthews and Herb Smith, a friend that Mr. Matthews ran into at the auction, huffed up the stairs behind us carrying the cabinet with the sewing machine. Auntie Odie and Mrs. Matthews followed. Mrs. Matthews explained that she had an illness which made her tire easily, so she had to take stairs slow.

The troublesome woman, Mrs. Gazz in apartment E, snapped open her door. In pink curlers and a housecoat printed with flowers the size of Grams' flapjacks, she frumped and frowned, but said nothing, for once.

Mr. Matthews smiled at her over the cabinet and then continued down the hall.

Mrs. Gazz left her door ajar and watched us.

The men placed the cabinet under the south window next to the floor lamp. Mama set her mouth in a straight line like a dash. She was nervous with all these people in our tiny place, and maybe embarrassed. Olivia Matthews and Auntie Odie helped her sort through the sewing supplies and put them away in the cabinet.

Mama's dash turned into a parenthesis on its side curving up, and a light shone in her eyes. She twisted a strand of her hair. "I-I want to thank you all." I was surprised when she walked up to each person with her little smile and shook hands, even with Martha.

Martha acted so sophisticated for a nine-year-old. She half-curtsied and said to my mama, "It was my privilege to help, Mrs. Snow."

By the time our helpers left, Mama had two more part-time jobs. One, working for Mrs. Matthews—housecleaning, laundry, ironing, and sewing—and, two, mending clothes for Mr. Smith's customers. He owned Smith Dry Cleaning across the street from Akin School.

Even I got a job. Mama and Mr. Smith agreed that I would check in at the dry cleaners every day after school. If there were any clothes to be mended, I'd carry them home for Mama to mend. Mr. Smith would pay me a nickel a day for checking in with him.

Mr. Matthews said he'd be happy to drop off the quilt and mending from Auntie Odie so Mama could get started.

Mama gently closed the door after them, then turned around in slow motion and leaned flat against the door. She sighed then smiled. "We're gonna make it, Ponia."

My heart did a little two-step. Mama looked so pretty there, her face relaxed, cheeks as pink as calamine lotion, thin lips curved upwards. Caught up in the longing to wrap my arms around her waist, I took a step toward her, and then halted.

Maybe, like a bubble drifting, Mama's happiness would last a little longer if left untouched.

So I just stood there, awash in the moment, and smiled.

Chapter 11

39 Below

Freezes

Up Weld

—*Greeley Daily Tribune*, p.1, Thurs., Feb.1, 1951

★ ★ ★

Residents Out and

About In Warmer

Temps, Melting Snow

—*Akin Scoop*, p.1, Thurs., Feb. 8, 1951

Thursday's high 66°, low 26°; mild 45° in evening

In the play yard at lunch recess most kids had discarded their coats. A few of us hung onto ours to use as padding behind our knees for twirling on the bars.

In the low-bar line, Martha stared off toward the icy blue and snow-capped mountains in the distant west. She'd been sad and distracted all morning. Out of the blue she said, "My brother's coming home from Korea."

Pascal, the tallest boy in our class, grabbed her arm. "You mean he's done with the war? Done fighting?"

"You don't mean it!" Clyde said.

Martha shook her head. "No, he'll be home for thirty days, and then he has to go back."

"Keen!" Clyde said.

"Aren't you happy Nate's coming home?" I asked.

Sarah frowned. "What's the matter, Martha?"

"My mother's worse again. That's why they're letting Nate come home." Martha turned to Pascal. "My brother doesn't actually fight. He's an army dentist. But he's close to the front."

Mary Joy scowled. "You mean all he does is fix teeth?"

"Sometimes he goes where they bring in the wounded GI's." Martha's nose grew pink and she wiped away tears. "I'm worried that they're flying Nate home because our mother's going to… pass away."

All I thought about the rest of the afternoon was that Mrs. Matthews might be dying.

As soon as the dismissal bell rang, I dashed to Smith's Dry Cleaning. Whenever Martha, Sarah, Clyde, Mary Joy, and Harry Roy came with me, we chatted and joked with Mr. Smith for a few minutes and sucked on our free suckers, but today I ran to the cleaners without them.

Mr. Smith held out a small bag and smiled. "One item today."

I ran all the way home, dashed up the stairs, and bumbled into the apartment, huffing and puffing.

"You're early," Mama said, without looking up.

The south-window light gilded the sewing machine and Mama with a golden glow. She was working on a dress I had seen on Mrs. Matthews—deep yellow, like ripe sweet corn from Gram and Grampy's garden.

After I caught my breath, I asked Mama what she was doing.

"Olivia's hired me to shorten some of her dresses."

That didn't sound like a dying woman.

I watched the needle thump up and down as Mama treadled her machine.

"Did you know Nate Matthews is coming home from Korea?" I said.

"Mm-hm."

"Is he coming because his mama's sick?"

"Mm-hm." Mama guided the folded-back hem under the foot as she treadled the machine slowly, the needle just catching the edge. Then she raised the foot, tied and snipped the thread. She stood up, shook the dress, and held it against herself. Mama's mouth curled into a little smile.

"Your pink gabardine is prettiest on you, Mama."

"I do wish I looked as good in yellow as Olivia does."

"Is Olivia going to die?"

"She's Mrs. Matthews to you."

I swallowed. "Is Mrs. Matthews going to die?"

Mama pushed a lock of hair back from her forehead, but it fell back over her eyes. She pulled the skirt over the wide end of the ironing board then pushed the iron across it, smoothing it with her left hand. The hot fabric smelled like Mr. Smith's dry cleaning establishment, a pleasant scent to me. It had smelled that way on ironing day at Gram's too.

"*Is* she, Mama?"

"Yes."

I took in a sharp breath.

Mama ironed faster now in short strokes. "Everybody's going to die. Sometime. Olivia included."

"But is Mrs. Matthews going to die *soon*? Maybe while Nate's home?"

"She might. Did Mr. Smith give you any mending?"

I held out the bag. "Don't you care that she might die?"

Mama's voice was low and calm. "Yes, I care. But there ain't nothing I can do about it if she does." She set the iron on the metal holder. The yellow dress slipped smoothly off the board and Mama hung it on a wall hook over other dresses. "There's graham cracker and milk, if you want it."

★ ★ ★

I found a place under the elm that wasn't bumpy with roots, and then sat against the tree. After the snow, ice, wind, and sub-zero temperatures in previous weeks, I relished the springlike day. The sky looked like blueberry-flavored cake with swirls of white-cloud frosting.

I broke off a piece of cracker and dunked it in the milk.

"Hey," said a familiar voice. Pascal Bucholz rode up on his green Hawthorne and stopped on the walk in front of me. "Want your *Tribune?*"

He was a cute boy in a funny sort of way—tall, big ears, freckles, impish brown eyes, and the longest eyelashes in Weld County, probably.

"Okay," I said, standing up and taking the paper. As soon as Mama had started getting work, she subscribed to the *Greeley Daily Tribune* and the *Akin Scoop.* She didn't go much for books but she did like the news.

After Pascal left, I turned a few cartwheels and got my hands muddy. I rocked in one of the chairs on the wrap-around porch and thought about Mama's and my good luck in meeting Auntie Odie and the Matthews.

It was hard to imagine what it would be like for Martha and Nate and Fritz Matthews if Mrs. Matthews died. I wished with all my heart that she would get well and live a long, long time. In the meantime, I would take pleasure in my "new" mama while she lasted, and hope she, too, would stay for a long, long time.

Chapter 12

Captain Nate Matthews
Returns Home To Akin
From Korea
—*Akin Scoop*, p.1, Sun., Feb. 11, 1951

★ ★ ★

Literary To Be Held At
Sintar Farm, Public Invited
—*Akin Scoop*, p.1, Mon., Feb. 12, 1951

Monday's high 34° (after yesterday's 71° high), low 12°; 23° at 1 p.m.; 5" snow

The springlike weekend tricked me into leaving my coat at home. At morning recess, it got cloudy, cold, and the wind fussed. Rain slanted down by the time the class went inside. I shivered the rest of the morning in my damp dress. Outside, the rain turned to snow.

Mrs. Kipp grumped because so many of us hadn't worn jackets to school. She fished a hanky from her skirt pocket, removed her glasses and cleaned them as she glared at each of the coatless.

I looked over at wise Martha whose red coat hung on a hook near the door. Her pink lips hinted at a smirk. I glanced back at Pascal who had also worn a coat. He sat up straight with his hands folded on his desk and looked straight ahead. No smile on his freckled face, but his large ears, which stuck out like pasture gates left open, were moving up and down ever so slightly.

A giggle spouted out of me, unbidden, and so did a wad of snot.

At lunchtime Mrs. Kipp told us we could stay in at recess since it was still snowing and it was plenty cold—our window thermometer read 24 degrees F.

She thrust her clenched hands on her hips. "This is a good eastern Colorado geography lesson. We live on the plains where anything goes as far as weather is concerned."

She snapped her fingers. "It can change just like that!"

By the time school was dismissed, it had stopped snowing. The friends who usually went to Smith's Dry Cleaning with me took off for home because of the numbing cold. I blew through the door, the bell jangled. I froze in my pink-and-white feed-sack dress—stiff as a paperdoll cutout. Ah, humid warmth and the smells of cleaning chemicals and hot fabric.

Mr. Smith grinned. "Here she is!"

I waited behind Mr. Smith's customer but then recognized her. "Mama!" I hugged her. Just like that. Real quick, before she knew what had happened.

She scowled and handed me my coat and hat.

Mr. Smith laughed. "You have to be prepared in fickle Colorado, little one. You should *always* carry a wrap with you until June—no matter what the weatherman says."

I giggled. "That's just what Mrs. Kipp told us today."

He eyed my frayed, too-small coat. "Say, Ingrid, I have a girl's coat in the back that someone left more than a year ago and never picked up." He disappeared before Mama could say a word.

He returned and held up a girl's royal-blue coat with silver buttons.

"Well, I don't know," Mama said.

Mr. Smith removed the paper covering, unbuttoned it, and said to me, "Here, try it on, little one. If it fits, it's yours."

It was big on me, but not so big I couldn't wear it. And it was beautiful. I twirled and it flared out.

But Mama looked doubtful. "How much do you want for it?"

Mr. Smith held up his broad hand. "Nothing, Ingrid. It's yours—Poni's. Please. I need the space on the racks."

Mama tucked a strand of brown hair behind her ear and adjusted her brown felt hat. She tilted her head and smiled just a little. "Well, I don't know how to thank you."

"Your smile is enough thanks." From under the counter he pulled out a woman's suit jacket for Mama to mend and pressed a nickel into my hand. I caressed the soft fabric of my coat.

He hurried around the counter and opened the door for us. "Drive careful out there. It's as slippery as goose fat on a pond of marbles."

★ ★ ★

Mama mended the tear for Mr. Smith's customer while I washed and dried dishes from breakfast. Then, while Mama fixed Kraft macaroni and cheese and opened a can of Sugar Belle peas, I read aloud from a reader that Mrs. Kipp let me keep at home.

We ate in silence for a while. I tried to see how many peas I could load onto my spoon. "Everybody's making a fuss about a literary thing that's going to happen in May. Silver Tongues Harvest they call it. Fourth graders on up can try out for it. Nearly everybody in my class is going to audition."

"Are you going to try out?"

"No! Not me."

"Why not?"

"I don't know any stories or poetry by heart, and I can't read good enough either."

"You read pretty good to me awhile ago."

"Mama," I said softly, "that's a first-grade reader." I scooted the last macaroni around the Poppyware plate with my fork.

Silence.

At the sink, her back to me, Mama said, "Come June twenty-first, I'm going with the Nimble Needles to Denver for a quilting fair." She ran some water into the sink. "I been invited to ride with Mary Ann Walters and Pearl Willis and Rachel Galante in the Walters' new Hudson Hornet."

"That's keen, Mama."

"If'n I get my quilt done, I'm going to register for the competition." She was rarely a woman of words, yet she rambled on for several minutes about the quilting fair. She had been dishing up a few surprises lately, but this one took the prize. I just sat and watched her talk, enjoying the transformation.

When Mama finally stopped for a breath I said, "Do I get to go?"

"Nope. Not enough room in the car. Anyway, it ain't for kids. We leave on June twenty-first, a Thursday afternoon. The fair'll last Friday, Saturday, and Sunday. You'd be bored to death with nothing to do." Mama wiped off the table, then rinsed out the dishrag.

This was exciting news. I had never stayed overnight at a friend's. "Should I ask Martha if I can stay with them?"

She removed her checked apron and hung it on the refrigerator handle. "Unless Olivia gets a whole bunch better, you ain't going to be staying there. June's still four months away. We'll figure it out by then."

Mama swept the floor as she talked. "I was at the Matthews' house cleaning today. Olivia and I talked about the quilt fair. As sick as she is, she kept saying how she was so glad I'm going to the quilt fair with the Nimble Needles. She thinks my Star of Bethlehem could win a prize."

I sat with my elbows on the table, my chin resting on my knuckles. I didn't want to do anything to risk changing Mama's mood.

"Martha's brother got home from Korea," she said. "Such a handsome young man, devoted to his mother. And he even joined in the conspiracy for me to go to the quilt fair in June."

I nodded. "Martha talked about Nate at school all day. She wants me to meet him." I dug out my spool knitting and brought it back to the table. "What else, Mama?" I hooked a violet thread over a nail in the spool, and then tugged gently at the tail hanging from the bottom of the spool.

Mama hung the broom on a hook in the corner, and then looked at me, hands on her waist. "Odessa Luckett has hired me to clean once a week for her, do some of the heavier housework. Maybe there'll be enough extra money one of these days to get you some decent shoes."

Whoopee! "That would be nice, Mama."

Things were looking up in the Ingrid and Poni Snow household.

Chapter 13

Chicago Deep Freeze
Woman May Point Way
to New Cancer Therapy
—*Greeley Daily Tribune*, p.8, Sat., Feb. 17, 1951

Francine's Fancies on Sixth
Ave. In Business
Twenty-five Years
—*Akin Scoop*, p.1, Sat., Feb. 17, 1951

Saturday's high 50°, low 20°

Mama laid the throw on the shiny wood floor in the Matthews' entryway and put the soap, Purex, sponges, and brushes under the sink. "Oh! The sheets on the line—come help me."

A slice of blue appeared above us among the gray clouds. We soon filled the basket with pillowcases and pajamas that smelled like Fab and fresh air—as fragrant as any flower.

I held one end of a sheet, crisp and white, while Mama unclipped the other end and dropped the clothespins into the clothespin bag.

Mama's face wore a mild grimace, like she was trying not to smile, but I knew it was exactly the opposite.

"Will you miss Olivia?"

We folded the sheet, working together, being careful not to let it touch the snow-covered ground. I lay the folded sheet in the bottom of the basket while Mama removed clothespins from the other sheet.

"I'll miss 'er all right." She sniffed and paused for a moment, head down, body in an S-shape, her long arms up, resting on the clothesline.

"Can I see her before she dies?"

"No."

"But I want to say good-b…"

"They don't allow no kids up there. No."

"So she is dying?"

47

"Looks like it."

Mama and I were folding the second sheet when a stiff gust came up and I lost my corners. Mama bunched up the sheet and dropped it into the basket. "We'll fold inside."

We heard men's voices as we entered the kitchen from the garage.

"I'll get changed and go back over," Mr. Matthews was saying.

"Dad, a half-dozen people from the church are there now, taking turns going in. Why don't you go back to bed for awhile?"

"Ingrid!" He clasped Mama's hand. "Poni! Sorry, Martha's with her grandparents. Nate, this is Poni, Martha's friend."

If a nine-year-old can become smitten with a twenty-six-year-old soldier within two seconds, I did. His bass voice was cradled in soft-spokenness, and the black-rimmed glasses looked insignificant compared to his strong, chiseled face and large muscular neck. My hand felt small and safe clutched in the strength of his large, long fingers when we shook hands. I could only wonder at that rich melted-chocolate shade of his eyes.

"Glad to meet you, Poni."

I could barely nod.

"Martha talks about you all the time."

She does?

Nate shook Mama's hand. "We meet again, Mrs. Snow."

She nodded. "Call me Ingrid."

"Ingrid. Nice to see you again." Then he excused himself and disappeared into a back room.

"Everything looks wonderful." Mr. Matthews glanced around the kitchen. "Thank you, Ingrid."

He wrote out a check and handed it to Mama, rubbed his hand over his thinning hair and took a weary breath. "You haven't been to the hospital yet to see Liv, have you?"

She picked up the basket at her feet. "No, sir."

"Do you want to?"

When Mama didn't respond, he said, "You know, Nate says she's a little better this afternoon, even smiled and asked for soup." He rubbed the dark stubble on his chin.

Mama just looked at him with that pinched look of hers.

He laid his hand lightly on Mama's shoulder. "Why don't you follow me over to the hospital, you and Poni. Come up to her room with me. Poni'll be okay in the waiting room for a few minutes. We'll go in together."

Mama's face relaxed. "All right."

Chapter 14

Institute Asks
Deferment for
Key Farm Boys
—*Greeley Daily Tribune*, p.1, Wed., Feb. 21, 1951

Akin School Orchestra
To Give Concert Tonight
—*Akin Scoop*, p.1, Wed., Feb. 21, 1951

Wednesday's high 54°, low 25°

I sat in the third row of the Akin School auditorium next to Auntie Odie. Martha sat on the other side of her, then Nate and Nate's long-time friend Ted Barnes Jr. and Mr. and Mrs. Barnes.

The high-school-student orchestra played "Rhapsody in Blue," accompanied by Rob Barnes, Ted's younger brother, on the piano. The most beautiful piece I'd ever heard, it rained joy over my soul's desert the way Auntie Odie's beautiful words did. Ted and Nate clapped and whistled above all the others in the audience. I knew some of the joy overflowing in our group was because Olivia Matthews was improving and would be coming home soon from the hospital—miracle of miracles.

"Our next number, 'America the Beautiful'..." The conductor straightened his tie and looked over the audience until he spotted Nate. "Captain Nate Matthews, please stand. Ladies and gentlemen, our next number is dedicated to Captain Nathan Matthews who is home on a thirty-day leave from Korea. Senior Bonnie Botanelli will sing the solo. Audience, please stand."

The chairs squeaked as the audience stood and clapped, then a hush settled over the room.

"Nate," the conductor said, "we appreciate you and all the boys overseas fighting for freedom."

Bonnie stepped up to the microphone and said in a sweet voice, "You're welcome to sing along as I sing, 'America the Beautiful.'"

In a red pillbox hat and red-and-brown jersey-print dress, Auntie Odie's eyes glistened, and her voice sang mellow like the cello in the orchestra—though off-key.

A Rogers and Hammerstein tune from Carousel, "June Is Bustin' Out All Over," concluded the program, and a happified audience departed into the cold Colorado air.

Trekking back to the cars, Mr. and Mrs. Barnes invited everyone to their home for hors d'oeuvres. Mrs. Barnes put her arm around me. "You're welcome to come too, sweetie."

Nate halted and looked down at me. I could see the brownness of his eyes behind his glasses, even in the parking lot lit only by a streetlight. "It's only nine-fifteen, Poni. Would your mother care if you came with us to the Barnes'?"

"She's not expecting me home before 9:30 or ten. That's when Martha told her I'd be home."

Everyone cheered so enthusiastically, I felt warm to my toes in spite of the cold. Martha and I walked on either side of Nate, swinging on his arms. I could feel his muscles, even through the thick sleeve of his army uniform.

Chapter 15

150,000 Yankees
Now Fighting in
Korean Action
—*Greeley Daily Tribune*, p.1, Mon., Feb. 26, 1951

★ ★ ★

Voted Best For Modern Design! 1951 Nash Rambler
—*Greeley Daily Tribune*, p.8, Tues., Feb. 27, 1951

Tuesday's high 58°, low 21°

The community hall and parking lot was situated among a grove of leafless trees. A handwritten sign was tacked to the streetlight pole, its message only periodically visible as it flapped in the cold night air:

Jaycees / Red Cross
CHILI SUPPER
Tues., Feb. 27, 6-8 pm
Army Capt. N. Matthews speaker.

Inside, the warm air was thick with aromas—chili and coffee and a hint of must, and echoes—children's squeals and giggles and adults' chatting voices and occasional peals of laughter. Over a loudspeaker, an elderly gentleman's voice announced directions for expediting the foodline and for entering drawings with proceeds going to the Red Cross.

The Matthews and Odessa Luckett had saved places for Mama and me at their table. People came by and greeted everyone at our table, especially Mrs. Matthews, with smiles and pats. She was frail but glowing in her red fitted suit and hat.

At seven o'clock the president of the Akin Jaycees, Bud Binger, stepped up to the microphone. I recognized him—the auctioneer at our farm sale. No ten-gallon hat tonight, just a head of white hair. "Ladies and gentlemen, thanks to all of you folks for braving the cold to come out and partake of fellowship and the best chili ever served in Weld County."

Applause.

He introduced and thanked various directors and officers of the Jaycees and the Red Cross for their diligent work. Each of them in turn praised the Red Cross volunteers and workers in the county, in Colorado, all across America, and overseas, especially in Korea.

He gestured toward Mrs. Matthews. "Olivia, we're deeply grateful that you're a survivor, and you're home from the hospital and have graced us with your presence here tonight."

The crowd applauded and whistled. Mr. Matthews clapped and gazed at his wife, tears in his eyes. Mrs. Matthews said something in Nate's ear and he nodded.

"Please," said Mr. Binger, "remember to support the March of Dimes and the fight against polio."

Applause.

"And now, the Jaycees and the Red Cross are honored to have Captain Nathan Matthews here tonight."

Applause.

"Nate, as Akinites know him, graduated from Akin School in 1942, later graduated from the dental school of Washington University at St. Louis, and was an interne at Fitzsimons Hospital before going overseas. He's been serving for four months as regimental dental surgeon for the fifth cavalry in Korea close to the front. We're happy to have him here tonight. Ladies and gentlemen, please welcome Captain Nathan Matthews."

Nate rose and strolled to the microphone accompanied by applause, shouts, and whistles. He pushed up his glasses, rubbed his hand over his close-clipped dark hair, and leaned down toward the mike. Bud Binger hurried to the front and raised the microphone, bumping Nate in the face. Everyone laughed including Nate.

"Uh," he began, "I work about five miles from the front in Korea, and I get into some tough situations." He rubbed his left temple. "But speaking in front of a crowd, now that's scary."

Laughter riffled through the gathering. Martha continued to giggle until her Grandmother Matthews nudged her and frowned.

"You're among friends, Nate!" It was a young man, standing and leaning against the back wall.

Nate smiled and nodded toward him. "Thanks." Then Nate addressed the audience. "What I'd like to do…" He wiped the palms of his hands on his uniform jacket. "I'll just say a few words then open it up to questions."

He talked about the Red Cross and all they did for GIs—how they wrote letters for the wounded, handled legal affairs for GIs, entertained patients at Fitzsimons Army Hospital—and about the annual fund drive that would be held in March. He said it was a good idea to buy U.S. Defense Bonds—"Economic power is as vital as military strength."

Across the table from me, Auntie Odie wore a narrow-brimmed maroon hat that matched her crepe dress and lipsticked smile. Her dangling pearl earrings barely swayed she was so intent on listening to Nate. The Matthews sat in rapt attention. And Mama too—her face appeared less drawn, even flushed, in her pink gabardine dress. She had trimmed her brown hair and was wearing it in a loose pageboy under her little navy hat with the white feather.

Soon Nate opened it up for questions and pointed to a man in overalls, plaid flannel shirt, and blue tie. "Gabe."

Gabe ambled up to the microphone. "Tell us about how you done your work over there and what kind of equipment you got available."

"We have a man in our outfit, a corporal, who takes care of upkeep on the dental equipment. He supplied the manpower for my footdrill."

Men, women, and children took turns at the microphone asking Nate questions. He told of experiences assisting in the collecting station where wounded GIs were treated. Nate's voice filled with emotion when he told of one of the casualties who came through—Lt. Charlie Thomas, one of his closest friends during his teen years at Akin School.

A little girl—about six years old—marched up. Mr. Binger lowered the mike. "Is it... Does it get cold in Korea?"

The audience chuckled.

"Yes, Daisy. It's a harsh, freezing cold." Nate smiled at the little blue-eyed girl then addressed the audience. "One of the most agonizing battles in Korea is the fight to stay alive in the bitter winter weather. Fierce Manchurian and Siberian winds howl across the landscape, turn the weather icy—it chews at your very soul. I never could've imagined how cold a place can be."

A teenage boy raised his hand. "Did you ever see any kids where you were?"

Nate's face flushed. He rubbed his palms together then gripped the microphone. "I—I hadn't been in Korea long when I was assigned, along with an interpreter and a colonel, to reopen a civilian hospital." Nate swallowed hard and glanced over at our table.

"I hesitate to talk about things in a group like this. But American citizens have a right to know." Nate swiped his temple and cleared his throat.

"The civilian hospital we helped open filled up almost overnight with Korean civilians, mostly women and children. Little kids were brought in or walked in, caked with mud, with gaping head wounds, often maggot-infested wounds, shot in the head or various parts of the body, sometimes limbs were missing or dangling." Nate coughed and slowly rubbed his temple. "That was one of the hardest things—the sounds of crying and moaning, the smells of blood and wounds and urine. And there were children who didn't cry, they'd just lie there, dazed, in shock, or unconscious. Those were the hardest things."

The only sound in the place was the hum of the heater and occasional sniffs. A dignified-looking, white-haired gentleman in a navy suit and red tie blew his nose, and then buried his eyes in his white handkerchief. Mama had a stricken look. So did the others at our table and, in fact, around the room.

Rosie Quintana from my class sat across the room with her parents, a little sister, and three older people who were probably grandparents. Mr. Quintana walked up to the microphone. "How would you say the war is going, Nate? Overall?"

"There are definitely days when we feel more encouraged than others. The Chinese communists are constantly infiltrating our operations. Being held in regimental headquarters right now are four men and two women—Chinese communists—who, armed with machine guns, infiltrated American lines."

"One more question," said Mr. Quintana. "Any ideas about when the war will end?"

Nate looked at the floor and shook his head. "I hear talk about it being over by Christmas. I don't see that happening." Then he broke into a broad smile. "But I hope I'm wrong. We'd be the happiest men on earth if we could all be home by Christmas."

Chapter 16

Capt. Nate Matthews Waves
Good-bye To Family, Friends
as He Returns to Korea
—*Akin Scoop*, p.1, Fri., March 16, 1951

★ ★ ★

Roy Hood Wins VFW Marble Tournament Title
—*Greeley Daily Tribune*, p.16, Mon., May 7, 1951

★ ★ ★

Silver Tongues Harvest Tonight
Community Invited
—*Akin Scoop*, p.1, Fri., May 11, 1951

Friday's high 78°, low 52°; fair

Folks arrived as early as six o'clock at the Akin School auditorium to reserve seats for the Silver Tongues Harvest. Men wore ties—with suits or clean overalls or jeans, and women wore high heels and dressy dresses or lo-heelers and clean housedresses. I wished I had thought to comb my hair and wash my face before I came.

I chose two places in the fourth row by the middle aisle. The wooden seats squeaked as people put them down or raised them up. Folks laughed and visited, and the sounds echoed 'round the high walls in a dissonant but pleasant chorus.

Along each outer aisle, six creamy white columns rose to the frescoed ceiling, connected by graceful arches high above. Tall arced windows glowed with late-in-the-day sunlight.

I amused myself by identifying smells: oiled wood, sweet perfume, and a man's cologne—maybe Old Spice like Grampy wore for special occasions. A breeze sailed in through the open windows—enough to ripple the gold-toned stage curtain, and the scent of apple blossoms sifted around me like fragrant talc.

I looked around for Mama. Mr. Matthews came down the aisle, greeted me warmly, and saved several seats next to Mama's and my seats.

"So Mrs. Matthews is well enough to come?" I asked.

The worry lines that had creased Mr. Matthews' forehead for so long had softened. "She says she wouldn't miss this for anything." He fumbled with his gray felt hat. "Nate's visit home seems to have revived her. She gets stronger every day."

I liked the way he talked to me, like I was a grown-up. I recalled Nate, tall and strong, the way he'd shaken my hand, firm but gentle, the first time we met and the softness in his brown eyes. "How is Nate?" I asked.

"Fine, fine, I think."

A man behind us laid his hand on Mr. Matthews' shoulder. "Fritz!"

Mr. Matthews turned around. "Why, Sal, Dora." He nodded to each, then said to Sal Santi, "How's the glass enterprise?"

Mr. Matthews and Mr. Santi got into a discussion about glassblowing (Mr. Santi's Firedrake business) and farming (both had farming relatives) and Mr. Matthews' drug store business and Nate and the war.

Dora Santi, Mr. Santi's mother, asked me about school. Pascal Buchholtz and Hetti Zimmerman from my class went up and down the aisles passing out programs to those who had arrived before the ushers. Pascal and Hetti grinned at me, said hi, and went on with their task. The smiles and cheer made me feel good inside. Akin was starting to feel like home.

Mr. Matthews' parents came, along with Mrs. Matthews who looked thin but happy and pretty in a mint-green fitted suit. Mr. Matthews moved down a seat so Mrs. Matthews could sit next to me. Her auburn hair was swept up into a loose bun under her crescent hat. I breathed in the scent of her perfume—roses?

She caught me staring at her and she winked. "Well, Poni, how is school going?"

"Good."

And it really was.

★ ★ ★

At five till seven the Silver Tongues Harvest participants filed in from a side door, along with several teachers, including Mrs. Kipp, and seated themselves in the front row.

The Matthews pointed and whispered when they saw Martha. The only indication that Martha was nervous was her stiff walk. She smiled in that slightly-crooked way of hers and looked like a ballerina in her full-skirted crayon-blue dress and her black hair pulled up tight in a bun high on the back of her head.

Auntie Odie entered behind Martha. Her royal-blue silk dress fluttered around her calves and her matching pillbox hat sparkled with jewels. She sat next to Mrs. Kipp who wore a flowery dress and white hat.

The stout and balding sixth grade teacher, Mr. Fraser, strolled up onto the stage and tapped the microphone. "Good evening." The microphone blared, Mr. Fraser stepped back.

"Good evening, ladies and gentlemen," Mr. Fraser said in a smooth voice. "Welcome to Akin School's twenty-first annual Silver Tongues Harvest. For the past few weeks, Akin's fourth through twelfth grade students have been competing in rounds of reading, storytelling, and poetry recitation." Mr. Fraser cleared his throat and looked at his notes.

"Mrs. Pamela R. Silverman, a former teacher at Akin School, consulted literary enthusiasts in the community and determined to revive and 'harvest' what she called 'the dying art of expressive oral reading and other forms of oral expression.' In 1930, to showcase and reward student talent and achievement in that endeavor, she and her committee organized and held Akin School's First Annual Silver Tongues Harvest in which six students participated.

"Since then, a number of Akin students have grown up and become successful writers, poets, dramatists, and speakers, owing their success in part to their youthful participation in the Silver Tongues Harvest."

The crowd applauded.

"We will begin with our first performer in the storytelling category. Fourth grader Frank Chavez will tell a tall tale of the U.S. of A., 'Pecos Bill and His Bouncing Bride.'"

The crowd applauded and whistled as Frank trotted up on the stage in a cowboy outfit, grinning, and waving his ten-gallon hat. I felt proud because Frank was in my class. He slung his shiny black hair off his forehead and replaced his hat as Mr. Fraser lowered the microphone.

As Frank "performed" the story, as they said in Akin, I grew a new respect for Frank—not only did he possess a rare, fun-loving intelligence, but a genuine talent for storytelling. When Frank told about the time Pecos Bill's horse, Widow-Maker, bucked off Slue-Foot Sue and she sailed up, up into the clouds, then came back down, landed on her bustle, then sailed back up again and that went on for a week, the crowd roared. Frank's voice sailed into the sky when Slue-Foot Sue did, then landed low, then high again, as Sue bounced up and down then back up again. Frank's voice, facial expressions—his entire body—told the story.

Frank bowed, deep and dramatic, to the audience. As the crowd applauded and cheered, Mr. Fraser hopped to the stage again.

"As you all know, each performer is allowed a maximum of seven minutes. It may be used in one category or divided between two.

"And now, ladies and gentlemen, please welcome Mary Joy Weatherby who will present us with her performance in the storytelling category, one of Aesop's famous fables, 'The Lion and the Mouse.'"

Mary Joy was very melodramatic, maybe trying too hard. It was funny that someone like Mary Joy would choose a story with the moral, "Little friends may prove to be great friends." But the crowd applauded for Mary Joy just as they had for Frank.

While people clapped after the fourth contestant's performance, an elderly man came down the aisle and insisted that I give up the seat I was saving. Rather than sit without a seat for Mama, I stood and gave a little wave to Mrs. Matthews.

I walked to the back where people stood along the back wall—no sign of Mama, and out to the vestibule. The loud speaker in the vestibule carried the young voices clearly.

Outside, the sky had darkened. I walked through the parking lot looking for our blue pickup. I watched for it from Sixth Avenue and Graham Way for awhile then decided to go back in. What was taking Mama so long?

Back in the building, the loud speakers announced that Martha Matthews would perform "A Mad Tea-Party" from Lewis Carroll's *Alice's Adventures in Wonderland* in the read-aloud category. I opened the door to the auditorium enough to squeeze inside. I found a place to stand so I could see Martha's performance. She walked lightly—nearly danced—up onto the stage.

At the microphone she looked down, her book at her side. Someone in the crowd coughed. A few people fanned themselves with their programs.

At last Martha slowly raised her eyes, opened her book to the marked place, and began.

> "There was a table set out under a tree in front of the house, and the March Hare and the Hatter were having tea at it: a Dormouse was sitting between them, fast asleep, and the other two were using it as a cushion, resting their elbows on it, and talking over its head. 'Very uncomfortable for the Dormouse,' thought Alice; 'only, as it's asleep, I suppose it doesn't mind.'
>
> "The table was a large one, but the three were all crowded together at one corner of it: 'No room! No room!' they cried out when they saw Alice coming. 'There's *plenty* of room!' said Alice indignantly, and she sat down in a large arm-chair at one end of the table."

Martha began gently, then gradually increased the pace of the reading. When she read Alice's lines, her voice flew, light and girlish, but when she read the March Hare's lines, her voice had a low, rough edge to it. And, indeed, her tone and pace changed to depict each character, but smoothed into her own voice for the narrated passages.

Once, when Dormouse and Alice talked back and forth to each other, Martha stumbled and got their voice depictions mixed up. I could hear a little frustration in her voice. She stopped, looked down for a moment, then continued and read the rest of the story perfectly.

As with the other contestants, the crowd clapped enthusiastically. I stood, mesmerized by what I saw that night. Kids my age and older telling stories, reading stories, and reciting or reading poems. But most of the contestants didn't just tell or read or recite. They performed. They grasped the audience by the lapels and flew it to other places and times. And the more practiced and polished the performer, the more real the places and characters became. We heard, smelled, saw, and tasted the sights. We were there.

It amazed me to think that so many people had left their work, evening newspapers, and radios in order to meet among the arches and columns and frescoed ceiling of this place to revel in and hold in high esteem the "silver tongues" of their young. And to think that they valued their children's "silver tongues" as much as their abilities in orchestra and choir, football and baseball.

Mr. Fraser bounded up on stage to announce the poetry competition.

Back in the foyer the ladies scurried to arrange cookies, cupcakes, and bowls of punch on long tables. As I walked toward a table, a petite, brown-haired woman, wearing a brown suit and matching feathered hat, held her hand protectively over a plate of brownies. "These are for after the Harvest, dear. Not now."

"I'm just waiting for my mother to come," I said. "I think she'll be wearing a blue-checked gingham dress and a navy hat with a white feather."

She looked at me as if I had described the Mad Hatter.

"She has brown hair this long." I pointed to my shoulder. "And she's kind of tall and kind of skinny and she'll be wearing brown loafers." I paused. "Have you seen her?"

"I don't recall seeing anyone like that," the brown lady said.

A pretty girl, about high-school age, smiled at me. "Maybe she's in the powder room."

But she wasn't. Back outside, I searched for the pickup again by the light of streetlights. At last I spotted it, parked on the street in the next block. So that meant Mama was at the Harvest, somewhere. I dashed back into the building, glad for the warmth. The air had turned cool.

Mama stood by a refreshment table. The lady in brown pointed in my direction. Audience applause reverberated through the loud speakers.

Mama walked toward me looking grim. She yelled so I could hear over the noise. "Did you save us seats?"

"They wouldn't let me save you a seat anymore."

Then the audience grew quiet and we heard a familiar voice.

"This zingy little poem by Emily Dickinson has become tradition at Akin's Annual Silver Tongues Harvest." Auntie Odie's voice was warm and full and so was the drawl. "This is the twenty-first time it will have been read at a Harvest."

The brown lady whispered to another refreshment lady, "They've had Odessa Luckett perform poetry while the judges calculate the winners for all the years I've been coming."

The other woman nodded.

The refreshment ladies opened the doors to the auditorium and crowded inside. Mama and I also squeezed through and found a place to stand where we could see.

Odessa Luckett stood at the microphone, the rich coffee-tone of her skin enhanced next to the royal blue of her dress and hat.

> "There is no frigate like a book
> To take us lands away,
> Nor any coursers like a page
> Of prancing poetry.
> This traverse may the poorest take
> Without oppress of toll;
> How frugal is the chariot
> That bears the human soul!"

The audience clapped, then,

> "Hope is the thing with feathers
> That perches in the soul,
> And sings the tune without the words,
> And never stops at all
>
> "And sweetest in the gale is heard;
> And sore must be the storm
> That could abash the little bird
> That kept so many warm.
>
> "I've heard it in the chillest land,
> And on the strangest sea;
> Yet, never, in extremity,
> It asked a crumb of me."

Pause and light clapping.

"'A Word' by Emily Dickinson." Auntie Odie smiled. The scent of apple blossoms swept in afresh through the high open windows, mingled with the poem, and left me breathless.

> "A word is dead
> When it is said,
> Some say.
>
> "I say it just
> Begins to live
> That day."

While everyone clapped, Mama turned to me and signaled me to follow her. We headed back through the door to the vestibule then toward the outside door.

"Where are we going?"

"Got to get home. It's late."

I lagged behind. "But you just got here." I wanted to linger in this place and bask in the images the words had strewn 'round my head. "Can't we stay and find out who the winners are?"

"You'll find out on Monday at school." Mama pushed open the door. "It'll be in the Sunday paper too." She held the door open and waited. "Come on. Now, Ponia."

I gave a longing glance toward the auditorium and toward the tables laden with sweet-scented refreshments.

"Please, Mama, can't we stay?" I felt my throat constrict, and heat behind my eyes burned.

"Please shut that door," said the brown lady.

Mama held the door open for me, silent.

My heart plummeted to bedrock as I trudged through the door and followed Mama. As the door snapped shut behind us, so, too, did the sounds of the Silver Tongues Harvest. Birds warbled their last lullabies in the cool night air.

But the Emily Dickinson lines Auntie Odie had recited sung in my head.

> Hope is the thing with feathers
> That perches in the soul,
> And sings the tune without the words,
> And never stops at all.

Chapter 17

Rain and Chill Do Not
Dampen Students' Spirits as
1950-51 School Year Ends
—*Akin Scoop*, p.1, Fri., June 1, 1951

★ ★ ★

Composting Provides
Inexpensive Source for Humus
—*Akin Scoop*, p.2, Tues., June 12, 1951

Tuesday's high 78°, low 53°; widely scattered afternoon and evening showers

Martha showed up at our door and invited me to spend the day with her. Mama let me because she had so much to do—errands and work and such.

Close to her house, Martha said, "Let's take a shortcut through the vacant lot."

I trailed behind. A meadowlark sang. Mustard weed and dandelions made my nose itch. Milkweed swayed beside the ditch bank, and insects hummed from all directions. Then something caught my eye. "Martha! Look at this."

She hurried over. "What?"

I pointed towards a small object dangling from a milkweed leaf. "A cocoon. It looks like a jewel."

Martha bent close and whispered. "We studied butterflies last fall. That's a chrysalis."

"A chrysalis? Why are we whispering?"

"This is something like a holy moment."

I shifted to get a better look. "There's a little flap sticking out at the bottom. It's trying to escape."

"Emerge."

Martha's hair had blue highlights in the morning sun and I saw the bottom of the well of brown in her eyes.

"He's not a prisoner escaping," she said, "just a butterfly whose time has come. A caterpillar forms a chrysalis around himself. When he emerges, it's like being born all over again." Martha's eyebrows raised in two dark arches. "We read all about it last September, before you came."

We knelt in the weeds and watched the small crumpled mass work to free itself from its cellophanelike covering.

Martha giggled. "Don't get your face so close. You'll scare him."

"He does look like a prisoner trying to escape," I said.

"Prisoners escape, maybe to go back to what they were before. But butterflies emerge. They're reborn into a new life and will never be the same again."

★ ★ ★

Martha threw the white gate open and ran, breathless, up to Auntie Odie. "You're back from vacation!"

Auntie Odie wore white anklets and tennis shoes, yellow-gingham dress, yellow-and-blue-flowered bib apron, and a wide straw hat pulled down over her hair. They hugged and laughed.

Was this the same Auntie Odie I'd met who wore big fancy hats, dangly earrings, and flowing dresses and quoted poetry and attended Nate's speech? *Across the street from Martha?*

Auntie Odie laughed, deep and breathless. "Glory be! Look who you brought with you!"

Martha looked back at me. "Come on, Poni."

I smiled and stepped through the gate. There my life became encased in a chrysalis. I would never be the same again.

I took deep breaths as though the sights could be absorbed through my lungs—a miniature heaven-world of fragrant flowers, shrubs, humming insects, and birds in concert. The marigold-yellow cottage, adorned with white gingerbread, nestled among the gardens like a prize bloom.

"You remember Poni Snow, don't you?" Martha said to Auntie Odie.

"Snow. A fitting name for a pindling towhead like you." Auntie Odie's voice rippled like water. "We meet again! Of course I remember! The angel at the library. And her mama cleans for me and did all that sewing for me and we sat together at Nate's speech." Slowly, softly she said, "Poni Snow." She offered her hand. "You should be a poet with a name like that."

I glanced at Martha and then looked down, smiling.

Auntie Odie grasped my hand, raised it up, and cradled it between two creamy palms. I studied the darkness of her skin, her large lips and broad nose. The smile, which dominated her dusky face, deepened the wrinkles, creating similar patterns in both her skin and her silver-dusted hair. "Now," she said, "what was all the hullabaloo over there in the weeds?"

"A butterfly is emerging!" I said.

"We'll show you the butterfly, but it'll take awhile to emerge," Martha said. "Could you show Poni your gardens first?"

Auntie Odie smiled.

"Your flowers are pretty," I said.

Martha poked her finger between the petals of a deep-magenta blossom. "Snapdragons are my favorites."

Auntie Odie flicked off a bug.

As birds fluttered among the feeders hanging from trees and mounted on poles, I questioned her. "What kind of bird is that?" "What flower is this?" "What's this tree's name?"

She answered with delighted patience. I heard the pleasure in her voice and saw it in the sparkle of her eyes.

"Do all colored folks know as much about plants and birds as you do?" I asked.

Auntie Odie stared at me, eyes wide. "Do all white folks ask as many questions as you do?"

Auntie Odie and I stared at each other for seconds, and then all three of us burst into laughter. When we'd settled down, I asked, "Is there anything you like more than flowers and birds?"

"Parades!" she spouted, then laughed.

And Martha laughed too. "We go to nearly every parade within fifty miles. If she can't find a friend to go with her, she goes by herself."

"I like parades," I said. "I'll go with you."

"Glory be, child! I'll be a-knocking on your door come Fourth of July."

"Don't forget me," said Martha.

"What else?" I asked Auntie Odie. "What else do you love?"

She gazed at some distant place. "Exquisite words uniquely arranged—poetry. Poems grow inside me like the flowers in my gardens. Poetry is a descant to life, to the ordinary day. And I love stories, skillfully told or read—whether true or moonshiny."

Of course.

"My favorite poets," Martha said, "are Robert Louis Stevenson and Rachel Field."

Auntie Odie chuckled. "I cotton to Emily Dickinson's poems especially. But I also like Langston Hughes' splendiferous poems and I get atwitter over Elizabeth Barrett Browning's rose pink. I read a lot of John Greenleaf Whittier and William Shakespeare." A fresh glint sparkled in her eyes. "Oh yes, and Agatha Jordan."

Martha grinned at me. "Rose pink is old-fashioned poetry."

"I've never heard of any of those people."

Auntie Odie rested her hand on my shoulder. I looked at it, knuckles enlarged and darker than the rest of the hand, skin creased with years and work. I liked the feel of Auntie Odie's hand alit there, as if it were a little bird ready to fly. *Hope is the thing with feathers / That perches in the soul.*

"If you cotton to my gardens, you'll cotton to poetry," Auntie Odie said. "You're welcome to borrow any of my poetry books any time."

"She doesn't read very well, *yet*," Martha said, eyes bright, motioning toward me. "I'm helping her read better."

"Splendiferous!" Auntie Odie spouted. "Get her going with poetry and well-written tales, Martha. She'll be reading in no time."

"Say an Emily Dickinson poem for us," Martha said.

Auntie Odie thought a moment then squared her shoulders, head erect.

> "A bird came down the walk:
> He did not know I saw;
> He bit an angle-worm in halves
> And ate the fellow, raw…"

"Ew-ew!" Martha and I said in unison, noses crinkled.
But Auntie Odie barely slowed in her recitation.

> "And then he drank a dew
> From a convenient grass,
> And then hopped sidewise to the wall
> To let a beatle pass.

> "He glanced with rapid eyes
> That hurried all abroad,—
> They looked like frightened beads, I thought;
> He stirred his velvet head

> "Like one in danger; cautious,
> I offered him a crumb,
> And he unrolled his feathers
> And rowed him softer home

> "Than oars divide the ocean,
> Too silver for a seam,
> Or butterflies, off banks of noon
> Leap, splashless, as they swim."

Just like at the library last winter, Auntie Odie's easy voice and the way she enunciated the words pulled me along like a sled on powdery snow. I understood little, but loved the sound of the words cast out on Auntie Odie's rippling voice, and I loved the lights in her eyes and the gestures of her long arms, the way it took all of her to create the full effect of the poem.

"And here's a real favorite of mine," Auntie Odie volunteered—"'A Blackbird Suddenly' by Joseph Auslander:

> "Heaven is in my hand, and I
> Touch a heart-beat of the sky,
> Hearing a blackbird's cry.

"Strange, beautiful, unquiet thing,
Lone flute of God, how can you sing
Winter to spring?

"You have outdistanced every voice and word,
And given my spirit wings until it stirred
Like you—a bird!"

"Oh!" I said like a gasp. "That's beautiful." *How do I know it's beautiful? I don't understand it. I don't know—I just know.*

Auntie Odie's eyes glistened as she smiled down at Martha and me. We smiled back.

★ ★ ★

Martha and I walked to the vacant lot on either side of Auntie Odie as she held our arms.

Nearing the milkweed plant, we stepped softly.

"There it is," I said. "It's out!"

The empty chrysalis swayed in the light breeze. Clinging to a stem with six long black legs was the monarch. Its long, slender abdomen trembled in the warm stirring of air. Sleek black-and-orange wings waved their patterns against the backdrop of blue sky.

Auntie Odie clasped her hands together. "Lollapalooza!"

"It looks like the white polka-dots are embroidered on the black edges of his wings," I said, "and he has one curly feeler."

"That's his little drinking straw," Martha said.

"His proboscis," Auntie Odie said. Then she squinted and leaned closer to the monarch. "Look there."

We all leaned close.

"What? What do you see, Auntie Odie?" Martha asked.

"No dark spots on the rear of the wings, no scent sacs."

"Does that mean he's not a monarch?" asked Martha.

Auntie Odie chuckled. "It means he's not a he. He's a *she.*"

Entranced, we leaned over the milkweed, arms and hands braced on our knees, eyes wide, mouths open.

"So it's a girl?" I said.

Auntie Odie straightened and rubbed her back. "See how vivid the veins on her wings are? Not like a male's."

Just then the monarch took flight. It wheeled and dipped, lit on a flower, then fluttered away. We oohed and ahed.

Auntie Odie waited while Martha and I trailed after the butterfly. At last it flew over the ditch and out of sight.

★ ★ ★

The three of us put our arms around each other's waists and walked back toward the cottage. Auntie Odie, her drawl pronounced and melodramatic, spouted forth Lewis Carroll's "Jabberwocky."

> "'Twas brillig, and the slithy toves
> Did gyre and gimble in the wabe:
> All mimsy were the borogoves,
> And the the mome raths outgrabe.

> "'Beware the Jabberwock, my son!
> The jaws that bite, the claws that catch!
> Beware the Jubjub bird, and shun
> The frumious Bandersnatch!'

> "He took his vorpal sword in hand:
> Long time the manxome foe he sought—
> So rested he by the Tumtum tree,
> And stood awhile in thought."

Auntie Odie's voice rolled and slid from one expression to another throughout the nonsense poem, and the words took on a life of their own. Martha and I giggled and squeaked to the last verse.

> "And, as in uffish thought he stood,
> The Jabberwock, with eyes of flame,
> Came whiffling through the tulgey wood,
> And burbled as it came!

> "One, two! One, two! And through and through
> The vorpal blade went snicker-snack!
> He left it dead, and with its head
> He went gallumphing back.

> "'And has thou slain the Jabberwock?
> Come to my arms, my beamish boy!
> O frabjous day! Calloch! Callay!'
> He chortled in his joy.

> "'Twas brillig, and the slithy toves
> Did gyre and gimble in the wabe:
> All mimsy were the borogoves,
> And the mome raths outgrabe."

Martha giggled in delight then clasped her elderly friend's hand. "Now tell us a story about the slaves that could fly, the folktale your mother taught you."

Auntie Odie brightened. "Let's pour up some lemonade and go sit on the bench swing. I'll tell it there."

In Auntie Odie's sunny, flower-filled kitchen she put ice in glasses and poured lemonade from a glass pitcher decorated with horizontal bands—red, then orange, yellow, green, and blue—and handed us yellow napkins with oatmeal cookies tucked inside.

Movement in the doorway caught my eye. A huge, yellow-orange cat ambled in to meet us. On the farm, Gram and Grampy had fed leftovers to cats that made their home in the barn, but they were wild and untouchable. This cat rubbed against my legs and purred like distant thunder.

Auntie Odie smiled.

"Does he chase the birds?" I asked.

"She—Emily—only goes outside when I'm working in the yard. If she gets atwitter over a bird, gives it one longing glance, she knows I'm a sockdolager—she'll be sentenced to the house." Auntie Odie leaned down to pat her cat. "But you've been a good girl for a long time now, haven't you, Emily?"

Martha leaned down and stroked Emily too. "She's named after Emily Dickinson the poet."

We strolled out to a bench swing hanging from the maple. On the way, Auntie Odie recited.

"The bee is not afraid of me.
I know the butterfly;
The pretty people in the woods
Receive me cordially.

"The brooks laugh louder when I come.
The breezes madder play.
Wherefore, mine eyes, thy silver mists?
Wherefore, Oh summer's day?"

I wished I could do poetry like that, and I wished I understood poetry more.

Emily cuddled on the swing between Martha and me, purring awhile then snoozing awhile. Martha and I sipped lemonade and savored each chewy bite of cookie and listened to our storyteller.

On the silver flow of her words she wafted us back to another time, another place. Her voice became a violin, a flute, a cello. The words became notes. Martha and I sweltered in the hot sun picking cotton. We suffered the blows on our backs and dreamed impossible dreams of freedom as the old voice carried us through her tale on the wings of her words.

At the end we sailed right up into the sky on freedom's back along with the other slaves, raptured by the magic and the music of her perfectly chosen words. When the story ended, several moments passed before anyone spoke, could return from that freedom sky.

The ice rested cold on my lip. I savored the last of my tart-sweet lemonade and the lingering joy of the freedom sky.

★ ★ ★

I tiptoed into the apartment at five o'clock. Mama, asleep on the couch, mumbled and turned over. Humming softly, I stepped to the kitchenette and made two peanut-butter-and-grape-jelly sandwiches. Happy to discover a new bottle of milk in the fridge, I poured up two small glasses and sat at the table.

"Supper's ready, Mama. PB and Js."

I had eaten half my sandwich and drank my milk by the time Mama woke up. She sat up and pushed her brown hair back from her face. "How long you been home?"

"A little while." I popped in the last bite of sandwich and chewed. "Guess what, Mama?"

Mama slumped and stared, sleepy-eyed, at me.

"Martha and I found a chrysalis today. We watched the butterfly get out." I walked over and sat beside my mother. "Auntie Odie watched with us. We got to watch the monarch stretch its wings and fly away."

Mama yawned and stretched. "You made sandwiches?"

I leaped in front of her and curtsied. "Yes, I did, Queen Ingrid."

Mama sat at the table and drank down the milk.

"Auntie Odie showed us her gardens. Did you see them yet?"

"I work for her. 'Course I did."

"Auntie Odie gave us lemonade and cookies and told us a folktale about slaves that flew away. I met Emily the cat too." I smiled. "Emily's named after a famous poet named Emily Dickinson. Auntie Odie says with a name like mine, I ought to be a poet. She knows all kinds of poems by heart and she makes stories come to life when she reads and she knows birdcalls and…"

"Ponia, please!" Mama held up her hand. "Don't jabber so. My head's exploding."

I funneled my hands around my mouth like a megaphone. "Jabberwocky! That's me!" I laughed and twirled. "'Twas brillig, and the slithy toves / Did byre and gimbles in the wabes…" I couldn't remember any more of it, so I repeated the lines as I danced around the room.

Mama shook her head and rubbed her forehead.

"Martha's family and Auntie Odie have been friends for a long time," I said. "They're like family to each other."

Mama yawned and stretched. "I know that." She stared at the sandwich, frowning.

Someone knocked and I ran to the door.

It was John Kimpell from apartment B downstairs. Round-faced, squinty-eyed, he shook his finger at me. "I'll thank you to be more quiet, young lady. When you run around like that, my ceiling sifts flour. Remember, there's people living downstairs."

Mama appeared beside me. "It ain't going to happen again, Mr. Kimpell." She glared down at me. "What do you say, Ponia?"

"Sorry." I noticed that the few strands of dark hair he had on top of his head were mussed.

Mama nudged me. "Sir."

"Sir," I said.

After Mr. Kimpell left, Mama picked up her sandwich, held it in front of her mouth, then set it back down. "No more stomping around in this apartment. Understand?"

I sat down across from her and nodded. "Sorry."

"Now…" Mama said harshly.

I blinked at Mama.

Her eyes took on that dark-cloud look. "No need to be going over to Odessa Luckett's when you visit Martha. You stay away from there, unless you're with me when I clean."

I stood up, knocking over the chair. "But, Mama, why?"

"She's a nice enough woman." Mama sucked in her breath. "But she *is* colored, after all."

What? "Mama!" I stepped back, fell over the toppled chair, and hit my side on the chair rung. I held my side, breathing in small gasps.

Mama pulled me up and squeezed my shoulders. "Ponia, you've never lived around coloreds before. But here's the way it is. They have their place and they should stay in it. And we whites have our place and we should stay in it."

"But the Matthews are white. And they love Auntie Odie. They go to each other's houses all the time."

"Ponia! You listen." Mama's voice scraped at my heart. "I can't speak for the Matthews. I speak for us. And, nice as she is, you ain't going no more to her house. Do you hear me?"

"But she's my friend," I shouted. "*Our* friend!" I placed my foot on the overturned chair, shoved with my foot, and sent it scooting across the linoleum floor.

Mama yanked my arm and scrunched her face in front of mine, our noses almost touching. "Ponia Glass Snow! You listen to me."

Bang! Bang! "Open up in there!" Mr. Kimpell growled outside the door.

Mama stomped to the door, yanked it open and yelled, "Leave us alone!"

John Kimpell raised his fist, then lowered it slowly. "I'll leave you alone when you stop the racket!" Some of the bark had gone out of his voice, facing Mama like that. He turned and stomped down the hall and down the stairs. Mrs. Gazz opened her door and stuck her head out. The pink curlers in her hair shook as she tried to speak, "O-o-o-h!" and then she slammed her door shut.

Mama slammed our door. "Now look what you've done!"

"Please let me visit Auntie Odie sometimes. She's my best friend. She…"

"Your best friend?" Mama twisted her mouth and the words came out like spittle. "A Negro you hardly know is your *best* friend?"

"No, Mama!" I drew in my breath. "I mean, yes. She's a good person, and the most interesting person I've ever met in my whole life."

Mama took a big chomp of her sandwich and chewed hard. "Don't you hang 'round her no more. That's final!"

A searing ache sliced through my heart, but I did not look away from my mother's glare. It was as though an archer held me against his bow, pulled me back, and was aiming me straight at Mama.

She shook her finger in my face. "Promise me you'll never go near Odessa Luckett's house again unless you're with me."

"Mama…" My chin trembled. The rest of me felt suspended, apart from my mind and soul. "Please tell me a good reason."

She stepped toward me and bumped the table. The plates jumped and clattered. "I've already given you reason enough. Since you're so smart, give me one good reason why I should let you."

My hands clenched. "Because… because when you tell me I can't see Auntie Odie anymore, it feels like a knife is cutting me inside, like… like when Gram and Grampy died."

Mama swallowed, straightened, and tipped her glass to her lips, but the milk was gone.

"She's your friend, too, Mama. Remember how she bought the Singer so you could…"

Mama threw her half-eaten sandwich back onto the plate. "*That* was a business deal! And I worked my fingers to the bone doing her sewing and I done paid my debt to her and then some."

"But you still work for her. You clean for her. She pays you good, you said so yourself."

"That's the way it is!" Mama yelled. "But the way it should be is she should be working for me!"

"Mama!" My throat and the backs of my eyes felt like dams holding back falls. My voice seemed to be calling from another room. "She told Martha and me about how her people were kidnapped from their homes in Africa a long time ago and made into slaves. Her mama and daddy were slaves, and all her older brothers and sisters. They were beat up and called names and…"

"Stop it!" Mama's voice was shrill like the sound of Grampy's windmill when the wind blew hard. "Stop this instant!" She lunged toward me then spun away, her face as red as ketchup. She paced back and forth, hands clenched, then opened the door. Scents of garlic and onion from the hallway filled the room. Her voice was low and hoarse. "I'm going for a walk. When I come back, you better be in bed for the night with your face to the wall. I don't want to see your face anymore today."

Then she left.

I slumped to my mat–bed, hands cupped over my face. Tears, unbidden, leaked into my palms and down my forearms. Outside a car sped by, and two men, engrossed in loud discourse, walked past. Faint voices and music from a radio drifted up from downstairs. Periodically, someone clomped up the stairs or along the hall to use the bathroom. None were Mama.

Gram and Grampy had taught me to follow their orders. Disobedience brought swift justice. When Mama was present, I followed her orders because that's what Gram and Grampy told me to do, but she had paid very little attention to me and made few demands.

What would Gram and Grampy do if they were here? Would they agree with Mama, that I shouldn't spend time at Auntie Odie's house? Or would this be one of those times when they would overrule Mama's wishes? At first I couldn't think of a time when Gram or Grampy had interacted with a Negro in my presence, but then I remembered Mister Henry. He was a colored man we used to see now and then around Greeley. Almost everybody knew him. Mister Henry was a custodian at a school, folks said, and he was an upstanding citizen and family man. "Hello, Mister Henry," they would say, friendlylike. But sometimes they used a slur-word in place of *Mister*. Mister Henry always greeted them back, a broad smile on his face, no matter which name they called him. And when Mister Henry introduced himself to someone new, he would say, "Howdy-do. I'm Mister Henry." And sometimes even Mr. Henry used the slur-word instead of *Mister*. I didn't know why.

Gram had told me never, ever, ever to call him by the slur-word, even if everybody in town did—even if Mister Henry himself did.

It hadn't been that long ago, come to think of it—maybe it was last summer—that Gram and I went shopping for new socks for me at Greeley Dry Goods. Mister Henry stood at the street corner, greeting various folks as they passed by.

The man ahead of us said, "Hello—" and greeted him with the slur before his name. "Nice day, ain't it?"

"Howdy-do, Ed, sir." Mister Henry tapped his forehead in a casual salute toward the man.

Gram's whisper had a sharp edge to it. "I hope never to hear you call anybody that."

"Hello, Ma'am, little 'n'." Mister Henry greeted Gram and me with a friendly smile.

"Hello, Mister Henry," Gram said vigorously. "Nice day, isn't it?"

"Oh, yes, Ma'am, indeed it is."

"Hi, Henry," I said.

"*Mister* Henry," Gram corrected.

"Hi, Mister Henry, sir," I said.

But would Gram have let me go to a colored person's house—a person like Auntie Odie, who loved gardens and poetry and storytelling and birds and… all kinds of interesting things?

Yes, she would, I decided. And Gram would like Auntie Odie as much as I did. Gram might even come with me to see the flowers and birds. Gram would not like Mama acting the way she was about Auntie Odie, and she'd tell her so. But Gram wouldn't like it if I disobeyed Mama either.

Footsteps on the stairs—Mama's?—propelled me to lie down and face the wall. Down the hall a knock, a door opening—not ours, voices, the door shutting again, then quiet. Weariness flooded me and tears flowed. And a thought pierced my mind for the first time since Mama walked out.

What if she never came back?

★ ★ ★

I awakened as Gram and Grampy's wall clock struck nine. I rubbed my aching eyes, and then closed them against the light over the table.

I lay on my mat on top of my quilt in my dress and shoes. Sounds of crickets drifted in through the open window. The moon shone through the window from a darkened sky, and the apartment was still empty of Mama. An ache gnawed at my insides.

Soft footsteps sounded on the stairs then in the upstairs hall. Mama! I faced the wall and shut my eyes, my heart thumping so loud I wondered if she would hear it.

The door creaked open. I listened to Mama walk to the kitchenette, push in the chairs at the table, and set the plates in the sink. She ran water, then it grew quiet. I figured she was drinking her nightly glass of water. Then I heard a click and the light went out. The soft rustle of her nightgown as she dressed for bed filled the room. A few minutes passed, and then her bare feet padded across the linoleum. A board creaked in the floor near my head.

Mama's knees grazed my back as she kneeled on the mat. Then she scooped me up, rolling me towards her, and cradled me in her arms. I felt Mama's warm breath and wet kisses on my eyelids, forehead, and cheeks. Hot tears spread onto my face like warm glaze on a cake. Then Mama's arms hugged me so tight it hurt, and I heard the sobs stuck in her chest. A breeze from the open window cooled my wet face.

Mama choked then fished hankies from the pocket of her nightgown.

I opened my eyes to tiny slits. Lights from the street cast a gray light across Mama's face. She placed her hand over my ear and pressed my head against her chest. It was as though I heard Mama's heartbeat, her racking sobs, and her short breaths through a megaphone.

★ ★ ★

Mama relaxed and laid me back down on the mat.

She pulled off my shoes.

I rolled to my back and whispered, "I'm glad you're back, Mama."

"Do you want to get under your quilt?"

"Not yet."

"G'night, Ponia." Mama rested her hand on my curls then padded to her bed on the couch. She blew her nose.

I swallowed and took a deep breath. "I love you, Mama." *Do I?*

Soon Mama breathed deep and steady.

Her touch lingered there on my hair. Her tears still cooled my face. I raised my hand to wipe them away then changed my mind. They would dry soon enough. I smiled into the darkness. Mama's embrace had filled an empty place in my heart I didn't know was there. What would Mama be like tomorrow when the sun rose on a new day? And what about Auntie Odie? Would Mama relent and let me spend time with Aunt Odie again in her house, in her garden?

Thunder rumbled far away. Soon came the gentle whisper of rain and the fragrance of clean, damp earth.

My eyes closed and I imagined myself a slave. The master pursued me, cracking his whip. The wind blew in my face, and I stepped right up on the air. Yes, I was aloft, drifting into the blue sky, far away from the master and all the troubles of the world. Far away, but so sleepy. I started to fall back to earth, and one of the slaves—a slave that looked like Auntie Odie—pulled me up, up.

"Sleep and I'll carry you," she said in a watery voice.

I rested in her gentle arms and we sailed into the endless blue of sky.

Chapter 18

Red Chinese Plan
To Conquer World
With Russia in 2 Years
—*Greeley Daily Tribune*, p.11, Fri., June 15, 1951

★ ★ ★

Weld County Farmers
Thankful for Rains
—*Akin Scoop*, p.1, Sat., June 16, 1951

Saturday's high in the 80s; fair; scattered showers in afternoon

We took turns riding Martha's shiny blue Schwinn then rested on the grass in front of her house.

"Let's go see Auntie Odie," I said.

"Her garage door's open," Martha said. "She's still at the store."

"How do you know where she is?"

"She goes to Piggly Wiggly every Saturday morning. She always asks my mother if she needs anything."

I rode Martha's bike up the Matthews' driveway and into their garage. "I'm saving my money for a pale-green and lavender bike I saw at Everybody's Store in Greeley."

"How much have you got saved?"

I parked her bike and put down the kickstand. "Three dollars and thirty-five cents."

"How much do you need?"

"Forty dollars."

I rubbed my hand over the handlebars, seat, and fenders, and then pushed the horn button. *O-o-o-g!* "If only I could collect enough Disney seals to win the Skylark Bread contest."

"I've been working hard to win." Martha put her hands on her hips. "We buy tons of Skylark bread. So does Auntie Odie and my grandparents, so I can maybe get enough end seals to fill the album."

I kicked her Schwinn's front whitewall tire. "How many doors have you knocked on, asking for Skylark end seals? How many loaves did you buy at Safeway with money you earned so you could get seals?"

74

Martha kicked the back tire, imitating me. "The contest is almost over. Neither of us will win a bike anyway."

"Why did you even try?"

Martha widened her eyes. "I just like winning."

"But you already have a bike."

"My birthday present. Maybe you'll get one for yours."

I stared at my oblivious friend. "Yeah. And a big party like yours too."

She smiled. Her voice softened. "Yeah. I hope I'm invited."

Words crammed into my throat, straining to be said. *You make me tired—you in your new dresses and lotioned knees. And your pretty mommy and happy daddy giving you everything you want, your shining home and your pink-and-white bedroom with shelves full of games and toys.*

Martha shook my shoulder. "What's the matter, Poni?"

I stood in the dim coolness of the Matthews' garage, feeling evil and angry.

Martha stuck her face three inches from mine. "Are you all right?"

Then the feeling drained away. "Yeah." But my heart thudded in my chest.

★ ★ ★

Pots and pans were stacked on the green Formica counter. Mama scrubbed at the copper bottom of a pan with Chore Girl Copper Cleaner, and Mrs. Matthews reclined in a lounge chair just beyond the kitchen.

"Good morning, Mrs. Snow." Martha was always so polite.

Mrs. Matthews' brown eyes lit up. "What have you girls been up to?"

"Just bike riding," Martha said. "We're hot. We're gonna play inside for awhile."

Mrs. Matthews lifted a thin arm and patted her daughter's shoulder as Martha bent to kiss her cheek. "Ingrid just finished cleaning the living room."

"We won't mess it up," Martha said.

Hot water steamed up around Mama's face as she rinsed a pan at the sink. She dried it with a tea towel, and glanced sharply in my direction. "Mind your manners, Ponia."

"Yes, Ma'am."

"You have such a darling daughter," Mrs. Matthews said to Mama as Martha and I headed down the hall.

Martha and I put up a card table in the living room. We punched out Esther Williams and Friends paperdolls and cut out their clothes. I heard parts of our mothers' conversation.

Mrs. Matthews spoke gently but articulated each word. "Oh, Ingrid, I can assure you that she is a good person—as safe a person as anyone can be."

"But, I just can't get used to... to thinking of a Negro like she's the same as us."

Mrs. Matthews perked a little laugh. "Ingrid! I can't believe you said that, after all Odessa has done for you. What finer friend could anyone have?"

"Let's design our own clothes for Esther," Martha said. "Come on."

I followed her into the kitchen. The women quieted—Mama swept and Mrs. Matthews set the table. Martha pulled white paper and a Deb shoebox full of scissors, pencils, erasers, and crayons from a bottom drawer and handed it to me. Shoe colors were listed on the end of the shoebox—Terra Tan was checked. I would've chosen one of the other choices—Golden Honey or Kelly Green.

Mrs. Matthews smiled and sat down. "Don't you two leave even one scrap."

"Not one scrap," Martha said.

Back at the card table in the living room I drew a pencil line around Esther Williams' shoulders, arms, and bodice. Martha drew around one of Esther's friends.

I added a very full skirt to the fitted bodice, puffy sleeves, and shoulder tabs. I drew a collar with lace around the edge and an apple pattern over the whole dress.

I heard Mama move the wastebasket away from the wall in the kitchen. "I suppose it is wrong for me to think that way." *Sweep, sweep, sweep.*

"Wrong, *yes!*" Then Mrs. Matthews' voice grew soft and I had to strain to hear her. "We all have our prejudices to overcome. Ingrid, Odessa is intelligent, kind, generous—you know that. And that's typical among her people, no matter what anyone says."

"I don't know what to say." I heard that edge to Mama's voice.

"You don't have to say anything, dear friend. Just keep your heart and mind open to goodness, to the truth that all people have intrinsic value, that we truly are created equal with certain 'inalienable rights.'"

Long pause. I knew exactly what was happening. The words *dear friend* were flying and spinning around in Mama's brain like whirlygigs. Just like Mrs. Matthews' words, *You have a darling daughter* had spun around in my brain. We weren't used to that kind of talk.

Then Mrs. Matthews said, "Odessa will be bringing groceries from Piggly Wiggly any time now. We'll have lunch together—all of us girls—if you'll help me make the sandwiches. Give you a chance to really get to know her."

"No. Thanks anyway." Mama had that tired hoarseness in her voice. "I'm 'bout done here, we'll be going home."

"Open the eyes of your heart, Ingrid. See what a lovely human being she truly is."

The doorbell chimed.

Martha ran to the door. "I'll get it!"

"Stay for lunch, Ingrid. Please."

I heard Mama quietly say, "All right."

★ ★ ★

I sat next to Auntie Odie, and Martha sat on her other side. Our tuna-salad-with-lettuce-on-Skylark-bread sandwiches and potato chips looked delicious. A polished red apple rested beside each of our plates. Mrs. Matthews poured milk for herself and Mama. Martha, Auntie Odie, and I chose Grapette, and since Auntie Odie preferred to drink hers from the little bottle, Martha and I did too.

Gram used to buy me six Grapettes once a month. I could have one anytime I wanted. "It's up to you how you drink 'em, little bee, but that's all you get 'til next month." Sometimes Grampy got a hankering for Grapette, and I'd give him one, if I had any left.

Mrs. Matthews smiled at Auntie Odie. "Odessa, would you ask the blessing with that sweet thanksgiving prayer by Mildred Edgington—and anything else you'd like to pray?"

"I'd be happy to." Auntie Odie looked down at Martha beside her. "You know it, too, don't you, child?"

Martha nodded, smiling.

"Pray it with me, child, would you?"

Martha nodded, bowed her head, and closed her eyes. Then we all bowed our heads, as Auntie Odie and Martha prayed.

"Thank You, Lord, for planting time, the fragrant earth is stirred.
Thank You for the golden sun and the song of a bird.
Thank You, Lord, for growing time, for each tiny blade of grain.
Thank You for the warm sunshine and the refreshing rain.

"Thank You, Lord, for harvest time—the grain is in the bin,
The fruit's in jars upon the shelf, the apples are gathered in.
Thank You, Lord, for winter time when everything's at rest.
Thank you for each season. Each one seems the best."

"And, Lord," Auntie Odie added, "bless each precious life at this table. May Your love and beauty and joy pursue us all the days of our lives. And we do so appreciate this nourishment and fellowship. In Jesus' name—and everyone said…"

"Amen!"

Sitting next to Auntie Odie, I heard her breathe and laugh, and chuckle in that funny way, and talk, and I smelled her talc that smelled like spicy honeysuckle. And she smelled something like the smell of earth and sweet flowers after rain, and the scent of green, if green had a scent.

Every so often her soft arm bumped against my bony one. That little touch by accident was so nice somehow.

I sneaked looks at her, especially when she talked or laughed. She'd removed her hat. Her dark hair, sprinkled with silver-gray, was shortish but curly and wild, like mine. A few short strands frizzed along her hairline, creating the effect of a narrow frame of mist around her large dark face.

Her nose was a wonder to me—glossy, kind of flat with wide nostrils, and it was so fitting that she had an enormous mouth with big, full lips—lipsticked bright pink today—to house all those words and thrilling tones and sounds that flowed from it. And the large teeth, which protruded slightly, made a grin that filled her face like a three-fourths full glass of milk. Her broad face, covered loosely with skin, looked soft to the touch, the many wrinkles like folds in soft, brown velvet.

When I spoke, Auntie Odie looked at me, eyes shining out of a big joyous face. I wondered if she was as interested in studying my features as I was hers. I would be a sorry sight to eyes that grew up in a world of mahogany faces and only a few white ones—probably none with skin and hair "as white as angels' wings" like Grampy used to say.

"Auntie Odie," Mrs. Matthews said. "Would you recite that beautiful praise poem, about God's mercy? I believe it's by Mildred Edgington too. I *love* the words."

The poet didn't need any arm-twisting. Auntie Odie drank the last from her Grapette bottle, and then began.

> "There's a wideness in God's mercy
> Like the wideness of the sea.
> There's a love in God's heart
> That reaches out to me…"

Auntie Odie's voice fairly sung the words. They reached right into my heart, and I felt God's love. It reached even me in that sweet moment. As Auntie Odie continued, God hugged me—that's what I think. A sweet warm zing swept over me. I closed my eyes and grinned.

> "There's a fullness in His service
> That no other joy can fill
> And He brought it down to man
> From a cross upon a hill.
>
> "So I will praise His name forever
> As eternal ages roll.
> He's the rock of my salvation,
> Blessed Savior of my soul."

We expressed our pleasure with warm smiles toward Auntie Odie. We ate in silence for a few minutes. But I couldn't stop grinning. The tuna sandwiches tasted extra delicious—the apple too.

Auntie Odie sighed. "Olivia, what've you heard from Nate?"

"Three letters since he got back to Korea." Mrs. Matthews smiled just at the mention of her brave son. "I really believe that's why I got better. It was wonderful having him home and safe for a whole month."

"Has he pulled any cupids since he went back?" I asked, hoping it was an intelligent question.

Everybody chuckled. Mrs. Matthews said, "Cuspids? I imagine he has."

We had just about finished our lunch, all but Mrs. Matthews. She swallowed with effort then looked at Mama seated next to her. "Now, when is that quilt fair in Denver that your Nimble Needles are going to?"

Using a potato chip as a plow, Mama scooted the other chips around on her plate. She cleared her throat. "I don't know as I'll be going."

"Oh, no!" Creases appeared on Mrs. Matthews' high taut forehead. She laid her hand on Mama's arm. "Now, Ingrid, if it's because you don't have anyone to watch Poni, she can stay right here with us. She'd be fine." She dashed a glance in my direction. "Wouldn't you, Poni?"

I gave her a few quick nods and smiled.

Mama shook her head. "I won't have Poni staying here while you're still—while you're recuperating. And anyway…"

"Well, I won't have you missing your quilt fair. You've worked so hard on that Bethlehem Star. And you deserve a get-away."

"I was thinking about asking Mrs. Gazz down the hall if Poni could stay with her."

I widened my eyes and held my breath. *Mrs. Gazz! Oh, no!*

Mrs. Matthews shook her head. "Oh, Ingrid, surely you're not serious. Not Mrs. Gazz."

"She's not so bad, now that we've gotten to know her some. She hasn't yelled or slammed her door for a few weeks now."

Martha piped up. "I'll make sure Poni is good. We'll be good together. Please let Poni stay with us."

"Poni will not be staying here." Mama's voice was taut and loud.

Auntie Odie raised her hand and waved it like a child in school. "Ingrid's absolutely right, Olivia. You're not up to taking care of Poni." She smiled at me and winked. "As dear and well-behaved as she is, she has no business staying here for four days. She belongs with me."

That little gasp I heard came from Mama.

Auntie Odie looked straight at Mama and talked with a lot of hand gestures. "Poni will stay with me! We'll check in with Olivia and Martha every day. She'll have a good time, and I'll have this wonderful child around to hack the loneliness out of a few summer days. And you'll get away and enjoy yourself with some nice friends, Ingrid. Won't that work for you?"

Mrs. Matthews tilted her head down and stared at Mama as if looking over the top of glasses. "Now that's a deal you can't pass up, Ingrid."

Mama's eyes widened, and her mouth poised, open, waiting for words. "I… Well…"

"Then it's settled." Auntie Odie's laugh cranked clear from her belly. Then she looked at me, her dark eyes large and soft like a deer's. "Would you *like* to stay with me, child?"

I glanced at Mama. Her cheeks were rosy-pink, and a sliver of smile relaxed her face.

"Well, would you?" said Auntie Odie. "Speak up, child."

All I could do was nod my head and let my mouth grin as big as it wanted to.

★ ★ ★

Mama spoke, her voice sharp. "I shouldn't have let them talk me into it."

"Who?" But I knew who.

Mama sighed. "Olivia and Odessa."

"But I thought you'd be happy about it."

Mama lifted the window, then leaned over and braced herself on the sill, the top of her head touching the wavy screen. "It probably won't happen anyway."

"Why?"

"Money," she whispered and closed her eyes.

"But I thought you were going to stay at Pearl Willis' sister's house. And ride in Mary Ann Walters' new Hudson Hornet—for free."

Mama raised up, pulled a hanky from her dress pocket, and dabbed her eyes. "Ponia." She looked at me, all soft and tired, her voice mellow, even tender. "I ain't gonna go without helping with gas and food. And besides…"

She blew her nose, and I waited, unmoving, not wanting to disturb the bubble.

"Some of the reason I was going was to enter my quilt in the competition."

"But you finished your quilt, Mama." It was spread out on the sofa, the Star of Bethlehem shining from the center in red, orange, and yellow calicoes. "Maybe you'll win the prize and get some money."

Mama blew her nose again. "Oh, little bee…"

My heart banged against my rib cage, every bit as hard as Mr. Kimpell from downstairs had pounded on our door. Mama never, ever called me *little bee*. That was dear Gram's—and only Gram's—pet name for me. I waited while Mama folded her hanky and slid it back into her dress pocket.

A sharp noise outside startled us. We looked out and saw a man in the front yard of the Victorian house across the street hammering in a For Sale sign.

I looked at Mama and waited.

She blinked and shook her head. "I can't remember what I was saying."

"I said maybe you'd get some prize money for your quilt."

"Rachel Galante said I could share her booth with her. Two dollars is my share of the five dollars it'll cost her. That's just to display my quilt. It costs five more dollars to enter the competition."

"How much money do you need altogether?"

Mama carefully folded her quilt and placed it at the end of the couch much like a rescuer would settle a fallen baby robin back into its nest. "Well, I've been doing some figuring." On the back of an envelope Mama had written numbers and cross-hatches. "I gotta have at least twenty-five dollars when I leave for Denver. That's for the fees to display and enter the competition, to help with gas and food, and a few dollars in case of an emergency."

"Twenty-five dollars!"

Mama threw the envelope back on the table. She flopped down on the couch, her head back. "And that doesn't even take into account paying Odessa Luckett or whoever watches you."

Auntie Odie, here I come! I plopped down by Mama on the couch. "Auntie Odie would like to have me for free."

"No."

"She's lonely. She likes my company. She really wants me to stay with her."

"I'd have to pay her something. I don't take charity."

"Maybe she'll pay *you* to let me stay with her." I grinned at Mama, and waited for her to smile, or maybe even laugh.

But a shadow had crossed her face. "I'm not going." She smoothed her dress and pushed her hair back. "I'll tell Odessa and the Nimble Needles tomorrow, and Olivia."

"How much do you have?" I asked, desperate.

"You mean money?"

"Yeah."

"You mean for the trip?"

"Yeah, in the Solitaire Coffee can."

"I think maybe, about twelve dollars."

Was I dreaming? Mama was actually sharing information with me, like I was a real partner with her in life. I counted on my fingers. "So you need thirteen more dollars."

"I could squeak by with twenty if I want to risk going without any extra money at all, no emergency money."

I did some more figuring. "So you're short at least eight dollars. Right?"

Mama's voice was hoarse, weary. "I guess so."

I ran to the bureau, got out my Lunch Box Sandwich Spread jar, and dumped its contents into her lap.

"Three dollars and thirty-five cents, Mama. You can have it."

She stared at the change as if she'd never seen coins before.

"There's still two weeks before you go, Mama. You can have everything else I earn from Mr. Smith between now and then. And Mrs. Matthews told Martha and me she'd pay us if we'd weed her window flower boxes out in front."

She scooped up the coins and dropped them back into her lap. *Clink, clink, clink.* "This is your bike money," she whispered.

Maybe a girl was walking into Everybody's Store right then, heading for my pale-green and lavender Schwinn. I'd had such fun just that morning on Martha's blue bike, speeding down the hill, wind blowing over me—an invisible sheet of energy. If I couldn't have my precious horse Maybelle, a bike was the next best thing.

Then I thought of all the sadness Mama had known. I'd probably never know all that happened between her and my dad, whoever he was, and why he left us. But it surely was some terrible sorrow. And Gram and Grampy.... Mama looked so fragile sitting there, like a glass goblet, empty, transparent, too close to the edge of the table. Her tender sorrow seeped from the shadows encircling her eyes.

"Folks need to see your Star of Bethlehem, Mama."

She looked at my worn-out oxfords, too small, tied with twine. "You need shoes."

"I want you to go, Mama. More than anything." And I meant it. Not just because I wanted a chance to stay with Auntie Odie, but because Mama's wellbeing hinged on this.

She dropped the coins back into the jar and stood up. She got fresh hankies from the bureau drawer, dabbed her eyes and blew her nose. At the sewing machine, in front of the south window, she began to mend a pair of men's black slacks. Earlier that morning I had fetched mending from Mr. Smith. I fished the nickel out of my sock and dropped it in the jar with the rest of the coins.

Mama stopped treadling and watched me open her top bureau drawer and place the jar of coins inside. I stood with my hand on the closed drawer.

She raised the foot on the machine, turned the slacks, treadled, and then stopped. "Go sweep, Ponia. Then you can play awhile before supper."

I lifted the broom off the hook and started to sweep, but Mama stared at me intensely.

I swallowed the knot in my throat. "I hope you make it to the quilt fair, Mama."

She turned back to her work. "We'll see."

Thump, thump, thump, Mama treadled her Singer, and *swish, swish, swish,* I swept the floor. "We'll see," she said again.

Chapter 19

Korean Action in Air,
On Land, at Sea
—*Greeley Daily Tribune*, p.1, Thurs., June 21, 1951

Time to Plant Tuberous Rooted
Begonias Started Inside During
Winter, Says Garden Expert
—*Akin Scoop*, p.1, Thurs., June 21, 1951

Thursday's high 79°, low 52°; scattered thunderstorms afternoon and evening

Mama and I rode in silence. Gray skies lounged just beyond the windshield.

Auntie Odie waited for us on the front walk in a wide-brimmed straw hat, blue-print dress, yellow-print apron, pink anklets, and white tennis shoes. She grinned and waved.

I had imagined myself leaping from the pickup when it was barely stopped and running into a sunbeam where Auntie Odie waited joyously, open-armed. We'd hug each other, and she'd twirl me 'round and 'round.

I slowly opened my side of the truck—*squeak*—took hold of my crackling grocery sack of belongings, climbed down out of the truck, and stood.

Auntie Odie opened the door on Mama's side. "Hello, hello," she bellowed. "Do you have time for tea?"

Mama smiled. "I'm late. What time is it?"

"About a quarter till two."

"Gotta get back," Mama said. "Mary Ann's picking me up at two."

A stiff wind blew and thunder cracked.

Auntie Odie wrapped her arms across her bosom. "It's gonna rain again, get poachy, maybe hail. Be careful, honeygirl."

I waited by the gate feeling nervous and a little afraid, but couldn't think why. Another gust whipped, delivering sprinkles.

Mama got out of the pickup, leaving the motor running, and walked toward me. Her hair whisked in the wind, her thin face flushed with the energy of her coming adventure. "Now you be good for Mrs. Luckett. Hear?"

I nodded and held up my hand in a little wave.

Auntie Odie's hand lit on my shoulder.

Hope is the thing with feathers.

"We'll be so busy adventurizing, enterprising, poeticizing and rhapsodizing, she won't have time to be anything but good."

I was petrified with gladness.

Mama pecked my forehead and brushed her fingertips under my chin—a demonstration for Auntie Odie, I was sure. "We'll be back Sunday afternoon." She pulled a piece of paper from her pocket and handed it to Auntie Odie. "Here's a phone number where we can be reached."

"Thank you, dear. Now you hustle and don't worry about a shebang. Get in out of the rain."

"Thank you!" Mama hollered over her shoulder and hopped up into the pickup. Rain mixed with hail pelted us. Auntie Odie and I ran for the house. At the door we waved at the back of the truck as Mama drove off.

I wished it wasn't raining. Maybe Mama would've stuck her arm out the window and waved. I recalled the day Gram and Grampy drove out of the farmyard at the Arrentz place, heading for North Platte. It was spitting snow, but Gram and Grampy waved out the windows of their gray Nash as Mama and I huddled beside the trellis and waved them off. I didn't dream I'd never see them again. What if Mama died in an accident too? A rush of love for her swept through me and I wanted her to come back. I wanted to hug her good-bye and kiss the soft hollow of her cheek.

I waved wildly in case she could see me in her rearview mirror. *Please, Mama, just a little wave.*

Auntie Odie waved, too, and recited,

> "If you were coming in the fall,
> I'd brush the summer by
> With half a smile and half a spurn,
> As housewives do a fly...."

She smiled. "I've forgotten the rest."

Mama honked the horn, *Toot, too-toot, toot, toot.* The truck stopped, turned the corner and was out of sight.

Toot, toot.

★ ★ ★

Auntie Odie showed me the daybed where I'd be sleeping. It was in "the writing nook" off the front room. I left my sack there and she took me on a full tour of her cottage. The first things I noticed, and loved, were all the little nooks and bay windows. Two bay windows at the front—in the front room and in the writing nook, and one on each side of the house—in the breakfast nook and in Auntie Odie's bedroom.

Auntie Odie and I sat across from each other in front of the kitchen bay window. Gray skies and rain did not dull the honey tone of the oak in the breakfast nook, nor the graceful glass vase full of yellow, white, and coral-pink roses from the garden.

We sipped our tea in silence. Auntie Odie's broad face reflected the peacefulness of a remembered time long ago. I sighed in glum joy—missing Mama but living out a secret wish.

Black-and-yellow-speckled linoleum, yellow-enameled cupboards, white appliances, and colorful plaques arranged on a yellow wall created a cheery atmosphere.

Auntie Odie gestured toward the window.

> "There came a wind like a bugle;
> It quivered through the grass,
> And a green chill upon the heat
> So ominous did pass
> We barred the windows and the doors
> As from an emerald ghost;
> The doom's electric moccason
> That very instant passed.
> On a strange mob of panting trees,
> And fences fled away,
> And rivers where the houses ran
> The living looked that day.
> The bell within the steeple wild
> The flying tidings whirled.
> How much can come
> And much can go,
> And yet abide the world!"

I stared at her, smiling. How did she do that? Make words that didn't make sense to me so meaningful, so beautiful? I had tried to read poetry at school, but I could never get a flow, couldn't usually make sense of it.

"Emily Dickinson?" I asked.

"Yes indeed."

"Another," I said.

She looked out again. The rain had slowed to a light sprinkle.

> "A drop fell on the apple tree,
> Another on the roof;
> A half a dozen kissed the eaves,
> And made the gables laugh.

"A few went out to help the brook,
They went to help the sea.
Myself conjectured, Were they pearls,
What necklaces could be!..."

"I like that," I said when she'd finished the poem. And that was true—because of the sound of a beloved voice, more than for the message, which was lost to me.

A grin spread across Auntie Odie's face. Her eyes were not dulled by the gray day—but glistened warm and dark. My body grew restless, but my heart and mind wanted to listen to Auntie Odie's volcanic voice spout poetry the rest of the day. I sat sideways leaning against the bench arm, my back to the window, knees crossed, bouncing my top leg.

"Careful, child," Auntie Odie said.

"Okay. Do you know anymore poems about rain?"

"Aren't you going to ask who wrote them?"

"Who did?"

She drew out the name, long and dramatic, emphasizing the first syllables. "*E-Em-mi*ly *Di-i-ick*inson."

"Oh." I adjusted again, curling up on my side, my head on the arm of the bench.

"Knowing the poet is more important than knowing the poem," Auntie Odie declared.

"*E-Em-mi*ly *Di-i-ick*inson," I imitated. "But the poem is more important, isn't it? When I hear a beautiful poem, I don't care who wrote it."

She chuckled. "Oh, child! That's like saying you love nature but you don't care Who created it."

I swung my leg. "Maybe I don't."

Aunt Odie gazed out the window. A patch of blue sky in the south matched her dress and the tiny flowers on her bib apron. "I thought you were a much wiser girl than that," she said softly.

My face flushed—I felt it, felt the tingle in my cheeks. "Did *E-Em-mi*ly *Di-i-ick*inson write any more poems about rain?"

She rubbed her brow, then gathered herself up.

"An awful tempest mashed the air,
The clouds were gaunt and few;
A black, as of a spectre's cloak,
Hid heaven and earth from view.

"The creatures chuckled on the roofs
And whistled in the air,
And shook their fists and gnashed their teeth.
And swung their frenzied hair.

"The morning lit, the birds arose;
The monster's faded eyes
Turned slowly to his native coast,
And peace was Paradise!"

"How... Where did Emily Dickinson learn to write new words like that?"

"*New* words?" Auntie Odie smiled. "She was a wordsmith in the finest sense, had a big store of words, rhapsodized like no other. She spoke the same language, used the same words we do, but she had a jim-dandy talent for choosing just the right ones and arranging them in surprising ways. Miss Emily wrote hundreds of poems—over seventeen hundred—so she practiced a lot. She loved words and paid attention to how words sound in the ear. And not just the physical ear, but the ear of the heart. That's one of the reasons I enjoy her poetry so much."

I sat up straight. "Seventeen hundred?"

"Seventeen hundred." Auntie Odie nodded solemnly, and then she giggled from somewhere deep inside. "She must've had a larky poetic life."

"Is that why you learned so many of her poems?"

Auntie Odie nodded and drank down the last of her tea. "I would memorize and recite Dickinson poesies, even if I didn't understand a word. She does make familiar words new. And the way she strings them together, it's music to my soul, a descant to an ordinary day—to life."

"Auntie Odie." I poked the teaspoon handle through the handle of my teacup, thinking about how to ask my next question.

Auntie Odie pointed at my spoon. "Careful, child."

"Do you think I could learn to say poetry like you do? I'm not good at memorizing." I raised the cup too far. It tipped and chipped the lip of the cup.

We jumped, gasped simultaneously.

"Sorry," I said.

"Well, that's your cup from now on when you visit."

"I'll pay for it. How much does it cost?"

"Don't feel bad, child. Everybody makes mistakes."

"Especially me."

"The main thing is that you learn from 'em."

I sat up straight at the table, not sure what to do next.

Thunder crackled, announcing a new downpour.

Auntie Odie chuckled good-naturedly. "Definitely a day for squidge."

★ ★ ★

"Well now, this was a jim-dandy project for a squidgy day." Auntie Odie set our word tablets on a kitchen shelf right next to a pink glass candleholder.

"Can we take off our shoes and go 'vestigate, go see if mud really sounds like *squi-i-i-idge*?" Now I was feeling silly.

"Not while there's lightning, child." She stood beside me, tall and dark—and *noble*, one of the words I'd just added to my new-word tablet. For a second I saw my reflection in her eyes. "Would you like to play a game of Parcheesi? Or Monopoly?"

I shrugged.

"Or maybe you have a better idea, child?"

I shrugged. "A story?"

Auntie Odie laughed. "A told story or a book?" She took her empty teacup and saucer to the sink.

I followed her with my dishes. "I like both."

"How about we start *Little Women* by Louisa May Alcott then? I think you'd like that."

"Do you have any books or big poems about slaves?"

"Henry Wadsworth Longfellow wrote a 'big poem' about a slave's dream."

"Say it!"

"Now that one I don't know by heart." She smiled and headed for the front room, to the floor-to-ceiling bookshelves beside the fireplace. "But it's in this book...right..."—she pulled *Favorite Poems of Henry Wadsworth Longfellow* from the shelf—"here!" We sat on the sofa, and then she read with diligent passion.

"The Slave's Dream

"Beside the ungathered rice he lay,
His sickle in his hand;
His breast was bare, his matted hair
Was buried in the sand.
Again, in the mist and shadow of sleep,
He saw his native Land..."

Auntie Odie read on, and I sailed with her in my heart and mind—from phrase to phrase, note to note, all the way to the last verse.

"...He did not feel the driver's whip,
Nor the burning heat of day;
For Death had illumined the Land of Sleep,
And his lifeless body lay
A worn-out fetter, that the soul
Had broken and thrown away!"

The reader closed the book, I stroked the cover.

"Such a sad poem, Auntie Odie."

Her lips squeezed together, flattening her chin. She stroked my curls. "Yes, child."

"Now, read me a story—a whole book—about slaves."

She raised a brow. "Why would you want a book about slaves, child?"

"I just wonder how it happened, what it'd be like to be a slave. I want to know more about your people."

She looked at me with such an odd look, I thought at first she might be irritated, but her voice was cheery. "Well, I have a book about the life of Frederick Douglass. He was a slave. And there's *Uncle Tom's Cabin*. But they're awful hard, tragic stories—sad to hear."

"I want a true story about a real slave."

Auntie Odie slid her finger along a shelf and whispered, "Narrative... *Narrative of the Life of Frederick Douglass*. Here it is." She pulled out a tattered book and thumbed through it. "Now, child, this is not a child's book. It's harsh at times—might be mumbo jumbo to you."

"Let's try it." I tried to sound noble.

"If you get tired of it or don't like it, you just say so, and we'll stop."

"Okay." Aunt Odie couldn't know how different my interests were from other kids my age, how determined I was to hear that story. Martha read fairytales and Nancy Drew mysteries. Sarah had a collection of comic books that filled three drawers, from Donald Duck to Little Lulu, and that's all she wanted to read. I wanted stories about the time of slaves.

We cuddled up on the sofa. As if a bugle had blared, Emily padded into the room and hopped up beside Auntie Odie. "Ma-a-aw."

I patted the sofa and made room for the purring cat between Auntie Odie and me. Emily strolled across Auntie Odie's lap and settled down between us.

Auntie Odie opened the book and gathered herself up. "'*Narrative of the Life of Frederick Douglass: An American Slave*, written by himself, copyright 1845.'" Auntie Odie looked at me as she turned the page. "That's one-hundred and six years ago."

I tried to whistle. Auntie Odie chuckled. "Chapter one." She read a minute or so. Auntie Odie paused and took in a deep breath. "That's just the first paragraph, child. Do you want me to keep going?"

I mostly understood it so far, and the sound of Auntie Odie's voice took on the resonance of various stringed instruments as she read. An iron glided over some place inside of me, smoothing my spirit. I grinned at her. "I like it."

She settled back, holding the book with one hand, her other across my shoulders while I stroked Emily. She read about Mr. Douglass' family—he was pretty sure his father was a white man. And all his mother's children were separated from her when they were babies. *No! That can't be true.* But that's what Mr. Douglass wrote about right there in his book.

And so I was seized—suspended—by that thread of time, by the words of the author-slave and the voice of the daughter of slaves beside me. She read on as cumulonimbus scrubbed away the afternoon, as "There came a wind like a bugle; / It quivered through the grass, / And a green chill upon the heat / So ominous did pass."

★ ★ ★

At four thirty the rain surrendered. The largest, darkest clouds departed to distant horizons and posed as cuddly animals asleep on the Rocky Mountains. Auntie Odie placed a bookmark and laid *Narrative of the Life of Frederick Douglass* on the coffee table.

"Auntie Odie?"

"Yes, child."

"Can you find that poem that Mr. Douglass quoted of John Greenleaf Whittier's—the one about the slave who lost her children?"

"It's just a few pages back from where we left off."

"Could you read it one more time? It's so sad… but so beautiful somehow."

"… Here it is. Read along with me, child. Put your heart into it."

Together we held the book and lifted our voices. Emily opened her eyes and gazed up at us as though profoundly stirred.

> "'Gone, gone, sold and gone
> To the rice swamp dank and lone,
> Where the slave-whip ceaseless swings,
> Where the noisome insect stings,
> Where the fever-demon strews
> Poison with the falling dews,
> Where the sickly sunbeams glare
> Through the hot and misty air:—
>> Gone, gone, sold and gone
>> To the rice swamp dank and lone,
>> From Virginia hills and waters—
>> Woe is me my stolen daughters!'"

Tears gilded Auntie Odie's eyes. We held each other a long time.

"I'm sorry about your mama's stolen children, Auntie Odie, and all the sad days of your family."

She puffed a sigh. "Doesn't do anybody any good to bemoan the past. And to hold onto grudges is like grappling with grizzlies—the grappler is always the one who loses the match."

"I'm glad you were never a slave, Auntie Odie."

"Oh, but I was."

I stared up at her.

"Still am for that matter." Then she chuckled. "I'm a slave of goodness—Christ's slave. Chapter six of Romans, verse eighteen, says,

'Being then made free from sin,

ye became the servants of righteousness.'

"That word *servant* can be interpreted as *slave.* So I once was a slave of sin. Now I'm a slave of Christ by choice, a slave of rightness—goodness. And within that very slavery He bestows an extravagant, spacious freedom. He frees me from the bondage of self-pity and hopelessness and unforgiveness—through his daily tender mercies."

"I'm not going to be a slave of anything."

"There are some things you need to know about God. He is good—He is love. He is fair and just. And He declares we're either slaves of sin or slaves of rightness—one or the other."

"I don't choose either."

"Not choosing is choosing—to be a slave of sin. Without God's insight revealed in His Word, we're helplessly deceived by the enemy of God and man."

"I'll have to think about that some more."

She chuckled. "Yes, you think on it some more. And pray. Ask God to help you uncover the Truth He has written on your heart."

"Okay," I said. *Huh?*

Together we gazed out the living room bay window where it looked like an ambitious laundress was giving the sky a slow, top-to-bottom rinse with bluing. The placement of Auntie Odie's cottage at the top of a gentle hill, with a vacant lot directly across the street, gave her a wondrous view.

"You live in such a pretty place," I said.

She answered with a poem.

> "At summer eve, when heaven's aerial bow
> Spans with bright arch the glittering hills below,
> Why to yon mountain turns the musing eye,
> Whose sunbright summit mingles with the sky?
> Why do those cliffs of shadowy tint appear
> More sweet than all the landscape smiling near?
> 'Tis distance lends enchantment to the view,
> And robes the mountain in its azure hue.

"That's 'Hope' by Thomas Campbell," she said. "I believe he was describing a place in Scotland, where he lived—more than a hundred years ago. Aren't the images lovely?"

I grinned. "Jim-dandy! But you were talking different—kind of funnylike."

"Oh, that's my Scottish brogue," she said in her Scottish brogue. "Do you like it?"

I nodded. I felt so peaceful somehow, there with Auntie Odie like that.

"I don't want to make you bumptious, child, but it's been a wonderful afternoon for me, talking about the Holy Friend I cherish, and sharing poetry and literature with a beginning wordsmith— someone who's interested and appreciates it so much."

"I feel kind of like a monarch coming out of my chrysalis. I'm getting a good look at some things I could really love to do. And be."

Auntie Odie got that distant look in her eyes. Another poem was about to bloom into the room.

"From the Chrysalis

"My cocoon tightens, colors tease,
I'm feeling for the air;
A dim capacity for wings
Degrades the dress I wear.

"A power of butterfly must be
The aptitude to fly,
Meadows of majesty concedes
And easy sweeps of sky.

"So I must baffle at the hint
And cipher at the sign,
And make much blunder, if at last
I take the clew divine."

Before I could ask, she answered. "Yes, that's an Emily poem."

"I like it," I said, "but I don't know why."

She smiled tenderly. "You don't have to know why to enjoy it, child."

We both stroked Emily and her purrs escalated.

"When will we read the slave book some more?" I asked.

"Maybe tomorrow, maybe tonight at bedtime."

Emily jumped down and sauntered toward the kitchen—and her feeding dish, more than likely.

Auntie Odie sighed. "Well, the Nimble Needles should be in Denver by now, settled in at Pearl Willis' sister's house."

"I hope Mama wins a prize at the quilting show."

"I do too, child. I do too."

Martha showed up at five o'clock. We accepted her family's invitation to their house for casserole supper at six o'clock.

★ ★ ★

"We better get titivated, child."

Auntie Odie tried her best to tame my curls, but the rainy weather had sprung them into a tangent. From her dresser drawer she pulled out a milk-chocolate-cherries box filled with bobby pins, hairpins, hair clips, and combs. She took a bobby pin and corralled the flock of curls that hovered over my eyes. It looked funny clipped back from my high forehead, but it appeared to please Auntie Odie, so I held my tongue. I wished Auntie Odie were my real auntie. If we were relatives, we'd stay in touch for the rest of our lives, no matter what happened or where we lived.

But as it was, our friendship felt fragile to me. It could be taken from me at any moment upon a random whim of Mama's, or Auntie Odie could move away.

Auntie Odie changed into a nylon jersey dress—blue with green and navy geometric designs all over it. "Now what earbobs should I wear, child? You choose."

I hunted through her assortment and pulled out clip-on earrings that were small blue rhinestone daisies with pearl centers. "These."

"I like the dangles-and-spangles kind the best," she said. "Try again."

She liked my next choice, long loops of sparkly blue and white beads.

"Can I wear the daisies then?"

"Just this once, since we're just going to the Matthews' house."

"Could I wear these too?" I held up a pair of white high heels with gold buckles.

"I can't wear 'em no more. Guess you might as well."

And she let me wear her Hawaiian-print duster, cinched at the waist—wrapped twice around with a silver belt.

"Martha will laugh," I said, giggling.

"Give us all a laugh."

The hat I chose for Auntie Odie was a wide-brimmed, blue-straw affair with a white band and immense bow in front. She chose a hat for me—a yellow, small-brimmed, straw hat with pink, blue, and yellow flowers. It was too big, but it "matched" my "dress."

Banana-nut bread from Auntie Odie's fridge, cream cheese for the bread, and fresh flowers from her yard—white daisies and marigolds—were our offerings for the host and hostess.

Fritz Matthews answered the door. "Well, now look at these getups!" He shook my hand. "Welcome, Miss Poni. Don't you look, er... lovely? And you too, Auntie Odie." He hugged her. "Come in!"

But even when he smiled, a sadness possessed his face. Martha giggled and commented over my outfit, yet she wasn't her usual bouncy self. The supper smelled beefy, delectable.

Mrs. Matthews rested in a recliner with a cotton-print lap robe tucked around her. "Come in, come in, dear friends."

A round of laughter erupted when Auntie Odie bent to kiss Olivia's forehead and her hat tumbled to the floor.

★ ★ ★

"Stay right here, Liv." Fritz Matthews pressed his wife back into the recliner. "Martha'll fix the water glasses and I'll get the casserole and the salad on."

"Oh, Fritz, you treat me like an invalid." Her brow creased and her coral lips curved down.

"You worked all afternoon putting together the casserole and salad. Now it's my turn." There was an unfamiliar scolding tone in Mr. Matthew's voice. "I may be clumsy in the kitchen, but I can handle it."

Auntie Odie jumped up from the sofa. "Fritz is right, Olivia. You've done enough. Let me help, Fritz."

Martha and I followed Auntie Odie and Mr. Matthews into the kitchen.

Once everything was ready, we found Olivia asleep. Auntie Odie and Mr. Matthews exchanged glances.

"Liv." When Mr. Matthews took his wife's hand she stirred.

She had grown weaker, but no one would know it by looking into her eyes—bright and determined as a healthy youth. She rose and shuffled to the table.

Mr. Matthews prayed the blessing on the food and asked for God's protection over Nate and the other boys in Korea.

Auntie Odie tasted the casserole. "Glory be! This is delicious. What's it called, Olivia?"

"Six-Layer Dinner. It's a family recipe—since 1925. I can't believe I haven't served it to you before."

Auntie Odie parted the layers with her fork. "Ground beef, tomato, green pepper. Ah! Rice. I'm in hog-heaven."

"And potatoes," Martha said. "I helped peel 'em."

"The trick is covering the dish tightly and letting it bake slowly at two-hundred and fifty degrees for two and a half or three hours." Mrs. Matthews' voice was strong and cheerful. Her auburn hair fell in smooth waves around her face but was mussed and flattened in the back from resting in the recliner. Her sallow skin turned rosy in the chandelier's soft light and in the presence of friendship.

Auntie Odie took a helping of tossed salad and set the bowl beside my place. "Pass the saltcellar please."

"Saltcellar?" I said. "That's what my gram always called the salt shaker."

"It's a good old word." Auntie Odie giggled and sprinkled her salad generously. "Any new news from Nate?"

"A letter yesterday," said Mr. Matthews, "dated almost two weeks ago. He's concerned that the war is just going to drag out. It's taking its toll. But he says he's healthy and enduring well. And he said to give his dear Auntie Odie a bear-hug—which I will deliver right after supper."

Auntie Odie displayed her white-fence grin. "Emily said, 'A letter is a joy of earth.'"

"How true, Odie dearest," Mrs. Matthews said, "especially when the letter is from a loved one on the other side of the earth."

Auntie Odie swallowed and sipped her water. "Dear Nate. Every day I pray for his safety, and for God's protection over all those boys."

I could barely hear Mr. Matthews. "We also."

Olivia nodded.

Gray gauze veiled our spirits.

Then Auntie Odie said, "I like to pray Psalms seventeen, verses eight and nine for Nate—'Keep Nate as the apple of Your eye, hide him under the shadow of Your wings, From the wicked that oppress him, from his deadly enemies, who compass him about.'"

"Let's stop for a moment," Mrs. Matthews said. "Auntie Odie, lead us all in that prayer. We'll pray it, right now, for Nate."

Slowly and with great feeling Auntie Odie led, and we all prayed as one. "'Keep Nate as the apple of Your eye, hide him under the shadow of Your wings, From the wicked that oppress him, from his deadly enemies, who compass him about.'"

How I wished I had known that prayer to pray for Gram and Grampy. Maybe they would be alive right now, and I'd be home on the Arrentz place with them. My child-heart swelled with faith—faith in the God I was only beginning to know, and faith that God would keep Nate safe from his deadly enemies and someday bring him home to eat Six-Layer Dinner with us.

I took a bite of casserole. "What's the sixth layer?" I asked.

All eyes looked at me.

"Potatoes," said Martha.

"We already said potatoes," I said.

Mrs. Matthews laughed. "Thin-sliced onions is the layer no one mentioned."

There was more discourse about Nate and the war, and whether President Truman could bring it to a close and whether Truman'd be re-elected in '52—or even want to be.

"McArthur promised he'd 'bring the boys home by Christmas,'" said Mr. Matthews. "Well now, Christmas has come and gone—six months ago. Truman asks for eight and a half billion dollars to help end the war, casualties are still rising. Yes, we've made progress, but there have been setbacks, and cost."

"Monday will be the war's one-year anniversary." Mrs. Matthews buttered a slice of white bread—Skylark, no doubt. "Only God knows how much longer it will go on. God help us all. Have some more, Auntie Odie. There's plenty."

"Gladly!" Auntie Odie dished up another helping. "Today's *Tribune* says the rain clouds over Korea have brought air attacks nearly to a halt. And it's the first time in five days no Communist warplanes were up flying."

Through the dining room window we saw that the rain had subsided again but the plate of sky remained dark-plum gray. In the west, golden sunlight gilded billowing clouds.

"Wonderful rains we've been having," Auntie Odie said.

"Too bad it can't rain like this every year," said Mrs. Matthews. "Can you imagine what that would do for the sugar-beet harvest—for all the farmers?"

"Mom and Dad have had a good year so far," said Mr. Matthews. "But they're getting too old to farm. Dad's talking about retiring, moving into Akin, just having a garden."

After the supper dishes were rinsed and put to soak in the sink, Auntie Odie spread cream cheese on slices of her banana nut bread and butter on some. Martha and I were asked to brush the crumbs off the tablecloth. Mr. and Mrs. Matthews worked together making coffee, getting out cups and saucers, and pouring cream into a cream pitcher.

"Now rest, Olivia." Mr. Matthews tried to lead her by the arm. "I'll serve up the coffee." Barely an inch taller than his wife, he eyed her.

"Fritz, I can serve the coffee. You sit for awhile."

"You've already overdone it today, Liv." Mr. Matthews slipped his arm around her and guided her toward the living room. "I'll take care of everything."

Mrs. Matthews stopped and removed his arm from her waist. Something like lightning flashed in her eyes. "Fritz, I've always served our guests coffee after supper."

Mr. Matthews raised his arms in surrender. He smiled an impish smile. "Yes, dear."

Auntie Odie giggled. "I'll settle this. You two go smooch in the living room while the girls and I serve up the dessert and coffee."

Martha chimed in, "Yeah, we'll serve."

"Yeah," I said.

But a shadow of sorrow darkened Mrs. Matthews' face. As Mr. Matthews helped her to the recliner, he whispered, "It's okay, sweet Liv. 'This too shall pass.'"

She sighed. "It already has."

★ ★ ★

After dessert, Mrs. Matthews said, "Auntie Odie, how about a verse of Scripture?"

That gathering-look swept over Auntie Odie. "Psalm one-hundred thirty-nine, verses one through eighteen…

> "O Lord, thou hast searched me, and known me.
> "Thou knowest my downsitting and mine uprising,
> thou understandest my thought afar off.
> "Thou compassest my path and my lying down,
> and art acquainted with all my ways.
> "For there is not a word in my tongue, but, lo, O Lord,
> thou knowest it altogether."

Olivia rested her head on the back of the chair and joined Auntie Odie.

> "Thou hast beset me behind and before,
> and laid thine hand upon me.
> "Such knowledge is too wonderful for me;
> it is high, I cannot attain unto it."

Then Mr. Matthews added his voice to the psalm.

> "Whither shall I go from thy spirit?
> or whither shall I flee from thy presence?
> "If I ascend up into heaven, thou art there:
> if I make my bed in hell, behold, thou art there.

> "If I take the wings of the morning,
> and dwell in the uttermost parts of the sea;
> "Even there shall thy hand lead me,
> and thy right hand shall hold me.
> "If I say, Surely the darkness shall cover me;
> even the night shall be light upon me."

The Matthews stopped, but Auntie Odie continued, her voice swelling, not unlike my new-birthed faith. A light from within radiated from her face.

> "Yea, the darkness hideth not from thee;
> but the night shineth as the day: the darkness and the light
> are both alike to thee.
> "For thou hast possessed my reins:
> thou hast covered me in my mother's womb.
> "I will praise thee; for I am fearfully and wonderfully made:
> marvellous are thy works; and that my soul knoweth right well.
> "My substance was not hid from thee,
> and when I was made in secret, and curiously wrought
> in the lowest parts of the earth.
> "Thine eyes did see my substance, yet being imperfect;
> and in thy book all my members were written,
> which in continuance were fashioned,
> when as yet there was none of them.
> "How precious also are thy thoughts unto me, O God!
> how great is the sum of them!
> "If I should count them,
> they are more in number than the sand:
> when I awake,
> I am still with thee."

Mrs. Matthews sighed. "This is how we should've begun the evening."
Martha and I had settled on the floor with a box of paper dolls, but they remained untouched.
"I like the part about the wings of the morning," I said.
Everyone nodded in agreement.
"Will you help me memorize that?" I said to Auntie Odie.
A look of sweet joy spread across her face. "You know I will, child."
"Me too," Martha said.
"Of course. You too, child."
"We can all work on it together," Martha said.

Mr. Matthews put his feet on the footstool and settled back in his easy chair. "Auntie Odie, what are those verses in Isaiah about being bore up on eagle's wings?"

"Isaiah forty," Auntie Odie said. "The first verses Arda Moore taught me when I was a child." Auntie Odie got up, walked over to Mrs. Matthews, and laid her hand on her shoulder.

> "He giveth power to the faint;
> and to them that have no might he increaseth strength.
> "Even the youths shall faint and be weary,
> and the young men shall utterly fall:"

Mr. and Mrs. Matthews' voices joined Auntie Odie's in a triumphant wave.

> "But they that wait upon the Lord
> shall renew their strength;
> they shall mount up with wings as eagles;
> they shall run, and not be weary;
> and they shall walk, and not faint."

★ ★ ★

Auntie Odie and I strolled along the gravel path, drinking in the rain-scented fragrances of roses, pink and white sweet pea, and lily-of-the-valley.

Lavender and pink cloud-tassels glittered in the far-west sky. Spilled pieces of cloud glowed overhead like neon confetti, and in the east a rainbow arched over the plains like a fantasy bridge to some faraway, mythical place. I pointed, Auntie Odie nodded.

Plunk, plink, plunk. The rain had stopped, but Auntie Odie's garden sounded like an underground chamber as moisture, collected during the rain, dripped from eaves, leaves and blossoms.

> "On this long storm the rainbow rose..."

Auntie Odie's eyebrows raised, her voice, light like the air, sped over the words.

> "On this late morn the sun;
> The clouds, like listless elephants,
> Horizons straggled down.

> "The birds rose smiling, in their nests,
> The gales indeed were done;
> Alas! how heedless were the eyes
> On whom the summer shone!"

"Emily Dickinson?" I asked.

She nodded. "That's an Emily."

"I like it. What's that part about the elephants again?"

> "The clouds, like listless elephants,
> Horizons straggled down…"

I gazed up at the dimming sky. "That's just what it looks like." I pointed toward a dark lumbering cloud to the west, faintly edged in gold. "That one looks like an elephant, with a trunk and big ears and everything."

Auntie Odie chuckled softly. I knew her thoughts were far away. Soon she said, "I'm remembering a poem about a family at the end of day—'Evening Song,' a Mildred Edgington poem."

I waited. "Say it, Auntie Odie."

> "When shadows are long and twilight is near,
> A voice in song and prayer I hear.
> I hear my daddy whistle as he does his evening chore
> And Mother getting supper. How could I ask for more?
> There's my brother and my sister a-laughing as they play.
> All these are songs of evening at the closing of the day."

"I wish I had a daddy and a brother and sister," I said.

Auntie Odie looked down at me so lovingly. "You have a Daddy, child—your Father in heaven. We both do." Smiling, she continued. "And the folks we spent the evening with are among our brothers and sisters."

"I like that," I said. "We're all part of our Daddy's family."

I clasped her hand. "Were those poems?"

She didn't answer right away. She lifted off her hat and swung it as she stepped along like a young girl. She tilted her broad face to the twilight sky, breathed in the fragrant air, smiled.

"Poems?" she said at last. "What about poems?"

"Were those poems you said over at Martha's after supper? About going away on eagle's wings?"

When at last she looked down at me, her face took on a look of surprise. "Stay right there, youngling." She stepped back, studied me.

"What's the matter?"

"There you go, looking like a little moonshiny, wild-haired angel again. The sunset sky is shining a raspberry-colored flashlight behind you. Flickering through your wayward hair, it looks like a halo." She laughed. "Seems as though you could open your wings and fly away."

"I wish I could." I turned toward the western sky of spilled tropical juices.

"Where would you fly to?"

I thought for a moment. "Here."

"Here? To this house?"

I nodded. "And to this garden. To you. I wish I could live with you forever, Auntie Odie."

"You don't mean that, child. I'm an old woman. Why, you'd get homesick for your mama. You'd get so sad and miserable."

"I'm not with Mama now and I'm not sad and miserable."

She laughed. "Your mama's only been away a few hours. Just wait a couple days. Then you'll know what homesick is."

"I won't get homesick. I like it here."

"That's nice," she said softly.

We circled around the oval garden of rosy-pink lambs'-ears, white dwarf phlox, and lavender lilies and followed the path where asters and gaillardia, honeysuckle and hydrangea colored the backdrop for the petunias, pansies, and snow on the mountain. She told me the names of those I didn't know. I touched and sniffed the blooms I could reach. Each flower was a miracle—like a little chip of heaven that had broken off and fallen to Earth.

I again took Auntie Odie's hand. "Say that poem again about riding on an eagle."

"The Scripture about mounting up with wings as eagles?"

"Yeah. You mean it's a Bible verse? Not a poem?"

"It's a Bible verse, but it's poetry. God wrote some of the most beautiful poetry ever written through His people." She settled her hat back on her head.

> "But they that wait upon the Lord
> shall renew their strength;
> they shall mount up with wings as eagles;
> they shall run, and not be weary;
> and they shall walk, and not faint."

"Who shall do all those things?" I asked.

"The people who wait upon the Lord."

"Who are those people? And what are they supposed to do while they wait for Him?"

"They're people who spend time reading God's Book, talking it over with Him, and doing what it says—building a love relationship with Him. We need to love God with all our hearts, love others, and trust God completely to work everything out in His way and in His time—I think that's some of the ways people 'wait upon the Lord.'"

"Do you wait upon the Lord?"

"I try to live my life waiting upon the Lord—because I love Him more than anyone or anything, and I'm grateful for His salvation through grace."

"So when you mount up with wings as eagles, can I watch? Can you take me with you?"

She laughed. "It's figurative. When God gives us strength to mount up with wings as eagles—as we trust the Lord completely *no matter what*, as we wait upon Him, we inspire those around us to do the same."

"Auntie Odie, you know the folktale you told about the flying slaves?"

"I do, child."

"Is that what those slaves were doing—mounting up with wings as eagles? Was it God that gave them strength to step up on invisible stairs and fly away to freedom?"

As we circled back to the maple and draped the towels we'd carried with us over the bench swing, Auntie Odie explained that the flying-slaves story was made up by the slaves to help them get through the miserable days of slavery, to help them think happy, and to give them courage and hope. She sat down and I gave the swing a good push then hopped on beside her. Birdsong hushed to murmurs. The fireworks of sunset passed and the sky turned midnight blue. A smattering of stars appeared between the inkblot clouds. I studied Auntie Odie's expressive face, softly highlighted in the faint glow of the porch light. She was barely more than a stranger to me, yet I felt such a kinship with her, like I had known her all of my life. Her shadow reached back over all my previous days and was, in some profound way, a part of them.

I leaned forward to look back into her face. "Is the Lord going to give Mrs. Matthews strength to mount up with wings as eagles?"

"Yes."

"When?"

"I believe He already has and continues to do so."

"Then she's not going to die. Right?"

"I don't know, child." The swing slowed to a tremble. Auntie Odie wrapped her long, soft arms around me. "I do know that even if she has to go through the valley of death, the Lord will give her strength to do that, and she will mount up with wings as eagles, and she will run and not be weary, and she will walk and not faint in that valley. Olivia truly loves the Lord and waits upon Him. She knows it's by His grace alone that she'll spend eternity with Him. Because she loves God so much, she lives a life of obedience to Him and trusts Him."

"How can somebody die and mount up with wings as eagles at the same time?" I pulled away to better see Auntie Odie's face in the dim light. "I try never to think about Gram and Grampy's dead faces in their caskets. It didn't even look like them. Death is awful."

"'Precious in the sight of the Lord is the death of his saints.' From God's point of view, death is Homecoming for His kids. God's whole purpose for each one of us is to have relationship with Him—forever—because He loves each of us so much. He wants us to love Him back with all of our hearts, souls, minds, and strength. When death paraded in on the arm of sin, God gave the world His Son Jesus. Now death has wings for those who live in the Son. If they believed in Him and waited on Him during their lives on earth, their lives are full of light. There will be a celebration in heaven. How beautiful is a life that's filled with God's light, as opposed to darkness."

I bet I looked puzzled. "So is that Scripture really about death—the one about eagle's wings? And what it's like to die?"

"I think the psalmist may have been referring to both—living and dying. Living life on earth in a love relationship with God *is* mounting up with wings as eagles. But so is living out that love relationship with God in the life hereafter—living forever with Him. I believe the psalmist meant that if we love and trust the Lord daily, His tender mercies will lead us through all our troubles in this life on earth, *and* He'll lead us in the life to come. In our hearts, we will always 'mount up with wings as eagles.'"

"What are tender mercies?"

"Oh… God's gentle kindness. He treats us kindly, even when we've hurt Him, disobeyed Him."

I nodded, but it was a lot to think about.

She patted my knee. "God's Book is full of Scriptures about His tender mercies. I've memorized a lot of them because they strengthen me."

"Tell me some."

"My favorites are these—Luke one, verses seventy-eight and nine:

> "Through the tender mercy of our God; whereby the dayspring from on high
> hath visited us, To give light to them that sit in darkness and in the shadow of
> death, to guide our feet into the way of peace."

She tilted her head up and looked down at me across her wide cheeks. "When Jesus Christ becomes our Lord, we become God's child—not just His creation. When we 'wait upon the Lord,' we can relax, knowing that God will work out everything, even sickness, even death, in a way that is good and purposeful in the end."

"Even death." I said.

"Especially death. When Jesus rose from the grave, He put wings on death."

She pushed with her foot, setting the swing in motion again. I swayed forward and back to keep it going, then sunk back in the swing and sighed.

She laughed. "End of sermon. Let's go in."

"One more poem. Please?"

> "…warm, sweet day
> Lapse tenderly away…"

I waited. "Is that all?"

She chuckled. "No. But I can't recall the rest of it. Let's see. Give me a minute…. Oh yes, I remember it's from the third verse of a poem called, 'The Last Eve of Summer.'

"I sit alone, and watch the warm, sweet day
Lapse tenderly away,
And, wistful, with a feeling of forecast,
I ask, 'Is this the last?'"

"Emily D.?"
"John Greenleaf Whittier."
"I like that, Auntie Odie. Especially the part you remembered first—'warm, sweet day…'"
"'Lapse tenderly away,'" she finished.
I tried to make my voice sound soft and rich like hers as we spoke it together.

"…warm, sweet day
Lapse tenderly away…"

"Ah-h-h," I said, exaggerating a sigh. "Just like today. One more, Auntie Odie."
Eyes closed, head back, she began. "'Stars' by Agatha Jordan:

"Stars sing praises,
    Gleaming in the sky.
They know Who to thank
    And so do I.
Stars praise their Maker
    As they swing through the night,
Glad to be lovely
    And my delight."

A breeze rustled the trees. We strolled along the garden path to the front step where the porch light bathed us in sweet, yellow light.

Chapter 20

Truman Warns
U.S. Cities Open
To A-Bombing
—*Greeley Daily Tribune*, p.6, Fri., June 22, 1951

Two New Cases
Of Polio in Akin
—*Akin Scoop*, p.1, Fri., June 22, 1951

Partly cloudy Friday; high in low 80s; more scattered showers and thunderstorms

The writing nook, varnished in the clean gray light of early morning, doused my eyes with wonder. Here I was, curled up on a deliciously soft daybed and enveloped in a cotton quilt that smelled like rain air—in Auntie Odie's cottage!

"Sleep as late as you want," Auntie Odie had said the night before when she tucked me in. "You're a princess while your mama's away."

Sleep still tugged at my eyes, so I closed them and soaked in my surroundings with my other senses. The birds sang so zealously, they sounded like they were perched in the room. Drifting through the open window, too, were the scents of flowers—too many and too blended to name. And other aromas wafted in from the kitchen. Coffee, and something else. Pancakes? No, different. Something bready, but not quite. And music! Auntie Odie's rich voice hummed along with the classical orchestra music—violins, flutes—probably coming from the Motorola on which she had played Louis Armstrong and Benny Goodman the day before.

Near my ear a purr started up and whiskers tickled my cheek. I smiled as I felt Emily snuggle down beside me. The more I stroked, the louder she purred.

At last I opened my eyes. Sheer yellow curtains across the west-facing window sifted the new morning light and sprinkled the room with a gray-gold glow. My daybed was along the wall opposite the bay window, my head near the arched doorway to the living room. Auntie Odie had pulled a paisley curtain across the doorway to the living room for the night. I snuggled my face in Emily's fur. She gazed at me with her ever-changing eyes—flat, olive-lime plates with clear, glasslike bowls inverted over them.

Dark-ivory shelves, floor-to-ceiling along the north wall, were laden with books interspersed with artful pieces of glassware. Auntie Odie would face the shelves when she sat at her mahogany desk, which she called a davenport. She'd left a narrow walkway between the davenport and the wall of shelves. Next to the davenport stood a small table with wheels on which sat an Underwood typewriter. A rose-colored, winged easy chair and a matching hassock faced the foot of my daybed. A small antique bureau with curved legs, ivory drawer knobs, and beveled mirror ornately framed, graced the southwest corner near the bay window.

The paisley curtain across the doorway parted and Auntie Odie peeked through. "Well, bejabbers! Good mornin', child!

> "Hey! It's morning time!
> I don't wanna sleep all day.
> No, no, I'm gonna get up
> And sing and work and play.

"Want some grits?"

★ ★ ★

At the breakfast nook Auntie Odie prayed a Mildred Edgington poem over our breakfast.

> "Good morning, God.
> You're ushering in another day, untouched and freshly new,
> So here I come to ask You, God, if You'll renew me too.
>
> "Forgive the many errors that I made yesterday,
> And I'll try again, Dear God, to walk closer in Thy way.
>
> "But, Father, I am well aware I can't make it on my own,
> So take my hand and hold it tight, for I can't walk alone."

Auntie Odie had stacked phonograph records on her Motorola so we could have music during breakfast—classical music was playing now. With milk and warmed maple syrup poured over the grits, they were delicious, and I asked for a second helping. But there was no question as to why that gritty cereal was called grits.

Auntie Odie peered out the south-facing bay window of the breakfast nook. "Another splendiferous morning." Then she looked at me across from her.

> "I'll tell you how the sun rose—
> A ribbon at a time.

The steeples swam in amethyst,
The news like squirrels ran.

"The hills untied their bonnets,
The bobolinks begun.
Then I said softly to myself,
'That must have been the sun!'"

I thought she was finished. "What does 'The steeples swam in amethyst' mean?"

But she continued with the rest of the poem, and then bowed her head, signalling it was finished.

I clapped. "Sometime maybe you could explain some poems to me."

She raised her eyebrows, her eyes twinkled. "I can explain what I know. But I'll tell you right now, child, I don't know all the meanings of what I quote."

"You don't?"

She shook her head. "I memorize things that I like the sound of, even if I don't understand them all. Funny thing is, every time I recite them, they make a little more sense."

I just sat and smiled at her.

"Anything special you'd like to do today, beamish child?"

"Work in the garden."

Auntie Odie laughed. "Really?"

The needle on the phonograph clicked in steady rhythm.

"Every so often that thing sticks," she said and disappeared into the front room. Shortly, the clicking stopped and she reappeared. "I worked outside some before breakfast. It was just poachy enough that the weeds came out lickety-split. Tomorrow we'll work in the garden together if you want, but today we got to do something special. What would you like to do, child?"

Working in the garden is special. I wanted to dig in the wet earth with Auntie Odie and plant some seeds. But I could wait until tomorrow. I thought a minute. "Tell stories?"

"Who? You or me?"

I grinned. "You."

"We'll do stories when that rain comes that the *Scoop*'s predicting for this afternoon or evening. And maybe that would be a good time to show you my scrapbook of zingy news."

"Feed the birds?"

"I did that this morning too. Tomorrow I'll wait for you to feed 'em."

I shrugged my shoulders. "Type on the typewriter?"

Auntie Odie looked doubtful. "Oh, child, that old Underwood's seen better days. It sure is touchy." She studied my face. "Jumps and skips."

I smiled small. "And runs and hops?"

★ ★ ★

Auntie Odie had pulled up the easy chair for herself, and she let me sit at the davenport in the desk chair that swiveled. She rolled the little table on wheels toward us, so all I had to do was swivel left and I was in front of the Underwood.

Bdreet-bdreet. She rolled in a sheet of white paper.

"The trick is," she said, "the typist has to push down on the keys firmly, bravely. Prepare your little fingers for a long ride because it's a long way down." She demonstrated with a long weathered finger. The letter *a* appeared on the page.

I pushed down on the *j* letter, hard, I thought. The carriage rumbled to the end and stopped—"Ting!" and a stuttering *j* appeared. My "little fingers" hadn't pushed down on the key "firmly, bravely" enough.

Auntie Odie showed me how to return the carriage with the silver handle. I pushed down on the *L* key, pushed it all the way to the bottom "firmly, bravely," but forgot to let up quickly. *Gr-r-r-r*, the carriage growled and moved along until I let up.

Then the phone rang.

While Auntie Odie answered it, I punched at the keys trying to get the touch.

Soon she was back with a smile. "Poni, someone wants to talk to you."

It was Mama. "Did you sleep good last night?"

"Uh-huh." *Really, really good.* "Did you?"

"Sort of. Tonight will be better."

"Did you get to sleep in a bed?"

"Well, yes. The four of us done slept in what used to be Maude and John's kids' bedroom—a big room in the basement with two double beds."

"That sounds like fun, Mama."

"Not quite." Then she whispered into the phone. "I got kicked and jabbed a dozen times."

"Oh."

"And enough snoring to blow the roof off. Good thing we're in the basement."

I giggled.

"But there's a bathroom down there, and there's even a fridge and a hotplate if we want to fix something. But Maude cooked us up a wonderful breakfast."

"Who's Maude?"

"Pearl's sister."

"You sound happy, Mama."

A long pause. "It's nice to get away. No offense."

I couldn't think of what to say.

"Are you being good for Odessa?"

"Yep."

"You better."

"I'm typing on the Underwood, and we're gonna work in the garden tomorrow."

"Oh, they want to leave now. Gotta run."

"I miss you, Mama." *Do I?*

"Be right there." She must've been talking to one of the Nimble Needles.

"I... I... love you." I squeezed the words out like so much toothpaste from a near-empty tube.

Long pause. "I gotta go now, Ponia."

"Will you call me tomorrow?" I asked.

"No more calls. No more money. Bye." *Click.*

And then a steady buzz.

I trudged into the nook where Auntie Odie waited.

She took one look at me and wrapped her arms around me. "Well now, that was a nice surprise."

"Yeah."

"Did you catch the mopes?"

"I didn't think I would," I said, and sniffed.

"Want to type some more?"

"Okay."

I poked at the keys. After a few more tries I got pretty good.

"Had enough?" Auntie Odie asked.

"I'll write you a note, okay? Don't look."

Auntie Odie soft-whistled a wavy tune, twiddled her thumbs, and looked at the ceiling.

I giggled and typed: iii lllllliik yuu ttttank youuu 4 liiii king me

When I handed it to Auntie Odie, her smile faded like a flower wilting. Her lower lip curved down and, at the same time, pushed up into her upper lip. Her chin quivered and flattened, nostrils flared, and her eyes took on that deer gaze. She sighed, scooted back in the chair, and held out her arms.

When I didn't move, she tilted her head toward me, turned her palms up, then curled and uncurled her fingers. "Come here, child." She patted her lap.

"I'm too heavy."

"Flumadiddle!"

I turned sideways and slowly sat down, feeling awkward—too big, too bony.

Surprised by her strength when she lifted me under the arms and brought me closer, I relaxed. Auntie Odie wrapped her long soft arms around me and held me snugly against her bosom. "It's easy to like you, child."

"It is?"

"As easy as scrambling eggs or planting a seed." She sighed. "As easy as breathing." Her long fingers patted my back. "Who wouldn't like a little white butterfly like you?"

My mama. Pressure built up behind my eyes and my throat constricted. I squeezed out the words, "Sometimes... I think... Mama wishes she didn't have me to worry about."

"Your mama loves you, child. I know she does."

But I knew different. An agonized whimper leaked from my throat.

"Lully, lully," she whispered. Then she spoke, her voice soft and stirring like the murmur of a brook.

> "To fight aloud is very brave,
> But gallanter, I know,
> Who charge within the bosom,
> The cavalry of woe.

> "Who win, and nations do not see,
> Who fall, and none observe,
> Whose dying eyes no country
> Regards with patriot love...."

A sob exploded from my chest. I clung to Auntie Odie and cried. And cried and cried. And she held onto me as if I would slide off a cliff if she let go.

Every so often, in her cello voice, she said, "That's it, little thumbling. Turn loose of that bunglesome sorrow and all those wild-and-woolly thoughts—let them gush from your soul and away."

She reached around, pulled open the top drawer of the davenport, and took out some hankies. She handed me one, then she settled us back into the chair. And I cried and cried some more, wondering if I would ever be able to stop. I used all the hankies—soaked up every one. Auntie Odie gave no indication that I should stop, or that she wanted to move on with the day. She never once said, "Now don't you cry" or "Big girls don't cry." I wished I would never have to leave that safe and loving place in Auntie Odie's arms.

"I'm sorry," I managed to say.

"No need to be, child. You squinny till you're dry." She sighed, deep and long, and spoke slowlike and thoughtful. "Life is hardscrabble sometimes, that's for sure."

Even when we both grew too warm from the rising temperature in the room, I stayed in her lap. Perspiration beaded above Auntie Odie's lip, but she hung onto me like a long-lost treasure she'd just reclaimed. Emily meandered in and viewed us with eyes the color of weathered bronze then strolled to the bay window, stuck her head between the sheers, and hopped up into the window seat.

When the doorbell rang, Auntie Odie and I looked at each other.

"Shall we ignore it?" she said softly. "Need more time?"

I shrugged and buried my eyes in a hanky trying to push back tears that still wanted to come.

Auntie Odie cupped my face in her hands. "How's about if I mosey on out and answer it, just to make sure it's not something urgent with Olivia, and you stay here with the hankies and Emily 'til I get back?"

I nodded and got off her lap.

Auntie Odie returned a few minutes later with Martha. By then Emily was cuddled in my lap, just as I had cuddled in Auntie Odie's minutes before.

"Are you okay?" I knew Martha spoke to me, even though she was patting and looking at the big orange tabby in my lap.

I sniffed and blew my nose on an already-soaked hanky. "Yeah."

"You wanna ride my bike?"

I glanced up at Auntie Odie, a soft smile lighting her face. I shook my head and whispered, "No thanks." I wanted to spend the whole day alone with Auntie Odie, soaking up her love and comfort and soft spirit. I felt possessive of her time and didn't want to share her with anyone, not even Martha—at least, not yet.

After Martha left, I held onto Emily as Auntie Odie gathered me back into her lap. She rubbed my back as I leaned against her, stroking Emily. With each of my hiccups and sighs, Emily purred louder.

"My poor sad mama," I said, dabbing my eyes. "My poor dead Gram and Grampy." More tears. "Mama hates me." Sobs and tears.

"Lully, lully, little thumbling. Lully, lully. You must know your mama loves you. She's just a troubled soul. Like a balloon full of air, her heart's stretched full of heartache and trouble—and loneliness."

I studied Auntie Odie's face. "*You* like me."

"'Deed I do!"

More deep crying from my soul.

Auntie Odie had surged into my life like rain on the desert and showered me with acceptance and love. What made her that way? What made her able to like me—a stranger, a nobody? How could she be so content to just hold me, a big ten-year-old girl, in her lap for an hour or more, an ugly white girl, not beautiful and dark like herself? We were as different as keys on a piano—ivory and ebony.

Once I settled into breathy sighs, Auntie Odie said, "How about you go rinse your face in the washroom while I pour us some lemonade?"

I nodded and stirred. Emily jumped down.

"Or would you rather have a Grapette?"

"Grapette."

I skipped through the front room and through the kitchen, face swollen, eyes burning, but my heart as light as if bay windows had been installed on all sides.

Auntie Odie came in while I was still rinsing my face. She moistened a pink washcloth, wrung it out, and then gently wiped my face.

"Better now, child?"

I nodded then hugged her, and she hugged me back.

She rubbed her hand over my head of curls. "You're my little dandelion gone to seed. My dandelion angel."

We giggled.

"Grapette's waiting," she said.

Then we promenaded into the kitchen, arm in arm.

★ ★ ★

Emily, Auntie Odie, and I cuddled in the bench swing in the big old maple. A soft breeze stirred the garden. Irises and daylilies swayed, and the marigolds and impatiens danced. Sweet pea, honeysuckle, and bicolored carnations along the north fence caressed us with their robust scents, and the petunias, too, with their odd, sweet smell.

Birds flew from tree to tree, feeder to feeder, and sang us a whole concert of song—a little classical and a lot of jazz. The robins—well, they sounded like beginners practicing two notes in the parlor.

Auntie Odie smiled, growing her cheeks into plums. "Where would our spirits be without all that cheeky chirping?"

The sunshine played hide-and-seek with the rain clouds gathering in the west, and the smell of distant rain and verdant fields mingled with the blooms' scents—an enchanted place. I half-expected to catch sight of fairies or elves frolicking among the blooms.

I would've been content to stay forever with Auntie Odie in her garden, and weed, plant, and prune—and listen to her recite poems and read stories, or sway with her in the bench swing. Her voice charmed my imagination. And I fell in love with the spoken word, especially the way Auntie Odie spoke it. When I asked her if it was something she was born with, her talent for saying words in a way that brought other worlds to life, she said she had only a little talent, but what she did have she spent her life cultivating.

"What's *cultivating*?"

"Child, cultivating is hard work. If you cultivate a plant, say, you cultivate the soil first, get the soil ready. You turn the soil, hoe it, weed it, add some fertilizer, some compost, and mix that in. You dig a hole bigger than the plant. You pour water in it. Then you hold the plant at just the right place—not too low, not too high—and scoop the soil back into the hole under and around the plant, being careful with the roots. You water it until the soil is poachy. Then you have a party when rain comes, you hope the sun shines, but not too much. Through the seasons you prune it, weed it, water it, protect it. When the blooms come, you cut off a few just so, arrange them in a glass vase and set it on your table. *Mazel tov!* You have beauty in your life because you cultivated a plant."

I wiped pretend sweat off my brow. "Whew! You did a lot of cultivating to make this garden so pretty, Auntie Odie."

She smiled. "Isn't it amazing how God made things so they'd flourish only in the right conditions?" She waved her arm dramatically. "All this wouldn't be here if I hadn't cultivated with what the Creator provided.

"Chew on this, child. God could've fixed everything so all we'd have to do is sit around with our feet up. Some seeds fall in just the right place to grow without help from us humans—in the mountains and meadows and fields. But it's teamwork that makes a garden beautiful. God does His

111

part—makes sunshine and rain, and seeds packed full of potential, gives us muscle and bone and passion and brain, then, using all those things, we cultivate."

She giggled like she held a secret. "A garden like mine didn't happen by chance. It took little ol' laughful, befuddled, muddled me, to plan it and cultivate it. I had the fun of taking a seed and, following God's rules for that seed, planting it where it would thrive and look pretty with the other flowers around it. No one else in the world has a garden designed exactly like mine. Like an artist uses paint to create a picture, I use plants to create a little world of beauty for myself and for all who come to visit."

She squeezed my shoulder then laid her arm across the back of the bench swing.

I tilted my head back onto its warmth and softness. "I wish I could talk."

She raised her eyebrows and looked down at me. "What do you mean, child?"

I thought for awhile. "I wish... I wish I was a storyteller and poem-maker and a good reader, and I hope I have a garden of my own someday—just like yours, Auntie Odie. And I wish I could get good at reading and poetry in time for next year's Silver Tongues Harvest."

"Glory be! Don't you know you can, child? If you're willing to work—to cultivate your potential—you can accomplish all those things, including being in the Harvest."

"But I wish I could talk."

"You can talk, child." She winked at me. "You're a little chatterbox sometimes."

"I mean talk like you. I wish I had a big mouth and big lips all full of words, like you do."

A full-bodied laugh burst from Auntie Odie till the swing shook.

"I mean it, Auntie Odie. I wish I was a Negro. Is it being colored that helps you talk?"

She laughed loud and long. I laughed at her laugh.

Then she laughed again, a little unlaugh with no turning up of the mouth. "Oh, child. You don't know what you're sayin'."

"But I do!"

"Being a Negro has its challenges, child. Even in Akin, being colored can cause a kerfuffle. God couldn't make everybody colored, because only the strong of heart can be colored and survive in this world—at least them that's in this here America where they say freedom rings."

"So my heart wasn't strong enough for God to make me colored?"

"I don't mean that exactly, child." She straightened her straw hat. "You do have a strong heart. You're strong in heart enough if God had wanted you to be colored."

"Why didn't He then?"

She sighed. "Well, just maybe He figured you'd have enough troubles just being a little white girl with a sad mama and grandparents that died. Maybe the kerfuffle that comes with being colored would've been more than you could bear along with everything else." She pushed a curl out of my eyes. "The good Lord says He won't allow us more than we can bear."

"Did He really say that?"

"I read it in His letters to us, dear child."

I folded my arms.

Her voice dropped to a rumbling deepness. "O-o-o-oh, child. What my people have gone through." Then she sang, slow and deep, and a little off-key.

> "Nobody knows de trouble I've seen,
> Nobody knows but Jesus;
> Nobody knows de trouble I've seen,
> Glory, hallelujah!

> "Sometimes I'm up, sometimes I'm down;
> Oh! yes, Lord!
> Sometimes I'm almos' to de groun'; Oh! yes, Lord!
> Oh! Nobody knows de trouble I've seen,
> Nobody knows but Jesus;
> Nobody knows de trouble I've seen,
> Glory, hallelujah!
> If you get there before I do, Oh! yes, Lord!
> Tell all of my friends I'm coming too, Oh! Yes, Lord!"

"But why did they have so much trouble?" I really wanted to know.

Auntie Odie spoke slowly, her eyes half closed. "'Cause we were colored dark brown and black—not like those who captured us and wrestled us here to be slaves. And some folks, they don't know that a hollyhock or dahlia or peach tree or rose or marigold adds as much beauty to a garden as a lily. They just don't know. Some folks think the whole garden should be lilies. Can you imagine what the world would smell like if it was filled up only with lilies?

"Pugh-ee!" She shook her head. Then her voice became light. "But when they're blended with the fragrances of roses and honeysuckle and lilac and even the odd-smelling daffodil, why... why, no one can measure the loveliness of that heavenly scent!"

I leaned against Auntie Odie and breathed in her scent—morning dew and honeysuckle and damp earth, and green—if green had a scent.

My heart bulged with thankfulness that Auntie Odie's fragrance was part of my world.

★ ★ ★

"Let's go see if we can find you some play shoes and maybe some peddle pushers." Auntie Odie changed from her tennis shoes to white, two-inch-high, broad-heeled shoes—she called them Brogies—that laced and tied high on the foot.

I cleared my throat. "I don't think Mama would want you to do that."

She paused in the middle of tying her shoe and looked up at me. "Not want me to do what, child?"

"Buy me things."

113

"That's why we're going to Mable's Second Hand Store and maybe Salvation Army. Nothing new. Nothing expensive."

I followed her into her bedroom—small, with simple furniture. An ivory chenille bedspread bedecked the ivory-painted iron bed. On the antique chiffonier and on the dresser, were bouquets from her garden in elaborate glass vases. Everything in the room was ivory and mahogany except the large spreading bouquets and an empty blue glass vase on a pier table.

"I've never had peddle pushers. I don't think Mama will let me wear anything but dresses in Akin. I wore overalls sometimes on the farm, but not here."

"Oh, bosh!"

Half of her closet was shelves full of hats, floor-to-ceiling. She searched for just the right hat and finally chose a red one with a modest brim and black-braided band. It was the same red that was in the poppies print of her jersey knit dress.

Because it had turned gray and stormy outside, the light from the windows glossed the room in gray pearl. On the pier table the graceful glass vase reflected in the pier glass behind it, and the ivory, crocheted dresser scarf upon which it rested appeared blue in the reflected light. I ran my hand over the cool, smooth contours of the vase.

"Careful, child."

I pulled my hand away quickly and the vase wobbled. Auntie Odie and I both gasped.

"Sorry." I gripped my hands behind my back.

She adjusted the vase. "That's all right, child. You were doing jim-dandy until I told you to be careful." Then she laughed.

She grabbed a hairbrush and brushed my hair with a vengeance until my eyes smarted. "Looks like you stuck your finger in the light socket, child." Then she combed the curls around her finger so they'd lay in smooth, short ringlets.

I liked the improved image in the mirror, but felt drowsy—my morning cry had worn me out. But I followed Auntie Odie through the kitchen, out the back door to the porch, and out toward the garage.

"We better take the Buick instead of walk," she said. "It's gonna get poachy."

★ ★ ★

At Mable's Second Hand three and a half blocks away, I handed Mable the bouquet Aunt Odie and I had picked for her from Auntie Odie's garden.

We put a pair of tennis shoes, peddle pushers, two striped knit tops, a yellow dress, and a white "church bonnet"—all for me—into the buying basket. Auntie Odie also found a hat she liked (Surprise!)—navy straw with a navy band—and small brim curving up.

"I need a conservative hat," she said. "There are just times when a body doesn't want to wear a big, flashy hat."

I giggled inside myself, wondering when that occasion might be.

The storeowner, Mable, was squatty and broad like a Texas watermelon but the color and texture of cantaloupe skin. Her little head blended right into her neck, shoulders, and body. But what a happy being she was. Auntie Odie and Mable bantered back and forth about the weather, exaggerating dialects and drawls—"Rain, and hail, too's, comin' fo' shor'." (That was Mable.) And about people they knew in town—"Yes'm, Grace is finally expectin' and her cute li'l hubby done jumped to the moon and danced with the cow a'fore he leaped back an' hugged 'er." (That was Auntie Odie.) And the laughin' that went on between those two—Boy-howdy! They giggled and tittered and chattered and every so often burst out laughing for a good long while.

I just watched them and grinned, my heart cheered.

Mable waddled to the front counter and added the cost of the items on a big old-fashioned cash register. "That'll be three dolla's and twenty-five cents, Odessa."

"Now, you sure you charged me 'nough, Mable dear? That don't seem like much for all this."

Mable laughed like a chimpanzee—a high, eeky sound. "Oh, it's all figured in all right… Say, did you notice that glass piece in the back window? Just acquired it yesterday."

"No! How did I miss it?" Auntie Odie whirled around and headed through a crowded aisle to the back of the store.

Mable waddled after her, and I followed. We looked like a little parade—the majorette marching in the front (Auntie Odie), then the big float wobbling on its truck bed (Mable), and, last, the clown running in circles and grinning big (me).

"Why, it's lovely!" Auntie Odie reached for the graceful form—heavy clear glass with tints of rose throughout. "How much you asking for it?"

"Oh, two dolla's."

Thunder cracked, and rain drummed on the roof.

"I'll take it!" Auntie Odie positively glowed.

★ ★ ★

"Some gullywasher!" Auntie Odie said. We headed home in her Buick as storm sewers filled and gutters overflowed. "What was that storm poem by Hilda Doolittle? 'You crash over trees…' How does it go? Let me think…"

I grinned at her. "I wish I knew as many poems as you, Auntie Odie."

"You can. Just do it. Write them down. Read them, say them, and the first thing you know—"

"Honest?"

"Honest. Collecting poems is a good thing. But I'm not so sure about collecting hats and glass. They sure do take up space."

"I'm glad you bought the hats for us, and especially the glass art."

She laughed. "Just what I need—one more hat and one more glass whangdoodle. My two weaknesses."

I smiled and looked at her sideways. "You have more than two weaknesses, Auntie Odie."

She feigned sadness. Rain and small bits of hail pummeled the windshield. The wipers whopped back and forth. "Well, I'm waiting for you to name my other weaknesses."

"Flowers, well, gardens really, and poetry. Well, words really, and birds and—" I scratched my forehead.

"There's more? I'm waitin'."

"And people—folks really."

"There's a difference?" Long pause. "So that's it? That's the whole list?"

"And me."

"You? Aren't you *folks*?"

"Yep. But I think I'm a *big* folks-weakness of yours."

We laughed.

"I'm nobody, but you like me anyway, huh?"

She winked.

> "I'm Nobody! Who are you?
> Are you nobody, too?
> Then there's a pair of us! Don't tell!
> They'd banish us, you know!"

I grinned. "Emily Dickinson?"

She nodded.

> "How dreary to be somebody!
> How public, like a frog
> To tell one's name the livelong day
> To an admiring bog!"

I snickered. "'An admiring bog.' How funny. I'll add that to my wordbook. What's a bog anyway?"

The gutters gushed with water, polka-dotted with hail.

"Our garden is a bog today, I imagine. If we walked in the garden soil right now, we'd sink. When the soil is poachy, that's a bog."

"I'll have to add *poachy* to my wordbook too," I said.

As we neared the top of the hill and Auntie Odie's cottage, she pointed up. "Looky there, Poni Snow. It's a magpie sky."

I looked up but didn't see birds of any kind. "Where?"

"All over the sky, child. See the black clouds over there and there and there? And white clouds in between there and there?"

"Auntie Odie!" I braced against the dashboard.

We jumped the curb, just missed a tree, and then swerved back toward the street. As the right side of the Buick dropped back off the curb and bumped the fender, we both shrieked.

"My lands!" sputtered Auntie Odie. "That was a boner and a half!"

She steered the Buick up her driveway and into the still-open garage. "Lucky I didn't run into Angela Fall's locust tree. I'd have never heard the end of it."

We checked the right fender and found a barely visible scratch. No dents.

"Mercy!" She looked up at the garage rafters and raised her hand. "Thank you, Lord, for watchin' over us."

I raised my hand and looked up too. "Thank you, Lord, for watchin' over us and giving us a magpie sky!"

Aunt Odie threw back her head in a belly-laugh.

More thunder, a gust of wind, and the rain blew in.

"Glory be! We need the moisture, but must it stagger down like it's sozzled?"

We pulled down the garage door, getting soaked in the process, and enclosed ourselves in the damp dimness of the garage.

I grabbed the sacks from the back seat. Auntie Odie took *Greeley Daily Tribune*s from the stack of newspapers in the corner of the garage and handed one to me.

"When we get our things carried in, can I play outside in the rain?"

"No, siree, child." A tone I hadn't heard before.

"Please, Auntie Odie. I want to hear a squidge like you talked about."

"They're saying polio might be brought on by getting wet and chilled through. We're not taking any chances, child."

"Is that how Mrs. Matthews got her polio?"

"They aren't sure. But she has other health problems too." She laid a firm hand on my shoulder. "How about a tea party? What do you say?"

I nodded. That sounded like more fun than getting polio.

Holding the newspapers over our heads, we dashed for the back door. We bustled into the enclosed porch and stood, dripping, on the multi-colored braided rug by the door to the kitchen.

We removed our sopping shoes and shook out the newspapers, which she stuffed into the trashcan. "I can't believe I didn't think to take umbrellas."

"I wish I could go barefoot in the mud."

She chuckled.

I opened the brown sack with my "new" things—red peddle pushers with white trim, a red-and-white, vertical-striped shirt, and a shirt that had blue, red, and yellow horizontal stripes. I held my dress up to me, its pale yellow the color of white corn.

"Glory be! That's a splendiferous color for you, child."

I thought of how Mama looked so washed out in any shade of yellow and figured I would too. "You think so?"

"I know so. It matches your hair and eyebrows, and your skin effloresces against that soft yellow."

"What's *effloresces*?"

"Guess you'll have to look it up in the dictionary."

Auntie Odie moved the bouquet from the breakfast nook table to the counter. Then she lifted her new glass whangdoodle from the sack and set it in the middle of the nook table.

Outside, the rain had softened to a soft sprinkle and the sun broke through the scattered clouds. As if someone had flipped a switch, light beamed through the bay window in a single ray onto the table and through the glass piece.

Whangdoodle was a good word for it because neither Auntie Odie nor I knew exactly what it was. It wasn't a vase, nor a bowl, nor a candleholder, nor a particular figure or shape. We agreed that, from one angle, it was an abstract form of an angel, but as Auntie Odie turned it, it looked like a butterfly in flight—in a way.

"Exquisite!" Auntie Odie said. "I've never seen anything like this before. I wonder who the artisan is—was. It looks like something Salvatore Santi might do."

"The art-son? That's another good word for my wordbook."

"The artisan—the artist, the glassblower who made it." She lifted the form and examined the bottom. "'Firedrake – '45.' It *is* Salvatore's! From six years ago. I can't believe it ended up in a second-hand store for two dollars."

"Auntie Odie, do you like glass as much as hats and flowers and birds and beautiful words?"

"I don't know." She squinted her eyes. "Maybe. Yes, I think maybe so. But in a different way."

"My name's Glass," I said.

"Really?" If she'd had doggy ears, they would've perked right up.

"My name is Glass—it's my middle name."

She stretched out the word like a rubber band and hissed at the end. "*Gla-a-s-s*? Your middle name's Glass?" Then she spelled, "G–l–a–s–s?"

I nodded. "Ponia Glass Snow. That's my whole name."

"And how did your mama come to name you that?"

I shrugged. "It had something to do with my dad. I think he named me—that's what Gram told me once. But Mama won't talk much about him. I remember Gram explaining to me once that my dad liked horses so he named me Pony, with a *y*, then he changed the ending to *i-a*. And his mom's maiden name was Glass—I think. Gram wasn't sure about that. Anyway, nobody ever calls me Glass, so I kind of forget about it."

"Hm," Auntie Odie said thoughtfully. Then she repeated my full name, articulating it slowly. "Ponia Glass Snow. I'm surprised you didn't tell me your name was Glass when you saw I like glass things."

I shrugged again. "I don't think of my name Glass as being the same thing as your glass whangdoodles and vases and such. It's just a name. Nothing to do with real glass."

She nodded slowly and pointed to the form glistening and reflecting light onto the tabletop. "Maybe one of your ancestors was a glass worker—a glassblower—like the person who made this."

Now that was an interesting thought. I raised my eyebrows. "You think maybe?"

"Maybe."

She got out fancy cups, saucers, and spoons and handed them to me. I set two places in the breakfast nook. The teakettle whistled and Auntie Odie held the teabag while she poured hot water into the teapot. She took two cupcakes from the bread box and set them on small plates. "Applesauce cupcakes, fresh yesterday from Branen's," she said. "Time for a tea party!"

Auntie Odie poured the tea—tangy lemon scent. "Careful. It's boiling hot." Auntie Odie took a bite of her cupcake. "You know what I think?"

I shook my head, my mouth full of cake.

"I think we need to take you, Poni Glass Snow, to meet the glassblower."

"What's a glassblower?"

"He blows into molten glass and makes glassware, glass art." She gestured toward the glass centerpiece.

"So *people* actually make this stuff?"

Auntie Odie laughed. "Well, Emily couldn't do it."

I giggled too. "I never thought much about glass, even if it is my name."

Auntie Odie got up from the table and marched into the front room, talking over her shoulder. "I'm going to call the Firedrake right now and see if Salvatore plans to blow tomorrow."

I grinned, picturing a big cloud named Salvatore blowing wind over the land, and this would happen tomorrow.

Ppppppp, t-t-t-t-t-t; ppp, t-t-t; ppppppppp, t-t-t-t-t-t-t-t. Auntie Odie dialed the glassblower's number on her black phone.

"Hello, Dora? This is Odessa Luckett." She paused and grinned. "Oh, I'm splendiferous! And you?" (Chuckle.) "Say, what I'm calling about is, I have a little girl staying with me for the weekend—Poni Glass is her name."

Odessa chuckled. "That's right. Poni Glass Snow…

"It is unique, isn't it? Well, we'd like to come and see Sal at work in his shop—tomorrow perhaps?"

I stood in the doorway between the kitchen and front room. Auntie Odie covered the mouthpiece and, grinning, whispered to me, "She's checking with her son the Firedrake."

She sat on the edge of the sofa. A smile broke across her face, and she laughed. "Wonderful!

"Thank you…. What time? We'll be there. Nine o'clock tomorrow."

Auntie Odie hung up, and stood with her hands on her hips. "Well, Ponia Glass Snow, tomorrow you're going to get a whole new look at your middle name."

★ ★ ★

"Heebie-jeebies, hog-wild child! Please don't swash so when you're in the tub. The whole washroom'll get poachy."

★ ★ ★

Auntie Odie left the window curtains open and the windowshade up so I could "twinkle back at the stars." She held up the sheet and I hopped in. It drifted down over me—I was a fairy snuggling down in a bed of grass with an oak-leaf coverlet. Auntie Odie rolled the desk chair to my bedside and seated herself so close I could feel her warmth and smell her talc. Because the doorway curtain was open, light from the small nightlamp in the front room spilled like bleary candlelight into the nook, softening and warming the shadows.

Utter contentment settled over me as Auntie Odie stroked my hair then gently rubbed my shoulders. She cleared her throat and gathered herself up. Her voice light like a flute, she said, "'The Plumpuppets' by Christopher Morley.

> "When little heads weary have gone to their bed,
> When all the good nights and the prayers have been said,
> Of all the good fairies that send bairns to rest
> The little Plumpuppets are those I love best...
>
> "The little Plumpuppets are fairies of beds:
> They have nothing to do but to watch sleepy heads;
> They turn down the sheets and they tuck you in tight,
> And they dance on your pillow to wish you good night!..."

I lay on my stomach, my head deep in the pillow. I wished that moment in all its purity and softness could be preserved forever. The sounds: Auntie Odie's musical voice casting words like notes upon the ear of my soul; her breathing; and, drifting through the window on the stir of rain-cooled air, distant thunder, crickets' whirring songs, and contented murmurs of mourning doves. The feel: Smooth sheets and soft pillow and Auntie Odie's long cool fingers upon my cheek. The smells: Lingering scents of flower gardens washed clean with rain, Auntie Odie's honeysuckle talc, and the provident perfume of books from the corner shelves. But most of all, the sense of being valued, protected, and cherished.

At last I summoned a whisper. "More."

I couldn't see Auntie Odie's smile—she was a black silhouette against the faint glow of light behind her, but I could hear it in her voice. Slowly, deeply she spoke each word like an artist strokes her brush upon a canvas. "Emily Dickinson...

> "I never saw a moor,
> I never saw the sea;
> Yet know I how the heather looks
> And what a wave must be.
>
> "I never spoke with God,
> Nor visited in heaven;
> Yet certain am I of the spot
> As if the chart were given."

My own voice sounded strange and far away. "Auntie Odie, is heaven real?"

Slow and deep, each word articulated. "Yes, child. Heaven's real."

"Is my gram and grampy in heaven?"

The silhouette leaned toward me. A faint light glimmered in her right eye and eyelashes and on the tip of her nose. "I can't say for certain, dearest Poni. Did they talk about God at all?"

I thought for a long time. "Every summer Gram said, 'God as my witness, my tomatoes is redder and bigger than they's ever been.'"

The silhouette sat back in her chair and waited.

I appreciated the way Auntie Odie gave me time to think. "And one time at Thanksgiving, Grampy prayed. He said something like—" I lowered my voice and tried to make it gurgly like Grampy's—"'Now God, as you know, we don't stop often enough to thank You for all You've provided. But we're stopping today.' And then Grampy pulled out his big red handkerchief and blew his nose and then he said, 'I thank You for Abb and Iggy...' That's Gram and my mama Ingrid. 'And for our little Poni. And for all You've given us, including the food. Amen.'"

Auntie Odie nodded. "Those are good memories, child. You hang onto them. Maybe write them down sometime soon." Then she waited some more.

"And we went to church once to celebrate Iggie's homecoming and Easter."

"Homecoming?"

"Mama came home to stay, she said."

"Did she stay?"

"A few weeks or months, then she left again."

"Where did your mother go?"

I shrugged. "While she was going out the door, Gram said, 'Don't be dawdling in and out. Don't come back and break this child's heart again. Stay away until you come back for good and be a real mother.'"

"So eventually she came back?"

I nodded.

"And she stayed."

I nodded. "Will Martha's mama go to heaven if she dies?"

"Olivia? Yes."

"For sure?"

"I was with her when she, and Fritz too, invited Christ into their lives. 'By grace we're saved,' she often says. I've watched them grow in their faith over the years and raise their children to love the Lord and I've watched them put God and others above themselves time and again."

"Is that why Mama said, 'Now ain't Olivia the kindest woman I've ever knowed?'"

The silhouette nodded. "Close your eyes, child."

I closed them and waited. After a minute, I peeked at my elderly friend. She sat straight in the chair, hands folded in her lap, face tilted down toward me. I closed my eyes again and felt all the tightness in my limbs drain away.

"Dear Father in heaven," Auntie Odie whispered, "please bless this dear child. May she come to know You for who You are—Holy Almighty God, Loving Father, Best Friend... Comforter and Love and Peace. May she be born into Your light."

Chapter 21

Has Korea Been
Worth Its Cost
—*Greeley Daily Tribune*, p.8, Sat., June 23, 1951

Gardens, Farms in Akin
Area Benefited by Rains
—*Akin Scoop*, p.1, Sat., June 23, 1951

Saturday's high 82°, low 51°; scattered thunderstorms in afternoon and evening

The neighborhood was a garden of giant geometric blooms—a street lined with pink, yellow, and cream-colored bungalows with brightly painted shutters. Some homes stood close to the walk, others hid among trees near the alley.

At the front of the Santi property—126 Dawson Way—Mrs. Dora Santi lived in a summer-sky-blue bungalow with white shutters shaped like ampersands. Auntie Odie explained that Mrs. Santi's bachelor son lived in the small gray house on the back of the lot.

Shelves across the inside of Mrs. Santi's picture window—much like Gram's—held glass bowls, vases, angels, and animals in an array of colors.

Standing by the gate staring at that window, I soaked in the memory of Gram.

A red-haired lady peeked around a blue vase, smiled and waved.

Auntie Odie, already up on the stoop, adjusted her white, flat-brimmed hat with red band. "Don't lollygag, child. Hustle along."

The door opened and Mrs. Santi peered at us over her horn-rimmed glasses. "Come in, come in!"

As soon as I smelled gingerbread and heard the whispery creaks in the floor, I knew we were in a good place.

During introductions, a rose-lipsticked smile framed Mrs. Santi's crooked teeth. Her short red hair curled around the top half of her face, like a pillbox hat. She was shaped like a summer squash, similar to Gram except Gram's squash shape had been with the large end up. Mrs. Santi's lipstick matched the whirly designs on her brown nylon dress. She led us toward the sofa. "Come sit here. Salvatore isn't quite ready to have you come out to the shop."

I glanced toward the window display.

She smiled. "Take a closer look at the glassware, hon. Pretty soon you'll meet the gaffer hisself."

"The laugher?" I walked over to the window.

Dora Santi tittered. "The *gaffer*. He's the boss glassblower. 'Course, he works by hisself now. He'd like to have an assistant, but it has to be a certain type I guess." She arched her brows above her glasses. "I'm certainly not it."

"So he *blows* glass?" I looked for balloonlike swells in the glass.

"Uh-huh." Her lo-heelers made a swishing sound on the paisley rug as she walked over to join me in front of the window.

The glass art stretched, crouched, and ballooned in their shiny poses on the shelves. Sunrays changed colors as they passed through the red and pink and blue and green glass. I longed to follow the smooth curves of a vase with my fingertips.

"Salvatore is quite the glassblower, all right. He's blown just about every glass piece in this house. Comes from a long line of glass artisans in Italy, but his father wanted to do something different like so many of the newer generations, and became a farmer. But Salvatore is reviving the glassblowing tradition." She paused then turned to me. "Would you care for some gingerbread and tea?"

Gingerbread.

Auntie Odie smiled. "We'd love some."

Mrs. Santi peered at me over her horn-rimmed glasses. Tiny rhinestones sparkled on the corners.

"Yes, Ma'am."

In her cozy, ginger-scented kitchen Mrs. Santi invited Auntie Odie and me to sit at a small table covered with a green and yellow oilcloth. She prepared three cups of tea, then on Blue Willow plates like Mrs. Myers', served generous squares of warm gingerbread mounded with dollops of whipped cream.

When we finished, Mrs. Santi headed out the back door to ask her bachelor son if he was ready for us to watch him blow glass.

Blow glass. How strange.

Soon she was back. "He's ready. Salvatore wants me to remind everybody to stay away from the furnace and to make sure Poni stays close to Odessa and me."

A nice current blew through the breezeway between Mrs. Santi's little house and the oversized garage. The house on the alley was shaded with numerous trees. An engraved wooden sign, *The Firedrake*, hung over the garage door. A furnace to the left filled the shop with fever and a muffled roar. Around the cement door of the furnace radiated an orange-white glow.

Mr. Santi wiped sweat from his face with a large red handkerchief like Grampy's and saluted. "Odessa, hello, hello." He was a giant of a man and talked gruff. But I knew from his expression he wasn't upset, that was just how he talked.

"Salvatore, wonderful to see you again." Then they all looked at me.

"So this is our visitor, ay?" He wiped his hands on the kerchief and studied me. Mr. Santi's mustache and beard were dark brown and gray, and his eyes were brown. He resembled Santa Claus, depending on the Christmas card. Santi was a good name for this man—Santi Claus.

Mrs. Santi said, "This here is Ponia, Salvatore. She was drawn like a magnet to the pretties in my window."

"She ain't the first, is she, Mother?" He chuckled then scowled. "Ponia, huh? Hello, young lady."

Auntie Odie placed a hand on my shoulder. "Listen to this, Sal. Poni's middle name is Glass. Ain't that name a whangdoodle?"

"Glass." Mr. Santi straightened and hooked his thumbs in the pockets of his dungarees. "How'd your folks come to name you that? Is your daddy a glassblower?"

"I don't have a daddy. Not anymore. He left Mama and me when I was a baby."

Auntie Odie squeezed my shoulder. "Name's a mystery, but isn't it splendiferous?"

Mr. Santi's faded chambray work shirt made a sharp contrast with his dark eyes, shadowed by a frown. "That shoulda been my name."

Mrs. Santi laid her hand on the gaffer's arm. "Are you going to make something, Salvatore, so Poni can see how it's done?"

Auntie Odie adjusted her hat. "Y' know, I never get tired of watching you blow molten glass into works of art."

Mr. Santi tugged on his beard. "I'll blow a little bowl. Won't take long."

Mr. Santi directed the three of us to stand by the gaffer's bench not far from the door of the shop. Orange-white heat glowed around the door of the furnace—a huge concrete cube, taller than I was with walls thicker than me. Mr. Santi opened the concrete door and, from the vat inside, "gathered" molten glass onto the end of his blowpipe, which was nearly as long as he was tall. We couldn't see the vat or the molten glass because the whole inside of the furnace radiated white-hot.

Even with a navy and white handkerchief tied around his head, sweat collected in the creases of his face and neck. Sometimes he spoke in low, gruff tones and at other times in a pleasant manner. He explained everything like I was the only visitor there, an important person who needed to know how to blow a bowl so that, as a result, everyone on the planet would be the better for it. He said my name lots of times—Poni this, Poni Glass that, and explained terms, like *vat* and *gather* and *marver* and *punty*. (Fine words to add to my wordbook.)

I leaned against Auntie Odie and she put her arm around my shoulder.

Mr. Santi brought the blowpipe out of the furnace then shut the furnace door, all the while rolling the pipe in his fingers. The molten glass glowed like a lightbulb, and it smelled… well, *hot*.

"Is it really, *really* hot?" I had to yell to have him hear me.

He nodded. As he worked, the wrinkles in his olive-skinned face smoothed out and so did his voice. "Two-thousand degrees Fahrenheit is really hot. Has to be to melt glass." On a marble table he rolled the gather which now glowed red to orange like a sunset. "Now I'm marvering it—cooling it some and shaping it on this here marble surface, what glassblowers call the marver." Then he rolled the gather in red and white glass shards.

Over the roar of the furnace, Mr. Santi spoke loudly, "Marvering tells me what the glass 'feels' like without actually touching it, and it allows me to blow and shape it."

He held the egg-shaped gather over the opposite edge of the marver, turned the pipe and blew. "I blow firmly into the pipe." He blew then turned it. "I force air into the pipe with my tongue—it's sometimes more of a pushing of air, than blowing." He pressed his mouth to the pipe again. Then he gathered more molten glass from the furnace and repeated the process, enlarging the balloon of glass.

Mrs. Santi led Auntie Odie and me to the side of the room opposite the gaffer's bench. Mr. Santi seated himself at the bench and, still turning the blowpipe, rested it on the racks. He "blocked"—shaped—the gathering with a water-saturated "paddle," continually rotating the blowpipe. "Turning keeps it symmetrical," he said, "and blocking with the paddle puts a thin skin on the glass." He explained that the paddles are made of cherry or apple wood because they're such hard woods and can stay wet all the time without softening. "The paddles would be ruined if they ever dried out."

Then back to the furnace where he gathered more molten glass—roll, block, blow. Sometimes he held his thumb over the blowhole briefly "to allow the hot air to expand the glass," then he swung the blowpipe in full circles to lengthen the bubble.

Beside the furnace was a smaller furnace. Mrs. Santi said it was called "the glory hole." Mr. Santi held the glass piece inside the glory hole, slowly turning, turning, turning it. Then back to the gaffer's bench to blow it and block it some more—shape and smooth it. He took a pillow of sodden (*poachy*, as Auntie Odie would say), folded newspaper and "papered" the glass by cupping the paper pillow in his hand and rolling the glass piece in it. This smoothed and shaped it more.

Even with two fans going, sweat rolled off Mr. Santi's face. Auntie Odie kept wiping her face with a hanky and Mrs. Santi did too. I wiped my face on my sleeve. Next came the process of attaching the punty to the opposite end of the glass form, detaching the blowpipe with "jacks," firing in the furnace again, then opening the bubble—in the place where the blowpipe had been— with the jacks. At last a red bowl-shape appeared on the end of the punty.

"Stand back." Mr. Santi held the punty about midway up the handle then swung it round and round like a propeller. The walls of the bowl became wavy.

"Oo-ooh!" Auntie Odie and I said in unison.

Holding the punty over large fireproof mitts, he scored the bottom of the bowl where it was attached. As he gently tapped the punty handle with a hammer, the bowl dropped into the mitts. He opened the door of a small oven—the "annealing oven," he called it, and slid his hands into the mitts under the bowl, then carried it to the annealing oven and set it inside.

Mr. Santi wiped his face with his red handkerchief. "Twenty-four hours in the annealer, an hour or so to cool on the shelf, and the bowl will be ready for someone's table or shelf."

I grinned. "Wow!"

"Sal." Mrs. Santi stepped to his side and said something to him, which I couldn't hear over the noise of the furnace and fans.

He nodded. "For a girl named Glass, I can do that."

He had us stand back over by the door. He didn't use a blowpipe this time, just a punty, much thinner than the others. From the vat he gathered molten glass on the end of the punty—just a small mass that looked like a nightlight. He maneuvered the hot glass with huge tweezers, pulling and stretching. Into the glory hole briefly, then more tugging out the tiniest strands of glass, pulling them out and back to the central mass—sketching in the air with glass.

Before our eyes he fashioned a butterfly, which he held up for us to see. Mr. Santi had taken it from its chrysalis of molten glass and formed it into a delicate creature with gossamer wings. Into the annealing oven it went before we could say anything more than, "Oo-ooh" and "Ah-h-h" and "Glory be!"

"We'll let it cool real slow for awhile so it don't break."

He wiped his face and looked at me. "But after it cools, it's yours."

★ ★ ★

It sprinkled rain, but we kept taking turns peddling and racing Martha's, Sarah's, and Margaret's bikes. Then thunder crackled like a giant with a chest cold, and lightning lit up the ceiling of clouds. When rain cascaded down, Sarah and Margaret rode home and Martha went to her house, but I stayed outside, leaned into the torrents and let it pummel.

"Lollapalooza, child! Look at you, all grubby and poachy. Don't you have 'nough sense to come in out of the rain?"

My shirt and peddle-pushers were soaked. All I had left to change into was the dress I'd worn to Auntie Odie's. I wanted to put on the yellow dress from Mable's Second Hand, but Auntie Odie said it was my Sunday-go-to-meeting dress for the next day, along with the hat we'd found in the bargain bin.

Auntie Odie hung my wet clothes on the back sun porch. "Don't you know, child, being out in the rain in a lightning storm is treacherous?" Auntie Odie's voice was low and calm, but I detected a breathless edge to it.

"But I was having so much fun."

"Every year somebody gets hit by lightning. Just last year, not thirty miles from here, a farmer got struck. Then there's the danger of catching polio from getting wet and chilled. Remember what I told you yesterday?"

Auntie Odie disappeared then reappeared and held out a housecoat. "Here. Put this on until you stop shivering, child."

I stood up and giggled as she dropped it over my head and I stuck my arms through. On me it nearly touched the floor, and three of me could've fit inside. The green, yellow, and red Hawaiian print fabric was gathered at the yoke and had short gathered sleeves that hung open like bells.

From the cupboard she took two wrapped candy packages. "Have a Cherry Mash, my favorite." She laid a package by my teacup—the one I'd chipped—and one by hers.

I scooted onto the bench of the breakfast nook. "Did he die?"

"Who?"

"The farmer struck by lightning."

"Yes, child, he died and left a wife and four children. At the first thunder or lightning, inside you go."

I opened my Cherry Mash and sniffed it. "Okay, Auntie Odie."

"And never try to hide under a tree neither. I've heard of many a soul struck by lightning who was standing under a tree to get out of the rain." She unwrapped her candy-round and took a slow bite.

"Yes, Auntie Odie." I took a small bite of my Cherry Mash. *Heaven.*

"Whillikins, Poni! Look at our beautiful garden, colors so vivid and clean."

"It's *efflorescence* in the highest degree." I burst into giggles.

Surprise doused Auntie Odie's face, then pleasure. "You looked it up. *Tch, tch.* You're a wunderkind!"

"It is splendiferous, Auntie Odie."

"The birdbaths are full to overflowing."

"Our birdie friends will love that."

"Now here's some nice, hot tea. Just sip it—it's too hot to swizzle."

"I'm not very cold." I shivered and hugged myself. "I'm just excited from having so much fun riding Martha's bike."

Emily sauntered in, eyed us for a moment then strolled over to her feeding dish.

I traced one of the big flowers on my housecoat outfit. "I never saw anybody wear anything this bright."

"You wore it to the Matthews for Six-Layer Dinner. Remember?"

I giggled. "Yep, I remember."

I twirled and the housecoat flared out. "I'm ready for the ball. You're invited, too, Auntie Odie. Let's go." I took her by the hand and tugged her into the front room to the Motorola. "Let the music begin."

Auntie Odie put on the record. "We need some swingy music. Here's Benny Goodman."

We held hands and hurtled around the room—not quite in time with the music. My feet got tangled in the housecoat and I stepped on Auntie Odie's foot. We giggled and laughed through "One O'Clock Jump" and "Sweet Georgia Brown" and "Goody Goody."

Auntie Odie, out of breath, wheezed, "Thank you, but my bunions can't take any more of this hoofing about."

"You're silly, Auntie Odie."

She laughed, put on a different record, and held out her arm. "How about joining me for more tea while Ella Fitzgerald jazzes us?"

I took her arm with my right hand, held out my "skirt" with the other, and we bebopped to the kitchen with Ella singing "A Tisket, A Tasket" in her smooth, easy voice—

"A tisket, a tasket, a brown and yellow basket. I sent a letter to my mommy and on the way I dropped it…"

Rain pattered on the roof and windows while we giggled and sipped tea. Auntie Odie hummed and sang along with Ella Fitzgerald. Even when Ella sang scat in "Flying Home," Auntie Odie scatted right along with her, so familiar was she with the recording. I was impressed, even if she was off-key. If Auntie Odie could've figured out how to sing in tune, she would've been just as good as Ella. When Ella was a viola, Auntie Odie was a cello, and when Ella was a clarinet, Auntie Odie was a saxophone. "Flying Home" ended and the next song began.

Auntie Odie flung up her hands. "Oh! One of my favorites." The pianist's fingers bubbled over the keys, the clarinet silked a few measures around the melody, and then Ella and Auntie Odie came in with the band—

> "'Cause my hair is curly
>   (oh, so curly,)
> 'cause my teeth are pearly,
>   (oh, so pearly,)
> Just because I always wear a smile, (oh, baby,)
> Like to dress up in the—
>   dress up in the latest style (I mean the latest style.)"

A saxophone purled over the scales murmuring a mellow melody. Then Ella came in for the finish, Auntie Odie accompanying her.

> "'Cause I'm glad I'm living,
> Take troubles smiling, never (wine or) whine.
> 'Cause my color's shady, Slightly different maybe,
> That's why they call (oh, baby,
> That's why they call) me 'Shine.'"

★ ★ ★

Auntie Odie relaxed on the sofa with a tablet and pencil, "jotting down some thoughts." I sat near her on the rug, the coffee table as my desk, writing in a tablet.

The way the sofa, coffee table, and two easy chairs were situated at angles, we could gaze into the fireplace or out the front bay window. Today we watched the storm pass through its stages.

"A splendiferous afternoon." Auntie Odie sighed. "The flowers are clean and bright, the lawn and trees verdant and fresh."

The rain had subsided except for an occasional sprinkle, and storm clouds whirled like dancers with billowing gowns across the pearly-gray stage of sky.

Auntie Odie took on a distant look. "Have you heard this one? 'Water' by Hilda Conkling." Her voice lowered and mellowed.

"The world turns softly
Not to spill its lakes and rivers.
The water is held in its arms
And the sky is held in the water.
What is water,
That pours silver,
And can hold the sky?"

"'What is water that pours silver, and can hold the sky?' Oh, those are good words, Auntie Odie."

Since we were invited to the Matthews' house for supper again, I was content to stay in with Auntie Odie that afternoon, watch the sky movie, and write down my thoughts as Auntie Odie was doing.

I enjoyed setting words down on paper, effort though it was. Pointing to each word, I read then made changes. I underlined words I'd look up later.

"What are you writing about, child?"

"The Firedrake."

"Nonfiction or fiction?"

I looked up at her and shrugged.

"Is it true or not true?"

I thought a minute. "It's true. Which one's that? Nonfiction?"

She gave a nod, smiling.

"It's nonfiction now, but it might turn into fiction."

She laughed. "You keep awritin' then, girl!"

"What's yours, Auntie Odie?"

"Nonfiction, like yours for now, but it might turn into something else too."

"Will you read it to me?"

"You read yours first, child." She patted the cushion. "Come sit by me. You read. I'll close my eyes and listen." She turned her tablet face down in her lap, folded her weathered hands upon it, and closed her eyes.

I took advantage of the moment to study her face, draped in lines and folds, so strong, yet so tender. The broad peaceful forehead and cheekbones, rich brown skin the color of dark rye, the slightly protruding mouth, maroon-red lipsticked lips curved in a smile, the large ears close to the head with oversized lobes from years of wearing "earbobs"—all were part of the face I'd come to love.

In her bass viola voice she said, "Well, child, you goin' to read or not? I'm awaitin' right here until you do."

I cleared my throat and read slowly.

"Today me and my best frend went to see a glassblower blow glass. Isn't that funny? I knew the wind could blow trees and peple could blow bubles, but I didn't know peple could blow glass."

I glanced up at Auntie Odie. Her eyes remained closed, her big lips smiled.
"I'm still listenin', child."

> "The moltin glass was very very very hot 2000 degrees hot. Mr Santi stuck a blowpipe into the molting glass in the furnas. He gatherd it up and took it out. He turnd the pipe and blue and turned and blue. When Im with Auntie Odie, my heart feels like its molting glass in a furnas. she taks her blowpipe and gathers my heart and blows into it and makes it into something bigger and better, maybe even something beutifull."

Auntie Odie sat still, her eyes remained closed.
"That's as far as I got," I said.
She opened her eyes and looked straight ahead. When she finally looked down at me, her eyes were liquid. "I didn't know you could write, child. Glory be!"
I blinked.
"That is lovely."
"It is?"
"I wouldn't lie to you, child. Emily Dickinson wrote, 'Truth is such a rare thing, it is delightful to tell it.' And I delight to tell you the truth now. What you wrote is lovely for a ten-year-old girl who's just beginning to grow the courage to write."
She put her arm around me and gave me a squeeze. "I love the way you said I take my blowpipe and gather your heart and blow into it. But you already had a beautiful heart, child. Want me to blow into some of your dreams and help you make them come true?"
"My dreams?"
She shifted so she could look at me and cupped her hand around my cheek. "You told me you wished you could read well and be a storyteller, good enough to be in next year's Silver Tongues Harvest."
I nodded.
"And maybe even get good at poetry?"
I scrunched my shoulders and nodded.
"And another of your wishes—your dreams—is to own a bicycle. You worked hard to try to win that contest so you could have a bike."
"But I won't win. The contest is almost over and I don't have all the Disney Seals from Skylark bread wrappers. And I don't know what to say in my sentence about Skylark bread."
"I could blow into your dreams—your wishes—of getting better with your words and earning a bike. I can help you make those dreams come true."
I rose, put a knee on the couch, and wrapped my arms around her neck.
She patted my back. "I believe in you, child."
As I sat back down I nearly sat on Emily. She jumped up on the back of the couch until I settled, then she nestled between Auntie Odie and me, purring loudly.

Auntie Odie folded back her tablet pages to a fresh page. "Let's write an agreement stating what each of us will do to make your dreams come true."

"We could call it 'The Dream Agreement,'" I said.

Auntie Odie grinned. "It's for you. You can call it whatever you want."

I pointed to myself—"I'm the dreamer with dreams like molten glass"—then I pointed to her. "You're the dreamblower."

Auntie Odie nodded. "You dream away, and I'll turn and blow, turn and blow." Her eyes sparkled. "William Butler Yeats wrote a poem at the beginning of this century. It could almost be your words since you've shared your dreams with me." She straightened.

> "Had I the heavens' embroidered cloths,
> Enwrought with golden and silver light...

"Let's see, how does it go?

> "...I would spread the cloths under your feet:
> But I, being poor, have only my dreams;
> I have spread my dreams under your feet;
> Tread softly because you tread on my dreams."

I must've looked puzzled.

She chuckled. "At this time in your young life, you have only your dreams, but you've spread them under my feet in a figurative sense. Now I must walk very softly because I'm walking on the dreams you've entrusted to me."

I liked the image.

Auntie Odie and I listed ideas and composed sentences, fussing over every word. Finally, Auntie Odie typed it up:

DREAM AGREEMENT
BETWEEN DREAMER, PONIA GLASS SNOW,
AND DREAMBLOWER, ODESSA LUCKETT

PONI'S DREAM #1:
<u>Read, tell stories, and recite poetry with expression.</u>
Dreamblower Auntie Odie will blow into Poni's Dream #1 by coaching her.
Poni will cultivate her Dream #1 by listening to what Auntie Odie teaches
and by practicing every day.

PONI'S DREAM #2:
<u>Own a bike.</u>

Dreamblower Auntie Odie will blow into Poni's Dream #2
by assisting Poni with memorization and
providing Poni with the bicycle of her choice after requirements are met.

Poni will make Dream #2 come true by:
reciting with beauty and expression ten verses (95 lines) from
"Hiawatha's Childhood" by Henry Wadsworth Longfellow
for an audience, small or large.

Signature: ——————————— Date: June 23, 1951
(Ponia Glass Snow)

Signature: ——————————— Date: June 23, 1951
(Odessa Luckett)

We inked our signatures and shook hands. Then Auntie Odie gripped my shoulders and looked deep into my eyes. "Child," she said,

"Your dreams are a treasure
    From heaven above.
Your dreams were honed
    From His heart of love.
Keep dreaming, dear one, dreams
    That chill and burn your heart,
That won't let go—and grab your soul.
    You say you don't know where to start?

"Water your dreams with persistence,
    With learning and work and prayer.
Your dreams will grow like trees, dear one—
    Large, lovely—delightful—to share.
As God rains His power on your dreams,
    And guides with His love like a star,
Your growing desire to love and please God
    Will motivate all of who you are."

I smiled. "By Emily... No, I bet that one's by Agatha Jordan."

"Yes, that's right." Then she prayed. "Oh, Lord, please bless this dear child bountifully. May she open her heart and mind to the splendiferous plans You designed for her even before You created the world. Amen."

★ ★ ★

132

From Auntie Odie's cottage on Jay Way, I pedaled down the hill on Martha's bike, venting the pent-up energy from the afternoon. The air smelled wonderful and the foliage shimmered in that wonderful green—the way the world can smell and look only after a rain.

I pumped back to the top of the hill and waited for a car to pass. Akin was a lovely sight spread out below me. The sun spoked around the rolling clouds and striped the fields and pasturelands with glowing lime and deep vivid greens all the way to the flat horizon in the east. The sky thronged vast, measureless. Clouds in every shade, from swan white to iridescent rock-dove gray, boiled around the sky. Even the darkest cumulonimbus was gilded in the afterglow of shy sun and rain. And beyond the clouds, eternity shimmered, clean and crystal blue.

I breathed deeply, enjoying every mite of oxygen. Recalling Auntie Odie's compliment about my writing and our Dream Agreement, I blushed with pleasure. Soon I would blow life into stories, I'd be able to read and speak so beautifully that I would hold an audience in the palm of my hand, just like Auntie Odie.

Martha and Sarah Fenderlupen relaxed on Martha's porch watching me. "The coast is clear, Poni!" Martha called. "Go on down."

Martha and Fritz and Olivia Matthews, along with Auntie Odie, had wedged into a new place in my life, and their lights shone across the dark void that Gram and Grampy had left.

"You have five more minutes," Sarah reminded me.

I hopped back on Martha's bike and coasted down the hill, the breeze sailing over me, whipping my hair. I turned right at the corner onto Eighth Avenue. At the next corner I waved at Clyde Nichlebaucher playing basketball with two bigger boys in his driveway. Clyde was a tall, skinny kid, wore wrinkled, soiled clothes, and his dark brown hair pointed out in all directions, porcupinelike. *I should talk.*

Suddenly I hit a large area of mud where a storm drain had clogged. I veered out of control and skidded into the curb. Over the handlebars I flew and bounced into darkness.

★ ★ ★

When I opened my eyes, Clyde and his friends were bent over me.

"Poni! You okay?" Clyde looked like a sun god the way the sunlight behind him glowed around his spiky hair.

I wondered why everything hurt, and why Clyde was there. Had school started?

"Come on, I'll he'p ya up." Clyde held up my arm. "Look at that!"

I stared at my arm, streaked with blood and burning like fire. My head throbbed.

"You gonna make it home okay?" another boy said.

I didn't remember riding the rest of the way back to Auntie Odie's front gate. Martha and Sarah tore across the street when they saw me, bloodied and covered with mud.

"Auntie Odie!" Martha yelled.

Martha and Sarah supported me and led me up the walk.

Martha hollered, "Auntie Odie, come quick!"

Hair wet, she appeared at the doorway in her Hawaiian duster and terry scuffs, and then she scurried to meet us and flung her arms around me. Her softness and the clean, raspberry scent of her bubble bath embraced me.

"You'll be all right, child," she cooed. "You'll be all right now."

A sob escaped from my throat.

"Let's get you in and cleaned up." Auntie Odie led me up the walk. "You can tell us all about it."

Olivia, leaning on her husband's arm, hurried across the street toward us.

"Is she okay?" Mr. Matthews ushered Mrs. Matthews through the gate. "Anything we can do?"

"She'll be fine, dears," Auntie Odie said, "but we might run a little late for supper. We'll get there as close to six-thirty as we can."

"I'm sorry, Poni," Martha said, and then she turned and stared at a big dark car that had slowed in front of Auntie Odie's house.

We all looked across at the car now pulling up in front of the Matthews' house. I raised my hand to shield my eyes.

Mrs. Matthews gasped and faltered.

Mr. Matthews uttered a guttural noise from deep in his throat then rasped, "Dear God!"

"Daddy, who is it?"

The sting on my arm felt like fire licking up from my wrist to my upper arm. My knee and head throbbed. A black sheet tried to slip down over my eyes.

Two men in military uniforms got out of the car and walked up the Matthews' walk.

"Nate!" Olivia cried.

Nate? Where?

Mr. and Mrs. Matthews reeled back through Auntie Odie's gate. They staggered toward the military men on their front steps.

Auntie Odie moaned from some deep place. "Nate," she whispered. "Dear Lord."

★ ★ ★

"Come in now, child. It's late." Auntie Odie stood in her front doorway, the porchlight spilling like apple juice over her and the front of the cottage.

I took one last look into the night sky, overcast except for a black pool of stars overhead, and one last turn of my ear toward the honey locust where I'd heard a mourning dove moments before.

"Auntie Odie, can we—"

"Sh-sh-sh, darlin'! People's asleep." She stepped out and stood beside me under the night sky.

"Can we sit in the dark in the garden swing and talk, Auntie Odie?"

Auntie Odie shriveled against me, her breath seeping out long and slow. "Oh, child, could you forgive me if we don't? It's been such a long day. I'm bone weary, aren't you?" Her right arm was around me, but she reached across and placed her left hand on my shoulder. "Poor, dear Nate." Then her voice rolled like rocks in a tumbler. "Poni, dear, I'm so tired and it's close to midnight. We must try to get some sleep."

★ ★ ★

134

While waiting for sleep, I stared through the nook window at the Matthews' house, the darkened and quiet windows, and wondered if they were lying awake or tumbling in their sleep, dreaming of Nate, or seeping tears.

★ ★ ★

Awakened by a sound, I lay still and listened. A car drove past. Silence. Then I heard it again, a muffled sound, almost like a throb in the darkness. Sitting up on the side of the bed, I froze, listening.

A wisp of light seeped around the paisley curtain and faintly outlined the desk and chairs.

I tiptoed through the front room and saw a faint glimmer of light under Auntie Odie's closed door. The sound—moaning?—came to my ears louder now.

My mouth close to the door, I said softly, "Auntie Odie?"

An eerie silence engulfed the house. Then she slowly opened the door. Her long white gown quivered as if she was cold, and with her hand on the doorknob, the nightlight gleamed faintly through the pit of her arm. Tousled hair, eyes swollen nearly shut, and her face twisted into such an agonizing form that I hardly recognized her.

"Auntie Odie!"

She turned her back to me, shuffled across the room, and sunk onto the side of her bed, her body curved like a *C*. "Oh, Poni!" she gasped.

I ran to her. "What's the matter? Are you sick?"

She clutched the yoke of her gown. "I'm sick all right. Heart sick."

I choked on the word. "Nate?"

Her rubbery face twisted all up again, lips stretched tight across her teeth in a grimace. "I've known that boy since he was born. Held him, burped him, fed him, and when he was older, we played Candy Land and Flinch and Monopoly." She crushed a hanky over her eyes. "He was the swee-ee-eetest boy anybody would ever want to meet. He liked to come and help me dig and weed and water—" deep breath, "and plant.

"And he stuck up for me like a man." She blew her nose. "One time when he was only eight or nine, Nate wanted to take me to lunch in Greeley for my birthday. The new owner, from someplace down south, had just taken over the café. She takes one look at me and says she doesn't serve colored. And that little Nate sticks out his chest and his lower lip, pushes up his glasses, and says, 'This is my Auntie Odie's birthday and I aim to take her to lunch. Are you sayin' you don't want our business... Ma'am?'" Auntie Odie chuckled, wheezy and deep. "And that lady pushes out her lower lip at him and tries to scowl him down, but he takes my hand and glares right back. I'm too amazed to do anything but stand there and smile at that cute little boy steeling himself against injustice, ready to do battle if need be."

Auntie Odie chuckled softly and blew her nose. "An old codger in a nearby booth says to the new owner, 'This is Greeley, Wanda. Not Biloxi.'

"Pretty soon, the owner—Wanda—glares at me and says, 'Your birthday, huh?' like she doesn't believe coloreds have birthdays. She turns away and signals us to a booth in the back. So what does

135

Nate do? He points to a booth by the front window, and he says, 'Auntie Odie likes windows.' The woman actually laughs. 'Looks like we're gonna serve a colored today—in the front window.'"

Auntie Odie's face smoothed at the memory. I ran and got her a warm washcloth, like she did for me on my crying day. She buried her face in it. "Oh, Nate, our beloved Nate. And dear Olivia and Fritz and Martha."

I sat beside her on the bed in the faint glimmer of the nightlight. We hugged each other and rocked, and her tears seeped through my curls onto my scalp. We adjusted positions and hugged and swayed some more.

I held onto her—or maybe she held onto me. We blew our noses. "I'm so glad you're here with me tonight, child," and she squeezed me tighter.

I waited, knowing the well was far from dry.

"Romans eight—starting with verse thirty-five." Aunt Odie raised her arm toward the ceiling.

> "Who shall separate us from the love of Christ?
> Shall trouble or hardship or persecution or famine
> or nakedness or danger or sword?...
> Nay, in all these things we are more than conquerors
> through him that loved us.
> For I am persuaded that neither death, nor life,
> nor angels, nor principalities, nor powers,
> nor things present, nor things to come,
> Nor height, nor depth, nor any other creature,
> shall be able to separate us
> from the love of God which is in Christ Jesus our Lord."

She bowed her head and closed her eyes.

"So nothing can separate Nate from God?" I asked.

She shook her head. "Nothing, child. Nothing can separate Nate or any other child of God from Him. What was it I just read this morning by Richard Baxter?" She clicked on the lamp by her bed and we squinted against the light. She opened to the marked place. "Here, child, Mr. Baxter wrote these words three-hundred years ago:

> "Christian, believe this, and think on it:
> you shall be eternally embraced in the arms of that love
> which was from everlasting, and will extend to everlasting;
> of that love which brought the Son of God's love
> from heaven to earth, from earth to the cross,
> from the cross to the grave, from the grave to glory;
> that love which was weary, hungry, tempted, scorned, scourged,

buffeted, spit upon, crucified, pierced;
which did fast, pray, teach, heal, weep, sweat, bleed, die;
that love will eternally embrace thee.

"And down further he says, talking about God—

"You are not dealing with an inconstant creature,
but with Him with whom is no variableness
nor shadow of turning.
His love for you will not be as yours was on earth to him—
seldom, and cold, up, and down.
He that would not cease nor abate his love, for all your enmity,
unkind neglects, and churlish resistances—
can he cease to love you, when he has made you truly lovely?"

"Mr. Baxter wrote that three-hundred years ago?"

Auntie Odie gazed at the ceiling, a sweet smile on her dry lips. "Oh, the power and breadth of the written word." Then she turned off the lamp and, until our eyes adjusted back to the wispy light of the nightlight, the room was pitch black.

I imagined a big, warm God embracing us. I tried to recall the verses in Psalm one-hundred thirty-nine I'd been memorizing. *Whither shall I go...*

"Whither shall I go from thy Spirit?
Or whither shall I flee from thy presence?
"If I ascend up into heaven, thou art there:
if I make my bed in hell, behold, thou art there.

"Uh...And..."

Auntie Odie prompted, "'If I take the wings...'"

I nodded.

"If I take the wings of the morning,
and dwell in the uttermost parts of the sea;
"Even there shall thy hand lead me,
and thy right hand shall hold me.

"And... and..."

Even in the dim room, I saw Auntie Odie's worry lines soften.

"'If I say...'" I began.

Then she joined me and we cradled the words on our tongues, declared them, sang them—flung them like darts to the dark corners of the room, to the night, to the heart of death's shivering sorrow.

> "...Surely the darkness shall cover me;
> even the night shall be light upon me.
> "Yea, the darkness hideth not from thee;
> but the night shineth as the day: the darkness and the light
> are both alike to thee."

Auntie Odie's long arms squeezed me so tight, I felt her heart beat. She rested her chin on my head. Finally, she said, "How well you've learned those verses, child. They'll shine like beacons in your heart the rest of your life."

The clock on her dresser showed two thirty-two. She redressed the wound on my arm, which had begun to throb. In the kitchen by the light over the sink, we sipped tea, and, still, Auntie Odie wept and quoted poems and verses, and we prayed. Finally, at three fifteen, Auntie Odie said, "I think I can sleep now, child. How 'bout you?"

I hugged her and we stumbled off to our beds. I didn't even remember laying my head on the pillow.

Chapter 22

Weld County Gardeners, Farmers
Welcome Unusual Soaking Rains
—*Akin Scoop*, p.2, Sun., June 24, 1951

Military Heroes' Families
Receive Medals from
General Omar Bradley
—*Akin Scoop*, p.1, Sun., June 24, 1951

Sunday's high 90°, low 49°; scattered showers and thunderstorms

The morning sun streamed through the open bay window. Mrs. Matthews and Auntie Odie and I gathered in Auntie Odie's breakfast nook.

"Fritz and Martha are sleeping. Finally." Mrs. Matthews wiped a tear from her blanched face. She tried to sniff, but her nose was clogged. "If I'd known you two were up at two o'clock after Fritz finally dropped off to sleep, I'd have joined you." She closed her eyes and allowed the steam to drift across her face as she sipped her coffee.

"I wish you had come, honey," Auntie Odie said.

Mrs. Matthews set down her cup, sighed, and traced the wood-grain lines in the table. Auntie Odie laid her hand over her friend's.

I studied the women as if through a fog and touched the bandage over my wound. How quickly everything had changed.

"Pray, Odie dearest," Mrs. Matthews said. "My heart is so sore."

We bowed our heads and waited.

Auntie Odie sighed. "Heavenly Father, sometimes this life is so dark… unsure—an empty shadow compared to the glorious life with You that awaits us…"

I peeked at Auntie Odie when she paused. Tears seeped from her closed eyes and chased along the deep creases of her brown cheeks. She straightened and tilted her face upward. "I admit it, Lord: I want to shout, 'Why? Why didn't You protect Nate? Why didn't You answer our prayers for his protection? We claimed You as Nate's shield, his refuge and fortress.'"

Auntie Odie and Mrs. Matthews hugged and bawled. I slid onto the bench next to Mrs. Matthews and wrapped my arms around her. They included me, then, in the circle of their arms and tears.

Why _didn't_ You protect Nate?

"Oh, dear Lord," Auntie Odie continued, "You say you are faithful, but sometimes You don't seem very faithful!" Her shoulders shook and she cried out, "Why did you let Nate die?"

Yeah, why?

"God, what do you expect us to think, to believe? What do you want from us?"

Defeat eked into the morning, so different from the surging strength of the previous night.

"Yeah, what do You want from us?" I echoed Auntie Odie's words. I wanted answers too.

Auntie Odie and Mrs. Matthews opened their eyes and stared at me through their tears.

Quiet, breathy weeping went on between the women, a few minutes of wiping tears and blowing noses, and then we piled up our hands in Mrs. Matthews' lap.

A teaching of Auntie Odie's came to me so clear, right into my mind like a light snapped on. "Trust," I said. "Trust, no matter what."

Auntie Odie held her gaze on me.

"That's what you said, Auntie Odie. Remember? You said we should trust God no matter what—*no matter* what happens."

Mrs. Matthews lifted my chin. "That's exactly what He wants from us, Poni."

"'The Lord gives,'" Auntie Odie quoted from the Bible, "'and the Lord takes away. Blessed be the name of the Lord.'"

We bowed our heads, and in that quiet morning sunlight thunder drummed from distant clouds. Silence. Then it thundered again. A meadowlark's notes trilled from the fence several feet away.

Auntie Odie gathered herself up, "We don't even know what to pray, Lord. So I pray your words:

"O Lord: let thy lovingkindness and thy truth continually preserve us.
Through the tender mercy of You, O God; whereby the dayspring from on high
hath visited us, To give light to us that sit in darkness and in the shadow of death,
to guide our feet in the way of peace.

"Father of Light, renew us, bring Your peace. We thank You that our dear Nate knew You and trusted You. You have allowed him to begin his life in heaven with You. That's wonderful for him, but so heartbreaking for us. Help us to endure this.

"We trust that You *are* faithful, even in these times when You do not seem faithful. Purify us as gold is purified in fire. We praise You, for You are holy and merciful. In Jesus' name..."

"Amen," we said together.

The meadowlark sang its lovely tune so close, it startled us. It had flown to the rose of Sharon bush beside the window. It cocked its head and sang again.

We all looked out at him through our tears and smiled.

★ ★ ★

> "All the way my Saviour leads me;
> What have I to ask beside?
> Can I doubt His tender mercy,
> Who thro' life has been my guide?
> Heavenly peace, divinest comfort,
> Here by faith in him to dwell;
> For I know whate'er befall me,
> Jesus doeth all things well…"

The Akin All Saints Community Church congregation sang as though they believed every word.

In spite of the sorrow—maybe because of it—the Matthews, Auntie Odie, and I had decided to attend church together. I glanced at Auntie Odie to my left, puffy-faced, wearing a plain, black, narrow-brimmed hat supporting a single black feather, her voice rustling out of her and spilling into the body of voices all around us. Next to me, Martha sang along with her parents, faces pale and creased with grief lines, tilted up toward the stained glass windows behind the choir loft. Mr. Matthews' parents stood on the other side of Mr. Matthews looking elderly and wan, singing half-heartedly.

Auntie Odie and Mr. and Mrs. Matthews took notes during the sermon. I wished I'd brought my tablet. The sermon was on Christ dying and then raising up and raining forever. That would be nice—no more drought ever again. And now this song about a Savior leading us—it was nice somehow.

> "All the way my Savior leads me;
> O the fulness of His love!
> Perfect rest to me is promised
> In my Father's house above;
> When my spirit clothed, immortal,
> Wings its flight to realms of day,
> This my song thro' endless ages
> Jesus led me all the way…."

I especially liked that line about the wings.

At the back of the sanctuary, when the minister spread out his arms, he looked like a bald angel in a black robe, proclaiming,

> "But the God of all grace, who hath called us unto His eternal glory by Christ Jesus, after that ye have suffered a while, make you perfect, stablish, strengthen, settle you. To Him be glory and dominion forever and ever. Amen."

★ ★ ★

It had been the strangest Sunday I'd ever lived through. I wondered if I had been kidnapped and taken to Country Odd. I'd only been to two church services in my whole life—now three—and after church, thunder pounded on the sky like it was a colossal drum. Mammoth, black, pointy clouds blew in and put up rows of black-cloud tents side-by-side across the sky and over the sun. It looked like twilight but it was only twelve thirty.

The Matthews family came to Auntie Odie's for Brunswick stew, which she'd put in the oven before we left for church. Everyone was so grief-stricken and so tired from not sleeping that, at Auntie Odie's dining table, people hardly spoke—mostly grunted—and hardly ate. If I'd been Auntie Odie, I'd have been offended at everyone's behavior, but she appeared not to notice. She was distracted and sullen too.

Martha and I went out and sat in Auntie Odie's garden swing, but Martha was listless and quiet. I brought my tablet and practiced the "wings" Scripture verse I'd written down. The wind came in gusts with points of rain, and blew our bench swing and made it swivel crazily, nearly driving us into the trunk of the maple. When we saw people driving up at the Matthews' house, we ran inside to report that they had company. The Matthews left and Auntie Odie and I washed, dried, and put away the dishes. The house creaked in the wind, the windowpanes shuddered, and soon rain pounded the roof. Auntie Odie looked so sad, I didn't think I could stand to look into her face again until she was over her grieving. Her sorrow left me insecure, uncertain, cold.

I put my shoulders back, took a deep breath, and tilted my chin up, just like Auntie Odie did when she gathered herself up to recite a poem or verse. I spoke carefully, recalling the words just ahead of my spoken ones.

> "But they that wait upon the Lord
> shall renew their strength;
> they shall mount up with wings as eagles;
> they shall run, and not be weary;
> and they shall walk, and not faint."

As though from some deep place of sleep, Auntie Odie awakened and turned to stare down at me. She opened her arms to me, and so very, very grateful, I walked into them.

★ ★ ★

Just as we settled on the sofa in the front room to watch the storm, the phone rang.

"May I answer it, Auntie Odie?"

"If you do it like I taught you."

I picked up the receiver, black and heavy. "Good afternoon. Odessa Luckett's residence. Ponia Snow speaking." I was surprised by the starkness of my image in the mirror over the phone table—my eyes a crisp, invading blue in contrast to the room behind me, colorless in the gray light of the storm.

"Ponia Snow? Ingrid's daughter?" the woman's voice asked.

I nodded my head. "Uh-huh."

"This is Mary Ann Walters, sweetie, your mother's Nimble Needle friend. I need to speak with Odessa."

Auntie Odie had stepped to my side. I handed her the phone.

"Hello... Yes... Hello, Mary Ann... As good as can be expected... Yes, a terrible shock."

Then Auntie Odie's face changed. She glanced at me, then looked down and tugged at the phone cord. "I see.... Glory be..."

Mama!

"Where is she now? ...I see... Oh, absolutely, yes! Poni can stay with me as long as necessary..."

I took hold of Auntie Odie's pleat. She looked down at me and smiled in a way I hadn't seen before—her eyes with the lids low, her large mouth in a slight curve.

"Yes. Thank you, Mary Ann. We'll be waiting for more news." She hung up slowly.

Before I could utter a word, Auntie Odie reassured me. "Now Poni dearest, your Mama's gonna be all right. She'll be home in a few—well, after a little while."

"She's not dead?"

"No, child."

"Did she run away?"

"No, child, your mother's not dead and she didn't run away. She's in St. Joseph's Hospital in Denver being well taken care of. She got appendicitis and they did surgery. She's in recovery right now. In a few weeks she'll be as good as new."

My face must've been a mess because she sat me down on the sofa, put her arms around me and said, "Now, child, you have nothing to fear. You have a home here with me until your mama gets well."

"Mama's going to be all right?"

"Absolutely."

"I'm going to stay here with you?"

"Yes, child, right here with me."

"She won't be home for awhile?"

"That's right, child."

I suppressed a smile. "How very sad."

Chapter 23

Mock Enemy Bombers Reached
Virtually Every Vital Location
In Northern U.S., Report Says
—*Greeley Daily Tribune*, p.7, Mon., June 25, 1951

★ ★ ★

Nearly Two Million
More Americans
in Arms than Year ago
—*Greeley Daily Tribune*, p.3, Wed., June 27, 1951

Wednesday's high 85°, low 54°; partly cloudy; scattered late afternoon showers; precipitation .01"

We yanked weeds in Auntie Odie's garden and watered and sweated and laughed. The wilted petunias we pinched off, and the pansies and moss roses too. For house bouquets we snipped roses, lilies-of-the-valley, daylilies, and daisies.

After we filled the birdfeeders, we rested in the swing. Besides sparrows and robins and house finches, we saw a house wren, blue grosbeaks and even a lazuli bunting which Auntie Odie and I identified by looking in her bird-guide book. The house wren didn't go to the feeders—Auntie Odie says house wrens prefer insects—but he gave us a concert. And a meadowlark sang-sang-sang silly songs from the vacant lot next to Auntie Odie's cottage—"Sweetie, Johnny Chucklehead," "Here Comes Kate and the Children," "Sweetie, Here's your Sugarpill," "I'll Stay Here Forever," "Very Peculiar People," and "Lookie Here! Lookie Here!" Each time he sang a song, we imitated him.

And when a thunderstorm blew in, we watched it from the front room, then from the enclosed back porch, like it was the best movie we'd ever seen. There had been thunderstorms all week and even a tornado in Holyoke. I described a thunderstorm, in detail, in my tablet.

"My!" Auntie Odie said. "This is the wettest year I believe I've ever seen in Weld."

"I like it," I said. "I have lots to write about."

Auntie Odie "performed" stories and African folktales and Bible verses and poetry, and I filled up my spiral and a Big Chief tablet with poems and Bible verses, and stories of my own—some true, some fiction. I worked on memorizing Henry Wadsworth Longfellow's ninety-five lines from "Hiawatha's Childhood." Every time I learned a verse and could perform it almost as good as Auntie Odie, gushing the words from my mouth like a waterfall, or sending them trickling in soft streams, a place in me grew more satisfied.

That week after Nate died the Matthews had a constant flow of visitors, so Auntie Odie and I didn't visit them much. Auntie Odie said they'd need us more after everybody went home, back to their normal lives. We prayed for the Matthews, we read the Bible and talked about what we read. The funniest Bible story was when God made an ass talk to a man named Balaam so Balaam would perk up and listen to what God was telling him to do. I felt funny saying *ass* because it sounded like cussing. When I told Auntie Odie that, she just chuckled.

She and I made more visits to the Firedrake's shop—"to watch him maneuver glass," as she put it.

Mr. Santi made a pony. "A glass pony for Poni Glass."

The pony stayed in the annealing oven, but I brought home the glass butterfly. I wrote all about it in my Big Chief. Auntie Odie said she'd help me edit and revise my stories, then I could copy them into a new spiral she'd buy me.

Auntie Odie sure kept busy so she wouldn't remember that Nate wasn't ever coming back.

I had been memorizing Emily Dickinson's poem, "I Never Saw a Moor." Now was the time for me to recite it for Auntie Odie—I just hoped I could say it right.

"'I never saw a moor,'" I announced. She turned, wide-eyed, and gazed down at me, listening.

> "I never saw a moor,
> I never saw the sea;
> Yet know I how the heather looks
> And what a wave must be.
>
> "I never spoke with God,
> Nor visited in heaven;
> Yet certain am I of the spot
> As if the chart were given.

"And Nate is there waiting, isn't he, Auntie Odie?"

She hugged me real tight for a long time. I gave her a hanky from the davenport drawer because she needed one.

"Thank you, dear, *dear* child."

Chapter 24

33 Soldiers Killed Daily in
Korea, While Automobile Deaths
Averaged 99 A Day, Study Shows
—*Greeley Daily Tribune*, p.16, Thurs., June 28, 1951

Memorial Service for Capt. Nathan
Matthews Set for Tomorrow at
Akin All Saints Community Church
—*Akin Scoop*, p.1, Thurs., June 28, 1951

Scattered showers and a few thunderstorms Thursday; high 87°, low 53°

Auntie Odie and I titivated, as she put it, before going to catch up on washing at Landry's Laundromat. She pinned a cameo brooch on her dress—the one I'd seen on her coat at the estate sale.

"That's pretty," I said.

She adjusted it until it was centered under her chin. "Ivory on ebony. It is fetching, isn't it, with its lacy gold frame."

"Why are you wearing a cameo with a white lady on it?"

"Why shouldn't I?"

"Well, seems like maybe you'd wear an ebony lady on ivory."

"I don't know if one exists." Auntie Odie removed the cameo again and pinned it a little lower, among the folds on the yoke of her dress. "I'd buy an ebony-on-ivory cameo if I ever saw one, but I sure wouldn't trade this one for it."

I sat in Auntie Odie's wing-backed chair and watched her as she studied her hats, deciding which one to wear. "Why wouldn't you trade it?"

She sat on her bed and rested the chosen hat—gray with pink feathers—in her lap. "Long ago, this cameo was given to me by Mrs. Arda Moore." Auntie Odie sighed and gazed at the ceiling. "She was the mistress of the house where Mum worked from the time I was five."

"Who's Mum?" I asked.

"That's what I always called my mama—Mum. The Moores were good to us and helped us get on our feet. Up until we went to live at the Moores', Mum hated whites, thought they were all hateful, mean—thought they all whipped and overworked their slaves. Remember? I told you I had seven older brothers and sisters, all born into slavery near Concord, North Carolina. When some of my siblings were taken from her and sold, her heart was broken. She wondered about her lost children and cried for them until her dying day."

I watched, my mouth dry and empty of words, as Auntie Odie traced the profile on the cameo with her long finger. She raised her eyebrows, creasing the high forehead, and sighed deeply. "When my mother was sixteen, she gave birth to Sarah. That was 1854. Then came Horace, then Samuel—sold when they were in their teens. Then came Mary. Sarah was just fifteen when she died of typhoid. Mary disappeared when she was twelve—no one ever knew what happened to her. Then came George, the next year Juliet, and in 1864, the year before the Civil War ended, Mum had Moses."

I kept track on my fingers. "Moses was number seven."

Auntie Odie nodded. "And they were freed from slavery by the Union victory in 1865."

I brightened. "Well, that's good."

Her lips formed a sad smile. "Yes, but real freedom didn't come for many years. In fact, even now, eighty-six years later, scads of colored folks can't say they live lives of liberty—free from fear and prejudice. Colored folks in the South still can't go into 'white' restaurants or use 'white' drinking fountains and restrooms." She rubbed her brow. "Even in the west, even right here in Akin, new people come to town and sometimes they'll walk way around me on the sidewalk, or make me cross to the other side of the street. They say, 'Don't come close to me—' and then they call me an insulting name. Things like that."

I took her hand. "But why?"

"They don't know any better, child. How can they if they don't have the Author of Justice and Mercy in their hearts?"

"I bet you just hate those people."

"If I claim Jesus as my Savior, I can't hate 'em, child. He's Author of Love too. I have to love my enemies—and forgive, just like He did."

"Love them? And forgive them too?"

She closed her eyes. "Have to. God says I must forgive others if I want to be forgiven and if I want to be healthy and whole. No backpedaling, no ifs, ands, or buts. Unforgiveness pumps poison into our spiritual veins, kills our spirits. God hates things that destroy us because He loves us so much."

"I could never do that, Auntie Odie. I'd never forgive people for treating me bad."

"Careful. That's prideful, child. That's like saying you've never done anything that needs to be forgiven, that you're perfect—sinless."

"Those rotten people don't deserve to be forgiven."

"Forgiveness isn't for them. It's for you. To remove the poison in His temple."

"His temple?"

"Your body, God's temple—house—when He lives in you. Don't pump poison into it."

I furrowed my brows—didn't like Auntie Odie's talk.

She continued, "Pride lurks in unforgiveness."

"What?"

"Pride. Unforgiveness. They're poison. They kill unless they're gouged out of the heart and life through prayer—repentance."

I folded my arms. "I don't want to talk this way anymore. Let's talk about your family and your cameo and Mrs. Arda Moore."

Her tender gaze and the catch in her voice shamed me. "All right, child. Where were we?"

"Talk about you, Auntie Odie. You were born after the slaves got freed?"

She nodded. "I was born ten years after the Civil War ended." She looked at the cameo in the mirror, caressed it with her fingers. "My family—Mum and Daddy and George and Juliet and Moses—eventually got a farm and eked out a living. Then Horace located the family and helped on the farm too. I was born on the farm in 1875, when Moses was eleven—my mother was thirty-seven. My hardworking Daddy died at age forty-nine. I was only four. He had a lot of health problems from the beatings he got as a slave. I have very little recollection of him." She sighed. "But I do remember one time—he was moaning, and I stood on a stool behind his chair and rubbed liniment on an old back injury."

As Auntie Odie and I went about our day, she told me more about her life. At Landry's Laundromat—surrounded by the smells of soap and bleach and the squeals of children playing while their mothers chatted and washed clothes—Aunt Odie said, "Mum became sickly after Daddy died. She couldn't work long days in the fields. While my brothers kept the farm going, Mum took me—I was five—and moved to Concord, North Carolina where she took a job as a servant—seamstress and cook, mainly—for a white family, the Moores. Arda Moore loved and pampered me, along with her own three children, and saw that I was educated. Arda Moore read to us children, and my mother told us stories and folktales of slavery."

Watering and pulling weeds in the garden, Auntie Odie continued, "Mum died when I was fourteen, but the Moores continued to treat me like their own daughter and sister. They finished raising me, and sent me off to school where I was trained to be a high school teacher. Later, I taught literature in a Negro college. Over the years I kept in touch with the Moore children—Betsy, who shared my birthday but was two years older, and Elizabeth, two years younger than me, and Richard who was my age. Mrs. Arda Moore was a cuddling, cheerful, hardworking woman. She worked alongside my mother, cooking and housecleaning. Dr. Floyd Moore was fun-loving and supportive, but worked long hours because of the demands of his practice."

Resting in front of the fan and drinking iced tea Auntie Odie said, "Mother Moore became ill while I was teaching in Pennsylvania. Dr. Moore treated her. He called in other doctors, but there was nothing anyone could do. She was dying. Betsy, Richard, Elizabeth, and I were called home to her side. We took turns entering the room, each spent a few minutes.

"At last it was my turn. Mother Moore was so weak, she could barely whisper, 'Get the cameo in my jewel box.' I returned to her side with the cameo that she had worn every day until her illness. She took the cameo, pressed her lips to it, placed it in my hand and closed her hand around mine. 'Always remember you were loved with full hearts by a white family.' She paused and smiled sweetly. 'Especially me. Odessa, I couldn't love you more if you were formed in my own womb.' She tried to lick her lips, her breathing was labored, but she held onto my hand with strength born of courage and resolve. 'Remember there is potential for both good and evil in the hearts of us all—young and old, colored and white, master and slave.' Mother Moore gasped and closed her eyes. I cried out and the rest of the family rushed in. She opened her eyes one last time and, still clasping my hand, her eyes large and gray and pleading, said to me, 'Odessa... dearest... promise me... you will not hate, you'll put away all bitterness and anger toward those who did evil things to your family. Do not give refuge to unforgiveness. For your own sake. Promise me.'

"My tears fell onto that beloved face," said Auntie Odie. "I could only whimper, 'I promise.' She smiled, then her hands relaxed and dropped to the sheet."

Auntie Odie caressed the cameo, her eyes like pools in spring, browned by streams of soil and melted snow. "That's why I wouldn't trade it for anything."

An ache had slowly coiled around my heart as Auntie Odie told her story. That evening I wrote on several pages of my Big Chief tablet about Auntie Odie and her family and the Moores. I wrote until my fingers throbbed. I wrote until the ache loosened, straggled down through my arm and hand and pencil, then out onto the paper in harmless, gray strings.

Chapter 25

High Korean
Official Says
Truce Is Near
—*Greeley Daily Tribune*, p.1, Fri., June 29, 1951

Matthews Family Claims
Strength to Endure Sorrow
Comes from Faith in God
—*Akin Scoop*, p.1, Fri., June 29, 1951

A few showers and thunderstorms Friday; high 60°, low 51°

Nate's memorial service was held in the midst of thundershowers and some hail. People packed out the All Saints Community Church. Some overflowed to the front steps under the awning where they huddled together against the storm.

There was something even sadder about Nate's memorial service than Gram and Grampy's. Nate was so young and smart and strong and had his life ahead of him. The grief endured by the Matthews family and Auntie Odie pierced me too.

"He laid down his life for freedom," Pastor Charles proclaimed. "What a gift to give the world. In fighting to bring freedom to South Korea, the whole world will be freer, safer. Thank you, Nathan Frederick Matthews, for paying the ultimate price."

Then the pastor talked about Jesus Christ's sacrifice, how He lovingly laid down His life so everyone who believed in Him would live forever like Nate was doing now. He said if anyone wanted to receive Christ, they could confess their sins, be forgiven, and be made right with God. He said in a soft, earnest voice, "Then the Son will come into you and live in you and you will live in Him—just as Jesus and the Father live in each other. If you want to know more about living in Him, you can call me at J123. There's nothing—absolutely nothing—in your life of more eternal significance."

J123… Jesus 123.

Chapter 26

Huge Crowd Overflows All Saints
Church for Nathan Matthews'
Memorial Service Here Yesterday
—*Akin Scoop*, p.1, Sat., June 30, 1951

★ ★ ★

Largest Non-segregated
Audience in Atlanta's
History Hears Bunche
—*Greeley Daily Tribune*, p.11, Mon., July 2, 1951

"Lost" Yellow-Rumped Warblers
Spotted in Groves Near Pretty Pond
—*Akin Scoop*, p.2, Mon., July 2, 1951

Monday's high 94°, low 54°; scattered afternoon and evening showers

Martha and I snuggled against Auntie Odie, and Emily on her lap, in the garden swing for our final reading session of *Narrative of the Life of Frederick Douglass: An American Slave*. Auntie Odie dabbed her forehead with a hanky but made no complaint about the heat, nor did she push anyone away.

If a voice can possess jubilant and sorrowful qualities at the same time, Auntie Odie's did. She read as bravely as Mr. Douglass had spoken at the anti-slavery convention at Nantucket in 1841. I wished I had as much courage as Mr. Douglass did. Sadly for me, the book ended. But before Auntie Odie could close the book, I put my fingers in the place. "Wait, there's more."

"Just the Appendix," she said.

At Martha's and my persuasion, Auntie Odie read the Appendix. Mr. Douglass wrote that the American Christian is like the scribe and Pharisee of the Bible. There was "the widest possible difference" between the religion of America and the Christianity of Christ—"so wide, that to receive the one as good, pure, and holy, is of necessity to reject the other as bad, corrupt, and wicked."

Auntie Odie read like she was reading a work of fiction, her voice expressive and earnest. I had trouble—and by the expression on her face, Martha did too—understanding all that Auntie Odie read. But I was captured by the idea that here in 1951 I was hearing the words of a black slave written over a hundred years before. My legs longed to run, my body wanted to squirm, but I held fast to my overly warm place beside Auntie Odie, drinking in her scent, the sound of her voice, the thrum of words, and the wonder of new knowledge—thinking on things I'd never thought about before.

But a melancholy embraced me as Auntie Odie read the last sentences of the Appendix.

Auntie Odie closed the book slowly as though meeting with great resistance.

"Are there any actual slaves left in America anymore?" Martha asked.

Emily burst into a loud purr as Auntie Odie stroked her. "Oh, indeed there are."

I sat up and cocked my head at Auntie Odie. "Honest? No! They got rid of slavery."

She chuckled softly. "Just what we've been talking about. In Second Peter, second chapter, nineteenth verse, Peter says that we're all servants—slaves—of sin unless we've joined Christ and received the freedom of being righteous in Him. Really, Frederick Douglass was saying the same thing Peter said.

"While they promise them liberty, they themselves are the servants of corruption: for of whom a man is overcome, of the same is he brought in bondage."

Alarmed, I raised my voice. "But there aren't real slaves anymore, are there? Abraham Lincoln made the slaves free, didn't he? There was the Emancipation Proclamation." We'd been learning about that in school.

Auntie Odie spoke of "slaves of hate and bitterness." She said her mother had such hatred for whites when she was a slave, she became fiercely bitter, took on a meanness. So her mother had been enslaved in three ways—physically, emotionally, *and* spiritually. "All of us," Auntie Odie said, "are slaves of either good or evil."

"Are you a slave then?" I asked her.

"I used to be a slave to sin," Auntie Odie said. "But now, I'm a slave to goodness. Remember? We've talked about this before. The Bible says we're all slaves to sin until Christ frees us. No exceptions. If my mother had allowed hate to grow and fester, that would've been as devastating to her as physical slavery was."

"So the slave owners were slaves too," Martha said.

"In a spiritual sense—true." Auntie Odie paused and looked up at a noisy flock of starlings flying in a broad circle above us. "They were as much slaves to their evil ways as their slaves were by their chains. Abe Lincoln's regiments couldn't fight that kind of slavery. It's fought in the heart. God identifies and hates evil because it makes people slaves to it. Evil—sin—destroys people."

Emily stood in Auntie Odie's lap, poised to jump down, but I took hold of her and brought her to my lap. Starlings lit in the locust tree by the house. Their cries sounded like dozens of children bouncing up and down on a bed with squeaky springs.

"Why didn't the Lord step in and save the slaves from all that meanness?" I asked.

"He did."

"Why did he allow slavery in the first place? Why did he let them suffer so long, so many years?"

"Life is a test for all of us." Auntie Odie couldn't hide the sorrow in her eyes. "God never promised we wouldn't have troubles, but He promises to lead us through our trials and give us strength. He promises not to give us any more than we can bear."

"But losing your mom or dad when you're sold *is* more than anyone can bear," I said.

"Or watching them get beaten," Martha said, "or being beaten yourself."

I snuggled my face in Emily's fur. "I'd never forgive anybody who hurt or killed my family."

Auntie Odie's whole face turned down. "If it's happening to them and if Christ dwells in them, they can bear it."

That's not true! I felt tears crowd my eyes. "But some couldn't bear it. Some died."

"If their hope was in the Lord, even a tragic death—a loved one's death or their own—was not too much to bear. They know—really *know* with all their heart—they have a forever-future with Him."

Emily insisted on hopping down. Rather than getting clawed, I let her go. I shook my head. *You're wrong on this one, Auntie Odie.*

She continued, "Death is the bridge to eternal life with God. All who repent and believe, no matter what happens to them in this life, will be free—saved—and will spend the rest of forever with Him."

"It isn't fair!" I cried. "God should stop people from doing bad things to other people."

"Life in this world isn't fair, our enemy isn't fair," Auntie Odie said, "but God is fair, whether we recognize it or not. The Bible warns that someday every person who hasn't received Jesus and His gift of forgiveness will stand before God—one at a time—and answer to Him for every wrong."

I chilled in spite of the heat of the day, remembering my silent wish that Mama had died instead of Gram and Grampy.

"Why doesn't God just make people be good?" Martha asked.

"God won't *make* us do anything. He allows circumstances, good and bad, in our lives, and he watches us make choices, but He doesn't make us make the right decisions. He offers counsel, comfort, strength, and direction to those who seek Him and who read the Instruction Manual, to those who love and honor Him by the choices they make, by the way they live their lives."

Auntie Odie's face had smoothed of the worry wrinkles.

I patted her arm. "God must be awful happy when He looks at you, Auntie Odie."

"I'm saved by grace. Not by the things I do or don't do. Sometimes I disappoint Him, sometimes I please Him, but he does know I love Him. Psalm seventy-nine, verse eight says,

"O remember not against us former iniquities: let thy tender mercies speedily prevent us: for we are brought very low.

"That verse teaches us that, when we're 'brought very low,' His tender mercies prevent us from the kind of anger and bitterness that enslave and destroy us. And Psalm one-hundred three, verses two and four says,

"Bless the Lord, O my soul… Who redeemeth thy life from destruction; who crowneth thee with lovingkindness and tender mercies…."

"But your people were slaves," I said. "Your family was ruined. They weren't redeemed from destruction."

"Oh, yes they were," Auntie Odie said. "The members of my family who loved God and lived in his daily mercies, were redeemed. They're with Him right now. God led them through to eternal life."

Martha nodded.

"I don't get it," I said. "If God really loves people so much, He'd protect them."

Martha nodded at everything Auntie Odie said and all that I said too.

"I know. It is hard to understand," Auntie Odie said. "Sometimes I lose my perspective and I question God. But He didn't promise that we'd always understand, that we won't be hurt, abused, maligned, spat upon, made fun of—even killed. After all, all those things were done to Jesus. There was a higher purpose. When those things happen to us, God does see and care. His greatest purpose for all people in this life is to turn to Him, to know Him, to love Him as He loves us, to be saved by His grace, to consider Him our friend, to obey Him and trust Him with strength and courage—no matter what. To trust Him, we can't go by feelings or circumstances. It's an act of faith. We must believe what He said, even when we don't feel His comfort and love."

I hopped off the swing and faced Auntie Odie. "But He said He *would* comfort us."

"Sometimes the comfort is in the knowing through His Word that no matter what happens in this life, we'll end up with Him in a good place—no matter how bad things get here. The comfort is in knowing—not feeling."

"But He said He'd *protect* us," I said. "You said so yourself."

"We don't even realize all the times we've been protected, rescued, restored, prevented from harm, healed. But when God allows us—those of us who welcome Him as Lord—to go through the fire, even death, we are protected from eternal punishment and we're welcomed into the home He's prepared for us."

Martha hopped off the swing, picked up a red, odd-shaped rock, sat back down beside Auntie Odie, and fingered it as she spoke. "So I get comfort when I remember that Nate's with God? And when I believe what God told us about heaven? And when I remember I'll see Nate in heaven someday?"

Auntie Odie nodded. "But if you and Nate hadn't received Him and come to know His truths, you wouldn't have that comfort."

"God ought to zing everybody who's been bad," Martha said.

"That's you and me," Auntie Odie said. "All of us."

"But He ought to rescue the people who believe Him," I said.

A smile grew on Auntie Odie's full lips and her eyes twinkled. She was enjoying our questioning. "There are times when God rescues us from bad situations, like when He sent an angel to rescue his follower, Peter, from prison. But there are times when He doesn't rescue us from our prisons and He allows us to be miserable and mistreated. Paul, another of God's faithful followers, spent several years of his life in prison. He was even put there while doing God's will."

"God should've rescued Paul." Nothing Auntie Odie could say would convince me otherwise.

"Do you know what Paul did while he was in prison?" Auntie Odie asked.

"He sang!" said Martha.

Auntie Odie stood, adjusted her skirt and hat, and strolled along the garden path. "Yes, songs of praise and thanksgiving to God. And he wrote letters of love and encouragement to the churches— letters we still read today. He could do that because he was living God's purpose. He was at peace because he knew God's truth and was comforted by God's truths—in spite of being chained in a filthy prison. God was pleased with him and that was all that mattered to Paul. He knew God had a reason—a larger purpose than his own comfort and pleasure—for everything that happened to him. Eventually Paul was released from prison, but he endured terrible hardships in and out of prison."

I walked with Auntie Odie while Martha skipped ahead of us.

Auntie Odie squeezed my hand. "Paul also had an illness—'a thorn' he called it—that he asked God to heal, but God didn't heal him. God gave Paul strength to endure it instead. God's tender mercies are available to us so that we can go through anything—and I mean *anything*—God doesn't rescue us from. People should be able to look at us, see how God strengthens us during difficult times, and be inspired to trust God too."

The starlings, all at once, flew off in a black cloud and left the garden still. Martha skipped back to us and took Auntie Odie's other hand.

"Who else didn't God rescue?" I asked.

Auntie Odie tilted back her head in that thinking look. "John," she said. "John the Baptist was doing God's will, preaching the Good News, and baptizing believers—all the things he was supposed to be doing."

"But they put him in prison." Martha knew a lot about the Bible. She'd grown up going to church and Sunday school and spending time with Auntie Odie.

"Yes, indeed," Auntie Odie said. "And when John found out that the king had ordered him killed, he sent someone to ask Jesus, 'Are you the Christ, or shall we look for another?' John's faith sure was tested that day. He wondered if he'd misunderstood his calling. He couldn't believe that Jesus—if He was who He said He was—would allow him to die, would not rescue him from prison and death. Jesus sent word back to John: 'Blessed is he who does not lose his faith on account of me.' In other words, 'You will not be rescued, John. You will be killed. Will you keep your faith in Me, love Me—trust Me—to your last breath even if you're not rescued?'"

"What happened then?" I asked. "Did Jesus rescue him after John promised to love Him, no matter what?"

"Did God rescue John? Not that day. John was rescued from eternal death and punishment on the first day he believed. Was God with him through his physical death? Yes. Was John comforted by God? Yes. If he didn't allow circumstances to cause him to lose his faith, he was comforted, even if disappointed, when he got Jesus' message. Jesus' answer was not what he thought—and hoped—it would be. But in his heart, he knew who Jesus was, he knew what God had promised to those who believed."

"So John was killed?" I asked. I still couldn't believe God would let that happen.

Martha whacked the side of one hand onto the palm of the other. "*Whack!* They chopped off his head. Just like that."

I shuddered.

Auntie Odie nodded. "John was beheaded, his head set on a platter and brought before the king who commanded it. Did God rescue John that day? No. Did God lead him through it? Yes. John is in heaven now, in God's holy presence forever, having heard the words, 'Well done, thou good and faithful servant.'"

"Glory be!" I said.

"There were many Christians through the ages who were rescued while on earth," Auntie Odie said, "who were led through great trials and came out alive to go on with God's work until a ripe old age. But there were also many Christians who were tortured, beaten, burned, stoned, fed to lions, starved, and humiliated. But those whose hearts were God's, who believed in Him even though they faced a chopping block or a noose, were led through to eternal life with God. Even Peter, who was rescued from prison, was eventually crucified upside down because he believed in and preached Christ."

"Glory be!" Me again.

"The same is true of many slaves in America," Auntie Odie continued. "God led many slaves through their misery, giving them strength and guidance. Those who loved God fought the enemy of hate and revenge. For some, God allowed relief through kind masters, but they were still slaves—until God raised up the President who would fight to abolish slavery."

Auntie Odie let go of our hands, and extended her arms around our shoulders. "If trial or tragedy causes us to lose our faith, our enemy rejoices—he has deceived us. He has won. But if we hold fast to God, to our faith, and do not lose it—no matter what happens to us—*we* have won, not the enemy, no matter how it looks in the physical world."

The three of us meandered to the back porch, Emily leading the way.

"Want some lemonade?" Auntie Odie asked.

"Seems like God has His favorites," I said, "rescuing some and letting others suffer."

"He rescued us all when He came and laid down His life for us."

Martha opened the door into the kitchen. "I'll have some."

As we washed our hands and Auntie Odie got down glasses, she said, "It's like a fantasy, isn't it? We're expected to trust God when we can't see Him, when we can't feel His presence, when we have to just believe what He's told us even when what He's told us doesn't feel true, when everything around us is falling apart and sad, and when some people have life easy and others have it difficult and even die awful deaths."

Martha dropped ice cubes into the glasses. "Like Nate getting killed and Mother being so sick."

Auntie Odie poured the pink beverage over the cubes. "This life is a fleeting shadow compared to the life that awaits us with the God of the Universe. *Nothing* is worth losing eternal life with the God of lovingkindness and tender mercies. Always remember: Dying wasn't part of the life God originally designed for us. He created us immortal. When sin entered the world, everything changed."

"Yeah," I said. "Death paraded in on the arm of sin, like you taught us, huh, Auntie Odie?"

Auntie Odie smiled with a little nod. "But...

"God is faithful, by whom ye were called unto the fellowship of his Son Jesus Christ our Lord.

"That's first Corinthians one, nine. Nothing is more important than being saved by God's grace, knowing Him personally, believing, and obeying His promises, so we can be comforted, even when everything around us is upside-down and backwards."

Martha gulped her lemonade then licked her lips. "Nothing is more important."

"Nothing is more important," I echoed.

But I really did wonder if all that Auntie Odie said was true.

Chapter 27

Truce in Korea
Will Not Affect
Preparedness
—*Greeley Daily Tribune*, p.1, Tues., July 3, 1951

Many Literaries Held
In Akin Vicinity
—*Akin Scoop*, p.1, Tues., July 3, 1951

Tuesday's high 88°, low 60°; widely scattered afternoon and evening thundershowers

With Mama's return to Akin a feeling of melancholy swept over me.

She was still weak and needed to avoid stairs, so she agreed to stay with Auntie Odie—and me—for several days while she recuperated. My melancholy left the moment I realized my time with Auntie Odie wasn't over yet. But I would no longer be sleeping in the nook. Mama slept on my daybed in the nook, and I slept on the couch in the front room. Mama liked that daybed, I could tell, and spent a lot of time in it.

With fans in each room and trees shading Aunt Odie's cottage, it stayed comfortable. In Mama's and my apartment, when Auntie Odie and I went to check on things and get Mama's other gown, it felt like the Firedrake's furnace.

Auntie Odie and I worked in her gardens in the early morning and filled the birdfeeders. When it stormed, we watched from inside, tended to Mama's needs, did housework, and read and memorized poems and Bible verses. The list of words and definitions in our wordbooks grew like summer flowers. Armed with our latest new words, we jousted in repartees like house finches banter with birdsong.

★ ★ ★

"Child, would you look on the third shelf there, and fetch that little brown book of poesy?"

"Will you read some out loud, Auntie Odie, so I can delectate?"

"Ecstatically delighted to."

"Here it is," I said. "I hope it's zingy poesy about gardens and comradeship and such."

"It is, thumbling, it is."

★ ★ ★

We had Auntie Odie's neighbor to the south, Mrs. Angela Fall, and Olivia and Martha over for lunch. It rained, roaring down like a waterfall for about fifteen minutes, and we sweated like steam engines with all the windows closed and all that humidity.

Mrs. Fall had shivering eyes, and she was tiny everywhere, except for her lips and teeth. She talked the whole time about nothing and everything, usually with her mouth full. We were informed that she had an allergic cousin in Chesapeake who had a habit of sneezing into his bowler. When the bowler got too crusty he just bought a new one. Mrs. Fall also mentioned that just that morning she had pulled out two white hairs from a single pore on her chin and puss oozed out. Mrs. Fall also mentioned that five years ago her sister Gretchen in New Jersey used Corn-Gone on a corn on her third toe and died six months later from infection that had set in.

But according to Auntie Odie and Olivia Matthews, Mrs. Fall was one of the most wonderful human beings on earth.

"Poor dear," Mrs. Matthews said after Mrs. Fall left, "she's so lonely. But what a good daughter she was to retire from her job and move to Akin to take care of her mother all those years—and all by herself. Not one of the seven siblings lifted a finger to help. *Tch, tch.*"

"That sure was nice of her," Martha said.

"I s'pose it was," said Mama.

"A person couldn't have a better neighbor," said Auntie Odie. "Why, for three weeks, when I had the flu one winter, she brought me soup every day and a bouquet of flowers from Bennie's Florals." Auntie Odie shook her head at the memory. "Oh, I was so sick, and she was so kind. Even slept on the sofa one night she was so concerned. Now that's love."

Glory be.

★ ★ ★

While Mama rested, Auntie Odie and I went to catch up on the laundry. Landry's Laundry in Akin was closed for remodeling, so we drove to Greeley's Wash-O-Mat. Afterwards, we got to go shopping in Greeley. Auntie Odie bought Mama two new housedresses and a new pair of slippers at Greeley Dry Goods. Francine's Fancies in downtown Akin had a hat sale, so Auntie Odie bought new hats—one each for Mama, herself, and me.

Mama sure did like her new hat—white, wide-brimmed. White and yellow daisies encircled the crown. She smiled—really smiled—for the first time in a very long time.

★ ★ ★

Mama was asleep for the night by nine o'clock. After a brief rain, Auntie Odie and I meandered through her garden just looking and listening. We sat in the garden swing and breathed in the wondrous aromas of damp earth and satiated flowers. A mourning dove crooed nearby.

159

I whispered, "Auntie Odie, what's that Emily Dickinson poem about the bird passing the window?"

Her voice was soft and low and curdled like the song of the mourning dove.

> "Heart not so heavy as mine,
> Wending late home,
> As it passed my window
> Whistled itself a tune,—
>
> "A careless snatch, a ballad,
> A ditty of the street;
> Yet to my irritated ear
> An anodyne so sweet...

"...Is that the one?"

"Uh-huh."

She cocked her head like she was listening—perhaps for a bird, but they had quieted. In the distance a train whistled and a dog barked. Beneath our swing a cricket practiced a single fluid note on his violin—over and over. The darkness settled down upon us, sweet and warm.

"Auntie Odie." I tapped her hand. "Is that the end?"

She sighed. "No, child..."

"You going to finish?" I waited.

At last...

> "...An Anodyne so sweet,
> It was as if a bobolink,
> Sauntering this way
> Carolled and mused and carolled,
> Then bubbled slow away.
>
> "It was as if a chirping brook
> Upon a dusty way
> Set bleeding feet to minuets
> Without the knowing why.
>
> "Tomorrow, night will come again,
> Weary, perhaps, and sore.
> Ah, bugle, by my window,
> I pray you stroll once more!

"Your turn," she said, "then we'll turn in."
I smiled up at her. "My favorite one of Emily Dickinson's:

> "A word is dead
> When it is said,
>   Some say.
>
> "I say it just
> Begins to live
>   That day."

Chapter 28

Crops, Wheat, Homes
Damaged by Storm
—*Akin Scoop*, p.1, Wed., July 4, 1951

100+ Degrees Expected
For Independence Day
—*Akin Scoop*, p.1, Wed., July 4, 1951

Partly cloudy Wednesday; high 101°, low 59°

The crowd sang the nation's anthem on that hot July Fourth evening, and I sang with them.

"O say! can you see, by the dawn's early light,
What so proudly we hail'd at the twilight's last gleaming?
Whose broad stripes and bright stars, thro' the perilous fight,
O'er the ramparts we watched, were so gallantly streaming?"

The Matthews sang, too, and Auntie Odie, Mama, and Mrs. Fall. The Firedrake and his mother Dora Santi joined us there at Island Grove Park in Greeley, along with the Fenderlupens—including Sarah and Margaret—and a few others from Auntie Odie's and the Matthews' neighborhood.

"…And the rocket's red glare, the bombs bursting in air,
Gave proof thro' the night that our flag was still there.
O say, does that Star-spangled Banner yet wave
O'er the land of the free and the home of the brave…"

The Matthews had decided that one way they could honor Nate's memory and celebrate his life was to join with friends for the Independence Day festivities. Mrs. Matthews said they'd never missed a Fourth of July together. It was Nate's favorite holiday of the year, and he had studied and learned every detail of the history of Independence Day.

So with sore hearts we sang the opening song, listened to announcements, and watched the fireworks light up the night sky. The finale of the evening of fireworks was a display depicting the American shield and the bursting of aerial bombs.

Mr. Matthews rubbed away a tear. "Nate would've loved this."

Chapter 29

6,000 See Fireworks
Here on Two Nights
—*Greeley Daily Tribune*, p.1, Thurs., July 5, 1951

Glass Menagerie, Winner of New
Work Critics' Award, Will Be
Little Theatre Play This Week
—*Greeley Daily Tribune*, p.11, Thurs., July 5, 1951

★ ★ ★

Weld Weather Can't
Make Up Its Mind: Heat,
Thunderstorms, Wind
—*Akin Scoop*, p.1, Sat., July 7, 1951

Saturday's high 104°–hottest July temperature of the last three years; low 62°

"Try not to be discouraged," Auntie Odie told Mama one Saturday. "That's only the second quilt you've ever made, you said so yourself. Why, you keep on making quilts and getting better each time, you'll soon be winning contests and selling quilts right and left."

Mama scowled. "I been thinking about all this sewing business."

I sat in Auntie Odie's desk chair and fiddled with the book on her desk, *Mr. Jones, Meet the Master!* by somebody named Peter Marshall. I opened it to the bookmark and my eyes fell on pencil-bracketed lines. I read silently:

The poor shall not always be poor.

"Things will get better," Auntie Odie said. She sat on the daybed and patted the place beside her. Mama sat down like an obedient lamb.

Auntie Odie rested her hand on the space between them and leaned toward Mama. "Just what *have* you been thinking about the sewing business?"

First the Cross—then the Crown.

"I'm not cut out for making quilts," Mama said.

"Glory be, you got to expect a struggle. It takes time to…"

Mama covered Auntie Odie's hand with her own. "Now, Odessa, I am serious about this. I been worrying and thinking a lot about it."

First the sorrow—then the joy.

Mama and Auntie Odie leaned toward each other and spoke in strong, earnest voices.

"I'll never be able to come close to making a quilt as fine as Mary Ann's."

"Now, Ingrid…"

"No, Auntie Odie!" Mama held up her free hand and waved it, like a flag of truce. "I… I don't want to do this, not really. I like being around the Nimble Needles, but… I… I don't really like sewing all that much. I only took it up because my mother was big on it, and it was a way to belong. But now I want to try something else."

"Why, of course you do!" Auntie Odie touched Mama's shoulder. "You have talent galore just waiting to be discovered."

The lowly shall be exalted.

"You honestly think so?"

"I know so."

The mourners shall be comforted.

Auntie Odie patted Mama's hand. "May I say a little prayer for you?"

What could Mama say to an offer like that? She nodded and closed her eyes.

"Dear loving Father—" Auntie Odie's viola voice glistened in my mind's eye. "Lead this dear young woman to the path for which You created her. Open her eyes to Your endless love. Thank You. In Jesus' name, amen."

Auntie Odie smiled, Mama took a hanky from her pocket and wiped her eyes, and I just sat at Auntie Odie's desk, feeling proud that I'd just read all those hard words right down to the last line of the chapter.

Through Him we are more than conquerors.

Chapter 30

Corn Estimate
Below Call for
Defense Needs
—*Greeley Daily Tribune*, p.1, Tues., July 10, 1951

★ ★ ★

Literary at Wilsons'
Place Attracts
Large Crowd
—*Akin Scoop*, p.1, Wed., July 11, 1951

Wednesday's high 56°, low 52°; steady drizzle; precipitation .28"

"What's your table made of?" Mama hollered over the roaring furnace.

The glass glowed at the end of the blowpipe. Mr. Santi rolled it on the table in glass shards. "Marble. Blowers call the table a marver."

"Does it have to be marble?"

Mr. Santi nodded. "Or steel. I prefer marble myself." He held the blowpipe back in the roaring furnace.

"Are you dipping it back into the molten glass?"

Glory be!

He nodded again. "I'm gathering more."

Out came the blowpipe again, with Mr. Santi slowly turning it. He blew and the glass swelled.

"Is it hard to blow into that hot glass?" Mama's eyes glinted with a new light.

"I'm blowing some, and forcing the air into the pipe with my tongue."

Mama took a deep breath, licked her thin lips then formed them into an *o*. In her brain, she was probably blowing into a blowpipe with a wad of molten glass on the end of it.

Auntie Odie chuckled. She'd noticed Mama's enthusiasm too. "Make somethin' wild and fancy for Ingrid, Sal! I'll buy it from you."

"You in a hurry?" he asked.

"We got all the time in the world, glassman." Auntie Odie dabbed her face with a hanky then fanned herself with her hat. She turned to Mama. "You still doing okay, honeygirl?"

Mama was sitting on a backed stool that Mr. Santi had pulled out for her. She looked peaked and fragile and comfortably warm. Since her operation, she'd had trouble keeping enough body heat, even on the hottest days. She leaned forward, her lips formed in the deepest curve of smile I'd seen in a long time. "Doing fine, Odessa, just *fine.*"

"I've been imagining a form for awhile now," Mr. Santi said. "Been sketching it and even dreaming about it."

"Make it!" Mama hopped off her stool and yelled like she was rooting for a player running for a touchdown.

Mr. Santi glared at Mama. "Risky. Haven't figured out how to do it yet." The glassblower sure was thinking hard about her suggestion.

"Well, just try it!"

Was this *my* mama? Auntie Odie and I exchanged glances. That left eyebrow of Auntie Odie's raised way up. She was happy, too, about how well the day was turning out.

"I'd need an assistant to do it right," said Mr. Santi. "It'll probably flop."

"We'll still know you're good," Mama said.

"Don't like to do flops in front of people." Mr. Santi had finished forming the hourglass-shaped vase. Now he worked to detach it from the punty.

"What do you call those long skinny pliers?" That was Mama again.

"Jacks." He worked with the jacks, scoring the bottom of the vase where the punty was attached, adding drops of water. A tap on the punty, and the vase detached and dropped onto a large, soft, fireproof mitt.

"Annealing oven," Mr. Santi said before Mama could ask, and he set the vase inside. "In the annealer, the piece cools slowly over several hours. Keeps it from shattering."

We all smiled, nodded.

"Just like us," Auntie Odie said.

Mr. Santi pulled off the mitts and laid them on the marver. "How's that, Miss Odie?"

"Just coming out of a fiery experience, God has to set us in the annealer for awhile before we can get on with life."

Mama and Mr. Santi looked at Auntie Odie with questioning looks.

She fanned with her hat. "We wonder why we're sitting in dark, prisonlike places. We think God has deserted us, lost track of us. But He knows if we go full-thrust into his will, before we're prepared, we'll shatter, come apart. We need the quiet, dark times to cool down—to grieve… pray … think… prepare—so we can face life again out in the cold world."

Mama looked puzzled.

Mr. Santi studied Auntie Odie, the brownness of his eyes escaping momentarily as he raised his dark, ample brows. "Hmmm," was all he had to say. He pulled off the bandana-band around his head, and threw it into a basket by the door. From a stack of folded bandanas, he grabbed a navy-blue, rolled it into a band, and tied it around his head.

"You going to jump off?" Mama asked him.

"Jump off? Wha...?"

"Give your idea a try?"

"You wanting to watch me crash and burn?"

"I'm wanting to watch you work, see you do the process again."

Mr. Santi folded his arms across his chest. "Seems as though you could blow somethin' yourself bein's as how I done told you just about all I know." Then he chuckled.

"It really does look easy," Mama said. "Dangerous, but easy. But I bet it's not."

"Well." He looked at me. "What do you think, Ponia Glass Snow?"

I shuffled my feet. "Yeah."

"Yeah what?"

"I wanna see you try it too," I said. "I won't laugh if it doesn't work."

"Promise?"

I nodded. "Cross my heart, hope to die, stick a needle in my eye."

"Oh, don't do that. Just don't you laugh at my whangdoodle or whatever it turns out to be."

Auntie Odie slipped her arm around me. "We might titter at the whangdoodle, Sal, but we won't laugh at you."

"I'd like a whangdoodle," and I meant it.

"I would too," Mama said.

"I already said I'd buy it for you, Ingrid," Auntie Odie said, "if the Firedrake's willing to sell."

Mama half-smiled at me. "If Poni wants it too, we'll draw straws for it."

For the next forty-five minutes the Firedrake worked to create the piece he'd imagined. What he finally created was a crystal-clear to pewter-gray glass object, partially hollow, that, from one angle, resembled a muscular male figure leaping and reaching as if he were trying to catch something in flight above him. From another angle, it looked like a woman—maybe a princess—in a long, flowing dress diving toward Earth.

Dora Santi joined us as he finished. She couldn't see anything but "just shapes." Mama couldn't see the woman. She said it was a dolphin diving back into the sea, most of its snout already in the water.

"Nice dolphin," Mama said.

"Splendiferous," Auntie Odie said.

"Beautiful princess," I said.

"Nothing like I imagined," Mr. Santi said. "I'll train an assistant then try it again."

Auntie Odie paid Mr. Santi for the piece, now in the annealer, with the agreement we'd come and fetch it in a couple of days.

Back at Auntie Odie's, we drew straws.

"The long straw gets the glass piece," Auntie Odie said.

"You keep it, Odessa," Mama said. "You done paid for it."

"I bought it for one of you. Now don't argue with your elders, dear girl."

Mama drew the long straw. She won my princess.

I wasn't sure why, but I was glad.

Chapter 31

United States, Australia, New
Zealand Sign 3-Way Defense Pact
—*Greeley Daily Tribune*, p.1, Thurs., July 12, 1951

Play, Glass Menagerie,
Tonight in Greeley at
Little Theater of the Rockies
—*Akin Scoop*, p.1, Thurs., July 12, 1951

Thursday's high 88°, low 55°; cloudy; morning damp and misty; occasional showers or drizzle throughout day and night

The Matthews drove Mama, Auntie Odie, and me to Little Theater of the Rockies at Greeley High auditorium to see the play, "Glass Menagerie." Auntie Odie and Mr. and Mrs. Matthews prattled on and on about a man named Tennessee Williams—how he was such a great playwright and how he won the Pulitzer Prize.

Once I read the program, I knew why everybody had blabbed so much about Tennessee Williams. He was the one who wrote "The Glass Menagerie."

My favorite character was Laura who had a collection of glass animals. She loved them and played with them all the time. I would've loved to have a glass menagerie of my own. Maybe Mama would learn how to make glass animals at the Firedrake's shop, and maybe she'd make me a collection. Laura was played by a young woman named Jane Ambrose, and I loved her in the part. She made Laura so real.

Amanda Wingfield, Laura's mother, was played by Lois Halladay—a wonderful actress. The audience chuckled when she shrieked for her son Tom to get up. "Rise and shine!"

Tom didn't like his mother much. I didn't either, but I felt sorry for her. She lived in the memories of her past when she was a Southern belle. Amanda Wingfield reminded me of Mama, but I wasn't sure why. Mama was no Southern belle, but a poor, Colorado farmer's daughter. Maybe it was because both were haunted by their pasts, and they were both pathetic somehow.

Sometimes the audience laughed—especially Auntie Odie. She had a way of enjoying everything in life, double. I'd never met anybody who not only found the good in tough or sad situations, but uncovered serendipitous joys in simple and ordinary events.

When the play was over, we eased up the aisle with the crowd to the lobby. Someone had opened the front doors and fresh rain-air swooped over us.

"Well, well, well! Look who's here." It was the Firedrake with his mother, Dora Santi.

Everybody shook hands. When Mr. Santi got to me, he said, "Well now, Miss Glass, how did you like the play?"

I scrunched my shoulders and smiled. "I liked it."

"And what did you like best?"

I found my voice and my courage. "Guess!"

He laughed. "Laura and her glass animals."

I grinned and nodded.

As he worked his mouth when he laughed, his beard took on a life of its own. "I knew it! I suppose you'd like a glass menagerie of your own."

My heart skipped a beat. I nodded.

He winked at Mama. "Well, we'll just have to see about that."

Chapter 32

102 Degrees
Here Sunday
—*Greeley Daily Tribune*, p.1, Mon., July 16, 1951

Heavy Rain, Hail
Damage Wheat,
Sugar Beets
—*Akin Scoop*, p.1, Mon., July 16, 1951

Monday's high 90°, low 57°; precipitation .12"; afternoon downpours; more hail

"Well, howdy-do! How's one of my favorite girls?" Denton Daleshaw kissed Aunt Bella on the forehead and clasped her hand. He greeted Mama and me, too, and offered his hand to Auntie Odie.

"And this is Odessa Luckett," Mama said.

"They say she's a fine storyteller and poet," said Aunt Bella.

"Yes, she is," said a sweet voice behind us. "I've heard you many times, Mrs. Luckett, and I'm always enthralled when you recite poetry." Mr. Daleshaw's assistant, Alice Cane, introduced herself to Auntie Odie, hugged Aunt Bella, and greeted Mama and me.

Aunt Bella eyed the empty birdcage. "Where's my Wordsie?"

"Wordsie?" croaked a voice behind us.

Aunt Bella laughed. "Wordsworth!"

"Favorite girl! Favorite girl!" said Wordsworth, and he flew from a small table in the corner of the office to Mr. Daleshaw's shoulder.

Mr. Daleshaw chuckled. "Odessa Luckett, storyteller and poet, meet Wordsworth, Assistant Director."

"Why, lookie there," Auntie Odie said to me, "a cockatiel that looks like you, only smaller and with wings!"

"Auntie Odie!" I scolded. But I didn't mind. I'd thought the same thing myself.

"He has the same hair-do as you, child," and she laughed. "Nice to meet you, Wordsworth."

"Favorite girl!" squawked Wordsworth. "Favorite girl!"

"Mr. Daleshaw," said Mrs. Cane, "How about if we play Wordsworth's favorite marching song—'Caisson Song'—on your record player?"

Hooking one thumb under his belt and stroking his chin with the other, Mr. Daleshaw appeared to be in deep thought, but a sly smile appeared beneath his mustache. "Good idea, Alice." He chuckled and she headed for the phonograph in the corner of the office.

"Over hill, over dale, we have hit the dusty trail…"

Mr. Daleshaw and Mrs. Cane sang exuberantly with the record, along with Wordsworth who squawk-whistled the tune. Aunt Bella and Auntie Odie joined in with gusto. I hummed along some (I didn't know the march) but enjoyed the show, especially Wordsworth, who was not only whistling, but also keeping time with his wild-hairdo-like-mine head.

> "…And our Caissons go rolling along.
> In and out, hear them shout: 'Counter march!' and 'Right about!'
> And the Caissons go rolling along.
> Then it's hi! hi! hee! in the field artillery,
> Shout out your numbers good and strong,
> Where e'er you go, you will always know,
> That those Caissons are rolling along…"

Leave it to a bird to transform a dreary, rainy afternoon into sunshine and fun.

Chapter 33

Rolfe Humphries, Poet And Teacher, To
Give Lecture, "The Art of Poetry," For
Fine Arts Festival This Afternoon at CSC
—*Akin Scoop*, p.1, Tues., July 24, 1951

Fair Tuesday; high 100°, low 55°; widely scattered afternoon and evening thundershowers

Auntie Odie stretched out on her sofa in front of the fan, lemonade in hand. "I hope your mama knows what she's a-doing, housecleaning this soon after her operation."

"No stairs. It's light work, like she told us." I sat in the easy chair and drank down my lemonade. "She's going to Mr. Santi's shop this afternoon to watch him blow again."

"Really? When did she tell you that?"

"While you were taking a bath this morning. Mama says the Firedrake asked her if she'd like to learn to assist him when he's blowing. He wants to experiment but needs help."

Auntie Odie sat up. "And she said yes?"

I nodded and gulped down the last of my lemonade.

Auntie Odie balanced her glass on her knee. She was thinking hard about Mama being Mr. Santi's assistant. "That day we went to watch Salvatore, your mama sure was interested in every detail about blowing glass. Yessir, this is a good development for your mama."

I slid an ice cube down the glass into my mouth and chewed. "M-hm."

Auntie Odie looked at the clock and stood up. "When's your mama due back, child? I got to get ready to go to a lecture—'The Art of Poetry.'"

"Can I go with you, please?"

"You'd be bored to death, child. Dry as a bone. It's for adults interested in poetry."

"I'm not a grown up, but I love poetry. I'll sit still and be quiet, even if I'm bored to death. Only please, just let me go with you."

Her eyes sparked, like someone lit matches in them.

She sighed. "We'll see."

I brought a pencil and my spiral and took notes. Auntie Odie was proud of that fact, I could tell by her smile. Folks sitting around us glanced at me and then smiled at Auntie Odie.

I wrote the date, July 24, 1951, and the name of the speaker, Rolfe Humphries, at the top of the page. Auntie Odie helped me spell it. Mr. Humphries was a nice older man who would've made an excellent grandpa. He taught poetry and creative writing classes at an academy in Long Island. His translations and anthologies had been published, and he'd written a book of poetry titled *The Wind of Time*. I got tired of sitting still and trying to understand everything. But I wanted to be able to talk intelligently about the lecture with Auntie Odie afterwards.

The audience laughed when Mr. Humphries said the football yell is primitive poetry and the cheerleaders provide the dance element. He described the difference between romantic and classical poetry. He said most poetry today is romantic poetry.

On the way home, I told Auntie Odie I wished I owned Rolfe Humphries' book, *The Wind of Time*. She said she had a copy.

"Will you read it to me, Auntie Odie?"

"Splendiferous idea, child! We'll read it together."

Chapter 34

Rain, Thunder,
Lightning, More Rain
—*Akin Scoop*, p.1, Thurs., July 26, 1951

Akin Polio Victims
Meet With Weld Nurses
—*Akin Scoop*, p.1, Thurs., July 26, 1951

Thursday's high 100°; scattered afternoon and evening thundershowers; brilliant lightning display

Salvatore and Dora Santi took Auntie Odie, Martha, Mama, and me to see the Little Theater of the Rockies' Pulitzer-Prize-winning play, "Harvey," at Greeley High School auditorium.

Martha and I loved Elwood P. Dowd's invisible rabbit. After that play, we pretended Harvey came to see us for visits.

We decided we'd like to be actresses someday and be in a play together—maybe at Little Theater of the Rockies. But then I decided I'd rather write plays. Martha could act and win acting awards. I'd be the playwright and win Pulitzer Prizes. I wanted to write down words on paper in such a way that people would laugh, cry, and live experiences they wouldn't have otherwise.

I went home after "Harvey" and wrote my first play—"Geneva." Geneva was an invisible mare whose owner, Garrett, created glass creatures—unicorns, half-rabbit-half-giraffes, things like that. Geneva made Garrett's glass creatures come to life, then Garrett had to find homes for them. Only the people who believed the creatures were real could adopt them—mostly children because adults had trouble believing. All the animals got good homes except one—a half-rabbit-half-giraffe—so Garrett kept it for himself. At first Geneva was jealous, but eventually they became friends.

After I finished that play, I decided to stick with stories and poems. Word choices weren't nearly as important in plays. I liked words—as much as Auntie Odie's flowers, as much as the wild birds that came to her feeders. I could plant words in my brain and let them rest there while I watered them with strong thinking and let them warm in the sunshine of new ideas. After the words sprouted, I'd pick them, and arrange them in story vases or poetry jars where they'd shine out from the paper like sunrays. The word-bouquets would be so beautiful they'd inspire and thrill folks.

Auntie Odie said Pulitzer Prizes were given for other great pieces of literature besides plays. Someday maybe I'd win a Pulitzer Prize like Tennessee Williams and Mary Coyle Chase, only mine would be for writing an exhilarating novel.

Or a book of poems as lovely as Emily Dickinson's, as fine as Langton Hughes', or as beautiful as Agatha Jordan's.

…Keep dreaming, dear one…

Chapter 35

Some 40 Bushel
Wheat at Nunn
—*Greeley Daily Tribune*, p.1, Fri., July 27, 1951

Raisins And Other Fruits,
Suet, Bread Attract Northern
Mockingbirds to Gardens
—*Akin Scoop*, p.2, Fri., July 27, 1951

Generally fair; isolated afternoon thundershowers; high 96°, low 64°; precipitation .08"

"Poni child, I've got to get those blowballs out of the grass today. Will you help?"
"I'd be right jollified to, Auntie Odie. For pay."
"What do ya charge?"
"Cherry Mash, Grapette, and a storiette."
"Whizbang! It's a deal!"

Chapter 36

Korean Casualty's
Funeral in Windsor
—*Greeley Daily Tribune*, p.1, Sat., July 28, 1951

Famous Choir
Here Aug. 8
At Gymnasium
"…world renowned Negro choir…"
—*Greeley Daily Tribune*, p.8, Sat., July 28, 1951

Saturday's high 97°, low 64°; generally fair, isolated thunderstorms

The tiny, share-one-bathroom-with-a-dozen-people, glassblower-furnace-hot apartment would be no fun to go back to after living in Auntie Odie's pleasant cottage for a few weeks. But I was determined to make the best of it, be cheerful, and not complain.

I'd promised Auntie Odie.

After Mama and I climbed into the truck and Mama started it up, Auntie Odie settled her hand on the sill of Mama's open window. "Poni dearest, you're welcome in my garden, my heart, and my home, morning, noon, or night—always. I *love* your company." She stretched out *love* like a long satin ribbon. "And, Ingrid dear, you too. You're *always* welcome here."

Mama nodded. I smiled, too choked to speak.

"You girls come see me. Hear?"

All at once a gust whipped up, the heavens opened, and rain pummeled down. Mama threw open the pickup door, scooted to the middle, and Auntie Odie hopped in. We rolled up the windows and waited, chatting and giggling as the windows steamed up. Then marble-sized hail beat like rhythmless drummers on cars and roofs, and our pickup.

"Your poor flowers," Mama said.

Trees, shrubs and flowers whipped crazily in the wind and quailed under pelting hail. Auntie Odie shook her head. "*Tch, tch.*" It finally let up and she sighed. "I best be getting into the house while it's just a sprinkle."

Mama's crescent sliver of a smile appeared. "Thank you—for everything."

"My pleasure." She took Mama's hand in hers, reached across Mama's lap, and took my hand too. She closed her eyes and smiled. "Heavenly Father, please go with these two dear children. When life's storms blow, keep them sheltered beneath Your wings. Please open their eyes—and their hearts—to Eternity. Amen."

Chapter 37

Gardeners, Farmers
in Weld Vicinities
Undergo Hail Damage
—*Akin Scoop*, p.1, Sun., July 29, 1951

Literary Tomorrow
at Judson Place;
Come One, Come All
—*Akin Scoop*, p.1, Sun., July 29, 1951

Sunday's high 102°, low 62°, partly cloudy; scattered showers

I stared out of the spotty window of our apartment, past the trees and the Victorian house across the street, over the roofs of the neighborhood, to the Sunday morning sky.

"'Please open their eyes—and their hearts—to Eternity.'" I squinted, and then opened my eyes wide. Where was Eternity?

Blushed-apricot cords of cloud swung upward from the northern sky, curved overhead, and widened into blazing furrows to the south. The eastern horizon—glowing peachblow—washed up to lavender then to watery blue.

Eternity could wait. Auntie Odie needed help in her garden before church—and before it got hot.

★ ★ ★

I found Auntie Odie at the back fence dressed in overalls and white shirt, a red handkerchief tied around her head, and a large straw hat with red flowers. She fervidly pruned back morning-glory vines and talked away—to no one that I could see.

I took my time along the garden path, enjoying the rollicking birds, the colors and scents of flowers, and the delicious shade cast by the maple and locust and weeping willow trees.

As I neared, I heard her words. "'For thou art my lamp, O Lord: and the Lord will lighten my darkness.' Yes, Lord, please lighten my darkness. Lighten this darkness, please, Lord."

"Auntie Odie?"

She whirled toward me. Poised there, her pruning shears glinting in the morning sun, she looked like a fierce black warrior maid, weapon in hand. "Glory be, child! You sure snuck up on me like a li'l ol' mouse on a piece of cheese." Then she laughed and held out her arms to me. "Good morning! You look like sunshine herself in that yellow shirt."

We hugged, and then I looked into her face. "Don't you like your color anymore, Auntie Odie?"

Her eyes widened, eyebrows raised. "What are you talking about, child?"

"I heard you praying."

She nodded. "And…?"

"Why were you asking the Lord to lighten your darkness? Don't you like your color anymore?"

Her eyebrows flew down, forehead smoothed out, and a hearty laugh burst from her. She bent over and slapped her knee. "Well, glory be! The Lord has done answered my prayer, yes, indeed." She raised her hands toward heaven and shouted, "Thank You, Lord!"

"You're still the same color," I informed her.

She hugged me close and explained that she was quoting a Scripture as a prayer, asking the Lord to ease the darkness of her sorrow. "It's figurative."

"Oh."

"And He done answered my prayer, child." She squeezed me so tight, and it hurt so good. "He sent you over to lighten my darkness for awhile."

"You're sad, Auntie Odie?"

"Oh, Poni." She placed her hand across her forehead, thumb on one temple, fingertips on the other. "Losing Nate has hurt so much. Sometimes, when I think of that wonderful young man never coming home, I can barely breathe. My sadness isn't only for me, but for Fritz and Olivia and Martha."

I loved it when Auntie Odie shared her thoughts and sorrows with me like I was a grown-up.

"And I see Olivia slipping away from us too." She wiped away a tear with her thumb. "And sometimes I still grieve over my child that died, and the other children I never had." Then she looked straight into my eyes. "And that's not all. I can't begin to tell you how much I've been missing you, dear heart, and your mama." She gripped my shoulders and looked down at me. "But you, dear child, have helped me put my sorrow aside for awhile. You made me laugh."

We giggled and hugged, and I recited the first twenty-two lines I'd memorized from "Hiawatha." After she declared me the brightest child on Earth, we cleared her garden of hail damage.

Chapter 38

102 Degrees
Here Sunday
—*Greeley Daily Tribune*, p.1, Mon., July 30, 1951

No Progress in
Kaesong Talks;
War To Go On
—*Greeley Daily Tribune*, p.1, Mon., July 30, 1951

Partly cloudy Monday; widely scattered showers and thunderstorms; high 92°, low 62°; precipitation .10"

"Now, child, I'm going to a literary coterie today. Want to tag along?"
"What kind of literary?"
"Home-grown stories mostly—some poesy."
"You in it?"
"Storyteller."
"Bejabbers, Auntie Odie! 'Course I do."
"You wait here by the fan while I change."

★ ★ ★

"Lollapalooza, Auntie Odie! That's rakish toggery if I ever saw it."
"Thank you, child."
"Razzle-dazzle hat, too, Auntie Odie."
She bowed—caught it before it fell off. "Do ya like my raggle-taggle earbobs?"
"They're laughful—splendiferous."
"Reckon I ought to dress down a little, child?"
"Flapdoodle!"
"Then let's skedaddle."

Chapter 39

Cease-Fire Line
Argued 5th Day
With No Result
—*Greeley Daily Tribune*, p.1, Tues., July 31, 1951

Record Growth Corn
Crops in Akin Vicinity
—*Akin Scoop*, p.1, Tues., July 31, 1951

Tuesday's high upper 90s, low mid 60s; fair; scattered afternoon and evening showers

My audience sat in Auntie Odie's front room. Air from the fan ruffled Martha's dark bangs, the plume on Auntie Odie's Robin-Hood-green hat, and the frilly neckline of Mrs. Fall's flowered dress. They sat primly, while I "gathered" myself like Auntie Odie always did when she was about to recite. Emily yawned and snuggled between Auntie Odie and Martha.

I took a deep breath and launched into the poem I'd come to love for its rhythm and imagery. Eyelids closed, I imagined myself there, let the words flow from my mouth like water from a spring, like water singing on the shores of Hiawatha's Big-Sea-Water:

> "By the shores of Gitche Gumee,
> By the shining Big-Sea-Water,
> Stood the wigwam of Nokomis,
> Daughter of the Moon, Nokomis.
> Dark behind it rose the forest,
> Rose the black and gloomy pine-trees,
> Rose the firs with cones upon them;
> Bright before it beat the water,
> Beat the clear and sunny water,
> Beat the shining Big-Sea-Water.
>   "There the wrinkled, old Nokomis
> Nursed the little Hiawatha,

Rocked him in his linden cradle,
Bedded soft in moss and rushes,
Safely bound with reindeer sinews;
Stilled his fretful wail by saying,
'Hush! The Naked Bear will hear thee!'
Lulled him into slumber, singing,
'Ewa-yea! my little owlet!
Who is this, that lights the wigwam?
With his great eyes lights the wigwam?
Ewa-yea! my little owlet!'
    "Many things Nokomis taught him
Of the stars that shine in heaven;
Showed him Ishkoodah, the comet,
Ishkoodah, with fiery tresses;
Showed the Death-Dance of the spirits,
Warriors with their plumes and war-clubs,
Flaring far away to northward
In the frosty nights of Winter;
Showed the broad, white road in heaven,
Pathway of the ghosts, the shadows,
Running straight across the heavens,
Crowded with the ghosts, the shadows...."

I paused and licked my lips. *Perfect so far.* Like the Firedrake gathering molten glass on his blowpipe, I gathered the words, hot and glowing and pliable, on the blowpipe of my mind. I breathed deep, and forced the molten words into the beautiful, translucent images Henry Wadsworth Longfellow created a hundred years before my birth.

    "At the door on summer evenings
Sat the little Hiawatha;
Heard the whispering of the pine-trees,
Heard the lapping of the waters,
Sounds of music, words of wonder;
'Minne-wawa!' said the pine-trees,
'Mudway-aushka!' said the water.
    "Saw the fire-fly, Wah-wah-taysee,
Flitting through the dusk of evening,
With the twinkle of its candle
Lighting up the brakes and bushes,

And he sang the song of children,
Sang the song Nokomis taught him:
'Wah-wah-taysee, little fire-fly,
Little, flitting, white-fire insect,
Little, dancing, white-fire creature,
Light me with your little candle,
Ere upon my bed I lay me,
Ere in sleep I close my eyelids!'
    "Saw the moon rise from the water,
Rippling, rounding from the water,
Saw the flecks and shadows on it,
Whispered, 'What is that, Nokomis?'
And the good Nokomis answered:

The fan blew over me. I trembled. This last part was not as familiar. Martha smirked, trying not to giggle, Mrs. Fall fanned herself with a folded *Akin Scoop*, and Auntie Odie, that whitewashed-fence grin on her face, fanned with her hat. Emily snoozed, resembling a basketball.

"You're doing beautifully, child," said Auntie Odie. "Keep it up."

I looked at the ceiling.

"'Once a warrior, very angry,
Seized his grandmother, and threw her
Up into the sky at midnight;
Right against the moon he threw her;
'T is her body that you see there.'
    "Saw the rainbow in the heaven,
In the eastern sky, the rainbow,
Whispered, 'What is that, Nokomis?'
And the good Nokomis answered:
''T is the heaven of flowers you see there;
All the wild flowers of the forest,
All the lilies of the prairie,
When on earth they fade and perish,
Blossom in that heaven above us.'

"Then… no, When…Then…"

My audience waited.

"Oh, yeah…

"When he heard the owls at midnight,
Hooting, laughing in the forest,
'What is that?' he cried in terror;
'What is that?' he said, 'Nokomis?'
And the good Nokomis answered:
'That is but the owl and owlet,
Talking in their native language,
Talking, scolding at each other.'

"When… Then…" Next, Hiawatha would learn the animals' names. I faltered and then stammered on, confusing parts, turning phrases around. I finally stopped. "That's all I remember," I said, and bowed.

My listeners clapped and smiled.

"You did well, child!" said Auntie Odie. "I'm amazed at how smoothly and beautifully you recited that, up until the last stanzas. Just some polishing in the last section and it'll be perfect."

"That's swell," said Martha. "I could never memorize that much. That's why I enter the reading division at the Silver Tongues Harvest."

I sighed. "No bike yet."

Auntie Odie stood up and hugged me. "I'm proud of you, child. You've achieved far beyond what I expected in these five weeks since we signed the agreement."

"My brain just gets muddled up."

"I couldn't memorize that much," Martha repeated.

I looked into my friend's brown eyes. "Yes, you could if you didn't have a bike and wanted one real bad."

"You'll get there," Auntie Odie reassured. "Besides, the bike isn't the only reason you're doing this. It's for the love of words. I see it in your eyes and hear it in your voice."

"Really?" I said.

"Let's see, this is July thirty-first." Auntie Odie looked at invisible numbers on the ceiling. "You'll have the rest smoothed out beautifully within two weeks. Before school starts."

Mrs. Fall joined the circle around me. "You'll be better at reciting poetry than Odie before you know it." Then she twittered.

"I don't want to be better than Auntie Odie," I said. "I just want to be as good in my style as she is in hers."

Auntie Odie laughed from that deep place. "Oh, child, you will be! I know it from the bottom of my soul—you will be."

And I believed her.

Chapter 40

Flowers from
American Bomber
Dropped on Ruins of Hiroshima
—*Greeley Daily Tribune*, p.5, Sun., Aug. 5, 1951

★ ★ ★

Junior Fair Champions
Happy Over Awards
—*Akin Scoop*, p.1, Tues., Aug. 7, 1951

Tuesday's high 90°, low 52°; partly cloudy; thundershowers in a.m.; precipitation .24"

Auntie Odie was right—except I did it in one week instead of two. After two more tries, I recited the ten verses—ninety-five lines—from "Hiawatha's Childhood" by Henry Wadsworth Longfellow, for an audience of seven—Auntie Odie, Mr. and Mrs. Matthews and Martha, Mrs. Fall, Mama, and a purring Emily.

★ ★ ★

"Let's skedaddle!" Auntie Odie said.

She drove me to Everybody's Store in Greeley. I loved the way the floors creaked and the way it smelled too—a blend of rubber, wood, and new.

"Oh-h-h, I took too long to get 'Hiawatha' right," I said. "It's not here—not the pale-green and lavender one." My throat tightened with disappointment.

Auntie Odie chuckled. I was surprised at her, laughing at me when my heart was so sick.

"Well, I've been expecting you." It was *Bart McFee- May I Help You?* according to his name tag. He was small and thin and had kind eyes. "I see you finally made it back with your young friend, Mrs. Luckett." He grinned at me. "I reckon you're here because someone earned a bike. Right?"

"You've got it right, Mr. McFee," Auntie Odie declared.

Then Bart whistled as he headed for the back room.

That Auntie Odie. She'd gone in to Everybody's Store clear back in June after we signed the Dream Agreement and put my pale-green and lavender bike in layaway.

Glory be! Now that's faith and hope.

And love.

★ ★ ★

Mama stayed busy—cleaning houses, mending clothes for Smith Dry Cleaning, attending the Nimble Needles meetings, quilting, and learning to be the Firedrake's assistant.

Auntie Odie liked when Mama worked because that meant I spent time with her. We worked in her garden early mornings and evenings—when it wasn't raining. I helped her do dishes and laundry, added new words to my wordbook, and learned to identify six new birds of northeastern Colorado and their calls—nuthatch, goldfinch, northern flicker, red-tailed hawk, red-winged blackbird, and northern harrier. We helped each other memorize more poems. I committed to memory long ones, like "Paul Revere's Ride" by Henry Wadsworth Longfellow, and short ones, like "Splinter" by Carl Sandburg.

Once I got started learning poems by heart, I couldn't quit, didn't want to. Auntie Odie said I memorized things even faster than she did when she was young. She told me, if I kept up like that, I'd be a world-class storyteller and poetry performer.

"'Hope is the thing with feathers,'" I said.

"'Keep dreaming,' child."

"I do, Auntie Odie."

We read books together—*Uncle Tom's Cabin*, *Old-Fashioned Girl*, and *Pinocchio* (only half of *Pinocchio* because it was an awful story), we watched Mama assist Mr. Santi in glassblowing, and we went places—Boy! Did we go places. Sometimes Martha went with Auntie Odie and me, sometimes we went with the Matthews or Mrs. Angela Fall. When Mama could, she came with us, but mostly it was just Auntie Odie and me. That's when I liked it most.

And, of course, I went bike riding with Martha and Sarah and I rode my new pale-green and lavender Schwinn. Our favorite bike ride was out to the edge of town to an old deserted farmhouse—windows knocked out, door swaying on one hinge, narrow creaky stairs, cobwebs, years of dust and sand. I made up a scary story about the "haunted" house and why the people left. Martha and Sarah finally told me to stop. They shivered down to their toes even though it was as hot as the Firedrake's glory-hole in that old house.

Chapter 41

Parents Urged
To Be Calm in
Polio Season
—*Greeley Daily Tribune*, p.15, Thurs., Aug. 9, 1951

Weld County Fair
Final Performances
Tonight
—*Akin Scoop*, p.2, Thurs., Aug. 9, 1951

Thursday's high 90°, low 55°; partly cloudy; widely scattered afternoon and evening showers

The Matthews, Auntie Odie, the Fenderlupens, Mama, and I rode in Mama's pickup truck to the final evening performance of the Weld County fair in Greeley. Mr. Fenderlupen and Mrs. Matthews rode in the cab with Mr. Matthews who drove, and the rest of us bumped along in the back of the truck. Auntie Odie and I recited poetry—"By the shores of Gitche Gumee..."—but, mostly, everybody sang and laughed a lot.

Once we got to Island Grove Park in Greeley, we headed for the stands.

"Well, look who's here!" a man shouted.

It was Mr. Myers, our former neighbor on the farm, with Mrs. Myers, Maizy and Marvin, and Mr. and Mrs. Hill and their boys. What a greeting we got—hugs and handshakes and laughter. Mama and I introduced everybody. Mr. Matthews knew the Hills and the Myers some as customers in his drug store. We found enough places in the stands to sit together.

Mr. Matthews figured three thousand or more people were there. Sitting with my friends, old and new, that night was better than a year's supply of Cherry Mash. The parade at the beginning was the best part for me—all those exhibitors with their livestock—and for Auntie Odie, too, the parade-lover. Then came the 4-H executive council, leaders, and club members. Champion showmen were chosen from several categories—beef, dairy, horses, and swine.

Ha! Swine! They'll always be pigs to me.

During the showmanship finals, each contestant had to show his or her own animal, as well as an animal from each of the other departments. The grand champion steer, an Angus, was chosen

188

and shown by "Miss Dorothy Harden from Nunn, Colorado," according to the loud speaker. Her sister Ruth had the reserve champion Angus steer.

I imagined myself raising animals, belonging to 4-H, and entering the county fair. I missed Maybelle and the chickens and our cows Polly and Pie. I missed having farm animals, but I decided that, more than anything else, I wanted to be a "wordsmith," as Auntie Odie put it. Like her, I wanted to be a storyteller, a reader, a writer, and a reciter of poetry—"a literary" who'd perform at literaries. And someday I'd have a flower garden, too, with feeders to attract birds of all kinds. Like Auntie Odie's.

Keep dreaming, dear one.

Chapter 42

Reds Drive
U. N. Forces
From Hill
—*Greeley Daily Tribune*, p.1, Wed., Aug., 15, 1951

★ ★ ★

Polio Outbreak
Might Surpass
'46 Epidemic
—*Greeley Daily Tribune*, p.1, Thurs., Aug., 16, 1951

Generally fair Thursday; high 98°, low 52°

"Child, I got to get some cream at the drugstore. Want to come?"

"Cream? For your coffee? At the drugstore?"

"Face cream—Pond's. I got to slather it on my poor ol' parched face before it effloresces."

"Faces don't bloom, Auntie Odie."

"Aren't you a snollygoster! Read *all* the definitions when you look up a word, child."

"Glory be!"

"Auntie Odie."

"Yes, child."

"Is your face 'changing from crystalline to a powdery state through loss of water,' or is it 'developing a powdery crust because of evaporation?'"

"A little of both. Now you comin' or not?"

"Am I titivated enough, Auntie Odie?"

"You're plenty dandified for a drugstore."

"I'm done lollygagging then. Let's skedaddle!"

Chapter 43

Seven-Block
Parade Feature
Of Pickle Day
—*Greeley Daily Tribune*, p.1, Sat., Aug. 18, 1951

Many Akinites
Head for Platteville
For Pickle Day
—*Akin Scoop*, p.1, Sat., Aug. 18, 1951

Generally fair Saturday; high 98°, low 51°; few isolated afternoon thunderstorms

"I'm late! I'm late, for a very important date…."

We sang that crazy rabbit's song from "Alice in Wonderland," as Auntie Odie drove Martha and me in her Buick the twenty miles to Platteville for Pickle Day. We talked about all the things that happened to Alice in the Walt Disney animated movie, which we had seen—and Mama too—at the Chief in Greeley the night before.

Platteville Pickle Day started off with a parade. The float that won first place and got the fifty-dollar prize toted a big sign, "Platteville's Cream of the Crop." A life-sized cardboard cow—white with black spots just like Pie—stood on top eyeing a monstrous bottle of milk. Pickles, sugar beets, red beets, potatoes, cabbage, and grain crops were displayed on a platform around the cow and bottle of milk.

After the parade we toured the displays. A woman in a bright-pink housedress sold decorated straw hats of all sizes and styles.

Auntie Odie's eyes lit up. "Pick, girls! I'll buy."

Geranium-pink flowers vined around the sweeping brim of my hat choice. Martha's was a dyed-red straw with bright-yellow pears imprinted on the broad flat brim. Auntie Odie switched from the big white hat she was wearing, to her newly purchased affair—yellow straw with a crown made to look like a bird's nest. A small, lifelike robin perched in the nest, mouth open as if chirping.

Its wide-eyed mate "flew" above the nest, bobbing and doing loop-de-loops on its wire support. I figured Auntie Odie just bought it for laughs. We giggled till our sides hurt.

Sporting our new hats, we visited other displays and ate pickle samples—sweet, dill, Kosher-style, lemon pickles, bread-and-butter—all kinds. Auntie Odie bought pickles, potatoes, and ears of corn. The winner of the Weird Beard Contest received a twenty-five-dollar war bond and a free shave at the local barbershop. The sun shone hot and shade was scarce, so after lunch—hotdogs and Pepsi Cola—we headed back to Akin. When we'd ridden to Platteville, Martha got to sit by Auntie Odie, so I sat by her on the way back home. Auntie Odie and I recited Mr. Longfellow's "Hiawatha's Childhood" in unison.

Back at Auntie Odie's cottage, still wearing our hats, we sat in her breakfast nook and devoured huge scoops of Cloverleaf Dairy Fresh Peach Ice Cream. The bird on Auntie Odie's hat jiggled in the fan's breeze and fresh giggles assailed us. We croaked out the *Alice in Wonderland* song, "All in a Golden Afternoon," and named ourselves the Birds-of-a-Feather Trio.

Martha grinned and stretched. "I wonder how we came to be such good friends."

"Emerson said, 'The only way to have a friend is to be one,'" Auntie Odie said. "I suppose we're good friends because we each know how to be one. And that's why we can safely be Jesus' friend—He's the best friend anyone could ever have."

She gazed at Martha then at me with a soft light in her eyes.

"I bet you're thinking of a poem about that," I forecasted.

She thought for a moment, smiling, and then began, "'Proven Friendship' by Mildred Edgington...

"For many years I groped around, lost in the darkness of sin.
There was no hope in my heart, no joy or peace within.
Long did I wander here and there, no thought of God all day.
I thought it silly to read God's Word, I thought it worse to pray.

"Yet Jesus looked upon me, His heart full of pity and love,
And He offered to give me shelter and a home with Him above.
When I was heartsick and troubled, He came to comfort me.
When I was bound in sin, He offered to set me free.

"When I was lost and lonely, He led me to the fold.
When storms around me gathered, He sheltered me from the cold.
When I was alone and friendless, He took me in His arms
And offered me His friendship true and kept me from all harm..."

Auntie Odie paused. She swallowed and tears gathered in her eyes. Martha and I waited and looked at her with love in our eyes—I just know we did. At last she continued...

"Now if you should find this Friend so true, I'm sure that you would be
Just as happy as I am since He has set me free.
So come, ye, one and all. He offers this to you—
A loving heart and comfort and a friendship sweet and true."

I ran and got a hanky from the writing nook and brought it to Auntie Odie because she needed one. She thanked me then we hugged her—Martha and me, one on each side of her, in the breakfast nook. Auntie Odie's hat fell off in the process which got us all laughing again.

"Anyway, your tears don't go with your silly hat, Auntie Odie," Martha said.

Auntie Odie plopped her hat back on and shook her head to make the bird on the hat loop-de-loop every which way.

After all three of us enjoyed another good giggle session, I reached for *In Praise of Wings: A Flock of Poems by Agatha Jordan* on the sill in the breakfast nook and handed it to Auntie Odie. "Where's that poem you read the other day about our friendship being sealed by God, Auntie Odie?"

"It's on page five... Here it is," she said. "It's called 'God Made Us Friends.' Read it aloud with me, girls...

"God made us friends, I know for real.
He meshed our hearts, pressed on His seal.
We cry, we play, we laugh, we sing.
Our friendship song is a beautiful thing."

"'...Our friendship song is a beautiful thing,'" I repeated. "I like that."

"Me too," said Martha.

"Me three," said Auntie Odie.

Then the Birds-of-a-Feather Trio twanged and spangled their zingiest rendition ever of "All in a Golden Afternoon."

Chapter 44

Area Churches
Congregate to
Pray for Troops
—*Akin Scoop*, p.1, Mon., Aug. 27, 1951

★ ★ ★

19 More Polio
Cases in Colo.
—*Greeley Daily Tribune*, p.7, Tues., Aug. 28, 1951

Partly cloudy Tuesday; high 87°, low 53°

"There you are, you supine child! Out here in the grass relishing the cloud pageant?"
"Mm–hm."
"Lovely, isn't it, child?"
"Splendiferous, Auntie Odie! Want to be supine with me?"
"You up to some jiggery-pokery?"
"Nope. Just joy."
"Hold my hat. I'm comin' down."

Chapter 45

Thundershowers Continue
Area Crops Flourish
—*Akin Scoop,* p.1, Fri., Aug. 31, 1951

Half-Armistice in Korea Has
Been Life-Saver for Thousands of
War-Weary American Veterans
—*Greeley Daily Tribune,* p.4, Fri., Aug. 31, 1951

Partly cloudy Friday; scattered afternoon and evening thundershowers; high 82°, low 51°

"Know any riddles, Auntie Odie?"

She laughed. "Oh, a few."

"Try one on me."

"How about riddles with book-of-the-Bible answers?"

"I don't know any of the books," I said, "except Genesis. And Matthew, Mark, Luke and John. But I'll try."

"What did George Washington use to chop down the cherry tree?"

"Hm-m-m. An ax—Acts!"

"Glory be, child! I thought you only knew Genesis and the gospels."

"I forgot about Acts."

"Here's another. What book could you read to brush up on your arithmetic?"

"M-m-m. I give up."

"Numbers."

"That's a real book?"

"Yes, child. Why couldn't the coffee shop owner stop to answer the phone?"

"I give up."

"Hebrews."

"Huh?"

"He brews. Get it?"

We giggled.

"Another one, Auntie Odie."

"This one's hard," she warned. "What two sounds do horses make?"

"Hm-m-m."

"It's…"

"Don't tell me! Let me think."

"Give up?"

"Okay, Auntie Odie, tell me what two sounds horses make."

"Nahum."

"Nahum! Never heard of it. Doesn't make sense."

"Neigh-hum. All horses neigh and the talented ones hum."

"Oh, bejabbers!" I said, and we both had a good laugh. "Another one."

"You tell me one now, child."

"Don't know any. Tell me a real one."

"'Thirty white horses upon a red hill, Now they tramp, now they champ, Now they stand still.' What are they?"

"Teeth and gums!"

"That was quick."

"I forgot—Martha told me it. It's a Mother Goose, huh?"

"Yes, child."

"I cotton to you, Auntie Odie."

She closed her eyes, her eyebrows pushed up a tent-line in the middle of her forehead. "Oh, child, I cotton to you too."

Chapter 46

Thousands of Utah
Children Inoculated
Against Polio Virus
—*Greeley Daily Tribune*, p.7, Sat., Sept. 1, 1951

★ ★ ★

Akin School Students,
Teachers Begin First Day
of 1951–52 School Year
—*Akin Scoop*, p.1, Tues., Sept. 4, 1951

Cloudy Tuesday; scattered showers and drizzle; electrical storm, rain, and hail in evening; fields wet with standing rain; bean growers concerned about damp weather

Miss Maddsen gave Martha and me a brief smile as we handed her our bouquets from Auntie Odie's garden.

I sat next to Martha, but Miss Maddsen made me move. "In fifth grade," she said, "we sit in alphabetical order by last names."

Even in her spike heels, our teacher was only an inch taller than Pascal Buchholz who stood about five feet. The boys grinned and whispered about her prettiness—curvaceous petite figure, black curly hair and eyelashes, azure-blue eyes—but she ruled the classroom with all the authority of Napoleon.

★ ★ ★

I wouldn't have minded missing afternoon recess—it was off-and-on drizzle—but my teacher believed I was deliberately naughty during contractions review.

Miss Maddsen said, "she is," and chose Hettie Zimmerman to write the contraction on the blackboard.

She's, Hettie wrote.

"Are not," said Miss Maddsen.

Thor Blackburn wrote *aren't.*

"We are."

Imogene Schott wrote *we'r*, then changed it to *we're*.

Martha got to write *should've* for "should have." Laurence Dunkling meticulously printed *they'd* for "they had."

Contractions were confusing to me, so I fidgeted and worried until my turn.

Miss Maddsen handed me the chalk. "He will."

And I would've done just fine if only I'd remembered the apostrophe.

Chapter 47

Torrential Rain
And Hail Hits
Northern Weld
—*Greeley Daily Tribune*, p.1, Fri., Sept. 7, 1951

★ ★ ★

Storm Damages
Roads, Bridges
in Weld County
—*Akin Scoop*, p.1, Sat., Sept. 8, 1951

Saturday's high 93°, low 51°; generally fair; some roads still closed

I arrived at Auntie Odie's cottage Saturday morning just as the sun rose over the plains.

"You're here bright and cool," she said. She retied the bow of her scarf under her chin. "What a welcome sight you are, child."

Yank! Yank! Auntie Odie and I wrenched out the weeds that had flagrantly grown up in her gardens during recent rains. Next, we removed old foliage from the perennials and the dead leaves and decaying matter around them.

By ten o'clock it warmed, and we had good crops of sweat on our foreheads.

I was behind the garage loading up the wheelbarrow with straw when I heard Auntie Odie call. "Look here, child! A turtle."

Sure enough, a turtle sunned on a rock by the pond. After a few minutes of observing the little fella, Auntie Odie recited a poem by Vachel Lindsay about a little turtle.

"I want to learn that one," I said.

So while we spread straw around the perennials and filled boxes in the garage with sand, she helped me memorize "The Little Turtle." We took a break and practiced while we filled glasses with ice and water. We gulped down our water and continued going over the lines about the little turtle snapping at insects and minnows around him—but not at us, the quoters of the poem. Before long our little turtle-on-a-rock disappeared. Guess he was shy about having a poem recited about him.

"Let's dig up the canna now," said Auntie Odie.

I pointed to the crimson and baby orange lilylike flowers clinging to tall reedy stalks. "But, Auntie Odie, look. There's still some blooms."

"Got to get them out of the ground. Nights are getting colder. A freeze could come anytime."

So we dug them up and buried the rhizomes in the boxes of sand in the garage.

"Leave the sunflowers alone," Auntie Odie instructed, "and the black-eyed Susans and coneflowers. I know they look scraggly, but the fall and winter birds love them."

We gathered seeds from dried hollyhock and marigold blooms. Auntie Odie's face possessed that smooth delighted look in spite of her weariness. "We'll plant them next year." We gathered the remaining mint and chive from her herb garden, and some basil and parsley. "We'll dry some and have a good supply for the winter."

"I know you use the mint for your iced tea and lemonade," I said, "but what's parsley good for, and basil and chives?"

She wiped her moist forehead with the back of her gloved hand. "I consider a sprig of mint in my tossed salad a special treat, and I serve my Silvery Tea Cake Triangles with sprigs of mint when I've got it. Adds color."

"But what about the other herbs?"

"Oh!" She chuckled. "They go into lots of dishes, but especially— let's see, basil for ham and shirred eggs and for chicken gumbo, chives for my jambalaya and meatloaf, corn omelet, and my boiled fish, ah, and kidney stew. Parsley's good on or in about anything—but it's a sin to bake hominy-and-bacon casserole without it. And egg pilau would be insipid without parsley, basil, and chives for seasoning—takes all three as far as I'm concerned."

Mama came by and found us still working in the garden. "Here you are!" She sure sounded cheerful.

Auntie Odie greeted Mama warmly and we trudged inside to rest and cool off.

Mama held up two brown sacks. "I brought lunch."

"Really, Mama?"

"Really. Bar-B-Q sandwiches from Vic's. I cleaned a house in Greeley this morning. Thought Vic's would be a nice little treat for us." Mama took three plates out of Auntie Odie's cupboard and arranged a sandwich and potato chips on each. Out of the second bag she removed three large papercups. "And malts."

"Malts!" Auntie Odie guzzled the last of the water from her glass and looked over Mama's shoulder.

"I hope you like malts, Odessa."

"I rarely have 'em. Sounds good." She plunked a potato chip into her mouth. "I'll get my pocketbook."

"No!" Mama grasped Auntie Odie's arm. "No, Odessa. You do a lot for me." She glanced my way. "For us." She set the plates and malts on the breakfast-nook table. "Anyway, it wasn't much. Fifteen cents a sandwich is all. I been getting quite a bit of work."

At the table Auntie Odie took hold of Mama's and my hands and gazed upward. "Thank you, Lord, for able, work-hard bodies, the fragrance of sunshine on flowers, the love of treasured friends, and good eats. Amen."

★ ★ ★

Auntie Odie invited Mama to go with her and me to the one-fifteen matinee—*Uncle Tom's Cabin*—at Park Theater in Greeley, but Mama had promised the Firedrake she'd assist him with his glassblowing in the afternoon.

Mama was happy to let me spend the rest of the day with Auntie Odie.

"You deserve a reward," Auntie Odie told me, "for surviving your first week of school and helping me all morning in the garden."

On the way to the theater Auntie Odie taught me the first four verses of "The Highwayman."

> "The wind was a torrent of darkness among the gusty trees.
> The moon was a ghostly galleon tossed upon the cloudy seas.
> The road was a ribbon of moonlight over the purple moor,
> And the highwayman came riding—
>> Riding—riding—
> The highwayman came riding, up to the old inn-door…"

The matinee started with Lum and Abner in *The Bashful Bachelor,* then the main feature, *Uncle Tom's Cabin*. On the drive back to Akin, I vented my curiosity and concern about slavery.

"I just don't understand why slavery was allowed," I said. "All during our first week of school we've been learning about our country. Miss Maddsen said our government proclaims that everyone is created equal and everyone has unailable rights."

"Inalienable," Auntie Odie corrected.

"Yeah. Nobody can take anybody's rights away."

Auntie Odie smiled. "Right."

"Then how did slavery get started in America? Why did people steal the colored people's rights?"

"Some thought Negroes were like animals, to be owned and worked—for profit."

We slowed, then pulled around a farmer on his John Deere tractor.

Auntie Odie continued, "Without God in us, empowering us to empty our hearts and lives of greed and self-centeredness, we humans can be fooled into believing that the most base evil—even slavery—is a good thing."

"But why did God *let* people kidnap folks from their homeland and make them slaves? Maybe God's heart is no better than people's hearts."

Auntie Odie pressed her mouth into a knot and squinted. Was she crying?

"You know what, Auntie Odie?"

"What?" she said softly.

"Sometimes I wonder if there is a God. How can anybody know for sure?"

She laughed—a deep, long laugh from her belly. "Glory be, child! That's like standing in a well-lit room at night saying, 'I wonder if there is such a thing as a light bulb.' Or sillier yet, saying, 'I wonder if there really is such a thing as electricity.'"

"Huh?"

"Look around you, child! Why, there's evidence of God everywhere. A watermelon-red sunset over the mountains and a flame-colored leaf shimmering in the sun aren't any less beautiful or any less real because you take them for granted. Miracles become 'ordinary' to us because they are part of every day—sunrises, sunsets, the stars and moon, rain in spring, snow in winter, dew on the grass, a butterfly on a bloom, a rock, a grain of sand, a gnat, senses of sight, smell, and sound. We forget that each and every thing around us is nothing short of a miracle—evidence that God exists. The fact that you see all of Earth's beauty through the mini-universe of your eye is miracle enough—reality enough—to know there's a Designer, a Creator." She turned the Buick onto Sixth Avenue and headed into Akin.

I couldn't think what to say.

"Try this sometime, child: Ask somebody—anybody—how they know that a person designed this Buick, manufactured the parts, and built it. Ask them, 'How do you know a Buick-creator really exists?'"

I giggled. "They'd think I'm dumb. They'd say..." I lowered my voice, "'Open your eyes, girl! Use your brain!'"

"Do you need to see the Buick maker in person to know he exists?" she asked.

I flopped my head onto Auntie Odie's shoulder and laughed.

She drove the Buick up the hill on Jay Way and into the driveway. "Oh, looky there. Emily's in the breakfast nook again."

Yellow-orange Emily gazed at us with spring-green eyes from the kitchen bay window. She pawed rapidly at the pane with both front feet like she was trying to get out to meet us.

I got so tickled, I couldn't stop giggling. "Emily is proof that God does—how do you say it?—have us sing some hoomer."

Auntie Odie pulled into the garage and turned off the motor. Her facial expression had gone flat, puzzled. "'God has us sing some hoomer?'"

As the motor cooled, the car made sounds like popcorn starting to pop.

"You know, Auntie Odie. You're always saying God has a funny bone. He arranges funny predicaments and He designs comical things in nature—you said so yourself. You said God probably guffawed while He sketched some of His ideas. Remember? He gets a kick out of this earth. So God has us sing some hoomer—oh, that's not right. I can't remember now."

Then Auntie Odie's face opened up and she did laugh. "Do you mean *sense of humor?*—God has a sense of humor? Is that what you're talking about?"

"Yeah, maybe that was it. A sense of humor!"

Then we giggled all the way into the house.

While Auntie Odie made tea, I got down the cups and saucers.

"Auntie Odie?"

"Yes, child."

"If I don't believe there's a God, then, so what?"

"God says in his Book that anybody who says there is no God is a fool."

"A fool?"

She smiled at me in that loving way only Auntie Odie could. "In Romans one He says there's no excuse for not believing in the Creator because of all the things that He has made. People try to act and talk intelligent, but the minute they say, 'There is no God,' they're talking bosh."

"Well," I said. "I'm sure not one of 'em. Not anymore."

Chapter 48

UN Command Admits Its Fighter
Strafed Kaesong by Mistake
—*Greeley Daily Tribune*, p.1, Tues., Sept. 11, 1951

Less Corn,
More Wheat
In Forecast
—*Akin Scoop*, p.1, Tues., Sept. 11, 1951

Tuesday's high 95°, low 39°; partly cloudy; windy in afternoon; scattered showers and high winds tonight; precipitation .09"

After the Pledge each morning at school, we chorused Walt Whitman's poem, "I Hear America Singing," a little more smoothly and with more expression than the day before. If we didn't show improvement, we had to read it three more times. Miss Maddsen said if we chose not to improve our choral rendition of one of the finest poems of all time, we'd read it three more times—and three more times if necessary, and three more, through morning recess, lunch, and afternoon recess until the dismissal bell rang. She said if that ever happened, we'd have to show up on Saturday to do make-up work. If we didn't show up on make-up Saturday, we'd flunk fifth grade.

And we knew she meant it. Our parents signed notes agreeing to support her classroom discipline plan.

By the third day, I knew "I Hear America Singing" by heart. During the second week, she asked for volunteers to recite it, alone, in front of the class. I raised my hand. Overriding my nervousness was my desire to earn a hallowed place among my peers as the best-kid-reciter-of-poetry in Weld County.

Little lights twinkled in Miss Maddsen's eyes at the sight of my upraised hand, and I hoped I could keep them on with my performance.

"Come on up then, Ponia," she said.

Mary Joy snickered as I passed her desk.

"Mary Joy, I'll see you at recess." Miss Maddsen's comment sobered Mary Joy nicely.

"'I Hear America Singing,'" I announced as we'd been taught, "by Walt Whitman.

"I hear America singing, the varied carols I hear,
Those of the mechanics, each singing his as it
        should be blithe and strong,
The carpenter singing his as he measures his
        plank or beam,
The mason singing… singing his while sewing or washing…"

The class laughed, I groaned.

"You're allowed one falter," Miss Maddsen said, "before you're postponed to a later date. Start with the carpenter line again and think about what masons do."

I nodded then gathered myself up like Auntie Odie did.

"The carpenter singing his as he measures his
        plank or beam,
The mason singing his as he makes ready for
        work or leaves off work…"

Miss Maddsen smiled and nodded me on.

"The boatman singing what belongs to him in his
        boat, the deck hand singing on the
        steamboat deck…"

I continued on to the final stanza.

"Each sings what belongs to him or her and to
        none else,
The day what belongs to the day—at night the
        party of young fellows, robust, friendly,
Singing with open mouths their strong melodious
        songs."

A few in the class clapped.

After I was seated, Miss Maddsen said, "Ponia did well to memorize Whitman's poem." She paced down the first aisle and up the next. "But, Ponia, do not stop striving to improve. I hesitate to praise, lest you become satisfied with less than your best. There is a foe to excellence, and that foe is settling for 'good.' Don't strut when someone praises you. Strive to become even better."

At recess time, Miss Maddsen pulled me aside. "Ponia, you have the gift of memory and your love for words shines through. Continue working hard, and you'll qualify to perform in the Silver Tongues Harvest in March."

"Auntie Odie inspired my love of words. She helps me memorize poems and stories."

"Odessa Luckett?"

I nodded. "She's my mama's and my best friend."

★ ★ ★

"Reading aloud with expression is a dying art," Miss Maddsen said to the class after lunch recess. "It takes dedication and hours of practice to perfect, just like any other art form.

"The citizens of Akin will attend the Silver Tongues Harvest next spring, and they expect to hear the finest readers, storytellers, and poets of your generation. Our community is known in Weld County for producing exceptional oral expressionists and holding superior literaries. Whatever your preference—poet, storyteller, or reader—you must be, first and foremost, an excellent reader. From that, the others hinge.

"Therefore…" Miss Maddsen's petite figure paraded up and down the aisles, high heels tapping the wood floor. "Your ongoing homework assignment is to read with expression, for a minimum of a-half hour, five days per week. You must get your Weekly Reading Record signed by those who hear you read. It's due each Monday."

The class moaned. Martha and I looked across the room at each other.

At recess, with Sarah, Vanessa, Anna, and Florie gathered around her, Martha grinned at me. "We can do the reading thing, Poni."

"Yeah, we have Auntie Odie." I knew I'd learn to sing, roll, blare, whisper, and fly words off my tongue just like her. I danced across the playground like a ballerina on stage and laughed when Mary Joy and some boys pointed and taunted me.

"They're amazed at how I'm changing," I said to Martha as we lined up to go back into class. "They're starting to see the colors of my wings through my chrysalis."

★ ★ ★

Every day Martha and I read to each other and to an adult who signed our Weekly Reading Records. Mrs. Matthews, although ill, was among our faithful listeners. We read to Mama while she mended clothes for the dry cleaners or to Aunt Bella at the Akin Rest Home. But our favorite audience was Auntie Odie who listened with a smile as wide as the Platte River. She gave us pointers and often modeled reading our selections with all the drama of a Shakespearean play. Miss Maddsen would've been pleased to know that expressive reading was definitely *not* a dying art in the Matthews' and the Snows' households.

Life was good.

Chapter 49

Wilbert Winter
Killed in Korea
—*Greeley Daily Tribune*, p.1, Tues., Sept. 25, 1951

★ ★ ★

When Administered Appropriately
Spankings are Positive Discipline For
Kids Says Renowned Psychologist
—*Akin Scoop*, p.1, Wed., Sept. 26, 1951

★ ★ ★

Bums Admit Banging On Umps' Door After Hectic Rhubarb in Thursday's 4-3 Loss
—*Greeley Daily Tribune*, p.5, Fri., Sept. 28, 1951

Friday's high 72°, low 40°; fair today and tonight

"Delicious gumbo, Odie." Mr. Matthews devoured the last spoonful of his second bowl of the stuff.

"Best gumbo in Colorado," Mrs. Matthews said.

The Matthews family had years to get used to Auntie Odie's southern cooking. Martha, and even Mama, guzzled down the gumbo like starved gypsies.

I helped clear the table in hopes no one would notice my leftovers.

We took our beverages and dessert out to the picnic table in Auntie Odie's "friendship garden." Mrs. Matthews walked without Mr. Matthews' support. Birds bustled about the trees and feeders, and their gentle chorus sailed joyfully to our ears on the fragrant breeze of early evening.

"Oh, my, this is delicious pie, Odie," said Mrs. Matthews. "Another of your southern recipes?"

Mr. Matthews sipped his coffee then forked in the last of his pie. "Whatever it is, get the recipe, Liv."

"Sour Cream Pecan Pie," Auntie Odie said. "Clipped it out of the *Tribune* a couple weeks ago. Been wanting to try it."

"We've got about a month of *Tribune*s in the garage," Mrs. Matthews said. "Martha and Ponia can find the recipe for me—maybe tomorrow, huh, girls?"

"Sure," we chorused.

"I'll clip mine out for you," said Mama.

Mr. Matthews moved to one of Auntie Odie's metal lawn chairs, leaned back, and sipped his coffee. "I'm surprised at you, Odie—and disappointed."

Auntie Odie's mouth sort of popped open and she raised her eyebrows. "Why, Fritz? What did I do?"

"It's what you haven't done—yet." He took another sip of coffee.

We all gawked at Mr. Matthews. I thought he might have a little something up his sleeve. And yet…

"I'm waiting right here, Fritz," Auntie Odie said firmly, "until you tell me how I've disappointed you. I thought you liked my *Tribune* pie recipe.

"Oh, the pie was great! But one way it might've tasted better is if it had been accompanied by a well recited—and maybe even manly—poem." The only give-away in Mr. Matthews' expression was one raised eyebrow.

"So *that's* your complaint? And just what 'manly' poem would you want to hear?" I could tell Auntie Odie was suppressing a grin. She was pleased, all right.

"Well, as a matter of fact," Mr. Matthews said, "I haven't heard you recite that trucker's poem by Wilburt Robinett for a good long while. And I do believe it's one of my personal favorites."

"Really?" That was Auntie Odie.

Mrs. Matthews smiled toward her husband. "My man has always had a little bit of trucker blood running in his veins."

Mr. Matthews appeared pleased. "Mebbe so," he said.

"Don't you know the poem, Fritz?" Auntie Odie said. "You could probably recite it yourself, don't you think?"

"Mebbe. Some of it."

Auntie Odie was already gathering herself up for a mini-recital. "Then you recite with me, the parts that you know. Here we go. Start with me, Fritz…"

"'Reminiscings of a Truck Driver' by Wilburt Robinett," Auntie Odie and Mr. Matthews chorused.

So Auntie Odie and Mr. Matthews recited it together. I was surprised at how much Mr. Matthews knew. In one of the verses, Auntie Odie sort of forgot and Mr. Matthews was the one who remembered and got them both going again. Martha, Mrs. Matthews, Mama, and I made a wonderful, attentive audience, if I do say so myself. Even the birds quieted down for the recitation.

> "It's nice to be back home again after being gone so long,
> To be with friends and loved ones,
> To enjoy the fellowship in word and joyful song.
>
> "I've been to Chicago, Des Moines, to Fargo and Kalamazoo,
> To Kansas City and Nashville, to London and Peru.

"I've seen Rochester and Knoxville, Pittsburg and Harrisburg too,
To Bakersfield and Fresno and Sacramento to mention a few.

"I've seen the beauty of our country, its splendor far and wide
From our great majestic mountains to the oceans' rolling tide.

"In all our wooded forests and in the desert sand
I can see God's Handiwork all across our land.

"Still, in time it becomes a long and lonesome road
So far from all your friends, so far from your abode.

"But it helps so much to call back home and the voice you love to hear
Says over and over and over again, 'I still love you, Dear.'"

We applauded and whistled (the whistle was Martha's). "Bravo!" "Excellent!"

"Say the last two verses again," Mrs. Matthews chimed. "Please."

Mr. Matthews and Auntie Odie said them again, and the audience cheered again.

By then the reciters were standing. They grasped each other's hands and took their bows. Mr. Matthews wore a goofy grin I hadn't seen before.

"Thank you. Thank you," they repeated several times. Just like real celebrities.

Then Mr. Matthews sat back in the lawn chair and gazed over at Mrs. Matthews. "Remember those months when I was traveling all over the U.S. on business?"

Mrs. Matthews nodded and smiled at him, her eyes sparkling like she knew what he was going to say.

"I know exactly how the trucker in that poem felt," he said. "I looked forward to your I-still-love-you-Dears more than anything—*anything* else during those long trips away from you, Liv."

"Ah-h-h," the rest of us chimed at once, while Mr. and Mrs. Matthews gazed at each other like new lovers.

Moments like these with precious friends and genuine love on display filled me up. Pure happiness flowed from inside out onto my face, I was sure of it. I agreed with the trucker in the poem—it's a long and lonesome road when you're far from people who care about you. This moment, here, in Auntie Odie's friendship garden, was perfect. I was home, surrounded by love again at last.

★ ★ ★

"Odie," Mr. Matthews said, "did you see today's *Tribune* story about the umpire's door getting kicked in after the Dodgers lost to the Braves?"

"I saw it all right." She looked up as a house finch flew to a stocking of thistle seed and scattered the goldfinches that had been feeding. "You naughty finch! Go to your own feeder."

I laughed. "You usually don't get mad at the birds, Auntie Odie."

Mama appeared restless. She finished her pie then collected the dessert plates.

"What do you think, Odie?" said Mrs. Matthews. "Did Jackie Robinson kick in the umpire's door?"

Auntie Odie stood up and watched the goldfinches gradually return to the sock. One was sideways, another upside-down hanging onto the gauzelike feeder. "If he says he didn't do it, then he didn't do it. Even Preacher Roe swears Jackie had nothing to do with it."

"It was a bad call," Mr. Matthews said, "and it cost the Dodgers the game, but that's not a reason to vandalize."

"I'm with you, Odie," Mrs. Matthews said. "Jackie said he knew who did it, but it wasn't him. I believe him."

"Whew!" said Martha. "Jackie sure was mad. He said anybody who says he kicked in the umpire's door is a—"

"Martha!" Mr. and Mrs. Matthews and Auntie Odie erupted in a hot chorus.

"No swear words are appropriate—ever," Mr. Matthews scolded.

I chortled.

"Well," said Martha, "it was printed right there in the paper—what kind of liar they called him. They called him a..."

"Martha! That's enough!" Mr. Matthews again.

"I didn't say it." Martha began licking her plate.

"Martha!"—the three adults again.

I exulted in Martha's unruly bravery.

Mr. Matthews glowered at his daughter. "You don't have to repeat cuss words, wherever you hear them—or read them. And if you keep on licking your plate like a dog, you'll earn yourself a swat."

"Spankings are in fashion," I said. "I read that in the paper too."

Chapter 50

Allied Planes
Attack in Cold,
Steady Rainfall
—*Greeley Daily Tribune*, p.1, Sat., Sept. 29, 1951

Tonight's Carnival To Benefit
Akin Aviary Says Waterford
Perkins, Akin School Principal
—*Akin Scoop*, p.1, Sat., Sept. 29, 1951

Partly cloudy today and tonight; high 78°, low 43°

Martha, Sarah, Margaret, and I scurried from booth to booth at the school carnival.

First was the Spoonbill Relay. Each participant carried a hard-boiled egg in a spoon-shaped bird bill to a chalked line and back without dropping it. The fastest relay team won a prize.

At the Owl Pellet Toss, players worked in pairs. The partners' greatest challenge was to keep from laughing themselves silly while the owl pellets (Milk Duds) were tossed into each other's open mouths. Four misses and they were out of the game. Partners who caught and ate five pellets, won plastic owl knickknacks.

Players in the Egg Toss threw rubber balls into a papier maché pelican head with open bill.

Auntie Odie was the birdcaller for the Bird-Talk booth. Players sat in five chairs. Auntie Odie warbled or whistled a birdsong or call. The best imitation by a participant, according to the judges, Angela Fall and Dora Santi, was awarded one of Mrs. Waterford Perkins' vanilla-chocolate-caramel cupcakes. Any who whispered into a judge's ear the correct identity of the bird call, received a small bundle of birds' eggs (jelly beans).

Sal Santi the Firedrake and Mr. Waterford Perkins the principal were the masterminds and muscles for the Whooping Crane Ride. Attached to a small wooden platform were cardboard whooping-crane head and wings. Sarah, Martha and I waited together in line. Sarah's little sister, Margaret, climbed onto the platform and sat down between the wings. Mrs. Kipp, my teacher from fourth grade, blindfolded Margaret, and Mr. Perkins gave out his imitation of a whooping crane's trumpeting call. Margaret squealed as the whooping crane took off. Mr. Santi and Mr. Perkins soared the crane—and Margaret—up, up. A student helper handed Mrs. Kipp a book. She let the book touch the top of Margaret's head.

"She's flying into the ceiling!" Mr. Santi exclaimed.

"We'd better bring her down," said Mr. Perkins.

Another wild-whooping-crane call from Mr. Perkins, and Margaret came safely to rest in "the marsh."

Martha poked me. "You're next."

Mrs. Kipp, wearing a tan shirt that matched her glasses and hair, smiled. "You ready, Poni?"

Sweat beaded on Mr. Perkins' brow. "Ride the world-class, gravity-defying whooping crane if you dare, young lady!" He smoothed his squirrel-brown hair and wiped his face with a white handkerchief.

Mr. Santi grinned at me. "Hop on, Miss Glass!"

My heart atwitter, I climbed on. Blindfolded, I became disoriented and held onto the platform with vice grips. The crane took off. I jerked and gasped when Mr. Perkins whooped his crane call.

The noises from the carnival echoed in my head. I pictured myself flying up to the ceiling where I bumped my head. As the crane tilted in its soaring pattern, I let out a scream and grabbed onto its wing, which came off in my hand. The crane squawked, and laughter swelled into the cocophony of sounds around me. I landed in the marsh with a thump. I yanked off my blindfold and saw Mr. Perkins, red-faced—and bald—and I held in my hand...

"A toupee!" Mrs. Kipp's brown eyes waggled behind her glasses as she stared, first at the toupee and then at the principal. "Mr. Perkins! I didn't know... I... All that nice handsome hair."

No words came to me. I held the hairpiece behind me like one might hide sheets after wetting the bed.

Silence among the witnesses, and then Mr. Perkins let out a warwhoop—louder than his whooping crane call—and everyone laughed. Mr. Santi guffawed.

I handed Mr. Perkins his toupee. "I thought I was grabbing a wing, Mr. Perkins. I'm sorry."

He knuckle-scrubbed my curls good-naturedly and grinned. "No harm done."

Chapter 51

Former Conductors Will Feature
Philharmonic's 40th Anniversary
Concert at Gunter Monday Night
—*Greeley Daily Tribune*, p.1, Fri., Oct. 12, 1951

★ ★ ★

Dewey Says
Ike Will Be
Nominated
—*Greeley Daily Tribune*, p.1, Mon., Oct. 15, 1951

Generally fair and windy; partly cloudy Monday night; high 75°, low 36°

When I found out Auntie Odie invited Mama to hear the Greeley Philharmonic Orchestra and not me, I scowled.

I stomped around the apartment when Mama told me that Mrs. Gazz had agreed to come over and sit with me. She'd crochet while I slept. Mama even offered to pay her twenty-five cents an hour. Like I was a baby or something. And what an old crank Mrs. Gazz was.

"I'll sit still and listen—cross my heart, Mama," I said, "if only you'll let me come. I'll take a bath—no swashing—and comb my hair and polish my shoes. I won't squirm or nod off or swing my feet."

But the answer was no. A big arrow flew through my chest and gouged my heart when Auntie Odie said, "I know you'd like to go, child,"—she patted my shoulder—"but it's a school night."

And Mama acted all happy, put on her pink gabardine and the cute little hat Auntie Odie bought her last summer, and her black pumps and her hose with the black seams, and her hair all freshly washed and shiny in a pageboy. She didn't mind hurting my feelings. She said I got to do things with Auntie Odie all the time while she was working and she deserved a nice evening out. The Matthews went too, and Martha stayed with her grandparents. The Firedrake and his mother, Dora Santi, met them at the concert hall.

★ ★ ★

When Mama got home from the concert at eleven, I woke up. After Mrs. Gazz went home, Mama let me sit next to her on the sofa and she told me all about the concert. She giggled and said the music was beautiful but she got awfully sleepy and envied me, at home all curled up asleep and cozy.

"What music did you like best?" I asked.

"'Carmen.' No, I think my favorite was… what was it?" She opened the program and found the page. "Here—'From Sun to Sun (A Joyful Round)' by Dr. Cline, one of the directors. He wrote it for the Greeley Philharmonics' fortieth anniversary. It was lovely."

Lovely. Not a typical word for Mama. Sounded more like an Auntie-Odie word.

"Maybe even splendiferous?" I asked.

"Even splendiferous."

Mama handed me the program, said I could keep it.

"I'll read it tomorrow—all sixteen pages! Thank you, Mama."

"Now get back to bed, it's nearly midnight."

Mama settled on her sofa bed and turned out the light.

"Mama."

"Mm–hm."

"I'm glad you liked the concert. It's good you and Auntie Odie didn't have to deal with me."

"You got lots of years to go to concerts, Ponia."

"Uh–huh."

"I missed you." Mama's voice was barely more than a whisper.

I waited until the thumping pulse in my neck calmed down. "I missed you too, Mama."

"Thanks for being good."

"But I wasn't good. I acted terrible when I learned you were going to the concert without me."

"You were good for Mrs. Gazz and I appreciate it. Thank you."

"You're welcome."

The wind shuddered against the window and the floor creaked. The bathroom door down the hall closed, echoing in the hallway.

"G'night, Mama."

The wind subsided and the world grew still. Through the window, stars shone between the tree branches like silver berries.

"'Night, Ponia."

Chapter 52

Storm Delays
Harvesting of
Sugar Beets
—*Greeley Daily Tribune*, p.1, Mon., Oct. 22, 1951

★ ★ ★

Soprano Wylma Fletcher to Sing
Spirituals and Other American Favorites
7:30 Tonight, at 1ˢᵗ Methodist, Greeley
—*Akin Scoop*, p.1, Wed., Oct. 24, 1951

Generally fair Wednesday; partly cloudy tonight; windy; high 64°, low 30°

"'Swing low, sweet chariot—'" I tried to sing with smooth vibrato, my imitation of Wylma Fletcher. "'Comin' for to carry me home….'"

Auntie Odie, Mama, and Mrs. Fall joined in. "'Swing low, sweet chariot, comin' for to carry me home.'"

Sitting in Auntie Odie's breakfast nook at ten o'clock at night, we tittered, sipped tea, and savored moist bites of Auntie Odie's spice cake.

"At the concert I wished I could sing like Wylma Fletcher," I said.

Auntie Odie grinned and adjusted her river-blue hat. "Me too!"

Mama raised her hand and echoed, "Me too."

"Don't we all," said Mrs. Fall.

I washed down the last of my spice cake with tea. "But I've changed my mind. I want to use my voice in expressive ways to tell stories and recite poetry. And use words in new ways that no one has ever thought of."

"I'd rather sing," Mrs. Fall said.

"I second that," said Mama.

"Your manifest destiny, Ponia Glass Snow," Auntie Odie said. "Splendiferous decision!"

I pointed to Auntie Odie. "And I want to have a cottage like this one and create gardens like yours."

She clasped her hands under her chin. Her river–blue and white earbobs glittered like rapids in sunlight. "A lovely way to dandify the world!"

"And I'm going to have a cat just like Emily."

"For cryin' out loud!" Mama said.

Chapter 53

Weld Covered in Snow,
Beet Harvest Delayed
—*Akin Scoop*, p.1, Thurs., Nov. 1, 1951

★ ★ ★

Hooray! Spanking's
Now Back in Style
—*Greeley Daily Tribune*, p.2, Mon., Nov. 12, 1951

Monday's high 63°, low 31°; partly cloudy and windy

I wrote in my tablet at Auntie Odie's breakfast nook table while she clipped articles for her scrapbook. I loved it when Mama worked and she let me go to Auntie Odie's after school.

"Why are you cutting out *that*?" I asked. "You aren't going to keep that spanking article, are you?"

Auntie Odie nodded and smiled. "It's mighty interesting—right up there with the one about the cocker that saved his little mistress from a rattler. See? Right here: 'Gus, Cocker, Saves His Mistress, Linda, 5, When Rattler Strikes.' That was in August second's *Tribune* right on page one."

"You'd never spank me, Auntie Odie, would you?"

"I hope I never have to."

"You're not my mama."

"No. But you spend as much time here as if I were." She looked at me sideways and a smile pressed into her pursed lips. "I'm not complaining, mind you. I love your company."

"Do you think you'll spank me sometime?"

"I'd never spank you if I was really mad. I wouldn't spank you if a gentler discipline would work as well." She looked at the ceiling, thinking. "But if your offense was something that would put you in danger or ultimately dash your soul, I'd give you a good swat."

I grinned, got up, walked to her side of the table, and hugged her. "Thank you, Auntie Odie. I was hoping you'd say that."

Her eyes widened. "You were?"

"Yep. You must love me a lot. Not to spank me when you're mad. And give me a good swat if I'm in eternal danger."

"*Tch, tch.*" She clicked her tongue and laughed. "Oh, Poni child, you really are *something.*"

Chapter 54

No Parallel to Massacre of U.S.
Prisoners in Korea, Boyle Says
—*Greeley Daily Tribune*, p.1, Fri., Nov. 16, 1951

★ ★ ★

Lester Gains
Akin Pioneer Dies
—*Akin Scoop*, p.1, Sun., Nov. 18, 1951

Sunday fair; increasing winds; high 61°, low 13°

The Sunday morning before Thanksgiving, Gram and Grampy's clock struck six then someone banged on the apartment door. Mama threw on her housecoat and hurried to answer it.

"Ingrid! Forgive this intrusion." A man in a brown overcoat gripped his brown hat. My heart stopped. I hardly recognized Mr. Matthews, his face drawn, white as milk, and unshaven.

"Fritz! What's wrong?" Mama said.

The way he stepped into the apartment, as though he had pebbles in his shoes, pierced my heart with fear. I jumped from my mat, hurried to his side, and took hold of his wrist. It felt cold and hard.

He looked at me with glazed eyes, then at Mama. "It's… Olivia." His voice broke. "Could Martha stay with you while I take her to the hospital? Odie'll be in North Carolina a few more days and…"

"Yes!" Mama nearly shouted. "Where is Martha now?"

"In the car, with her mother. I'll send her up." He pressed a key into Mama's hand. "This is so you can get into the house. Make yourselves at home."

"Y-Yes." Mama stared up at him. "We'll go to your house so you can call and let us know…"

As he turned to go, Mama touched his arm. "Fritz."

He looked back at her.

"I'll be praying."

Glory be!

He blinked then headed out the door and down the stairs.

Chapter 55

U.S. Casualties
in Korean War
Exceed 100,000
—*Greeley Daily Tribune*, p.1, Wed., Nov. 21, 1951

Ridgway in Thanksgiving
Message To His Forces

Tokyo. Nov. 21 –(GP)—Gen. Mat-
tew B. Ridgway, supreme allied
commander, gave thanks…
"On this Thanksgiving day of
1951, we ask our allies of the United
Nations to join with us in our ob-
servance of thanks annually re-
newed to Almighty God, for the
bounty he has provided…."
—*Greeley Daily Tribune*, p.1, Wed., Nov. 21, 1951

Thanksgiving, Thursday, Nov. 22: Fair; high 60°, low 27°

Mama and I had planned to have our Thanksgiving meal at Akin Rest Home with Aunt Bella, until Dora Santi invited us to her house for Thanksgiving. Her glassblower son was there, and her other son Farley and his wife Becky and their two boys, Farley Jr. and Jimmy. Farley and Becky farmed over by Sterling.

Mr. Santi and Mama and I drove over to the rest home to fetch Aunt Bella at eleven-thirty. The wheelchair didn't fit in Mr. Santi's Bel Air, so he had to pick up Aunt Bella and put her in the front seat. Then he carried her from the car into his mother's house. He carried her from the sofa to a chair at the table, and, after dinner, back to the sofa. Lucky for him, Aunt Bella was pickle-skinny and had a strong bladder.

I felt sad and lost most of the day. How I wished Auntie Odie hadn't gone to North Carolina for Thanksgiving. The Matthews were feasting out at Martha's grandparents' farm. Thankfully, Mrs. Matthews was improving some and well enough to go. I did enjoy sitting at Mrs. Santi's dining room table in a mahogany chair with a striped, padded seat and a harp design on the back. When asked, Mrs. Santi explained that they were Duncan Phyfe chairs and the design was a lyre. I wondered how a harp could lie, but I was too shy to ask about it.

Thanksgiving. Mama and I had lived a whole year without Gram and Grampy. How did we survive? With a lot of help from Auntie Odie and the Matthews, the Nimble Needles, Mr. Smith at the cleaners, and the glassblower and his mother. And Aunt Bella, and Mrs. Fall. And God.

Dora Santi baked the turkey and all the trimmings just right, almost as good as Gram. Farley Jr. and Jimmy reminded me of the Hill boys. We played in the pile of sand out behind the glassblowing shop all afternoon, making roads and hauling dirt in the toy trucks Farley Jr. brought. That was a happy part of the day.

And Mama wore a little curve on her lips, and got along fine with everyone. Especially Salvatore Santi, the glassblowing man.

Chapter 56

Bitterest Cold
Wave Hits War
Front in Korea
—*Greeley Daily Tribune*, p.1, Sat., Dec. 1, 1951

★ ★ ★

Weld County
Cold and Windswept
—*Akin Scoop*, p.1, Thurs., Dec. 6, 1951

Downtown Will
Be Wonderland
For Parade Sat.
—*Greeley Daily Tribune*, p.1, Thurs., Dec. 6, 1951

Partly cloudy Thursday; scattered snow flurries; windy, diminishing tonight; high 35°, low 6°

Walking home from school, Martha said, "We're moving to Idaho."

"What?" I stopped in front of Mrs. Denou's gray house. "How come?"

Martha walked on, and then waited for me at the corner. "Mother is too sick to stay in Akin. She needs her family, my dad says—and Mother says so too. So we're going back to live near her family."

I caught up with her.

Her chin trembled. "They have a big hospital in Boise. Doctors there know how to treat her health problems. Christmas vacation is in three weeks. We'll move then."

"But what about your dad's drug store?"

Martha pursed her lips. "Mr. Sides will manage it. Daddy says Mr. Sides might even buy it. We'll see."

My voice was louder than intended. "You can't move! What about me? What about Auntie Odie? And your Grandma and Grandpa Matthews?"

Martha closed her eyes for a moment then looked at her feet. "I'll write to you if you'll write to me."

Her words scraped my heart. I thought of the single exchange of letters between Maizy and me since I'd come to Akin eleven months ago.

A lump formed in my throat. "Letters? That's it?"

"That's it," she said.

Chapter 57

★ ★ ★

Friday's high 54°, low 21°; fair today and tonight; windy

In their winter sleep, bushes and trees rattled—snored—in the wind. Birds chirped and sang greetings, feasted on suet, and pecked at feeders. The snow sparkled and icicles dripped in the warm-for-December sunshine.

"The seeds in the patches of snow look like freckles on snow faces," I said.

"I'll miss your word pictures, Poni," said Martha.

A wooden sign under the wreath on Auntie Odie's door said *Welcome*.

She opened the door.

> "I heard a bird sing
>   In the dark of December
> A magical thing
>   And sweet to remember.
>
> "We are nearer to Spring
>   Than we were in September,
> I heard a bird sing
>   In the dark of December.

"By Oliver Herford."

Oh, Auntie Odie, I love you.

Martha laughed. "It's not dark, Auntie Odie. It's sunny."

A mourning dove flew off with a gurgle of wings, knocking a clump of snow off a branch above Martha.

"Hey!" Martha brushed snow off her hat.

Auntie Odie laughed. "Come in, come in."

The cottage diffused scents of pine, hollyberry, apples, and cinnamon. Though Christmas was past, holiday knickknacks still snuggled among pine boughs, holly, ribbons and bows on the end tables, shelves, and mantle. Beneath the Christmas tree laden with tinsel and a medley of ornaments, nativity figures knelt in humble adoration before the Christ child. The fireplace crackled with fire, warm and yellow.

"I just wanted to say a special good-bye to two of my dearest friends in the world." Martha put words to my secret wish since my first day at Akin School—that I would one day be considered among Martha's best friends.

Auntie Odie sat in an easy chair. "Not 'good-bye,' Martha dear. Too final. 'So long' is better."

Martha removed her red coat and laid it over the arm of the sofa. "'So long' instead of 'good-bye?' They're both the same. Either way, I'll be far, far away from here—from home."

"You have heart-wings, child. You can fly back home to Akin in your thoughts and memories anytime you wish. Phone calls and letters will keep us close too. And who knows? You may even move back someday. *That's* 'so long,' not 'good-bye.'"

Martha and I slouched on the sofa.

"How about some milk or hot chocolate?" Auntie Odie asked.

Martha sniffed and rubbed her eyes. "No thanks."

Auntie Odie popped up from her chair and headed for the kitchen. "Jabberwocky! Since when do you refuse a cup of hot chocolate, child? Come along now."

Auntie Odie split bran-raisin muffins and laid them on dessert plates. "Just baked these a while ago. My heart must've known you were coming." She found a container of lemon curd in the refrigerator, warmed it up in her speckled, baby-blue enamel saucepan with the black handle, then spooned the curd over the muffin halves. "There," she said, "Odie's Surprising Mélange. But I've got oatmeal cookies, if you're in the mood for the customary." She added an oatmeal cookie from her depression-glass cookie jar to each of our plates. "Here. Now, where are your splendiferous smiles?"

Martha and I eyed each other then smiled at Auntie Odie.

"How we will miss you, Martha child. But distance will strengthen our friendship. Some of the finest lines of prose were written in correspondence between cherished friends."

"You will write to me?" Martha leaned into her long, open arms.

"I'll answer every letter. I promise."

They hugged and choked back tears.

"Say a poem," Martha said.

Auntie Odie thought a moment. "'The Coin' by Sara Teasdale…

> "Into my heart's treasury
>   I slipped a coin
> That time cannot take
>   Nor a thief purloin,—
> Oh, better than the minting
>   Of a gold-crowned king
> Is the safe-kept memory
>   Of a lovely thing."

The house creaked, and Emily meandered in, purring.

"Tell us a story, Auntie Odie," I said.

"Tell us your people-flying story," Martha said.

Auntie Odie pulled a white hanky from her apron pocket, dabbed her eyes, and headed toward the front room. "I love a chance to tell a story."

We nestled on the big sofa facing the fireplace. Martha and I made a place for Emily between us.

I smiled. "This is just like last summer in the garden swing—the four of us together, Auntie Odie storytelling us."

The story of slaves, invisible stairs, and flying into freedom sky was as powerful as the first time I heard it. Auntie Odie's words pulled me through the story with gentle hands that would not let go until long moments after the last phrase had been spoken.

When it came time for Martha to leave, we stood at the door, shoulders sagging.

Brow furrowed, Auntie Odie held Martha's hands. "We'll miss you, dear sweet neighbor. I'll keep praying for your mama."

Martha's face crumpled, tears fell. "I don't want to move away."

Auntie Odie and I wrapped our arms around her.

"Now," Auntie Odie said, "let's dry our tears and face this mountain, too, with courage."

We giggled at Auntie Odie's melodramatic tone.

"And now," she continued, "I quote for thee a poem by Agatha Jordan:

> "Until we meet again, dear friends,
> I'll dream of you when night descends.
> And when the sun comes over the hill
> I'll think of you, my heart will thrill.
> Wherever you go, whatever you do,
> Remember, dears, that I love you.

"And when this time of parting is through,
We'll still be friends, tried and true.
We three will be just as before—
Together–friends forevermore.

"Now be on thy way lest we all be swept away and drown in a creek of bitter tears."

Martha saluted. "And 'when this time of parting is through,' I will be back." She clasped Auntie Odie's hands. "I'll never forget you, Auntie Odie."

"Nor I you, child.

"Oh, better than the minting
Of a gold-crowned king
Is the safe-kept memory
Of a lovely thing."

Chapter 58

7 Ships Send
Out SOS in East
Atlantic Storm
—*Greeley Daily Tribune*, p.1, Sat., Dec. 29, 1951

Wind, Snow, Sleet
and Rain Saturday
—*Akin Scoop*, p.1, Sat., Dec. 29, 1951

Rain, sleet, and snow before noon Saturday; windy; highways snow-packed and slick, high 40°, low 29°; precipitation .39"

Mama, Auntie Odie, and I huddled against the blowing snow and waved as the Matthews pulled away behind the moving van. It had been suggested that they wait until the storm passed, but they were determined to get to Rock Springs, Wyoming—where Mr. Matthews' uncle lived—before nightfall.

We watched in heady sorrow as the three precious friends drove away from their empty house with the sign in front, *For Rent*.

Chapter 59

March of Dimes Drive in January
To Aid in War On Polio; Developing
Immunizations Part of Battle Plan
—*Akin Scoop*, p.1, Sun., Dec. 30, 1951

Literaries to be Held
At Community Hall
3 Evenings in Jan.
—*Akin Scoop*, p.1, Sun., Dec. 30, 1951

Sunday's high 39°, low 20°; very wet rain-and-snow storm; precipitation .05"

Auntie Odie eased west for three blocks along Eighth Avenue toward All Saints Community Church. At each intersection, the Buick slid to a stop. The snow and rain had diminished, but left the streets treacherous.

Auntie Odie gripped the wheel. "Maybe we shouldn't have come out in this." The snow had been scooped into hills along the east edge of the church parking lot.

"Whew!" she said. "We made it. Early, in fact."

She pulled her black felt hat down over her ears, which reminded me of my precious Gram. "I wish your mama would've come with us." Auntie Odie stepped gingerly out of the driver's side. "She seemed awful sad this morning."

"She's been crying and sleeping a lot," I said.

We held onto each other, and tried to avoid icy patches.

★ ★ ★

"…Great is Thy faithfulness! Great is Thy faithfulness!
Morning by morning new mercies I see…"

The All Saints congregation was small on that frigid Sunday after Christmas, but their faces looked toward heaven and they sang with fervor:

"All I have needed Thy hand hath provided—
Great is Thy faithfulness, Lord unto me!

"Summer and winter, and springtime and harvest,
Sun, moon and stars in their courses above
Join with all nature in manifold witness
To Thy great faithfulness, mercy and love.

"Great is Thy faithfulness! Great is Thy faithfulness!
Morning by morning new mercies I see…"

Halfway through the chorus, Auntie Odie closed her hymnal and whispered in my ear. "We've got to leave, child. Follow me."

In the Buick, heater blasting, we slowly headed south on Meadow Way for two blocks then turned east on Tenth Avenue.

"What's wrong, Auntie Odie? Why'd we leave in the middle of God's faithfulness?"

"I don't know. I'm probably overreacting. I just…"

"Just *what*?" I scooched to the middle and looked into her solemn face.

"Every time we sang, 'Great is Thy faithfulness,' your mama's face hovered behind my eyes like a dream. But of course, I was awake, standing next to you, singing along with the congregation. Your mama's face was as white as that snowman's head—see, in front of that red house? And her mouth was all twisted."

Auntie Odie dabbed her eyes with her gloved fingers and pulled into the parking space behind Mama's blue pickup.

The apartment door was locked. We knocked—then pounded. No answer. I'd forgotten my key. By the time Auntie Odie fished around in her purse and found the key Mama had given her, Mrs. Gazz, Lolly and Duke Pendleton from *D* next door, and Mr. Kimpell from downstairs had gathered around us.

"Is something wrong?" Lolly asked, smoothing her hand over her round belly.

Auntie Odie turned the key. "Ingrid's probably just out for a walk."

Duke Pendleton led his wife back toward their apartment. "Can't imagine why anyone would walk on a freezing day like this. Let us know if we can help."

Someone in the house was baking a beef roast—or beef stew. It smelled heavenly.

"Oh, dear," said Mrs. Gazz, pointing. "Over by the window— Looks like she fainted."

Chapter 60

1952

Precipitation
For Year Here
Above Average
—*Greeley Daily Tribune*, p.1, Wed., Jan. 2, 1952

★ ★ ★

Many Akinites Plan To Attend
JCC's Twelfth Night Festival
at Greeley High Aud. Tonight
—*Akin Scoop*, p.1, Sun., Jan. 6, 1952

Partly cloudy Sunday; high 24°, low 2° below zero

Because the radiator in the apartment wouldn't come on, Auntie Odie and I wore our heaviest coats.

Salvatore Santi and his brother Farley Santi had moved the sewing machine, suitcase, trunk, and some boxes to Auntie Odie's garage. Auntie Odie had hung Gram and Grampy's wall clock in the writing nook where I now slept. It was surprising how many things Mama and I had accumulated in the year we'd lived in Akin. Auntie Odie had made room for my small collection of books on a shelf in her front room.

"Stop dawdling, child. Let's knuckle down and get this place clean so we can get home and warmed up." Auntie Odie scoured the sink fiercely, like a sink-scrubbing machine. Clean rags were piled on the counter near her can of Ajax.

I rung out the mop and leaned it against the kitchen wall. "I'm done."

Breathless from her hard work, she said, "Good. Now, child, take one of these rags and dust that chest of drawers."

"Could we make some tea, Auntie Odie? I'm freezing."

"No time for lollygagging, child. We're almost finished. Anyway, how would we make tea?"

I sighed. "Oh, yeah. I wasn't thinking."

"Seems to me you're doing too much thinking and not enough knuckling down to your duties. Looka here, Poni Glass." She pointed toward the chest of drawers.

"What?"

"You missed this whole area around the chest with your mop, child. And we need to pull out the chest."

She tugged at the chest while I stood with my arms folded. She managed to move it out from the wall.

"There now, I did it *without* your what-would-have-been-kind help. Good thing you didn't dump out the mop water yet, little bee. And you'll need to sweep before you mop. See? All along the wall there."

"Why'd you call me that?"

"Call you what? 'Little bee?' I called you that because I thought it might smooth down some of your feathers." Her large mouth smiled, pushing her cheeks up into plums under her dark eyes. I knew she was as cold and tired as I was and longed to be home by her cozy fire—reading a book, writing in her notebook, clipping out special articles from the newspapers, or gazing out the bay window in search of beauty in this bitter winter day.

"Don't you call me 'little bee.' That's Gram's special name for me. Not yours." I jerked my head to a tilt and glared at my best friend in the world.

"All right, child." Her voice took on weariness as she walked toward the sink. "I'm sure you know what to do to make the floor clean. I'll leave you to it."

I longed for her to turn and look at me again with that gentle smile. I wanted her soft, dark eyes to stare through mine, down into that place behind my rib cage where an unnamed fear weighed hostile and heavy like a block of ice. I wanted her to melt it with her love—her tender mercies.

But when she did turn around and smile at me from the tenderest of faces, I flattened my chin and scowled at her. *Why am I acting like this?*

Then blue fire lit her eyes. "You keep giving me those cheeky looks, Ponia Glass Snow, and all that sky blue's going to shoot out of your eyes and leave nothing but black holes."

Our breath fogged between us in the frigid air. We stood, frozen, in our heavy coats and scarves, hands shoved into our pockets.

Why was I doing the opposite of what I wanted to do? I longed to run to Auntie Odie and squeeze her so tight we would meld to each other like hot glass touching molten glass. And she would always be in my life, never go away, and neither would I. Why was I piercing her with my beligerence? What were these benumbing, black waters that whorled in my mind, my heart? I abhored them, yet cleaved to them. I blinked, and looked down, away from her face.

"Lighten my darkness, Auntie Odie," I whispered.

She finally spoke, her voice light and the words hovering in the air between us like motes. "Child, are you struggling with what you want to do and say, but you can't do or say it?"

I just stared up at her.

"The Apostle Paul struggled with that. In Romans seven he said, 'For the good that I would I do not: but the evil which I would not, that I do.' Is that what you're feeling, child?"

I don't know! Nothing makes sense.

Auntie Odie held her arms out to me.

I got the broom and dustpan and swept along the wall. She stood there, arms at her sides now, and watched me struggle to hold the dustpan and sweep the dirt into it. I leaned the broom by the door and emptied the dirt into a grocery sack.

"Ponia… dearest," Auntie Odie said. Then she opened her arms to me again.

For some crazy reason—I didn't even know why, I burst into tears. Then I threw the dustpan. It struck the linoleum and bounced, hitting Auntie Odie's shin.

She took a small step back, but didn't flinch. There were tears in her eyes—at least, I thought….

But I didn't want to see them, didn't want to let go of the black fog, the meanness I felt toward her, toward Mama for taking all those pills, toward Martha and Olivia and Fritz Matthews for moving away, and, yes, toward Gram and Grampy for leaving this world without me. But now I had another chance to try to make Mama happy. Maybe she'd work things out with Mr. Santi and be his apprentice again. Maybe that would make her happy enough so she could conjure up a little love for me. But what if she tried to die again? Maybe the next time we wouldn't be singing "Great is Thy Faithfulness," and Auntie Odie wouldn't know she should go check on Mama.

How terribly cold the room was. I trembled.

"Come here, child." Yet again, Auntie Odie held out her arms. "Come to your Auntie Odie." I turned away from her, retrieved the mop with blatant movement, and mopped fiercely.

Auntie Odie walked to the sink, but this time she labored languidly and recited softly to herself. I strained to hear her words.

> "I shall know why – when Time is over –
> And I have ceased to wonder why –
> Christ will explain each separate anguish
> In the fair schoolroom of the sky –
>
> "He will tell me what 'Peter' promised –
> And I – for wonder at his woe –
> I shall forget the drop of Anguish
> That scalds me now – that scalds me now!"

My mind yelled, *Emily Dickinson!* But I wouldn't say it.

She gathered the rags and stuffed them into a sack.

The water ran gray-brown from the mop as I rinsed it in the sink. When it ran clear, I strangled the mop, hard work for my small hands, but I enjoyed it.

Auntie Odie opened the cupboard, stepped back to peer into the shelves, and then continued her inspection. She wiped her hand over surfaces and opened and closed the refrigerator. She gathered the cleaning supplies, scrutinized the main room, then pressed her forehead to the window and looked out. A wistfulness in her expression pulled my tear string, like a hotel guest might pull a rope in her room to ring a bell in the servants' quarters. But I, the servant, clutched the bell so it couldn't ring.

Her breath frosted the window.

I waited by the door. The place looked the same as last January on the day Mama and I moved in, only cleaner. I never liked it much, but now that Mama and I wouldn't be coming home to it anymore, sadness drenched me.

"Ready?" She turned toward me then. "Oh, Poni... I'm so sorry." Auntie Odie looked at me the same way she had that day after I hung up the phone from talking to Mama in Denver—the day I sat on her lap and bawled until I cried empty airdrops instead of tears.

"Come on over to the window for a minute," she said. "Look out here at these birds."

On a branch near the window, three sparrows huddled against the cold. One opened its beak every few seconds and let out a frail chirp.

"Their feathers are so fluffed up, they're curled," I said.

Auntie Odie whispered, "'Cause, my hair is curly..." then she managed an off-key squeak, "(oh, so curly)..." She gathered herself up, and with each line her voice sang stronger.

> "'Cause, my teeth are pearly,
>   (oh, so pearly,)
> Just because I always wear a smile, (oh, baby,)
> Like to dress up in the—
>   (dress up in the) latest style, (I mean the latest style...)"

Auntie Odie's face still looked drawn, but she forced a good smile, and danced around the room and sang off-key. She stretched her arms out and moved gracefully.

> "'Cause I'm glad I'm living,
> Take troubles smiling, never (wine or) whine."

I knew I was invited, but I walked toward the door, arms folded.

> "Just because my color's shady, Slightly diff'rent maybe,
> That's why they call (—oh, baby, that's why they call) me 'Shine.'"

Without looking I knew what she was doing—standing poised in her final dance step, arms out to the sides like wings, head back, big grin. *Was* she grinning? I turned to look, but she'd broken the pose. I gathered the mop, broom, and mopbucket containing Windex and Spic 'N Span and lumbered toward the stairs. Behind me was the rustling of the brown grocery sack of supplies as she jostled it, and the closing of the door to apartment C.

★ ★ ★

233

Auntie Odie handed Gertrude Fens the rent Mama owed and the keys to the apartment, then we hurried out to the car.

On the drive back to Auntie Odie's house, I thought she might try again to cheer me with a light-hearted poem or song, but she remained silent.

When we walked into Auntie Odie's cottage, Emily was curled up on the rug in front of the fireplace where only a few flickering embers remained.

★ ★ ★

I sat on the bay-window seat and looked out, stroking Emily.

Auntie Odie stood behind me, hands on hips, looking stern. "You mean to tell me, you finally get a chance to go visit your mama, and you don't want to?"

I ignored her.

Her hand gently pressed my shoulder. The edge in her voice had softened. "I know you're hurting, child. All this hullaballoo with your mama has been tragic and scary—for both of us."

Emily paced back and forth, rubbing against me as I petted her.

"Chew on this…" Auntie Odie sat beside me on the window seat. "The Twelfth Night Festival is tonight. You were excited about going to that—and so was I—before… before this happened, this incident with your mama."

"Before she tried to kill herself." I glared at Auntie Odie then looked back out the window at a crow alighting on the fence.

"Yes. Before that, your mama wanted to attend the Twelfth Night too."

Without wanting to, I brightened. "Can she leave the hospital for awhile? Can she go to Twelfth Night Festival with us?"

"Oh. No… no, child. I didn't mean that. She's not well enough for that, but…"

"Can we still go?"

"Do you still want to?"

"Uh-huh."

"We'll go then, but…"

"But, what?"

"Your mama needs visitors, needs to see people that care about her. We need to go gracing— love on her a little. You're not allowed in her hospital room, but she can come to the waiting room. A nurse's aide will stay with her—with us."

I folded my arms—a favorite stance of late. "I don't think I'll go."

"And why is that?"

"I don't care about her anymore."

But I did finally go see Mama that afternoon—and behave and smile some and not pout— because that's the only way Auntie Odie would take me to Twelfth Night.

I was glad I went to see Mama, even though she looked awful. Her skin had a bluish cast, as if it were white chiffon pulled tight over blue ice. Her cheeks were concave like she was sucking in her cheeks, and her dull eyes matched the purple-gray skin around her eyes.

When Mama saw me, little candles lit in her eyes and she held out her arms. When I didn't move, she stepped close and wrapped her bony, cold arms around me.

It's too late, Mama. I don't want your hugs anymore. I turned my head and saw Auntie Odie watching. She nodded toward Mama, her signal for me to return Mama's embrace. So I did, barely touching her, but was relieved when she released her arms. *Why?*

The nurse's aide sat next to Mama. Auntie Odie had me sit on Mama's other side, and she sat next to me. I looked for the candles in Mama's eyes but they had gone out.

We didn't stay long. Mama looked awfully tired. Auntie Odie said reassuring words—"Just think about getting well. Don't you go worrying about Poni—she's safe with me" and "When you're well enough to go home, you can come and stay with us. You girls can stay as long as you need. My *casa* is your *casa*."

Mama said very little and kept wiping away tears.

"I need to take you back up to the room, Ingrid," the nurse's aide said. "If you have anything to say, now is the time."

It took a lot of effort for Mama to stand up, look at us, and say, "Thank you."

Auntie Odie took Mama's limp hands into her own. "May I pray with you?"

Mama bowed her head.

"Dear Father, only You know and understand the ache, the incredible sorrow, in Ingrid's heart. She feels hopeless. Her world is darker than the darkest night right now. But, Lord, You are our Lamp. Please lighten her darkness. May she look to You and find hope, comfort, and, yes, even joy. In Jesus' name, amen."

★ ★ ★

At supper I asked Auntie Odie why she didn't quote Second Samuel twenty-two, twenty-nine for me that morning when I was so mad and so sad, and why she didn't pray for me like she did for Mama at the hospital.

"Would you like me to now?" she asked.

I held out my hands to her across the table, and she clasped them.

"Say the verse with me, child. You know it."

So we said it together.

"For thou art my lamp, O Lord: and the Lord will lighten my darkness."

Then Auntie Odie prayed for me.

★ ★ ★

The Twelfth Night Festival wasn't the fanfare of activities and noise I'd expected, at least not the first half. It was a rather solemn, religious service organized by the Greeley Council of Churches and was one of the Junior Chamber of Commerce's Christmas events. Rev. Jack Reeve explained that Twelfth Night is the eve of Twelfth-day, the evening before Epiphany. Epiphany, he explained, was a feast observed on January 6 to celebrate the manifestation of Christ to the Magi.

Auntie Odie closed her eyes and tilted her head toward heaven when the Elks Chorus sang, her mouth curved gently upward. When Marvin George, the director of the Elks chorus, announced the next song, "Jesus Calls Us," I positioned myself like Auntie Odie—closed my eyes, tilted my head up barely smiling—then listened intently to the words to see if I could understand what Auntie Odie was feeling and to see if I could be comforted.

> "Jesus calls us; o'er the tumult
> Of our life's wild, restless sea,
> Day by day His sweet voice soundeth,
> Saying, 'Christian, follow Me...'"

Tumult would be the next entry in my wordbook. I'd look it up when we got to Auntie Odie's. I understood that line about "life's wild, restless sea." Auntie Odie's head nodded in rhythm with the hymn. So I nodded too.

> "Jesus calls us; by Thy mercies,
> Savior, may we hear Thy call,
> Give our hearts to Thy obedience,
> Serve and love Thee best of all. Amen."

Rev. Merle Allen, Lacy Wilkinson, and Ralph Lindeen read during different portions of the service. I was fidgeting when the Elks Chorus' next song—"Breathe on Me, Breath of God"—was announced. Auntie Odie whispered, "Repeat the words inside your head while they sing. Think of the words as a prayer."

Auntie Odie closed her eyes and I followed her lead.

The thirty voices of the Elks Chorus sang,

> "Breathe on me, Breath of God,
> Fill me with life anew,
> That I may love what thou dost love,
> And do what thou wouldst do.

> "Breathe on me, Breath of God,
> Until my heart is pure,
> Until with thee I will one will,
> To do or to endure.

"Breathe on me, Breath of God,
Till I am wholly thine,
Till all this earthly part of me
Glows with thy fire divine.

"Breathe on me, Breath of God,
So shall I never die,
But live with thee the perfect life
Of thine eternity. Amen."

The candlelighting service, symbolizing the growth of Christianity, filled the auditorium with wavering glow and shadow—bleary gold and hazy-black velvet. Altar boys lit candles representing apostles, saints, and missionaries. People who represented churches in the region stood before candles as they were lit. Three men in kings' costumes roved down the aisle to the front.

The service ended with a boy and girl lighting candles to symbolize "the church of today." The Christmas season was officially ended when the candlelighters led everyone out into the frigid night to the mountain of discarded Christmas trees on the high-school field west of the building. They were set afire with candles, and an immense sphere of light illuminated around us.

The fire radiated a welcome heat. Adults and children laughed and rejoiced—I did too. But, so unlike her, Auntie Odie remained subdued. I huddled close to her, and we wrapped our arms around each other. At last. Auntie Odie sang gently—and off-key—close to my ear.

"Breathe on me, Breath of God,
Till I am wholly thine,
Till all this earthly part of me
Glows with thy fire divine."

Chapter 61

350 Persons
Attend Twelfth
Night Services
—*Greeley Daily Tribune*, p.5, Mon., Jan. 7, 1952

★ ★ ★

Akinites Mourn
Death in Korea
of Another Akin Soldier
—*Akin Scoop*, p.1, Wed., Jan. 23, 1952

Partly cloudy Wednesday; high 37°, low 13°

Jan. 17, 1952
Dear Poni,

I like my new school more and more. Jeanie is a girl in my class newer than me. I'm going to her house after school to play Jacks she's a good reader like me.

My mom keeps geting sick. The polio lets her catch colds and flu easy. Other stuff is wrong to. My dad is sad and me to.

Dad got a job filling preskiptions at a drug store. It's 5 miles away so I can't walk over and get sodas like we use to. Anyway he's not the boss anymore. Grandma and Grandpa come over and take care of my mom a lot.

We hired a housekeeper and cook. Her name is Ardonnis. Can you believe that? What kind of mother would name her kid that?

I'm sorry your mom is sick to. I hope she gets better soon. I miss you and Auntie Odie teribly. I miss feeding the birds to.

Love,
Martha

Jan. 23, 1952

Dear Martha

Tell Ardonnis hello. I like the name. Im glad you have a new freind. Tell Jeanie hello from me to. I don't have any special freinds since you left Just Auntie Odie. I see Sarah F. some. We rode bikes one day.

I hope your mama gets better. Auntie Odie and I pray for her.

My mama is better. She may get out of the hospitle soon. I think she will get well.

Love, Poni

Chapter 62

Families' Best Christmas
Gifts: Photos of POWs
—*Akin Scoop*, p.1, Tues., Jan. 29, 1952

★ ★ ★

Negro Sergeant Who
Sacrificed Life Gets
Congressional Medal
—*Greeley Daily Tribune*, p.9, Tues., Feb. 12, 1952

Generally fair Tuesday; light chinook wind tonight; high 54°, low 26°

"'Abraham Lincoln lived when photography was in its pioneer stage,'" I read. "'There were no candid cameras and taking a picture meant a "sitting." The need for these formal sessions im… mob…'"

"Immobilized," said Auntie Odie.

"'…immobilized his features and his friends said that many qualities of the man failed to get through to the photographic plates…'"

After I read the article aloud to Auntie Odie, we studied the nine photos of Abraham Lincoln, taken during the years from 1848 to1865.

"This is a good article for your scrapbook, Auntie Odie," I said.

"Clip it and glue it in if you want to. Don't forget to write in yesterday's date and the source, *Greeley Daily Tribune*."

She watched me clip, write, and glue.

"One of our poems at school for February is called 'Abraham Lincoln' and I already know it."

"Do you?" She pushed curls back out of my eyes. "Perform it for me. Good practice for the Silver Tongues Harvest."

With sun shining through Auntie Odie's front room bay window I recited all four verses of Mildred Plew Meigs' poem, "Abraham Lincoln." Auntie Odie's smile told me she was pleased—stupendously pleased.

I treasured these quiet times with Auntie Odie reciting poetry, helping each other memorize new poems, reading the newspapers, and clipping articles for her scrapbook. When I worked on homework she sat near me, cheered me on, and fixed us tea. I worried about Mama over in the hospital, but I didn't miss her much.

"I *love* your scrapbooks, Auntie Odie."

She chuckled. "I've been scrapping a long, long time."

I pulled a scrapbook from the shelf and turned the delicate pages. "My favorite is from 1930. Here it is: 'Woman Drank Lizard Egg; It Hatched: Live Reptile, Believed to Have Hatched in Stomach, Drawn From Woman's Throat.'"

I laughed and made a face and Auntie Odie gave me her white-fence grin.

"I clipped that from the *Grand Junction Daily Sentinel,*" she said, "back in the 30s when I visited an elderly friend over on the Western Slope."

"'April 29, 1930, page eleven,'" I read.

We took turns reading the article, and giggling and groaning.

"Can we take this to show my Aunt Bella?"

"Let's go," she said. "It'll give her a good laugh and us another one."

★ ★ ★

Aunt Bella questioned Auntie Odie and me all about Mama. Then she giggled and cooed and commented, looking through Auntie Odie's scrapbooks. She was especially taken with *Greeley Daily Tribune*'s December 23, 1950 article, "Scientists Predict Living Conditions in U.S. in 2,000." She read some of it, and then asked us to read some of it to her.

"'Amid war and rumors of war,'" Auntie Odie read, "'new terrors grip the world, but hopes and dreams of the future prevail…many millions of persons alive today will live to see peace, prosperity, health, longer life, more leisure and greater luxuries than ever were known…'"

With Auntie Odie helping me with some words, I read from the article's "Price of Peace" section. "'Students of history in the year 2000 will probably look back on the 20th century as the new era of blood and money.

"'Blood because the earth will still be reeking from the third world war.

"'Money, representing the material resources of the western world, because it will have outweighed the unfulfilled promises of Russian imperi…' You read it Auntie Odie."

So Auntie Odie read for awhile about the United States being "a new world unifying power" and a lot of scary stuff—like the third world war.

"My, my, my!" Aunt Bella clicked her tongue and shook her head. "Keep a'readin', Odessa."

"'Man-made Planet,'" she read. "'The first man-made star will be circling around the earth by the year 2000.'"

"Lands sakes!" Aunt Bella said. "How can they know all this stuff?"

"'This star's light,'" continued Auntie Odie, "'will be like that of the moon, reflected sunshine. It will be visible before sunrise and after sunset. It will circle 400 to 500 miles away from earth, or possibly farther…

"'Practical uses are numerous. One is a radar beacon. Another to reflect radio signals, for scientific study. Three of these small ships, high enough and evenly spaced around the earth might become relays to serve the entire world with television.'"

Aunt Bella laughed and shook her head. "Hogwash!"

"'...In 2000 we shall be able to fly around the world in a day. We shall be neighbors of everyone else on earth, to whom we wish to be neighborly...'"

"Listen to this, girls." Auntie Odie said. "'In the next century the nation's expenditure for food will be eight times what it is now....

"'Technical advances will be well distributed throughout the economy. For example, a housewife may use an electronic stove and prepare roast beef in less time than it takes to set the table.'"

"More hogwash," Aunt Bella said.

I tugged on the scrapbook. "Auntie Odie, may I read the 'Women for President' part?"

She laughed and placed it in my hands. "Have at it, dear young-eyed child."

"'The woman of the year 2000,'" I read eagerly, "'will be an outsize Diana, anthropologists and beauty experts predict. She will be more than six feet tall, wear a size 11 shoe, have shoulders like a wrestler and muscles like a truck driver.'"

I stopped to snicker then continued, "'Chances are she will be doing a man's job, and for this reason will dress to fit her role. Her hair will be cropped short, so as not to get in the way. She probably will wear the most functional clothes in the daytime, go frilly only after dark.

"'Slacks probably will be her usual workaday costume. These will be of synthetic fiber, treated to keep her warm in the winter and cool in summer, admit the beneficial ultra-violet rays and keep out the burning ones. They will be light weight and equipped with pockets for food capsules, which she will eat instead of meat and potatoes.

Her proportions will be perfect, though Amazonion...'"—Auntie Odie had to help me with *Amazonion*—"'...because science will have perfected a balanced ration of vitamins, proteins and minerals that will produce the maximum bodily efficiency, the minimum of fat...

"'She'll be in on all the high-level groups of finance, business and government. She may even be president.'" I looked at Auntie Odie, then at Aunt Bella. "Maybe I'll be the first woman President of America."

Aunt Bella laughed. "I don't think so."

"It's possible, child," said Auntie Odie. "Just depends on what's your calling, what you'll want to do to fulfill the Lord's purpose for your life."

"Hogwash!" Aunt Bella said for the umpteenth time.

Auntie Odie closed the scrapbook. "Child..."—she laid her hand over mine—"if the God of the Universe wants you to be President of the United States, and if you listen to His voice and follow His ways, you'll be President."

I looked into Auntie Odie's dark eyes and said, "I hope He doesn't want me to be President. I hope He wants me to be a storyteller and recite poetry. I want to be a wordsmith, like you."

Knock, knock. We looked toward the open door. A tall, elderly man in a gray suit stepped in. "Hello, Mrs. Chester."

"Chaplain Brenner!" Aunt Bella declared.

After brief introductions, we settled into a conversation with the chaplain about the world in 2000. I liked the chaplain's friendly, easy manner. Because he had difficulty hearing, he talked loudly, and we had to speak up. The conversation wound around to me and the fact that I was staying with Auntie Odie while my mama was hospitalized.

Chaplain Brenner said he had to leave but was going to see "the boss" first.

"Oh! We'll walk you to his office," said Aunt Bella an octave higher. "I haven't seen Wordsworth in a few days."

"Glad for the company." His voice had a jolly ring to it.

★ ★ ★

The secretary, Alice Cane, visited with us while Denton Daleshaw finished his phone conversation.

From atop the bird cage in the corner, a hoarse voice called, "Favorite girl."

"Here, Wordsworth!" I called, holding up my finger like a perch. But Wordsworth remained on his cage, eyeing us all.

The cockatiel flew to Aunt Bella's shoulder, to her delight, and then retreated to the top of his cage.

"Hey, Charlie!" Mr. Daleshaw hung up the phone, grasped Chaplain Brenner's hand and shook it. Then he greeted Aunt Bella, Auntie Odie, and me. "That ol' Wordsworth will warm up after a few minutes. We've had quite a few drop-in visitors this morning. He's a little tired I think."

Mrs. Cane made sure we all had chairs.

Mr. Daleshaw told Chaplain Brenner he was concerned about one of the rest-home residents, Gladys Zena. She had gotten up during the night and fallen, breaking a hip. Mr. Daleshaw repeated phrases for the near-deaf chaplain. Alice Cane told the chaplain that her daughter had fallen off her bike and broken her arm and was in a lot of discomfort. Aunt Bella brought up Mama's hospitalization and how Auntie Odie needed God's help in caring for me.

"My! A lot of needs today." Chaplain Brenner held his hands out from his sides. "Why don't we join hands and pray right now?"

"Excellent idea," Mr. Daleshaw said.

We gathered in a circle. I held Auntie Odie's cool, weathered hand and Alice Cane's warm, soft one.

"Dear heavenly Father," the chaplain said loudly, "You said that where two or more are gathered together, You would be in the midst of them. Here we are, Lord, gathered in Your name. We've come with our praise, and we've come with our needs."

The chaplain prayed for Gladys Zena, and Mr. Daleshaw—that he would be strengthened and encouraged in his work at the rest home, and he prayed for Aunt Bella, and Alice Cane's daughter, and Auntie Odie and me. While he prayed for Mama, I peeked at him. Right at that moment, Wordsworth circled above his head, stirring the air and strands of the chaplain's hair. Just as the cockatiel started to come in for a landing, Chaplain Brenner tilted his head to the other side.

"Glory!" the chaplain shouted.

Wordsworth continued fluttering around the chaplain's head, drawing strands of hair up on end.

"Thank You for Your Almighty presence among us," trumped the chaplain. "Hallelujah!"

Mr. Daleshaw opened his eyes. He grabbed for Wordsworth just as the chaplain opened his eyes. The chaplain ducked. Wordsworth squawked and flew off.

Everyone laughed.

The chaplain chortled and patted down his thinning hair. "Wordsworth didn't realize that the Holy Spirit needs no assistance."

Chapter 63

Colder in Colorado,
Some Light Snow
—*Akin Scoop*, p.1, Wed., Feb. 13, 1952

Two-Month POW
Exchange Limit
Agreed by Allies
—*Greeley Daily Tribune*, p.1, Wed., Feb. 13, 1952

Partly cloudy and windy Wednesday; high 42°, low 23°; snow flurries in afternoon and night

The class had just recited "Abraham Lincoln," when the principal strolled into the classroom. Miss Maddsen told us to read page 212 silently in our geography books.

Mr. Perkins talked quietly with our teacher then he walked to my seat and bent down. "Poni, I need to talk with you in the hall."

He didn't look upset or anything, so I wasn't worried, just curious. At the door, he signalled for me to take my coat from the hook. A shiver slid down my back.

Mama! Something's happened to Mama.

In the hallway, Salvatore Santi the Firedrake stopped pacing when he saw me, his ruddy face had turned pale, eyes sunken behind furrowed brows. He touched his temple to cover the visible pulse. "Poni, I hate to tell you this."

"Did Mama die? Did she get burned with hot glass?" Then I remembered she was in the hospital—hadn't been to the glassblowing shop for days.

"I don't want you worrying 'bout anything, little girl," Mr. Santi said, soft and low. "You'll be taken care of. You can stay with Mrs. Santi—my mother—and I'll help out some to make sure…"

"Where's Mama?"

"She's fine," Mr. Perkins said. "She's still in the hospital. Sal—Mr. Santi—and his mother are going to take care of you."

My heart stopped beating, and I couldn't breathe. "Auntie Odie!"

★ ★ ★

It was snowing again—sleeting—against the window as the wind blew.

I'd never had many toys, never cared much for them, but I clung to the cloth doll with red-yarn hair that Mrs. Santi had tucked in with me for the night. Her grandchildren slept in this bed when they stayed with her, she'd explained. She said she'd be sleeping in the next room, and I could call her if I needed anything during the night. I wished Mrs. Santi had prayed with me like Auntie Odie always did. It was a warm room, a comfortable bed, but I felt so cold. So cold. I couldn't stop shaking inside.

They'd told me Auntie Odie was in the hospital in Greeley. What was Auntie Odie going through right now? Was she awake? Asleep? Hurting? Was she aware of anything? Was anyone with her? A stroke. What was that exactly? Would she die? Would I ever see her again?

I pulled the covers up around my shoulders and the doll's, squeezed the doll's palms together, and closed my eyes against the darkness.

"Please!" I whispered. "God, please make Auntie Odie well. Please lighten her darkness. And mine too. Pleasepleaseplease don't let her die!"

★ ★ ★

"Mrs. Santi!"

Within seconds the snoring from the other room stopped and she was beside my bed. "I'm here, Poni. What is it?"

I sat up, shivering. "Mrs. Santi, I forgot all about Emily. She didn't get fed. She's all alone in the house."

"Emily?" Her hair in a hairnet snug against her head, and without her glasses, she looked odd, almost spooky, in the uncertain light of the nightlight.

"Auntie Odie's—and my—cat."

"That kitty'll be fine for tonight." She nudged my shoulders until I was back on the pillow then tucked the cloth doll in the crook of my arm. "We'll go see her tomorrow and feed her. Now you lie back down and get some sleep."

"And the wild birds…"

"They'll be fine too. But if it'll make you feel better, tomorrow we'll buy seed at Anderson Mill and Elevator to fill Odessa's feeders."

"She has a big supply of seed in the garage. I know where it is. I know how to feed them."

Mrs. Santi tucked the covers around the doll's and my chins. "They'll all be fine tonight. You and Sal can check on Emily and the birds on the way to school tomorrow."

"School?"

She smiled—at least, in the darkness, it sort of looked like she smiled. "Yes, school."

"But I have to go see Auntie Odie."

"That won't be any time soon, honey. Not while she's in the hospital. Just don't worry yourself. Things will work out."

I listened to the soft shuffle of Mrs. Santi's slippers across the rug, and on the hallway wood floor to her room.

Oh, Emily, what will become of us?

246

Chapter 64

Good Chance for
Korean Peace by
Spring, Acheson
—*Greeley Daily Tribune*, p.5, Thurs., Feb. 21, 1952

★ ★ ★

3 Weld County
Towns Skirted by
U.S. Highway 6
—*Akin Scoop*, p.1, Sat., Feb. 23, 1952

High Saturday 46°, low 14°, precipitation .01"

After showing Mama the well-stocked refrigerator and cupboard, Mrs. Santi wrapped an arm around her waist. "Now, do you think you two will be okay here by yourselves?"

Mama nodded.

Mr. Santi slipped on his big plaid jacket. "Let us know if you need anything, Ingrid." He tousled my hair. "You, too, sweetheart."

"Thanks," whispered Mama.

He stopped in the doorway. "If you're interested, I still need a good glassblowing apprentice."

"Thanks," Mama said.

A knock on the door—it was Mr. and Mrs. Herb Smith.

"I'm sorry this place is so small, and beat up by so many renters," Mrs. Smith said, "but it's pretty quiet back here behind the cleaners. Hardly any traffic in the alley."

"It's fine," said Mama. "Really it is. We're so thankful for it. It'll get us by until I can get back to work."

"It stinks good." I tried to say something positive.

They all gawked at me.

"The cleaners smell," I explained, "the hot clothes and the detergent. And the stuff you put on the clothes being dry cleaned."

After they left, Mama sat me down. "I know this has been hard for you, Ponia." She straightened and put her shoulders back. "But things will get better now."

I nodded, wanting to believe her.

"We're not always going to live in this place. I'm going to make a better life for us." Square lights from the only window reflected in her eyes. She covered my hands with her own long slender ones and looked me straight in the eyes. "Can you believe that with me?"

I finally nodded. "Yes, Mama."

Maybe. I'll try.

Chapter 65

War in Korea
Grinds into
21st Month
—*Greeley Daily Tribune*, p.1, Mon., Feb. 25, 1952

Weather Perfect
For Recording
Eclipse
—*Akin Scoop*, p.1, Mon., Feb. 25, 1952

Fair Monday and tonight; high 45°, low 8° at 8:00 a.m.

"All who turn in signed Weekly Reading Records," Miss Maddsen announced, "verifying that you have read at home, with expression, at least twenty-eight days in March, will qualify for a field trip to the county's first television showing, April seventeenth, at Weld Garage in Greeley."

★ ★ ★

I raced my pale-green and lavender bike to Auntie Odie's house to feed Emily and the birds, and then rode to Akin Rest Home to visit Aunt Bella.

I'd been visiting Aunt Bella every day to practice reading with expression. While she knitted, I read, and she'd scribble her signature on my Weekly Reading Record. Then I'd push her in her wheelchair to Mr. Daleshaw's and Mrs. Cane's office to visit our cockatiel friend, Wordsworth. We always left the office with smiles, no matter how bad Aunt Bella's arthritis ached or how deep the sorrow Auntie Odie's stroke had delivered to my life.

"Aunt Bella, guess what!" I dropped my book and papers and pulled off my coat. "I'm going to the first television showing in Weld County with Miss Maddsen by reading every day in March."

Aunt Bella was looking at something behind me.

I turned around and gasped. "Auntie Odie!"

In the corner bed—face sunken, the color of chimney smoke, eyes closed, mouth open, breathing in whispery little puffs—was my dearest friend in the world.

Aunt Bella's voice came from far away. "The ambulance brought her this morning from the hospital in Greeley. I requested her for my roommate."

I stepped to her bedside. "Auntie Odie, it's me, Poni."

A nurse's aide came in, straightened Auntie Odie's covers and fluffed her pillow.

"She ain't said anything since she's been here," Aunt Bella said, "nor opened her eyes."

"Will she wake up?" I asked.

The aide shrugged and shook her head.

"Will she talk someday?" I asked.

"No one knows for sure." The aide patted my shoulder, then left.

"How sad." Aunt Bella straightened her lap robe, and then looked up at me with those big, stary eyes of hers. "But aren't you glad she's here now? You can see your friend anytime you want."

I grinned, so glad Aunt Bella was being good about sharing her room—the first time she'd wanted to share for a long time. "Now I can visit both of you every day. And maybe I'll be here when Auntie Odie wakes up."

Aunt Bella chuckled her high bony laugh. "Ponia, you just scooch right up here beside me and read. You're getting to be *some* reader."

Aunt Bella clickety-clacked her knitting needles, smiled, and nodded as I read. Every so often I glanced over at Auntie Odie, still and gray. So different from the vibrant friend I once knew. But at least she was *here* where I could see her every day and have hope that she would get better soon.

Hope is the thing with feathers.

★ ★ ★

I rode my bike to Auntie Odie's house, held the grateful cat and petted her until I looked at the time. Five o'clock and starting to get dark. I rode past Martha's house with different people inside and puffed like a steam engine in the frosty twilight air as I peddled toward the tumbledown house behind the dry cleaners. Clouds that looked like see-through baskets of apples, peaches, and pears sat on the Rocky Mountains awaiting a jelly-maker.

Mama actually smiled when I came in the door. "What kept you so long, as if I didn't know?"

Something smelled good. I hung my coat on the hook by the front door. "Did you know Auntie Odie's at the Akin Rest home? In the same room as Aunt Bella?"

"I heard," she said. "I guess that makes you mighty happy. How does tomato soup and grilled cheese sandwiches sound—ingredients compliments of the Santis?"

"Sounds *good*. Have you seen Auntie Odie yet, Mama?"

"No. I'll go tomorrow after I finish at the glassblower's."

"I hope it doesn't make you sad. She's not awake. And she doesn't look good."

"I'll be okay. Don't you worry." She dished up the soup and sandwiches and poured two glasses of milk. "Come and eat before the soup gets cold."

Chapter 66

Negro Released 1 ½-Years
After He Was Acquitted
—*Greeley Daily Tribune*, p.3, Fri., Feb. 29, 1952

Hill Says New Modern
Weld Hospital in Greeley
Best in Colorado
—*Akin Scoop*, p.1, Fri., Feb. 29, 1952

Friday's high 36°, low 14°; winter wheat covered with snow; snow ending this morning; partly cloudy

After school I fed Emily and the birds and watered Auntie Odie's houseplants. Tucked inside my school tablet was a *Tribune* article I'd cut out the day before, "Lonely Vigil at Scene of Tragedy." It was such a sad photo and story, but I believed it was one that Auntie Odie would've clipped and added to her scrapbook. A man near Racine, Wisconsin had a heart attack and died while changing the tire on his car. His cocker spaniel stayed by his side for ten hours before they were discovered. I would tell Auntie Odie the story.

★ ★ ★

"There's our girl!" squawked Aunt Bella.

I hugged her then greeted Auntie Odie as if she could hear me and gently held her hand for awhile. I told her the cocker spaniel story, and about the reading assignment Miss Maddsen had given us for March, and about my goal to go to the Weld Garage in April to watch television for the first time. Today Auntie Odie's eyes were open, but they weren't seeing eyes.

I read to Aunt Bella and she signed my Weekly Reading Record. I recited all three verses of our February poem, "Washington" by Nancy Byrd Turner, with all the expression I could muster and hoped that, somehow, Auntie Odie heard it too.

"Bravo!" said Aunt Bella.

I searched Auntie Odie's face for some sign that she had heard.

But there was none.

Chapter 67

Dry Snow and
Chill Weather
Cover County
—*Greeley Daily Tribune*, p.1, Mon., March 3, 1952

★ ★ ★

Students Gear Up for 1952
Silver Tongues Harvest
Set For March 21st
—*Akin Scoop*, p.1, Wed., March 5, 1952

Partly cloudy Wednesday; high 47°, low 21°

I clasped Auntie Odie's limp hand and my stomach tightened. Behind an oxygen tent, her face was gray, sunken. "What happened, Aunt Bella? Why's Auntie Odie on oxygen?"

Aunt Bella's hands moved quickly, looping and catching the yarn as she knitted. "She had a spell today. But she's better now. The oxygen should get her back to the way she was."

"Guess what, Auntie Odie."

Aunt Bella rested her knitting in her lap, her eyes bugged in her pickle-shaped face. But I'd come to love her—and her face—during recent months. "Now, honey, you know she can't hear you."

"I know, but I have to try." I kissed Auntie Odie's hand. "Auntie Odie, I saw a pair of red-breasted nuthatches at your feeder today."

"Poni," Aunt Bella said, "why don't you scooch right up here beside me and read me your book?"

"I spotted the male in the spruce tree, upside-down on the trunk. He was so cute, just a little guy—red breast, bluish-gray back. And a sporty little black cap and black goggles."

Aides in the hall talked loudly about their night-before dates. The oxygen tent shimmered gently as oxygen filled it and Auntie Odie breathed.

"Come on, honey," said Aunt Bella.

"Then that little red-breasted nuthatch flew to the suet. His mate was already there partaking." *Partaking* was a new word I'd learned at school. I'd added it to my word book, along with *diaphanous*. But I didn't think I'd ever be able to use *diaphanous* in everyday talk.

I wrapped my hands gently around Auntie Odie's. I kissed the back of her hand again and stroked it. "Auntie Odie, aren't you proud of me for noticing different visitors to your feeders? And for noticing their details and listening to their call so I could look them up in your bird book? That's how I knew they were red-breasted nuthatches."

"Come on, Poni," Aunt Bella said. "Maybe she'll hear you when you read."

I pulled up a chair beside Aunt Bella and opened my school library book. "*Little Women* by Louisa M. Alcott. Chapter One.

> "'Christmas won't be Christmas without any presents,' grumbled Jo, lying on
> the rug.
> "'It's so dreadful to be poor!' sighed Meg, looking down at her old dress."

I paused and gazed at my dear Auntie Odie.

"Keep it up, Poni," Aunt Bella said. "I always heard about *Little Women* but never read it."

"I wish I had a book about slaves," I said. "I want to read about Auntie Odie's long-ago people—real stories about real people."

"Goodness, girl! What's gotten into you?"

"I'll go to Dunkling Memorial Library tomorrow and see what they have about American-Negro people." *Dear God, please! Make Auntie Odie well.*

"Read, Poni! Read!" Aunt Bella demanded.

> "'I don't think it's fair for some girls to have plenty of pretty things, and other
> girls nothing at all,' added little Amy, with an injured sniff...
> "'We've got father and mother and each other,' said Beth contentedly, from
> her corner..."

Chapter 68

Truman Warns
Farmers Against
Change In Govt.
—*Greeley Daily Tribune*, p.7, Tues., March 11, 1952

★ ★ ★

Ike Backers in
Colorado Are
Enthusiastic
—*Greeley Daily Tribune*, p.1, Wed., March 12, 1952

Partly cloudy Wednesday; high 44°, low 17°; fierce winds

Miss Maddsen asked me if I'd stay for a few minutes after school.

"Poni, you haven't signed up to try out for the Silver Tongues Harvest. I expected you would."

"Well…" I shuffled my feet. The windows shuddered as the wind whooped against them.

Miss Maddsen sat down eye-to-eye with me. "Is there a problem?"

I looked out the window at the cold day instead of into her pretty blue eyes.

"I think you'd do well. But it's only a week away. You need to try out by Friday."

"I want to, but I don't know if I can." I slipped into my coat. "Auntie Odie's sick and so's my mama sometimes."

Miss Maddsen smiled—a rare, genuine smile. "I've heard how devoted you are to the best storyteller and poet in the county, visiting her every day, taking care of her household."

Warmth filled my cheeks like hot water pouring into a hot-water bottle.

"What do you say, Poni? Shall we sign you up to try out?"

"I'm not good like lots of other people. Some kids don't think I have a chance."

"Who's to say? You could end up the dark horse—the winner people least expect."

I avoided Miss Maddsen's gaze by studying the bumpy texture of our geography books lining the shelf.

"It would make Odessa Luckett very proud if she woke up and heard how well you did at the Harvest. Don't you think?"

I smiled and looked at my shoes. "Mm-hm."

Chapter 69

Wind Storm
Whirls Large
Dust Clouds
—*Greeley Daily Tribune*, p.1, Wed., March 19, 1952

Akin Students
Eager For
Silver Tongues Harvest
—*Akin Scoop*, p.1, Wed., March 19, 1952

Snow disappeared Wednesday morning; generally fair; high 62°, low 32°; windstorm at 1:00 p.m.—huge clouds of dust; destroyed some wheat

I greeted Auntie Odie's still form and touched her hand.

"Ponia," Aunt Bella said, "you just scootch right up here beside me and read to your heart's content. What are you going to read today?"

I pulled up a chair from the corner of the room and sat beside her. "*When the People Soared Like Eagles*. It's a retelling of an African folktale I found at the Dunkling library, something like the story Auntie Odie told Martha and me last summer. I've been practicing and practicing it."

"Read it!" blared Aunt Bella, sweeping her arms in the air.

I worked to make my voice full and slow with expression.

"Some say that in the bygone days of Africa the people soared like eagles.

At least them that had the magic. Yes, they spread their arms and stepped up into the air like they was jus' climbin' stairs. But there came long dark days when they were stolen away for slavery. No time to gather wings. No way to hide them anyways on those dismal ships, full to their sterns with brokenhearted slaves."

Aunt Bella hummed and knitted, clicking her needles like fury. I moved my chair away a little.

"Of course, they still had the magic, them that could fly. In the slave land, they hid their secret deep in their hearts. But some forgot the secret. And some, born into slavery, weren't ever told they could fly.

"Johnny was like an old granddaddy that all the slaves loved. He never forgot that he could fly, even when the Driver opened his back with a whip. One day a young girl, Abby, got sick in the field. She did fall and could not get up.

"'Get up and back to work!' shouted the Overseer. The sun beat on Abby's back and so did the Driver.

"As Johnny helped her to her feet, he whispered, 'You have the power, Abby. Fly!'"

Aunt Bella's humming and knitting noises irritated me. I moved my chair close to Auntie Odie's bed. As the sun slowly set, the room dimmed, and I read on in the bleary light.

"...When at last Abby's feet left the ground, she mounted up like an eagle, soaring higher and higher. Then Johnny blew the magic words like a gentle wind over the slaves. A mother, holding her wide-eyed baby tight, and a young boy did step into the air and fly.

"How they did laugh and holler. The Overseer on his horse galloped after them grabbing for their heels.

"The other slaves jumped and shouted, 'They're flyin'! They're flyin' to freedom!'

"An old woman stepped up, and a man, and another. They did step right up on invisible stairs and fly away."

While I paused to look at the picture, a trembling pressure alighted on my shoulder.

I turned. *Auntie Odie!* But my mouth and voice froze.

Eyes open wide, she gestured, slowly.

I was scared at first. She didn't look real, but transparent—as if the white sheets were gray fog peering through her body. *Diaphanous.*

I rose slowly, treelike, then planted my feet beside her bed.

Her clouded brown eyes sparked and she beckoned me to come close.

"Auntie Odie, you're back," I was finally able to whisper. But so afraid it was a dream and I would wake myself.

Her lips formed words I couldn't hear.

"Aunt Bella, Auntie Odie's awake! She's trying to say something."

Aunt Bella stopped knitting and stared, mouth open.

I leaned down near Auntie Odie's face, held my breath, and listened.

"I... like... story." Then a small, one-sided smile formed on her wrinkled mouth.

I smiled and nodded. The chair bumped and thudded under my quaking hands as I faced it toward Auntie Odie. She looked so ill, but her eyes were new.

Aunt Bella wheeled toward the doorway. "I'll get a nurse!"

"Oh, Auntie Odie... I've missed you so much!" I choked on my words.

A nurse bustled in with two aides and Aunt Bella in tow. An aide turned on Aunt Bella's lamp.

"She's come to!" Aunt Bella blared. "See? Ain't I right?"

Auntie Odie's barely audible words thrilled me beyond anything I'd ever known. "Read... I... like."

"See?" Aunt Bella huffed and waved her arms toward her roommate. "She wants Ponia to read to her. Don't that beat all?"

"Odessa, my name is Candice. I'm your nurse. Can you tell me your last name?"

Aunt Odie slowly moved the focus of her eyes from my face to the nurse's. "Luck—" she finally managed to say.

"Her last name's Luckett," I said.

"Do you know where you are?" the nurse asked her.

Long pause. Auntie Odie whispered, "No."

"You're at the Akin Rest Home." The nurse's voice was loud in the small room, and she articulated each word. "Sandy, a worker here, is calling your doctor. You had a stroke, and you've been asleep for awhile. Your young friend's aunt is your roommate, Bella Chester."

Aunt Bella rolled her wheelchair into the circle of observers. "We're glad you're back, Odessa. This here little Ponia has missed you dreadful, been here every day to look out for you. She hasn't missed a day."

Auntie Odie studied Aunt Bella then looked back at me.

While the nurse took Auntie Odie's pulse and blood pressure, she said, "Mrs. Luckett, do you like Poni's reading?"

A half-smile formed and she moved her head up slightly then back down.

The nurse's eyes were bright, alert. She said to me, "Go ahead and read to her. I'll just watch."

I read, glancing up every few words to reassure myself that Auntie Odie really was back. At first, the words settled like rocks in my dry mouth and I stumbled over them.

Nurse Candice interruped me. "Sweetie, I've got to get some meds to some folks, and the doctor should be here real soon. Will you and Bella be okay alone with Mrs. Luckett for a little bit?"

"I'll call for you," interjected Aunt Bella, "or I'll wheel to the hallway and start yelling if there's any changes."

"Fine. Wonderful." The nurse looked at me and said, "You just read to her, sweetie. I'll be back soon."

After the nurse and aides left, I felt my neck and shoulders relax. "You still want me to read, Auntie Odie?"

She looked awfully tired, but she slowly blinked her eyes. I was pretty sure that meant *yes*.

"You ready, Aunt Bella?"

She was already knitting away. "You betcha, honey."

"…An old woman stepped up, and a man, and another. They did step right up on invisible stairs then fly away. You shoulda heard all the laughin' and hollerin' and singin' by those slaves on the ground and in the air."

The lines on Auntie Odie's face softened. I felt peaceful—carefree. Auntie Odie was back! *Make the words beautiful for her.* My tongue and voice wrapped each word like a gift. The words rose like violin notes then fell to textured whispers.

"The Master, the Overseer and the Drivers were confounded by it all, shoutin' and yellin' and chasin'."

Deep breath. My voice became a flute.

"Soon the field became shadowed by the people as they flew like one massive bird—soaring toward the clouds into the ocean of sky. Then the heavens opened up and welcomed them home to Freedom."

Auntie Odie's little one-sided smile stayed. Her eyes closed, but I knew she was still listening. Life spread over her countenance like the sunrise lights hills and valleys.

I read to an audience of two from that day on, Auntie Odie smiling half and Aunt Bella with needles clicking.

Chapter 70

Winter's Heaviest Snow Covers
County, Blocking Highways and
Forcing Most Schools to Close
—*Greeley Daily Tribune*, p.1, Fri., March 21, 1952

Due to Adverse Weather
Silver Tongues Harvest
Rescheduled For Fri., March 28
—*Akin Scoop*, p.1, Fri., March 21, 1952

Friday's high 22°, low 11°; snow and wind; drifting snow; precipitation .07"

Mama and I pulled the card table near the open oven door to warm ourselves. The chicken noodle soup and saltines tasted so delicious, I wished we had more.

"When the weather clears, could I go get Emily and bring her here until Auntie Odie is well enough to go home?"

"The cat's better off there than cooped up in this little room."

"I hope she's okay tonight."

"You gave her extra dry food yesterday, right?"

"Yep. And cleaned her cat box."

"She'll be fine."

I drank the last of the broth from the bowl. "I hope Auntie Odie's okay. This is the first day I didn't go see her at the rest home."

"They'll take good care of her and Aunt Bella."

"What if the nurses and cooks can't get through the drifts?"

"They'll get through. Somehow."

I enjoyed the school day at home with Mama, reading, memorizing poetry, practicing for the Harvest, and helping with the housework. Mama was even talkative at times. And pleasant. I had been afraid the dreary weather would get her down, make her sour.

"You disappointed?" asked Mama.

"What?"

"You know, that they postponed the Silver Tongues Harvest?"

"I'm glad. It's another week to practice."

"You doing 'Hiawatha?'"

"Mm-hm. I know it good from reciting it to earn my bike."

"Say it for me." Mama's eyes sparkled in the lamplight as she overlapped her sweater across the front of her dress.

"Now?"

"Sure, now. Pretend you're on stage at Akin School and five hundred people are listening." She sat, hands folded in her lap.

I stood the mop up in the mopbucket and braced books around it so the handle stood upright. Mama announced me and I walked to the "microphone."

"'Hiawatha's Childhood' by Henry Wadsworth Longfellow:

> "By the shores of Gitche Gumee,
> By the shining Big-Sea-Water,
> Stood the wigwam of Nokomis…"

Chapter 71

42 Degrees
Heat Reduces
Snow Banks
—*Greeley Daily Tribune*, p.1, Thurs., March 27, 1952

★ ★ ★

Community Invited to 1952 Annual
Silver Tongues Harvest
Tonight at Akin School Auditorium
—*Akin Scoop*, p.1, Fri., March 28, 1952

Fair Friday; high 65°, low 26°

"You walk on over to the school, Poni. Maybe I'll come later."
"Aren't you coming to the Harvest, Mama?"
"I'm awfully tired. I'll see."
Disappointment scalded the back of my eyes and forehead.

After what happened at the Harvest, I was glad Mama didn't come, and relieved Auntie Odie wasn't there either, for that matter.

Climbing up the stairs to the stage, I caught my foot on a step and fell. The audience gasped. My nose and forehead hit the floor so hard I couldn't move for a few seconds. Mr. Fraser, the emcee, helped me back down to a front row seat between Frank Chavez and a sixth grade girl. I touched my nose to see if it was bleeding. It wasn't. Just felt like it. Frank patted my shoulder.

They called up Hetti Zimmerman. She performed a poem, "The Ballad of the Harp-Weaver" by Edna St. Vincent Millay.

After Mr. Fraser announced me—again—and I stood to go up onto the stage, the audience clapped. At the microphone, I shook like I was standing on an earthquake, fumbled words, and couldn't get my body and mind under control. Finally, several lines into the poem, I simply turned away and headed off the stage. I hurried up the side aisle and out to the vestibule, pulled on my boots, grabbed my coat and hat and fled home—across the street to the little shack on the alley.

Light from a night lamp and Mama's gentle snores greeted me. She slept on the twin bed in the corner, facing the wall. I pulled off my boots and set them on the newspapers spread out by the door. I turned out the night lamp and felt my way to my mat bed on the floor. The room felt drafty and I chilled. With my clothes, coat, hat, and shoes still on, I crawled between the covers and cried myself to sleep.

Chapter 72

Nearly 600 people Attend
Silver Tongues Harvest
—*Akin Scoop*, p.1, Sat., March 29, 1952

★ ★ ★

Accidental Acrobat
—*Greeley Daily Tribune*, p.1, Tues., April 1, 1952

Partly cloudy Tuesday; high 56°, low 29°

"Here's a good one for your scrapbook, Auntie Odie."

Each day I brought *Greeley Daily Tribune* and *Akin Scoop* to read to Auntie Odie. Sometimes she slept through my visits, but most of the time she was awake enough to respond—a nod or a half-smile or a faint squeeze to my hand. But she hadn't spoken any more words since the day she awakened two weeks before.

I showed her the *Tribune*'s front-page photo—a boy walking his dog, the dog up on his hind legs. Auntie Odie studied the picture, half-smiled, and raised her left hand as if to point.

"Shall I read it to you?" I asked.

She looked at me and blinked slowly, appearing more listless than the day before.

"Accidental Acrobat
"Richard Marandola watches
proudly as his dog Rusty marches
along on two legs at Cranston, R.I...."

"I wonder what *R.I.* stands for," I said to no one in particular.

"Rhode Island," Aunt Bella said grumpily.

Uh, oh. I hadn't paid much attention to her, so I showed Aunt Bella the photo too.

She grunted and knitted furiously.

I stood by Auntie Odie again.

"…Both Rusty's front legs were broken when he was run over by an auto a couple of months ago. While they were healing in splints, Rusty learned to walk on his hind legs. Though he customarily uses four now, it's no trouble at all to use just two when his master tells him.

"Isn't that a good story, Auntie Odie?"

Her hand lifted in a little wave.

"Shall I cut it out and glue it in your scrapbook?"

Another lift of the hand and a half-smile.

After I read more newspaper articles, I said, "Mama went to Anderson Mill and Elevator and got more seed for the wild birds and cat food for Emily."

Auntie Odie half-smiled.

"Emily misses you, but she's doing fine. She stays real close and purrs when I visit her."

But when I described my experience at the Silver Tongues Harvest and said I never wanted to recite in front of an audience again—ever, Auntie Odie's eyes brimmed with tears. She raised her hand toward my face. I leaned close and she cupped her hand around my cheek.

She tried to speak, but couldn't. Found my hand and squeezed it.

I nodded. "I know… I'll try again—someday. Maybe."

The one-sided smile slid right up the left side of her face like spilled water on a sloped table. Then, she slowly winked.

"If Rusty can learn to walk on two legs," I said, "I should be able to walk up the stairs without falling next time." I grinned at her. "And you'll be well by the next Harvest, Auntie Odie, and you'll be able to come. Every day I ask God to make you better."

Chapter 73

Allied Airmen Tie
Down Planes in Wind;
DE Shelled, Unharmed
Seoul, April 17
—*Greeley Daily Tribune*, p.1, Thurs., April 17, 1952

Weld County Garage Hosting
First Television showing;
16 Students Earn Attendance
—*Akin Scoop*, p.1, Thurs., April 17, 1952

Scattered thundershowers Thursday afternoon and evening; high 71°, low 36°

The sixteen students who read at home twenty-eight or more days in March boarded the schoolbus with Miss Maddsen and rode to the Weld County Garage in Greeley for the live television show at two-thirty.

Hundreds of people situated themselves among ten screens throughout the showrooms. Visitors arrived from as far away as Wyoming. Radio and newspapermen conversed and set up equipment. I found the transmitters as interesting as the show on the television screens. I learned from reading the *Tribune*, it was transmitted by a DuMont transmitter through a shielded coaxial cable to the receiving televisions at the garage, rather than over the air.

Miss Colorado, Jo London, and talent from around Weld County performed in the show—soloists, vocal duets and trios, dancers, trumpet players, accordianists, pianists, song-and-dance acts, and bands. It would still be months before over-the-air television was available in Weld.

Later, I recounted the event to the elderly roommates at Akin Rest Home. Aunt Bella chuckled and asked a dozen questions. Auntie Odie smiled half and her clear dark eyes glistened like stars.

Chapter 74

Biggest Atom
Blast in U.S.
Set for Tues.
—*Greeley Daily Tribune*, p.1, Mon., April 21, 1952

Late Snow Ends
Weld's Early Summer
—*Akin Scoop*, p.1, Mon., April 21, 1952

Cloudy Monday with intermittent rain, clearing tonight; windy; high 40°, low 32°; precipitation 1.03"

"I want the language to be beautiful, special, and just right," I told Miss Maddsen, "like the poems in my Auntie Odie's poetry books."

Since April first, we had been studying and writing poetry. I had labored for two weeks, at school and at home, writing a poem for Auntie Odie. I chose some favorite words from my word-collection book and worked them into the verses. My teacher, impressed with my determination, taught me how to use a thesaurus and a rhyming dictionary, and she helped me revise.

Miss Maddsen remained sober but her blue eyes twinkled as she gave my arm a squeeze. "I'm amazed at how far you've come, Ponia."

After school I walked the two blocks to the rest home with my poem, along with a gift for Aunt Bella. I handed Aunt Bella a sack. "Some stationery for you I decorated with thumbprint flowers."

She pulled a sheet out of the bag. "Beautiful! Thank you, sweetie."

Auntie Odie watched us from her bed. I stepped to her side and kissed her forehead. "I wrote a Haiku poem for you, Auntie Odie. Would you like to hear it?"

She smiled her one-sided smile.

"The title is 'Tender Mercies.'" I articulated the words slowly and expressively:

"With tender mercies, each seed she sows,
bids each stalk and cheers
the blossom cameos.

"With feeders brimming, wild birds are fed,
　　her words and their songs
　　　　entwine like woven thread.

"With tender mercies, she teaches me,
　　bids each gift and cheers
　　　　my slightest victory.

"My mind brims with wisdom softly said.
　　Laughter, poems, and hearts
　　　　entwine like woven thread."

Aunt Bella clapped. "Great guns ablasting! Very good, Poni!"

Auntie Odie raised her hand and made a faint gutteral sound. And the good half of her face grinned.

Chapter 75

Newest Atomic Bomb Jolts People
10 Miles Away, Seen for 75 Miles;
Heat Singes Faces of Observers
—*Greeley Daily Tribune*, p.1, Tues., April 22, 1952

Storm Loaded
With Welcome
Moisture
—*Akin Scoop*, p.1, Tues., April 22, 1952

Cloudy Tuesday with scattered rain or snow; partially clearing in afternoon; high 47°, low 31°

After school, as usual, I ran to the nursing home to see Auntie Odie and Aunt Bella.

The nurses had seated Auntie Odie in an armchair.

"Poem…again," she said after she managed her half-smile.

"Auntie Odie!" I ran to her and embraced her. "You're talking again! And sitting up!"

Her face—especially her eyes—expressed all the love for me that she'd expressed in words and deeds when she was well.

I finally settled myself and recited my poem for Auntie Odie again. When I finished, cheering and clapping resounded behind me. Crowded just inside the doorway were Mrs. Angela Fall, Mama, Dora Santi, the Firedrake, Chaplain Brenner, and a nurse's aide.

"I'm a poet!" I laughed then took my bows.

Chapter 76

Eisenhower Backed By
Saturday Evening Post
—*Akin Scoop*, p.2, Wed., April 30, 1952

Start Seeds
Indoors To
Beat Weather
—*Greeley Daily Tribune*, p.3, Wed., April 30, 1952

Partly cloudy Wednesday; lightly scattered showers in afternoon; high 56°, low 43°; prec. .08"

"'Start Seeds Indoors To Beat Weather,'" I read to Auntie Odie from the *Tribune*. "'By Cynthia Lowry, AP Newsfeatures Writer.

> "There are two ways of acquiring tender young plants for the garden: obtaining them by gift, theft, or purchase, or by raising them from seed yourself. It seems only fair to warn the latter alternative is a time-consuming, fussy, worrisome—and fascinating— job to most gardeners, who use the 'sunny window' system.
> "The object of starting seeds in-doors, of course, is to get a head start on the weather…"

Auntie Odie wore a peaceful face as she leaned forward in her wheelchair and listened. The rosy-pink hue of the fancy hat and rhinestone earbobs Mama and I'd brought from her cottage reflected on her dark skin. Color was returning to the face I'd come to treasure above all others.

Aunt Bella glanced up from her knitting and smiled. Mama sat on Auntie Odie's bed. The visible signs of Auntie Odie's progress and the attentiveness of my audience warmed me down to some deep place in my spirit.

Whenever I came to a new subheading, I asked if I should stop.

Auntie Odie half-smiled each time. "Read, …dear… child."

When I finished reading, I asked Auntie Odie if she'd like me to start some seeds for her according to the directions in the seeds article.

"W–Work." she said.

"It wouldn't be work to me, Auntie Odie. I'd love to do it."

Mama amazed me when she knelt down by Auntie Odie's wheelchair and took her limp hand. "I could help Poni. We'd both enjoy it. We'll give you reports on the progress."

Auntie Odie placed her good hand over Mama's. "Splen…diff…."

Aunt Bella chortled. "And you can bring us summer bouquets once they're growing."

A shadow crossed Auntie Odie's face. She looked Mama in the eyes. "Where… live… you?"

"She wants to know where you're living," Aunt Bella interpreted.

Mama swallowed. "Herb and Betty Smith are letting us stay in the house behind their cleaners in exchange for my cleaning at the business after hours every weekday."

"Sh-sh-shack," Auntie Odie said. Then she began making noises, trying to speak. In her effort, she slumped over toward her paralyzed side.

"She needs another pillow under that paralyzed arm," Aunt Bella said.

Mama and I propped her up with the pillow from her bed.

Auntie Odie raised her good arm toward Mama's face. Mama leaned down and Auntie Odie cupped Mama's chin in her hand. "My house… your… house."

The sound of knitting needles stopped. "I think she wants you to live in her house," Aunt Bella said.

"Y–Yes!" Auntie Odie's eyes glistened as she looked first at Mama, then at me. "Yes!"

Mama rested her fingertips over her parted lips. "Well, I… Oh my, Odessa. We couldn't…"

"Yesyes!" Auntie Odie whispered forcefully, "Do! …Wait for… me… there."

"I'm your witness," Aunt Bella said. "Get movin', I'd say."

Something like a laugh forced its way from Auntie Odie's mouth. Her head flopped forward, and her pink hat tumbled to the floor.

The laughter in that little room made my body tingle like my spine was a sparkler on the Fourth of July.

Chapter 77

Twister Touches
Down on Beckett
Place South of Akin
—*Akin Scoop*, p.1, Thurs., May 15, 1952

★ ★ ★

Dooley Tells Memorial Day Crowd
at Linn Grove Cemetery There Is
Hope in Today's Troubled Times
—*Greeley Daily Tribune*, p.1, Fri., May 30, 1952

★ ★ ★

Reds Resume
Attack Upon
T-Bone Hill
—*Greeley Daily Tribune*, p.1, Fri., June 20, 1952

Partly cloudy Friday; scattered light showers in afternoon and evening; high 95°, low 57°

The seeds Mama and I planted in flats last April had come up beautifully and now bloomed in Auntie Odie's garden. Aunt Bella and Auntie Odie had been enlivened and entertained by the indoor-seed-planting reports.

Mama worked—cleaning homes and businesses, mending for Mr. Smith's customers, and assisting the Firedrake at his shop. Every day I rode my bike to the rest home to visit Auntie Odie and Aunt Bella, and Wordsworth too.

Slowly, Auntie Odie was overcoming the effects of her stroke. Mama and I loved living in her cozy cottage. I labored zealously in her gardens, yet it wasn't work to me, but pure joy. My heart's desire was for her to come home to a garden as lovely as if she were the gardener. But my hard work wasn't just out of love for Auntie Odie. It satisfied my budding passion for gardening. I checked out gardening books from the library, and, when it was too rainy or windy to be outside, read them by the hour. I read and memorized poetry. Sometimes Sarah Fenderlupen and I rode our bikes to the haunted house on the west end of Seventh Avenue. The ghost stories I told were more ghostly and ghastly out at that cobwebby, creaky old house.

"Oddball," "weird," "strange" were typical names I was called by other kids because I didn't spend much time playing with toys or games. And sometimes the Weatherby twins taunted me with unkind remarks because my best friend in the world was colored. But I didn't even care. Auntie Odie was the important one I wanted to please—not those immature and prejudiced Weatherby twins. My latest new word in my word book was *prejudiced*.

I'd received several letters from Martha, and I answered them all. The Matthews had hoped to travel to Akin to see Auntie Odie this summer, but Mrs. Matthews wasn't well enough for such a trip.

One Friday morning it became too hot to work anymore in the gardens, so I pulled several of Auntie Odie's poetry books from the shelf. I cuddled up with Emily in Auntie Odie's wicker rocker. It was comfortably cool inside the house.

One book, *In Praise of Wings: A Flock of Poems by Agatha Jordan*, overtook me. Whenever it was time to move the sprinkler, I raced outside, reset it, and raced back. There were poems about sunsets and birds, slaves and struggle, friendship and love. The book was like a neighborhood, each poem a lovely home, uniquely designed and constructed with skill. Characters strutted through the stanzas like proud owners, entertaining the reader with warmth and hospitality. Upon each reading, I longed to tarry and yearned to return to each house again and again.

"No wonder Agatha Jordan is one of Auntie Odie's favorite poets, Emily. I'm surprised she didn't name you Agatha." I laughed and pressed my face in her soft fur. "Guess what, Emily. I've decided on my most-favorite-of-all poet: Agatha Jordan."

Chapter 78

Rolfe Humphries Returns Here
for Last Four Weeks of Session
—*Greeley Daily Tribune*, p.15, Mon., June 23, 1952

Broad-rimmed Hats
Recommended For
Hot Sunny Weather
—*Akin Scoop*, p.8, Mon., June 23, 1952

High Monday 96°, low 62°

I was curled up in Auntie Odie's wicker chair reading a gardening book when Mama and Mr. Santi walked in and greeted me.

"I was leaving the Firedrake to come home for lunch and the truck wouldn't start," Mama explained. "Sal towed it to Zimmerman's Standard for me."

Mr. Santi chuckled. "Your mama invited me to lunch."

I left the chair and followed them to the kitchen.

"That's the least I can do." Mama even explained to me that after lunch they were going to the bank so Mr. Santi could loan her money for the truck repair.

While she fixed sandwiches, Mr. Santi and I set the table and poured up lemonade. Seeing a man help in the kitchen got me to giggling, especially when he tried to put ice cubes in the glasses and they stuck to his fingers.

"What's so funny?" he asked. "Ain't you ever seen a man pour lemonade before?"

I cackled. "No, I ain't never."

"I didn't laugh at you reading a great big gardening book," he said. "Why're you reading that?"

"I'm going to buy pansies with my cleaners money and plant 'em in the empty spots."

After lunch, Mama and Mr. Santi left. When they returned, they unloaded his car trunk, which was full of pansies, petunias, moss roses, snapdragons, and marigolds.

"All for you, Miss Glass," he said.

Like an ecstatic mole, I dug in Auntie Odie's gardens all afternoon—even when it sprinkled—preparing the just-right place for each bloom. *Ecstatic* was the latest addition to my wordbook, and

I'd recently learned from a library book that moles, who live underground, dig dirt with their shovel-feet.

That evening Mama and I walked to the Akin Rest Home. Auntie Odie glowed at the news of all the flowers that Mr. Santi had provided and I'd planted in her garden.

"Some...day," she said, "I'll...see."

Aunt Bella gave us her daily account: Auntie Odie responded well to the leg-and-arm-exercises. Although her speech was still slurred and slow, the doctor said he expected her to get better over time.

Mama wheeled Aunt Bella, and I wheeled Auntie Odie toward the office. Chaplain Brenner came out of a resident's room and followed us.

After the usual warm greetings from Mr. Daleshaw and Mrs. Cane, Wordsworth flew to Aunt Bella's finger. "Favorite girl!" he squawked.

"Mr. Daleshaw," I said, "Why'd you name your bird Wordsworth?"

Wordsworth flew to Mr. Daleshaw's head, fluffed up the dark hair with his feet and beak, which provoked laughter, then settled down as if nesting.

"Well," Mr. Daleshaw began, "the way this bird loves songs and poetic words, I figured I'd name him after a fine old poet, William Wordsworth." Wordsworth listened intently from his "nest." Mr. Daleshaw cleared his throat, slid his thumb under his belt, and adjusted his red tie.

I looked at Auntie Odie. "You've said some William Wordsworth poems to me, haven't you?"

Auntie Odie had a poem on her tongue, but it came in short pieces and slowly...

"Enough...if something...from our hands..."

She gestured slowly toward Mr. Daleshaw, signaling a request for him to finish.

"Of course," Mr. Daleshaw said. "I don't know many lines by heart, but I know that one...."

"Enough, if something from our hands have power,
to live and act and serve the future hour.

"Is that the one, Miss Odie?"

Her eyes warmed and smiled half. "Thank...you..."

"I sure do like that Wordsworth line," said Mr. Daleshaw. "And that's another reason this bird deserves a fine name like Wordsworth—he's a bird of great wisdom, like Mr. Wordsworth was a man of great wisdom."

"Wisdom is a treasure all right," Aunt Bella said, chuckling.

I folded my arms and said to Wordsworth, "I think you're wise enough—and cute enough—to be named after a wise and famous poet."

Mama looked at me in an odd way, but she was smiling her little crescent smile. Aunt Bella laughed, and Auntie Odie smiled her one-sided smile.

And then Wordsworth flew to my head, stirred up my curls, and whistled, "Favorite girl! Favorite girl!"

Chapter 79

Civil Rights To
Be Warm Issue
at Conventions
—*Greeley Daily Tribune*, p.4, Thurs., June 26, 1952

★ ★ ★

Humphries Says
Poem Must Have
Music, Meaning
—*Greeley Daily Tribune*, p.16, Wed., July 23, 1952

★ ★ ★

Most Negroes
Support Adlai
—*Akin Scoop*, p.1, Fri., Aug. 29, 1952

Partly cloudy Friday; high 90°, low 49°; precipitation .03"

It had been a pleasant summer in spite of Martha's absence and Auntie Odie's illness. Nourishing Auntie Odie's gardens, tending the birds, cuddling Emily, and taking long rides on my pale-green and lavender Scwinn smoothed the edges of lonely days while Mama worked. I visited the rest home every day, helped Auntie Odie do simple exercises, read and recited poetry to the two roommates, and basked in Auntie Odie's approval.

"Cotton... you," she whispered.

"Oh I cotton to you too, Auntie Odie. Thank you for never giving up."

Chapter 80

Some Dentists Will
Be Called for Armed
Forces in November
—*Greeley Daily Tribune*, p.1, Sat., Sept. 27, 1952

★ ★ ★

Akin Students Already
Preparing For Silver
Tongues Harvest in Spring
—*Akin Scoop*, p.1, Thurs., Oct. 9, 1952

Fair Thursday; high 80°, low 34°

I soared in sixth grade reading and writing. Mr. Fraser encouraged us to volunteer to "perform" readings in front of the class. I yearned for the courage to perform, but my hand would not go up.

Every day I read to Auntie Odie, Aunt Bella, Mama, and whoever else would listen. And I continued to memorize poems and Bible verses. Auntie Odie had setbacks but, overall, continued to progress slowly.

I prayed Second Samuel twenty-two, twenty-nine every night just before I drifted off to sleep. "'For thou art my lamp, O Lord: and you have lightened my darkness.' Thank You for making my Auntie Odie better each day. Amen."

Chapter 81

1953

Brutal Winds and Dust
Assault Weld County
—*Akin Scoop*, p.1, Tues., Jan. 20, 1953

Greeley Folks
Cluster Around
TV for Inaugural
—*Greeley Daily Tribune*, p.1, Tues., Jan. 20, 1953

Tuesday's high 57°, low 23°; partly cloudy; strong gusty winds

"The Silver Tongues Harvest is in March again," Mr. Fraser announced, "and tryouts will begin the first week of March. Let's be ready."

It was my turn to practice a reading in front of the class. The evening before, I'd read *When the People Soared Like Eagles* to Auntie Odie and Aunt Bella, to Mama at home, and to myself before going to sleep. But I still shook at the thought of reading in front of the class.

"Poni, it's your turn," said Mr. Fraser. "Come on up."

I walked to the front and opened the book.

> "Some say that in the bygone days of Africa the people soared like eagles.
> At least them that had the magic…"

I made it all the way to the end, and the class clapped.

After school, at the coat rack, Mr. Fraser said, "Poni, I think you should consider performing the folktale you read this morning for the Silver Tongues Harvest. What do you think?"

I fingered the silver buttons on my blue coat and looked out the windows.

"Poni?"

"I'd like to, but—" I tugged at my hat and pulled my gloves out of my coat pockets.

"But, what?"

"I did bad last year. I fell, and I couldn't remember anything."

"I remember, Poni. I was there. But this is a new day—a new year." He placed his hand on my shoulder. "You just have to read well, not memorize. They say that if you fall off a horse, you should get right back on and ride. If you don't, you may never have the courage to ride again."

"It's been almost a year. My courage is already lost."

"You got up in front of the class today and did a fantastic job. You're back on the horse. Now keep ridin'."

"Excuse me, Mr. Fraser. But I have to go by Smith's cleaners. I should go now. And my aunts are waiting at the rest home for me to read to them."

He grinned. "That's riding the horse."

I couldn't think of anything to say.

"I've heard about all you're doing for Odessa Luckett."

"She's done leaps and bounds more for Mama and me."

"Knowing what a fine storyteller and poet Mrs. Luckett is, and how she's mentored you and helped you through some tough times, the best thing you can do for her is to become the best reader and storyteller and reciter you can be. Show Mrs. Luckett what a good job she did teaching you. Show her your appreciation by shining at the Harvest."

My mind buzzed with all Mr. Fraser said. I took off my snowcap then put it back on.

"Well," said Mr. Fraser, "think it over."

"I don't have to think it over. I want to try."

Chapter 82

Akin School Closed
Due to Storms
—*Akin Scoop*, p.1, Fri., Feb. 20, 1953

★ ★ ★

New Cold Wave
Is Moving in
on Colorado
—*Greeley Tribune*, p.1, Mon., Feb. 23, 1953

Increasing cloudiness throughout Monday; high 47°, low 18°; 20–30 mph winds on eastern plains tonight

Except for afternoon naps in bed, Auntie Odie spent her days in the easy chair or wheelchair. She was slow speaking, slurred her words, but could speak sentences.

"Poni dear," she would say, "who… are you… today? Poet… gardener… author… reader… storyteller?"

My response was different each day. Today I answered, "Cat lover!"

Chapter 83

Many Seeds Survive
Despite Late Frosts
—*Akin Scoop*, p.2, Sat., Feb. 28, 1953

★ ★ ★

Strong West
Winds Start
Dust Clouds
—*Greeley Daily Tribune*, p.1, Thurs., March 5, 1953

Generally fair Thursday; windy; high 61°, low 24°

Auntie Odie haltingly told the tale of slaves that stepped up on invisible stairs. Aunt Bella and I rejoiced and applauded her—her first telling since her stroke.

Then I held out my library book—*When the People Soared Like Eagles*. "See, Auntie Odie? Your tale in a book."

"Read…child…"

So I did.

My chrysalis shimmered, transparent—wet, crunched wings in view. Soon they would emerge, become free, unfold, stretch. Maybe I would even fly.

When I gave Auntie Odie her parting hug, her one good arm squeezed me.

"You're getting better, Auntie Odie. I'm so happy!"

She smiled, not quite so one-sided. "My Emily is… waiting… Spring is coming. Time… for flowers."

Chapter 84

President Urged To Take Up With New Russian
Leaders Releasing 1,200,000 World War II POWs
—*Greeley Daily Tribune*, p.1, Sat., March 7, 1953

★ ★ ★

Mild, Pleasant Weather Predicted
for Tonight's Silver Tongues Harvest;
Far Cry From Last Year's Storm
—*Akin Scoop*, p.1, Fri., March 20, 1953

Partly cloudy Friday; high 68°, low 33°; brief thunderstorms late afternoon and night

When I walked into Auntie Odie's and Aunt Bella's room, what a surprise! The Matthews were there. I got the hug of my life from Martha who looked the same, only taller—black hair even farther down her back, deer eyes that could melt the hardest heart.

It was Martha's spring vacation and, since Mrs. Matthews was feeling better, they'd come to see Auntie Odie and Mr. Matthews' parents—and me.

Within minutes, Martha and I were giggling and chattering like old times. She patted my shoulder and smiled her pink smile.

"Tonight's the Harvest," I said. "Can you come?"

Mr. Matthews gripped my shoulders and smiled. "We'll be there! We heard you're in it."

Although thin and frail, Mrs. Matthews' face flushed with the excitement of seeing old friends. "How we've missed you, Poni dearest."

"We've missed you too." *Boy-howdy!*

Auntie Odie wore a three-fourths grin while we all chatted and got reacquainted.

I looked at the clock and winked at Auntie Odie. "Well, I better go home and titivate before the Harvest."

Martha squeezed me. "See you at the school—all titivated. We'll save seats for you and your mom. Sit with us after you perform."

Auntie Odie raised her hand toward me.

I stepped close and knelt down by her wheelchair.

"You… will… shine… like the… s-stars…" she said.

"Thank you, Auntie Odie." Then I kissed her warm cheek.

Everyone wished me well and I headed home. Mama would have supper fixed and she'd help me get ready and out the door early for the Harvest. That's what she'd said.

"And I'll come at seven," she'd promised.

I was careful not to mention who was in town. Boy, would she be surprised.

★ ★ ★

Hippos with wings thrashed around in my stomach. *What if I trip on the stage again? What if my mouth goes dry and no sounds come out? What if a sound does come out and it sounds like Polly mooing?* I had a long wait. I was last on the program.

The Akin School auditorium filled with jovial and talkative people. I peeked from behind the curtains at Martha and her parents in the audience. They smiled, laughed, and visited with the Fenderlupens, Mrs. Fall, Dora Santi and others around them, but I couldn't see the Firedrake anywhere. Or Mama.

Lights dimmed.

Mr. Fraser bounded up on the stage and raised the microphone. In a deep, enthusiastic voice he declared, "Welcome, ladies and gentlemen and boys and girls, to the 1953 Silver Tongues Harvest!" Everyone burst into applause and cheers.

As always, some students read, some recited, others told stories, but all poured heart and soul into their performances. The audience applauded and cheered wholeheartedly after each one.

The excitement of the audience filled me with determination to do better than my best. I scanned the audience again for Mama's face. She wasn't there. Yet. She'd come. She promised. She'd been in grand spirits when I'd returned home from the rest home. If Gram and Grampy were alive, they would be there. And so would Auntie Odie if she could. *Mama! Please hurry.*

"And now…" Mr. Fraser paused, looked backstage where I waited, and gave me a wonderful, warm smile. "Our next contestant this evening is a sixth grade student—from my classroom, I'm proud to say—who will read an old Negro folktale, *When the People Soared Like Eagles,* retold by June Lane Blair. Ladies and gentlemen, please welcome Ponia Snow!"

I stepped with elastic legs onto the stage. My damp, trembling hands gripped the book like suction cups. I swallowed. Standing in the spotlight, the audience became invisible in the dark auditorium, and a bright warmth encompassed me. I opened the book—

> "Some say that in the bygone days of Africa the people soared like eagles. At least them that had the magic. Yes, they spread their arms and stepped up into the air like they was jus' climbin' stairs. But there came those long dark days when they were stolen away for slavery. No time to gather wings. No way to hide them anyways, on those dismal ships, full to their sterns with brokenhearted slaves…"

The familiar words hovered like a sweet fragrance. My voice was a violin, then a flute, a cello—a young version of Auntie Odie's storytelling voice—as it rose and fell with the tide of words that had strewn stars in Auntie Odie's dark eyes.

"Of course, they still had the magic, them that could fly. In the slave land, they hid their secret deep in their hearts. But some forgot the secret. And some, born into slavery, weren't ever told they could fly.

"Johnny was like an old granddaddy that all the slaves loved. He never forgot that he could fly, even when the Driver opened his back with a whip.

"One day a young girl, Abby, got sick in the field. She did fall and could not get up.

"'Get up and back to work!' shouted the Overseer. The sun beat on Abby's back and so did the Driver. As Johnny helped her to her feet, he whispered, 'You have the power, Abby. Fly!'

"When at last Abby's feet left the ground, she mounted up like an eagle, soaring higher and higher. Then Johnny blew the magic words like a gentle wind over the slaves. A mother, holding her wide-eyed baby tight, and a young boy did step into the air and fly.

"How they did laugh and holler. The Overseer, on his horse, galloped after them grabbing for their heels.

"The other slaves jumped and shouted, 'They're flyin'! They're flyin' to freedom!'

"An old woman stepped up, and a man, and another. They did step right up on invisible stairs and fly away."

I was in that field, running from the Overseer with the other slaves, stepping up on those invisible stairs. At last I read the final lines.

"The field became shadowed by the people as they flew like one massive bird. They soared towards the clouds into the endless ocean of sky."

I, too, soared into the clouds, savoring the awesome joy of Freedom. My eyes spilled tears.

"Then the heavens opened up and welcomed them home to Freedom."

I looked down and half-bowed, as Mr. Fraser had instructed, to indicate I was finished. I was breathless with wonder—I had flown that Freedom sky.

Silence. My heart pitched. Had I made some terrible mistake?

Then the crowd exploded into applause, shouts, and whistles. They didn't stop until I had crossed the stage, bounced down the stairs, and hurried up the aisle and was seated next to Martha.

One of the many pleasures encased in that sweet evening was Martha's tear-stained face, her eyes shining over a smile as big as Alaska.

Martha stepped into the aisle and embraced me. Into my ear she said, "Remember the monarch, Poni? That's you!"

I sat between Martha and the empty seats for Mama and Mr. Santi. Everyone around me patted my shoulders and congratulated me. Mama's absence only slightly dampened my joy—because my Martha was there. And Mr. and Mrs. Matthews and Mrs. Santi and Mrs. Fry.

★ ★ ★

While the judges decided the awards, the emcee proclaimed, "Ladies and gentlemen, tonight we are truly honored to have as our special guest poet, Agatha Jordan."

A buzz went through the audience. Martha and I looked, wide-eyed, at each other. "Agatha Jordan!" I said. "My favorite poet!"

Mr. Fraser adjusted his tie. "When Agatha Jordan's first book of poetry was published in 1938, the publisher insisted she write under a pen name and not include a photo on the cover as is customary. They felt that many readers would not purchase her works if they knew she was a Negro. Since 1938, three more books have been published under the pen name, Agatha Jordan—the most recent, *In Praise of Wings: A Flock of Poems by Agatha Jordan,* published in 1949.

"Months ago, Agatha Jordan suffered a debilitating stroke and has since decided to allow her true identity to be known. The occasion of the 1953 Silver Tongues Harvest is her chosen platform to have it declared.

"Ladies and gentlemen!" Mr. Fraser shouted in his excitement. "We're highly honored—because of her accomplishments as a poet and because of her long, valiant struggle since her stroke—to have Agatha Jordan here tonight, who most of us know as neighbor, friend, woman of faith, storyteller, birder, and gardener extraordinaire. Will you please welcome Akin's own, Odessa Luckett!"

Heads turned. Murmurs. Whispers. There! Auntie Odie in her wheelchair. Dressed in royal blue, head to toe. Wheeled down the aisle by Mr. Santi! And Mama!

The audience leaped to their feet—clapped, cheered, whistled. I struggled to stand. My mind whirled in wonder and disbelief.

Mr. Santi and Mama lifted the wheelchair up the stage stairs and pushed her to the microphone. Still the crowd applauded, shouted, and cheered.

Auntie Odie waited, nodded, and smiled her new lopsided smile until, minutes later, the audience quieted and sat back down. She leaned toward the microphone and spoke. "This is… indeed… an honor… for me to be here… tonight." Speaking haltingly, and with great effort, she recited a poem I recognized from *In Praise of Wings*, but her recitation made it new, made it glitter with life and meaning. The audience clapped exuberantly.

"Earlier tonight…" she continued in her new halted, wavy style, "my friend, whom I admire more than words can disclose, read my favorite tale with beauty and skill. I will now recite a wonderful little poem she wrote for me. I hope to do it justice, for her words are, tonight, mine for her. Ponia Glass Snow, please come. Stand here with me as I bid your words back to you."

A fresh, deep trembling took hold of me as I made my way back to the stage. I embraced my Auntie Odie and cherished the discomfort of her blue-rhinestone earbob pressed into my cheek. Then Auntie Odie—Agatha Jordan—recited my own poem to me in front of the hushed audience.

> "With tender mercies each seed she sows,
> bids each stalk and cheers
> the blossom cameos.

> "With feeders brimming wild birds are fed.
> Her words and their songs
> entwine like woven thread.

> "With tender mercies she teaches me,
> bids each gift, and cheers
> my slightest victory."

Auntie Odie paused and swallowed back tears, lips quivering, then in a voice like rippling waters…

> "My mind brims with wisdom softly said.
> Laughter, poems… and hearts
> entwine like woven thread."

The audience sprang to their feet in a standing ovation.

Epilogue

2002

A few weeks later, on the condition that Auntie Odie would have daily assistance, her doctor released her to return to her cottage. Mama and I stayed, at her welcome invitation. We "earned our keep" by gardening, cooking, cleaning, and assisting Auntie Odie with daily personal needs—anything she could no longer do. A nurse came each week and helped bathe her, and assisted with exercises and medications. We all shared in Emily's care and kept the feeders full. For the next several years Auntie Odie and I basked together in the truths of God, images of poets, scents of flowers, and songs of birds.

After Olivia Matthews, Martha's beloved mother, passed away, Mr. Matthews and Martha returned to their home across the street, and Martha and I rejoiced in our reunion. Nate had been buried in Korea, but eventually Mr. Matthews and Martha arranged to have his body brought back to the United States—to Colorado—and buried in the veterans' cemetery.

One day, Auntie Odie fell asleep in her chair with Emily on her lap, and she never awakened.

She did step right up on invisible stairs and fly away. The heavens opened up and welcomed her home to Freedom.

That was many years ago. But every time I pray, tell a story, recite a Scripture verse or poem, give a speech, write a book, plant a flower, listen to birds sing, or stroke my cat Agatha, I remember Auntie Odie and give thanks for her life and the tender mercies she bestowed upon me.

Oh, better than the minting
Of a gold-crowned king
Is the safe-kept memory
Of a lovely thing.

Acknowledgements

Since the idea-seed for this book came to me (about 1985) and I began writing it (1996), many family members, friends, librarians, instructors, acquaintances, writing group members, critique group members, and Bible study groups have come alongside—some for minutes or hours, others for months or years. They've cheered me on, encouraged me, prayed for me, read manuscripts at various stages, critiqued, edited, taught, and assisted with research. My fear is that I will overlook someone who deserves special thanks—that's what happens when you take forever to write a book. Please forgive me if you have been supportive of me in some way and I haven't included you here.

Research assistance:

Special thanks to Jim and Cynthia Miller (Fireweed, Palisade, CO) and Sam Rushing (Ouray Glassworks and Pottery Company, Ourary, CO) for allowing me to watch you work and wield fantastic art in glass, patiently answering dozens of questions.

Karen McKee and other librarians at Mesa County Public Library as well as Anne Bledsoe at Colorado Mesa University Library (Grand Junction, CO) were extraordinarily helpful.

Thanks to Marie Filip (dear former writing group member who moved away). You loaned me Southern cooking books and other helpful information.

Super relatives, the Robinett clan: Thank you to my aunt and uncle, Wilburt and Inamae, who drove me to locations in Weld County pertinent to the book; to my cousin, Jim, who accompanied me on a short trip to a bird reserve in Weld County; and to cousin Shirley for being willing to go on a super early bird-watching hike in Weld, even though it didn't work out. And thank you to the family members (Wilburt, Inamae, Jim, Dan, Susie, and Shirley) who shared birdlore and other stories which helped set the tone for the book.

Many thanks to: Nancy Penfold, Curator, Fort Lupton Museum (Fort Lupton, CO) for invaluable information; my cousin, Carolyn Baylis (Schwinn bike info); my aunt and uncle—Elma McAvoy (Greeley stories) and Oliver McAvoy (in memory—Greeley stories); Bonnie Talbott (story); Carol Zadrozny ("literaries"); Therese Luellen and employees at UPS Store 1349 (for your patience and expertise in copying, sending, and receiving information on short notice); and Leif, Permissions Dept. at Nebraska Press (for your time spent answering my questions and offering helpful insight in Jan. 2013).

Reads, critiques, and edits of manuscript at various stages over many years:

Thank you to: My brother and sister-in-law, Earl and Carol McAvoy (for your useful edits and loving encouragement); Judy Rogan (for reading that early version of the manuscript years ago and providing such useful feedback); the board members of the former Western Slope Christian Writers Association— Steve, Linda Beckley (in memory), Debbie Brockett, and Rusty Morgan— (for amazing editing of an early version of the manuscript after it won a free critique at a WSCWA writing conference); Lauraine Snelling (one-on-one critique at a 2000 Colo. Christian Writers conference—such helpful edits); Sandy Dorr, 2003 Narrative class teacher (for your insightful comments on the 2003 version of the manuscript, as well as great critiques from class members— Bill Theimer, Danny Rosen, Drew, Emily Buchannan, Jackie, Jean Tyler, John, Marie Filip, Susan Paris, and Yvonne); Carolyn Lampman Brubaker (for your helpful and entertaining critique offered at the 2002 Jackson Hole Writers Conference).

How can I ever thank the Heart and Soul Critique Group enough? Sharon Bridgewater, Patti Hill, and Darlia Sawyer—I treasure you for all the wonderful and painfully truthful marks you have made on my manuscripts (including many versions and pieces of this book) since we began meeting in 2001. You are amazing critiquers and friends.

Linda Callison, a precious friend who knows a bunch about words and books and writing—you read the manuscript at an early stage and made invaluable suggestions. Thank you for your further comments, generous friendship, and many encouraging words through the years.

And thank you, dear son Steve Morley Jr., for your help in research endeavors. And your editing prowess amazes me. Thank you for reading the book in recent form and making such thoughtful and detailed suggestions, including asking important questions. Your loving willingness to give and use your expertise in reading and editing this book means more to me than you know.

Encouragement and assistance:

The Lord provided so many wonderful people (even our pets), using different methods to galvanize and inspire.

Four wonderful and helpful Coordinators at Inspiring Voices have made this journey, not only bearable but enjoyable. Thank you, Amanda Parsons, John Osredker, Erica Hookfin, and Ryan Carlberg. God blessed each of you with amazing patience and kindness, for which I am so grateful.

My dear friend, Barbara Milburn: I remember the first time I babbled on and on about my story idea while we waited for a table at Dos Hombres (1987?). One mark of your trueness as a friend is your great listening skills. In March of 2006 you read the manuscript and wrote two letters of praise and glorious encouragement, which I framed and hung on my writing-room wall. Numerous times I thought about giving up, but raised my eyes to your words on the wall and gathered strength to keep going. I've appreciated your continued words of encouragement through the years and, most of all, your prayers.

Heartfelt gratitude to Sandy Bergeron (Sandra Bergeron Creations) for allowing your delightful painting, "Sweetheart's Gate," to grace the cover of this book. May you be blessed abundantly for your kindness.

Special thanks to our precious daughter, Stephanie Haverstock, for your loving and encouraging words along the way. And to our son-in-law, Mark, for his vow to actually *read* this book when it's published.

Joyful thanks to: My brother-in-law, Paul Morley (your generous gifts of technology over many years made it possible to write this book); Tammy Martin (in memory—we swapped manuscripts and blessed and encouraged each other. I still miss you, Tammy); LoAn Callison (A+ encourager); Virginia Webb (I recall receiving your thoughtful note of writing encouragement at a time when I so needed it); Peggy Adams, Nursery Pastor at Canyon View Vineyard Church (for your kind words and prayers toward my writing efforts); my dentist, Dr. Darrel Blehm (for more than a decade now, when I've gone in for a checkup, you've asked, "How's the book coming?" Your interest in my book encouraged me, Dr. Blehm); Michele Soderborg (I don't see you very often anymore, but when I do, you usually ask about the book. Bless you, friend.)

The Bible study small group we belong to has extended encouragement to me and prayed for me during the last two years regarding the writing of this book. Thank you to Bonnie and Tom Campbell, Roxie Gallegos, Karen Grasso, Sharon Hancock, John and Judie Kenagy, Steve and Lynne Vaughan, Kay Wood, and of course Susie and Tom Vaughn our group leaders.

I've noticed that sweet glow in the eyes and smiles of my friends, Bonnie Talbott, Oneta Smith, and Della Fiske-Turner, at Pufferbelly breakfasts on Wednesdays when "the book" topic comes up. Thank you, friends.

I'm also grateful for The Lord's Write Hands (TLWH) writing group, which began meeting in Feb. 2002. I have enjoyed gentle, loving, and inspiring teaching and support. Dozens of you have come and gone, but I hold dear all of your contributions—offered directly or indirectly—toward the completion of this book.

Kimberly Carney, you sent me a card in 1996 that began, "You Are a Lover of Words—One Day You Will Write a Book…." I have kept that card in the front of my planner ever since, dear daughter. Your love, belief in me, encouragement, and willingness to assist along the way have spurred me on.

Since about 1992 at our monthly breakfasts, you—Marjorie Bristol, Linda Callison, Sue Greb, Pam Morris, Joyce Theyson, and Shirley Williams—began nudging me with, "How's your writing coming?" "Is that book finished yet?" "Don't give up." Thank you, dear friends. Later, Mary Cordova, Becky Karisny, Sharon Gartner, Mindy, and Maureen Reed joined the group and you've added your smiles of support. Thank you all for your love and encouragement and faith in me.

And last but not least—Stephen, dear husband, you have put up with neglect, untended household tasks, and glazed looks for many years and didn't complain. I love you for that. One time you listened to an early version of this story (which I had taped), and at the end you said, teary-eyed, "This book needs to be published." Thank you for that comment, dearest. Some time later you read a later version of the book and offered valuable suggestions in spite of the fact that you didn't think you had anything to offer as far as editing goes. And the other times you spoke words of encouragement, it meant the world to me—and you mean the world to me too.

Note: These acknowledgements make it sound like I did nothing but work on this book since 1996, but there were months and sometimes years when the manuscript lay in a file drawer hibernating, and maybe even sprouting some on its own.